W9-BBO-403

Also by Glyn Hughes

Published in America:

THE ANTIQUE COLLECTOR

Published in the United Kingdom:

Fiction

ROTH

THE ANTIQUE COLLECTOR

THE HAWTHORN GODDESS

WHERE I USED TO PLAY ON THE GREEN

Travel

MILLSTONE GRIT

FAIR PROSPECTS

GLYN HUGHES'S YORKSHIRE

Poetry

NEIGHBOURS

REST THE POOR STRUGGLER

BEST OF NEIGHBOURS

Plays

MARY HEPTON'S HEAVEN

THE RAPE OF THE ROSE

A Novel by

Glyn Hughes

SIMON & SCHUSTER
New York London Toronto Sydney Tokyo Singapore

SIMON & SCHUSTER
SIMON & SCHUSTER BUILDING
ROCKEFELLER CENTER
1230 AVENUE OF THE AMERICAS
NEW YORK, NEW YORK 10020

THIS BOOK IS A WORK OF FICTION. NAMES, CHARACTERS, PLACES AND INCIDENTS ARE EITHER PRODUCTS OF THE AUTHOR'S IMAGINATION OR ARE USED FICTITIOUSLY. ANY RESEMBLANCE TO ACTUAL EVENTS OR LOCALES OR PERSONS, LIVING OR DEAD, IS ENTIRELY COINCIDENTAL.

ORIGINALLY PUBLISHED IN GREAT BRITAIN IN 1987 BY CHATTO & WINDUS LTD.

DESIGNED BY SONGHEE KIM

MANUFACTURED IN THE UNITED STATES OF AMERICA

1 3 5 7 9 10 8 6 4 2

LIBRARY OF CONGRESS CATALOGING-IN-PUBLICATION DATA
HUGHES, GLYN, DATE
THE RAPE OF THE ROSE : A NOVEL / BY GLYN HUGHES.
P. CM.
I. PENNINE CHAIN REGION (ENGLAND)—HISTORY—FICTION.
I. TITLE.
PR6058.U35R3 1993
823'.914—DC20 92-39326 CIP

ISBN: 0-671-72516-5

THE DEFINITION THAT OPENS CHAPTER ONE IS FROM *THE SHORTER OXFORD ENGLISH DICTIONARY* AND IS REPRODUCED BY PERMISSION OF OXFORD UNIVERSITY PRESS.

to the memory of

my father

and for Jane

My happiness with her

has made possible the

writing of this novel.

THE RAPE OF THE ROSE

THE SICK ROSE

O Rose, thou art sick!
The invisible worm
That flies in the night,
In the howling storm,

Has found out thy bed
Of crimson joy:
And his dark secret love
Does thy life destroy.

William Blake
Songs of Experience
1789–94

Part 1

March - April 1812

CHAPTER ONE

March 12th

LUDDITE 1811 (Said [but without confirmation] to be f. Ned Lud, a lunatic living about 1779, who in a fit of rage smashed up two frames belonging to a Leicestershire 'stockinger').

A member of an organised band of mechanics and their friends, who (1811–16) went about destroying machinery in the midlands and north of England.

The Shorter Oxford English Dictionary

here there is fear, everything is fearful. Mor Laverock Greave, handloom weaver, village schoolmaster, scribe to a Luddite band, and "King Ludd's" messenger, returned twelve miles from his mission in Huddersfield to his home in Lady Well, walking over the hills, looking this way and that. If he had taken the twisting valley roads it would have been twice the distance. Also, he was safer on the hills, where he could see who was following him. He was not able to run quickly because his lungs were full of wool dust, his legs short and crooked, his knees bent from having been cramped over a loom since childhood. His work today, because of his association with machine breakers and for his treasonable statements against the King, might lead to his being transported or hanged.

The hills in their ceremonies of moving light were around him. The larks for the first time this year danced free in the air. Mor, climbing breathlessly up to Outlane Moor, and staring about him, turned his ankle.

In panic, he sat down, eased open his old leather coat, massaged his ankle and sat upright again. He removed his hat and wiped the brim. Though the weather was cool, his neck was damp with fear, under his unfashionably long, dark hair. He feared for his child, Edwin, his wife

Phoebe, and his elder son, Gideon. He feared for the whole of Lady Well.

Staring down the track he saw, caught in a swab of light, a couple of soldiers staggering from a public house. He saw an old woman who was reduced to doing a donkey's work of carrying warps on her back for the weavers. And there, in the distance, was a more mysterious fellow, talking outside a woolcomber's shop and pointing up the hill in Mor's direction: who was that?

Mor realized that he was an absentminded insurrectionary, careless in his speech. What a clown, what a fool he was! He had written and delivered his Luddite messages on behalf of his comrades, John Tiplady, Arthur Crawshaw and the others, because he was literate and they were not. But he had foolishly left clues behind him; especially at the Huddersfield hotel where the mill masters had been meeting. Placing his greasy bit of paper sealed with tallow, his message "to the manufactory owners when they come out of their room," into the hands of the lackey had left Mor with dried-up mouth and quaking shins. And later, a quarter of a mile out of town, he had foolishly chatted to a pothouse servant girl.

This sort of work doesn't suit me at all . . .

His ankle seemed to be all right. Relieved, Mor Greave leaned forward and plucked some small flowers that were growing on the bank. Frail and clean, their white petals were suffused with pale green lines: *Galanthus nivalis*—snowdrops! He wreathed some around his hat. He stood up and belted his coat again. He set off, more careful of the stones. He nodded to people and passed the time of day. It looked to the world as if he had done nothing wrong, but his heart was pounding like a steam engine.

Looking over his shoulder from time to time, he kept on climbing. Step by step, beckoned by the steely light over the moor, he felt cleansed of all that was superfluous, human, and wicked. On the hills he felt, as always, that layers were being shed from him.

Larks, airy symbols of his freedom, bulleted up out of the grass and flung themselves off the slopes. The sky was alive with them. It was indisputably their sky as they rose and dropped, or paused, hanging in vibrating feathers.

He walked a dozen miles. He climbed a wall and landed on a hard road. With relief, he was in sight of Lady Well.

Looking along this high, gaunt, exposed route between moor above and marsh below, Mor felt able to take off and glide, westerly into Lancashire, easterly to York, Hull, and the sea—somewhere away from Yorkshire, away from the pain.

A slow, heavy wagon, battered and dirty from travel, struggled along the road. Its cover was lashed down firmly but muffled cries could be heard from within, so Mor thought it was full of animals. It was pulled by four large, tired horses. They trampled the bright yellow celandines sprinkling the strip of grass between the ruts, while the iron-rimmed wheels tore other flowers from the bank.

The carter, a stranger, looked weary. His cloak shrouded him. His broad-brimmed hat was pulled down over his brow.

"Lady Well? Mr. Horsfall's manufactory?" the stranger asked. His voice, roughened from smoking and from the dust of turnpikes, was like the tumbling of gravel. He was too tired, or too contemptuous, to phrase his questions properly. He had asked for directions many times already and, in this "surly" part of the world, had been barely answered, or had been misled. In some villages they had thrown stones at him. He had discovered that they thought all strangers might be government spies. The people of the north were full of suspicion.

Mor, too, who could be gracious in his speech when the occasion called for it, pretended to be a boorish villager, with a heavy accent.

"Paradise Mills are at the bottom of the valley, mister. You've wasted your time climbing up here. You could have come straight along by the river from the turnpike. But you'd have to pay a toll, that way. Mr. Horsfall makes even his own workfolk pay for his road."

"God forgive me, I could do without losing any more time! I've been ten days on the road from London."

"That's a long way to bring us calves and lambs, sir."

The carter laughed. "Mr. Horsfall pays good money for my 'calves and lambs,' because my 'calves and lambs' come from the Hackney workhouse! Just take a look at 'em. But mind they don't bite! They're hungry beasts and are used to living like rats. Don't open too much, or they'll be off across the hills like a pack of jackrabbits."

Mor tentatively untied an edge of the covering. There came a smell of sweat and fouled straw. The face of a child, frightened and demented, was thrust into the gap. Other children, exhausted, stinking, dirty, bruised and bleeding from their long journey, crowded to the chink of light. One spat at Mor. A little girl, a wild look in her pale eyes, made a grab at the wild flowers in Mor's hat. She missed, as Mor pulled back, shocked.

"What's that?" she demanded. "Gi'it me!"

Mor raised his hat to her and gave her a flower. "Snowdrops, miss. *Galanthus nivalis.*"

She vanished with the flower, no doubt fearing that it might be taken from her. The carter laughed. From deep within the wagon, the little girl screamed with delight.

Mor, convulsed with nausea, leaned against the cart.

God forgive me, thought the carter, ***you'd be sick if you knew of the two who died and were buried; me bribing a parson and a magistrate so as to do it without death certificates, and having therefore to carry gold in my pockets, in these seditious times!***

"The mill doesn't need any more children," Mor said when he had recovered. "Our own young ones are already there. You should see my eldest boy's legs. He can hardly walk after a day's work. The youngest is set to grow the same way."

The carter laughed again and winked, but said nothing. He was intrigued by the flowers in Mor's hat, and other things he could not understand about this Yorkshire working man: such as the book sticking out of his pocket. Fortunately, the carter could not read the title. It was Paine's *Rights of Man*.

"Profit has to be made out of someone. Someone has to suffer, if we are to defeat Napoleon Bonaparte," the carter said.

"Then it's a pity, sir, that it must be children."

"Whoa! Whoa!" the carter shouted to the restless horses. "They are to be apprentices, by order of Parliament, so fasten down that cover now! They'd be off as soon as wink. I nearly lost two of 'em when I let them out for exercise near Cromford."

Mor had heard of Cromford in Derbyshire. That was where Sir Richard Arkwright was the first to employ children from five years of age, on day and night shifts. The children were brought from distant pauper houses, so that no one would be around to care about them. They were beaten to keep them awake through the twelve- or even fifteen-hour shifts, which were worked in sight of Arkwright's mansion.

His had been the first spinning mill in the world, and the first to be machine-driven—and the first to enslave children.

"Apprentices!" Mor scoffed. "You don't need to train craft apprentices to work a machine! It is no more than a legal device to enslave them until they are twenty-one!"

The carter looked at him suspiciously. "They say this is the most seditious corner of England, where King Ludd will finish you off as you lie in your bed. Have you seen any signs of this 'King Ludd'?"

"Oh, every place has its own 'King Ludd' in these parts," Mor answered airily. "He's everywhere at once and no one ever meets him. As soon as one is caught, another appears. I know nothing about him. It's all foolishness."

"They speak of a 'Lady Ludd,' too. Who's she?"

"She is one for upsetting stalls at markets. She's against the prices, so I'm told. I don't know anything about her, either. It's none of my business."

"Well, Mr. Perceval the Prime Minister is going to hang them all. *Queee . . .*" The carter made the gesture of a rope tightening around his neck. "They have a new bill to deal with machine breakers," he said. "Yet I see you have enough soldiers in Yorkshire already to save honest citizens from having their throats cut while they lie asleep. I've met whole regiments of militia marching here along the roads. Are you expecting the French to invade? I've heard that rumor in every public house from Hackney to Yorkshire, so perhaps it is true."

"We're up to our necks in fear in this country! There was a man in Lady Well who hid in a chicken shed for a week because someone had told him that the French were coming. They still don't think we've enough soldiers. They're still raising local recruits. Any man who has fewer than three children born in wedlock and is over five feet two inches tall is liable to be recruited. There's a notice on the church door about it. And I have but two children surviving."

The carter laughed. "You'll barely reach that height, though?"

Swaying and grumbling on its springs, the vehicle jolted into action, with its load of little boys, and little girls bringing their dowries of work smocks, aprons, and their two guineas each for prayer books and bedding, as arranged by contract with the London workhouse, two hundred miles for their marriages to Horsfall's Paradise Mills in the north.

"I'm five foot five!" Mor shouted after it.

The carter laughed.

Mor walked farther along the road. When, at the edge of Lady Well, he peered down the wooded slope toward Paradise Mills, he looked into a crimson pool formed by all the buds that were about to burst. The whole wood brimming out of the gorge was struggling into life; a corpse was striving to inhale.

He would have liked to cut through the woods, but was prevented from doing so. "Blood Wood," that wilderness named after an ancient, forgotten battle, where for centuries people had gathered firewood or nuts, cut bracken for animal bedding, fished and snared birds, or simply stared at the trees, had been enclosed. It was guarded by a force of gamekeepers, and notices had been put up: BLOOD WOOD ESTATE. PRIVATE. SPRING GUNS AND STEEL TRAPS SET HERE.

Be damned to the Horsfalls! Damn! Damn! Damn! thought Mor. *Why such alarm and fear?*

Throughout this day, the manufacturers had been meeting in Huddersfield.

A variety of frightening incidents had brought them together to discuss offering a reward for the capture of Luddites, who had now gone so far as to raid mill owners' homes in search of arms, as well as breaking into their factories. A wagonload of new machinery had been ambushed and smashed. A mill, not insurable against "acts of riot and civil commotion," had been burned down. One mill owner, who had skimped and saved to purchase a twelve-horsepower steam engine, had been afraid to leave his house as he listened to it being broken to bits. Another had been called from his bed to comfort daughters frightened by the sounds of Luddites conducting drills on the nearby moorland.

The meeting resolved on an appeal to be published in the *Leeds Mercury:*

> It appears to this meeting that a violent and determined spirit of insubordination has gained ground amongst the workmen. The Committee hereby offers a reward of one hundred guineas for information leading to the arrest of any one involved with "King Ludd" or with the breaking of machinery . . .

As the manufacturers were about to leave, they found Mor Greave's note awaiting them in the lobby of the hotel:

> Gentlemen, you have oppressed us beyond endurance, and have no notion of what you do. We assert our right to LIVE by our employment. Pull down your obnoxius machines. Pay fare wages to the weavers, their wives and children. Otherwise, sooner than see our numerus families of children cry and starve for bread, we will pay with our lives to reduce your property to ashes.
>
> Your obedient servant
> KING LUDD

What alarmed the manufacturers most about Mor's letter was not so much its content, which they were used to, but its literacy. An educated man could become a leader.

Therefore a spy, known as "B," was sent upon his trail.

"B" tracked Mor as far as Outlane, following clues given to him by a militiaman, a maidservant in a public house, and an old woman carrying warps for a living. The maidservant described him as "a working man with a gentleman's manners."

"B" had one other important clue. His quarry had a habit of leaving out the letter "o" at the ends of such words as "obnoxious" and "numerous."

CHAPTER TWO

March 14th

or, working at home two days later, alone, was hungry. There was neither meat nor fish available at the end of winter. His wife and children would return from the factory to find little but oatmeal, bread and some fruit preserves.

In Mor's mind was stuck an obstinate memory of a place on the river, on Horsfall's estate, where he knew there were trout. Finally, in the afternoon, Mor deserted his loom.

Avoiding the militia, he made his way down to the bridge. While waiting for passersby to disappear, he examined the water—its color, depth, density, and speed. New banks of weeds, which in a few weeks time would be flowing in the current, were beginning to prick the mud. He took some final, quick glances in every direction, climbed a wall, and darted for cover.

He knew everything about the water, and where there would be fish. Traveling downstream, trying to look every way at once, feeling for the edge of a mantrap or a spring gun prised to blow off his head, he made an arc through the woodlands, returning to the bank at a point where he was hidden from all directions.

A slow, curving shine of water lay before him. A clear brown color, it caught and rippled over stones, glided over gravel, or sulked in its deeper pools. Mor slowly worked his way upstream, watching, watching. There a trout rose. After a quick, excited *plop* as it broke the surface, it sank back again, leaving a glitter upon the water. Then another one tipped a nose to the river, leaving circles.

But Mor wanted a fish near the bank, and he knew where to go;

this was the spot he had been savoring at his loom. It was a deep place carved out by the swirling water. The fish were concentrating in the other direction, upstream, where the food came from.

Mor saw the lips of one touch and break the tight drumskin of the surface, sending out shivering circles of silver, to be swept away on the current's flow. He watched as the trout gently plucked the surface of the pool a few times. When it had sunk down again, he crept forward, feeling his way with the balls of his feet, so as not to crack a twig or rattle a stone. Nor did he throw his shadow over the river. His awareness of everything around him filled him with currents of joy, and the river's music was like a sweet gathering of fiddles.

Alert in every organ, listening out for the approach of gamekeepers, this was how an animal lived, he thought, its life concentrated, living in this moment only. A foot behind the trout's tail, Mor knelt, still keeping his shadow clear. His hands felt through the cold water, his fingers moving like pale weeds played by the current. Once or twice he touched the trout's sides, feeling its pulses of contained energy. He wrapped his fingers gently around the body. Then he gripped tightly under the gills.

The trout, ten inches long, in a sudden flurry was in his grasp, its tail swinging, trying to swipe at him, its speckled head gaping and gasping, its many little teeth glittering, its beautiful vermilion spots dimpling its flashing sides. It was like trying to hold oil. The more tightly he gripped, the more it thrashed, slipped, and squirmed.

For a moment it lay still, its eye regarding him without reproach, and as if it understood the value to him of its plump body. Then it tried to leap again. There was a throbbing between his palms. Gold and silver necklaces of water fell from it, as if it was disrobing for sacrifice.

He banged its head on a stone and the thick muscle that had been a fish became limp. Already, the gleam was drying and fading into a mist of gray scales. He thrust it into one of his deep pockets.

Traveling farther upstream, taking a chance near the bridge from which he might have been seen, he caught a second trout. Finally, there was a third one.

Three brook trout, although small, composed a feast, and Mor could be satisifed. The father of a hungry family had roamed, but now he could return home.

• • •

Night was falling and a sunset bled upon the countryside. Liquid drops like red communion wine fell upon the trees and darkened in the river. From across the bogs, or among the boulders, Mor heard rounds of shots fired. Out there, it was not the militiamen who were firing. Small gangs of Luddites were practicing, sure of their escape routes if pursued across the hills, or along networks of tracks which were unfamiliar to the soldiers, who had been brought in from faraway places.

Exposed for a moment upon a hillcrest, Mor glimpsed Lydia Horsfall, the manufacturer's wife. She was taking one of her frequent solitary walks. Always she avoided people. In her loose, dark velvet clothes she was like a black, soft-feathered owl, haunting the dusk. Why did she ramble so much? What restlessness pursued her? What dissatisfaction, that she could not bear to stay in her home? Everyone in Lady Well wondered about it. It was known that she carried two pistols, and in the Old Tup public house they said that she went to hunt Luddites. "Nonsense," others answered, for she was known to be a kind and sympathetic woman. But what other reason could they think of for a lady possessing wealth and every other comfort to walk so restlessly at night? What conceivable reason could there be?

Mor walked on toward Lady Well. On its narrow shelf below the hills, above the woods, it was no more than a stone huddle; a cluster of gray walls, heavy roofs made of thick stone tiles, and stone-paved alleys without trees or grass, veiled in a balloon of smoke.

The taint of smoke in the air grew thicker as Mor came close, but tonight it was not only from household fires. Mor saw, among the dim, gray shapes of cloth stretched to dry on frames in the fields on the edge of the village, that the weaving on some tenterframes had been burned. The embers were still smoldering. Which of the weavers would have their cloth burned? It was obvious who: the blacklegs. The traitors. A soldier, an anxious private of the local militia who did not like such a duty, was guarding the ashen rows.

As Mor climbed the street where his home was, he heard a voice singing from somewhere in a dark alleyway, the melody adapted from a hymn:

You heroes of England who wish for a trade
Be true to each other and be not afraid.

Though the bayonet is fixed they can do no good
As long as we keep to the rule of King Ludd.

Mor reached his cottage. It was in the center of the row. A short flight of stone steps led, above a cellar window, up to his front door, where an old gravestone formed one side of a small landing, separating his house from the next. Iron railings were on the other side, and they also flanked the steps.

Mor had once tried to grow a rose in a pot here from a cutting given him by one of Mr. Horsfall's gardeners; he trailed its branches over the railing, but eventually it had shriveled in the keen winds, and the ceramic pot that had held it cracked open in a frost.

Mor stood in the street for some time, afraid of something in there that might kill off what he had experienced out here, by the river, in the woods. That mystical feeling: it seemed too fragile to take into the human world. The shutters at the window above were not drawn, and he watched the candlelight and firelight flickering on the ceiling of his home.

Eventually, he climbed one step, reached up and closed the wooden shutters, with a squeak and a bang. His family within hardly looked up as dark wings folded over the glass. They knew who it was.

He climbed the remaining steps and entered. After pulling the door shut behind him, he used his heel to secure a rag that was laid along the bottom of the door to seal it against drafts. In the room, there was a smell of smoke, human staleness, the oil of wool and of machines. The cottage had a stone floor; furthest from the fire, the stone was dark from rising damp, while close to the hearth it had dried to a golden yellow. There were three stools, a chair with arms to comfort the man of the house, and a table so scrubbed that it showed ridges of harder wood where the soft parts had been worn away. There was a cupboard, ranged with wooden bowls and platters, but also containing Mor's violin, safe on its top shelf. There was a lidded barrel with a tin scoop, for oatmeal. A large brown jug filled with water stood on the floor. There were two brass candlesticks, and a couple of stoneware ornaments, loved by Mor's wife, Phoebe. One was a spotted dog, the other a huntsman. A geranium, at this time of year little more than a dead stick that was just beginning to sprout, stood on the windowsill.

Behind one door, a flight of stairs climbed directly to an upper room, another room lying beyond that one. Behind another door downstairs was the old scullery, cut into an earthen bank, very damp and used by Mor as his schoolroom. The room in which he stood would also have been damp, were it not for the big stone fireplace on his left. Crowded over the flames were a smoke-blackened pot, a pan of water, and a flat iron dish for heating oatcakes. A rack draped with oatcakes had been hauled by Phoebe up to the ceiling, to warm slowly above the fire. The fire had been allowed to sink low, in reproach, Mor thought, for his lateness. Like most villagers, they were preparing to go to bed, to save the cost of candles.

Mor's wife and two boys, all still in their factory clothes, sat close to the fire. Phoebe was a small woman, so thin that on his few opportunities to hold her, he felt all her bones, and it was frightening. She might break under the gentlest of touches. He still found her light movements sensual, especially if he could manage to make her laugh. More often, though, she moved with erratic jerks. When Mor entered, Phoebe hovered over the pot and guiltily pushed under it some sticks from the pile of kindling kept to dry on the hearth.

"So you've come back," she said in a voice prickly with hurt. "You left your wool piece unfinished, just like on Thursday."

"I've done enough for this week. I wanted to think out some lessons for the school."

"Hmmm!"

Their younger son, Edwin, nine years of age, squatted on the hearth, where he had been determinedly trying to count, using the cinders—a method his father had taught him. He also played with rows of roughly made and painted wooden soldiers, French and English.

Edwin's elder brother, Gideon, fifteen, always seemed crucifed by pain and guilt. He did not look up. Mor and Phoebe's "love child," for whose sake they had married, sat upon a stool rubbing his knees, through which the pain shuttled like the hundred needles of a spinning machine. Mostly it attacked him in the evening, after work. He had a candlestick nearby, to light up his Bible, and Mor suspected he had been taking the opportunity of his skeptic father's absence to read aloud to his mother.

At length, Gideon raised his eyes. "King Ludd set his men to burning cloth in the fields, while you were out," he said. "He asked why you were not there. He told me you are not going on the raid against Horsfall's shearing machines, either."

"No, I'm not! Crawshaw's a fool. It's one thing to prepare for a revolution, another to follow a blind idiot like Arthur Crawshaw who might lead us into a trap."

"But he's our King Ludd . . ."

"A raid in our own village, too! The first law of our operations is to carry out raids only on distant villages. Here anyone who happens to spot us will know who we are."

Mor hung up his hat, coat, and belt behind the door, leaving the fish in his pocket. He came to the fireplace. He smelled to his family of earth and river, quite different from their smell. He rubbed his hands over the fire, which was beginning to flare from Phoebe's sticks. Mor did not lift the lid of the pot himself; that was for the woman to do.

"We'll blacken our faces," Gideon said.

"Blacken your faces! Disguise yourselves in women's dresses! We've armed soldiers to face and a government looking to hang someone, lad! It's all right for Crawshaw, he's from another town and he's a bachelor. But I've you folk to think about. Does he know what defenses are planned for the mill? What soldiers will be on guard? He couldn't organize a Sunday School picnic, that one, let alone something that risks the lives of fathers of children! All he wants is to play the hero. A man sent in to organize us—he knows nothing about Lady Well."

By now Mor had turned to stand with his back to the fire, warming his hands behind him; the master, looking down. Edwin, at his feet, seemed to be concentrating on his soldiers, but he was listening.

"Well, Wrigley is to be asked to take your place," Gideon taunted. "You with your bold messages! They'll say that you're a coward."

"*And* he's superstitious, your 'King Ludd'—wanting twelve men for his raid!"

There were those who believed that the same number as Christ's apostles was necessary for success.

"He's read Tom Paine, or so he says, but he's a superstitious fool, still," Mor continued. "There are too many folk full of superstitions, of one kind or another. With magical Methodists waiting for the end of the world, for Christ to come again. Such are our ruin, not our salvation!"

"There might be some truth in it," Phoebe said quietly.

Mor took no notice. "Opening the Bible at random for guidance, because John Wesley did it. He calls that being a leader of men! I've no time for the chap. None at all. He'll have us all before a hanging judge before he's finished."

"We'll be seeing some hanging before all's done, that's for sure," Phoebe sighingly agreed. "The Lord knows who it'll be. I fear the day. There'll be no redemption."

To change the subject and to try to make her laugh, Mor joked, "Did you know, Phoebe, that Wrigley's got himself wed to Nancy Stott at last? He was drunk when he reached the church. 'What do you mean by bringing him to the altar in this state?' the parson asked, in his grand voice. 'Well, your reverend,' she replied, 'he will not come when he's sober!' "

Phoebe laughed. She lifted the lid of the pot, threw a nervous glance at her husband, then went to busy herself taking a wooden platter and spoon from the cupboard for him. When a husband comes home, no matter where from or what from, his stomach must be satisfied. Her mother had taught her that. There was not much food for her to offer; but it might be better tomorrow.

She knew that he had been poaching. Quick as a hungry animal, she had noticed something heavy pulling at the sides of his coat when he came in. She was afraid of the judgment of both man and God for such crimes, but she was also glad. For what was her family's usual diet? Apart from poachings, all she was ever able to put on the table was oatmeal, eaten as a porridge if they could afford milk, with treacle as an occasional luxury, or with dock leaves, nettles, or blood added, the whole baked into a cake. Sometimes there were potatoes, without greens, except maybe in summer; wild blackberries or whinberries; a little salted meat once in a while; and, as another rare luxury, a fruit preserve pie. They were nowadays forbidden even to gather nuts from the woodlands. So Phoebe had hoped all evening that Mor, when he arrived, would laugh and pull fish or game from his pocket; hoped and yet longed also not to see such a thing, for who knew whether the gamekeeper followed, and after him the hangman? Hunger conflicting with such fear wrought a very mixed happiness.

Mor rubbed his palm on Edwin's head. His hidden gift of food made him smile to himself.

"What's four times five?" he asked.

"Twenty!"

"Six times six?"

"Thirty-five."

"Thirty-six, you gobslutch! What's your head for? For nothing better than to carry your cap? You'll not change the world unless you can do sums." Mor laughed and shook the head out of which he hoped for so much.

Edwin caught sight of the platter and spoon placed on the table for his father.

"Have you brought us anything?"

"What could I bring?" Mor laughed.

Then Gideon interrupted with a story he had heard in the cropping shop about the mill engineer and the overseer. "Joshua Slaughter told Nathaniel Gledhill that a gentleman from the West Country had patented a method of raising water by means of fire. 'Eh?' says fat Nat. 'You can't raise water with fire. It would put it out.' 'By means of steam, you mophead!' Slaughter answers. 'By means of steam by means of fire?' says Gledhill, 'How . . .' "

Mor's own fun died on the air. He was reminded that he was a stranger to his family. Working alone and at home, he saw little of them, but they were together at the factory. It was in order to be with them a little that Mor often walked down with them to Horsfall's in the morning, before returning to his loom. His very house was filled with the smell of the oil of the machines among which they, but not he, worked. It had a rank, vegetable odor, being crushed out of rapeseed. As soap was something they could afford to use only rarely, their clothes and their skin reeked of machine oil. Mor was separated even by his smell, which was of the natural oils of wool, and also with something of the countryside in which he roamed.

Phoebe, seeing Mor turn impatiently back to the pot, recalled her wifely duty and again brushed past him, to reach the pot before he did. Their hands met, accidentally, over the fire, and she pulled away as if she had been burned.

She recovered quickly, but Mor remained shocked for some time. He moved from the fire to his comforting oak chair. He loved it; the ten bulbous spindles at the back, the shapely uprights, the legs that had been shortened for a man who was not tall. It filled him with warmth merely to look at it.

Phoebe filled his plate. She saw that his hands were shaking as he gripped the chair arms.

Gideon had observed the incident over the fire, the hands touching, and had smiled as his mother pulled away.

"Go on with the story!" Edwin demanded. "Tell us what happened to fat old Gledhill!"

" 'How?' repeats Slaughter. 'By means of an engine, that's how.' 'What sort of engine?' asks Gledhill, scratching his head. 'A steam engine driven by coals.' 'How can that be?' Gledhill asks. He couldn't understand a word of it."

Gideon was good at telling stories and he held their attention.

Mor, supping at his broth of turnips and other bits of vegetables, of whatever had come their way to throw into the pot, felt the weight of his marriage. He longed to touch and be touched by Phoebe, but she believed that his desire for contact was "unhealthy."

As Mor brought the spoon up to his mouth, he glanced possessively at his wife, whose laughter had ceased. Momentarily their eyes met; hers so large, in a drawn face.

He peered over his spoon at Gideon, who was rubbing his knee, while with the other hand he searched through his Bible. His hands were big, and still growing. From working in the cropping shop his wrists were powerful, and so would his whole body have been, had he not been underfed.

Mor took a loud suck at his food and looked at Phoebe again. He recalled that when she was a girl she had been like a weasel, lithe and alert.

Made nervous by his watchful eyes, Phoebe busied herself around the room. She never felt short of something to do. She did all she could to keep her house clean, neat, and comfortable, with a pathetic desire to please; especially to please Mor, through being as good a mother as possible.

When she looked at him again, she found him staring at his hand, the one which had touched her, and which was still trembling.

Gideon found what he had been searching the Bible for. " 'In the sweat of thy face shalt thou eat bread, till thou return into the ground . . .' "

Phoebe was at her happiest when listening to him. She often said that her son would make a wonderful preacher—if he was ever able to stand in the pulpit. Whenever she thought of the six-year-old boy she had taken, calming his fears, to the factory, her eyes dampened.

"That boy was once a proverb for straightness," she remarked, accusing Mor though she knew it was not his fault.

Indeed, when Mor realized how crookedly Gideon's knees were growing, he had wheedled and begged to break the boy's contract at Horsfall's, and got him apprenticed instead in his friend Tiplady's cloth-finishing shop, his "cropping shop."

Edwin's legs were still healthy. Mor hoped that he would be able to use them to escape Lady Well, and the boy had, indeed, inherited from his father a love of wandering. He liked to draw maps of Africa, America, or Greece, in sandy banks or in the ashes of the fire, as his father had taught him to do. But, as for most of the children of Lady Well, it was likely that in the end his bones would be crippled from standing at the machines, walking or crawling under them for up to twenty miles per day.

When Edwin heard his mother declare that Gideon had been "a proverb for straightness" he slowly, quietly, stretched first one leg and then the other, to test if they yet held the embryo of that typical, freezing pain. Yes indeed, a promise of suffering was sealed in them, like a demon trapped in a block of ice. Often Edwin had cried, just as Gideon had at the beginning of each day, thinking of what awaited him. He had cried the more as he saw that his mother had damp eyes when she pulled him from his bed, cuddling him but then having to slap him awake. But by now, at the age of nine, he had given up any trust in tears. He would have liked to have gone poaching with his father today. He would have liked to do as Gideon had done and get out of the mill. He did not cry about it anymore. He knocked over a toy Frenchman and pounded it with his fist.

His parents were always afraid that Edwin might, through tiredness or childishness, fall into the spinning frames, as had happened to their third child, their daughter Esther, when she was nine. She had been pulled out from the whirling steel rods, miraculously still alive, but only just. They had spent a few shillings on a surgeon, but could not afford a good one, nor one for long. For a week Esther had tried to hold her own mangled bones together as she lay in bed, before she died. The parents could never bring themselves to speak of this memory, but they longed for Edwin to reach an age that was beyond childish inattentiveness, and be safe.

Their second child, who had died before she could be given a name, had been born one year after Gideon, her misfortune having been to come forth in the winter. Phoebe had no milk, and so Mor had gone begging at the back doors of farms, at the vicarage, and at Mr. Horsfall's mansion for butter and eggs to feed the mother. Humbling himself, and promising to have no more to do with "radicals," had proved useless. So when, two years after Edwin, another son had been born, again in the winter—a child who would have been their fifth—Mor had said to himself, with grim realism, "Christmas baby, then go back to Christ." It wasn't worth being humble and telling lies to try to save a baby who was doomed anyway by the season in which he was born. "A child gone back is a poor man's blessing," as the proverb had it.

Phoebe then began to resent Mor for his pride that "allowed a baby to die." She would try, however hopelessly, to feed their children whom God, if not joy, had given them.

Ironically, here today was Mor's eldest son resenting him for "lack of pride."

Once, when Esther was five and Edwin nearly three years old, when there was a recession in weaving and Mor's schoolteaching had dried up with it, he had gone to the Lady Well Famine Relief Committee. They told him that they could give him nothing so long as he "kept at home" a child who could be employed at Horsfall's. Gideon already worked there, and it was Esther who was wanted. So it was that all Mor's children, with the others at Lady Well, had been put under contract to the mill. They had been lifted from their beds, in the dark for many seasons of the year, and were dragged or carried off, as Mor put it, "same as blind, helpless nestlings, or baby rabbits I might pluck out of hedgerows and tufts of grass." To break the contract for his children made the father liable to punishment in the House of Correction.

Such memories, haunting every day, made one into a revolutionary. Mor finished his turnip broth. He licked the spoon. Phoebe hovered nearby, wanting to play the housewife, the weaver's wife, and not a mere spinning-woman. She cleared away his plate.

"And now!" Mor announced, pleased.

At last he went to his coat and produced the first trout, dangling it by its tail. The spirit of water was a drab sight now, stained, limp, patchily bald of its scales, smelling, and its eyes glazed over, yet the room was transformed by it. He brought forth the other fish and laid them upon the table, reverently.

Edwin ran from the fireside to see them. His face, just reaching over the edge of the table, came eye to eye with the fish. Disliking his brother's sullenness, he was extra glad of proof of his father's care.

But even Gideon, without leaving his stool, peered in the direction of the trout.

From Phoebe, it was more than enough that she smiled.

The trout, in the dim light, had turned into religious objects: sacrifices borne to their altar. They were the tiny focuses of all their hopes and joys.

"There!" Mor said. "Three beauties!"

He was the proud father now; one who despite mill owners and the rest of them could care for his young.

With Edwin peering, Mor gutted one trout into a bucket. Candlelight shone on the scales and eyes. The mouths of all three fish had fallen stiffly open, showing rows of tiny teeth.

Edwin, nervous but fascinated, put forth a finger. He hesitated, then pushed it into one of the mouths.

"Why is its mouth open?"

"The muscles go slack when it dies."

"It's got a tongue."

"Fish 'aven't got tongues, you gobslutch," Gideon said irritably.

"So it has!" Mor remarked. "Fancy you noticing that!"

With a frown for Gideon, Mor picked up a second fish and carved a slit under the belly, from the gills to the tail. He scraped away blood and tissue down to the bone, carefully removing the chain of congealed black, bitter-tasting blood clinging to the spine; handling the knife carefully so as not to lift the hairlike bones out of their bedding in the flesh.

"You have a go at it."

Mor put the knife in Edwin's hand. Over the bucket on the floor, Mor stood behind the child's shoulders, his arms around him, to guide the knife in the third fish.

"Why don't we eat that?" Edwin asked as the offal slipped into the bucket.

"Stop asking questions," Gideon snapped. "You'll get a thick ear for it. Give him one, Father!"

"If you tasted it, you'd find out why. It's bitter, like poison."

"Don't crows eat it?"

"They'll peck at it, yes."

"Crows'll peck your eyes out," Gideon said.

To hide his fury at his elder son, Mor took the bucket of offal to the door and descended the steps. Edwin followed. Thin spears of light from the cracks in the shutters burst across the road before them. Beyond that, the dark folds of the valleys rolled into the night. They were illuminated by a new moon, slender as a nail paring; a bright yellow line. Stars were visible in gaps of cloud.

"Orion, Edwin! And there's the Plough! Do you remember the comet last year, eh? Do you remember?"

Edwin remembered it. He had been told that it forecast revolution.

Mor crossed the road and emptied his bucket over the wall. They could hear lambs crying.

"Look!" Edwin said.

They themselves were watched. From out of the dark fields, two sharp eyes, only inches above the ground, were filled with starlike flickerings; a spy out of the animal world. Man, boy, and animal hypnotized one another for a moment, then the two lights were extinguished, and a dark form rippled over the field.

"It's a polecat," Mor whispered.

It was a species that was almost extinct, and now frightened of the territory it had once owned. Yet, sniffing the air so carefully, in danger, a fugitive, it was alive, as the cared-for and comfortable but captive sheep were not.

They returned indoors. Edwin and Mor wrapped the cleaned trout in dock leaves and hid them under a bedroom floorboard until tomorrow. All went to bed happily; except that, while Mor was out, Phoebe had spat a little blood into a rag.

Mor and his wife always lay together, but did not normally stay awake for long. During the winter they removed only their outer clothes, so there was little of flesh to see or to touch. Neither did the rough bedding induce lovemaking. Phoebe would usually cough a little, with her dry sharp cough of which she did not like to speak. Then she fell asleep.

Mor often stayed awake longer, as he did tonight. He tried to keep still but at last his fingers could not resist stealing toward Phoebe. At first timid, he then gripped her dress tightly and desperately. He was like a man trying to save himself by grabbing at a frail clump of grass on the bank as he falls into a river. It did not wake Phoebe. Nor would he try to awaken her.

Once or twice, he heard the sounds of gunshots in the far countryside, and then he too fell asleep, still clutching the edge of her garment.

Sunday morning brought leisure. They all rose late, and stayed away from church—they were left to do so, because the Luddite villages of the north were regarded as too dangerous to be troubled much by Sabbatarians.

Mor and his sons spent an hour bringing buckets of water from the pump, which was fifty yards away at the end of the street, and heating the water over the fire. After using up much of their precious soap, they changed into clean clothes. Mor put on a shirt that had been darned many times by Phoebe's patient hands. She wore a flower-patterned dress, one almost bleached from washing, which Mor had bought her five years before, after taking his woven piece to market and getting a good price. Gideon and Edwin were in clean breeches and stockings. And all of them felt chilly, without the protection of their workday grime.

Mor, slipping a glove over his hand, went outside to the back of his cottage, where the land rose up to the chapel. From there, he could look down on his own roof. A cock blackbird landed on it, ran a few feet, lifted head and chest to break against the wind, and tried the chill day with a song.

That was joy! That was what joy was—it was when you could run and sing like that! Since the earliest spring days, before any other birds were singing, Mor had listened to the blackbird, marking how its tune grew daily from the merest wobble, feebly challenging rain and cold, to the full melody now.

He plucked some fresh young nettles. When he returned home, Phoebe was scraping and washing the trout again—unnecessarily, except as a way of giving herself to the fish, which had given up their flesh to her. She sprinkled them with dried thyme before grilling them. The stewpot, into which, all through the week, were thrown cabbage leaves, a turnip dropped from a cart perhaps, or a mutton bone, was put aside, like their working clothes.

Mor asked Phoebe to boil the nettles, and some old potatoes. He was as at home and confident today as if he had, in fact, possessed her during the night. They were both as happy as a pair who had made love all night long.

Meanwhile, Gideon was absorbed in his Bible. Edwin tried to help with the fish, getting under his parents' feet. He held a sprig of thyme to his nose and sniffed, lingeringly.

Mor touched his wife's dress, as if accidentally. She stiffened and leaped back.

Mor turned the fish over on the griddle. Phoebe, ruffled, fidgeted about, keeping her distance from Mor, trying to forget that he had touched her and that she had instinctively leaped away. Because Mor had taken over the fish, she tried to please him instead by tidying the house, rubbing at the pottery ornaments and turning the geranium around to the light. To remain still always made her feel guilty and ashamed. When Mor announced that the fish were ready, she took them to the table. The potatoes and nettles were in a steaming bowl.

They all sat down. Mor refused to join in saying Grace, but the others muttered together.

Mor filleted the trout. They would all have liked to drag out this meal, but were too famished. Phoebe would have enjoyed making a display, with tablecloth and china, instead of wooden platters. Mor also would have liked to take his meal slowly and with dignity, but he was forced to behave like a constable, coping with two squabbling boys and having to share three fish among four people.

"You two are as bad as the English and the French," he remarked.

"I'm the English!" Edwin shouted.

"You're a Frenchie! You'd eat frogs!" Gideon retaliated.

"I'm not!"

"Y'are, though!"

As Mor carved the fish, he avoided Phoebe's eyes, because they made him feel ashamed of his hands—so afraid was she of his touching her. But they could be as delicate as a woman's.

He fed the tastiest bits of fish directly into Edwin's mouth. When they had all finished, Edwin asked for the skeletons.

"What do you want them for? There's not enough meat left on them for a cat," Gideon jeered.

"I only want to look at 'em. I want to play with 'em."

"You can't have 'em. I'm chucking 'em onto t' fire."

He had already thrown one spitting onto the flames. Edwin, too proud to shed a tear at Horsfalls', was crying, then he was screaming, and in a flare of temper kicking Gideon's shins and clawing his sleeve, because he held the remaining skeletons over the fire.

"I'm not a Frenchie! I'm not! I'm not!"

"Thou'rt a Frenchie, 'cos thou collects old bones!"

"I'm not. Gi'em to me!"

Mor stepped between them. "Give them to the child."

"The kid doesn't want 'em. 'E's only going to play wi 'em. They'll stink on the hearth, and my mother's been cleaning. She 'as enough to do."

"Give them to Edwin."

"Shall not, Judas!"

"You call me Judas! Why, you—"

"I want 'em! I want 'em!" Edwin still screamed.

"What for?" Gideon sneered. "What do you want them nasty things for?"

"My collection. My anat . . . anat . . . anatocomical collection."

"Anatocomical! Anatocomical! Gobslutch!"

"Anatomical," Mor corrected. "Gideon . . ."

Mor's hand was raised. *Judas!* How it smarted!

Gideon dropped the skeletons from a height onto the hearthstones. One of them snapped.

Mor's blow fell across Gideon's ear. The boy continued to smile, with stupid fixity, maintaining his challenge, wanting to show that all this was beneath his contempt.

Edwin pounced. "Thanks!"

He laid out the unbroken skeleton neatly upon the stone at his usual place on the hearth, then tried to piece the other one together. Slender, delicate, pale-as-pearl bones. In the instant, Edwin had forgotten the tears and quarrels.

Mor was flushed and his heart was thudding. This was not what Sunday should be. Phoebe was awkwardly keeping her eyes turned away. They were all silent, subdued by Gideon's hate.

To calm the quarrel, Mor took his fiddle from where it rested, safe from children's hands and domestic carelessness, at the back of the cupboard. He lifted it out of its case and ran his trembling fingers several times up and down the strings. It was like the gesture of a man caressing the spine and shoulders of his mistress to excite her.

Edwin held the skeleton horizontally, his hands at its head and tail.

"Swish, swish," he said, and made it swim.

"Why 'as it two rows o' bones at the top and one at the bottom?" Edwin asked.

"The curved ones are at the top to guard the organs of the body. The row at the bottom is stiff to make a keel to balance it upright in the water."

"Why . . ."

"Stop asking questions," Gideon interrupted, trying to ignore his burning ear. "It's nought but God's universe, as He created it. 'Curiosity killed the cat.' Thou deserves a thrashing, asking questions."

Mor tucked his instrument under his chin. They all fell silent, with attentiveness now, instead of with anger. The schoolmaster had brought up his children to be respectful before music.

From the moment he bent his cheek upon it, the head of the man and the delicate body of the violin became one. The tune he played, running up from the sounding board and amok through his head, drove him crazy with delight.

If he raised his face he would see Gideon's distaste. The boy sat with his hand over his ear, humiliated, and ashamed of the mark. Mor was hiding his tears at having had to chastise a boy who already had so much to contend with.

Mor could feel, too, Gideon's dislike, or pretended dislike, of fiddle music.

He put down his instrument. "Nothing is so frail and light as a fiddle," he said. "A child can smash it. I've seen a parson stamp 'is foot through one because 'e did not like the music. Any brute can put 'is foot through a fiddle, yet the music survives. Like the snowdrops are strong, that come in the earliest days of spring. They look so frail, they bend, but they push through the frozen earth and flower in the cold, nevertheless."

Gideon sniggered. Mor began to play again.

The music stirred Phoebe. Mor recognized in her eyes a light like that of a couple of hours before when the fish were being prepared.

Then, from outside, there came several bars of a hymn tune, being tried out on the chapel's harmonium.

"Are you going to the Methodists this afternoon, Gideon?" Mor asked. "Mr. Whitehead from Halifax is taking the class. You'll not want to miss 'im."

Though addressing Gideon, Mor was smiling at Phoebe. On Sunday afternoons, Lady Well packed its children off to the Sunday School. It was the only time men had to lie with their wives when not exhausted. The Sunday School was therefore very popular, and many children had been conceived while their elder brothers and sisters were blessing the Lord's name.

"Can I go down to the river?" Edwin asked.

"Keep out of the wood, then. Don't go into the wood. Don't go in there."

"No, I won't."

"Promise me."

"Yes."

"You can go down to the bridge. Who are you going with?"

"My friends."

"Tell them the same, to keep out of Horsfall's game copses."

Edwin was already preparing to set off.

Mor bedded his violin and put it away in that cupboard which his children had been brought up to regard as sacred. He was tense and his hands were still shaking.

Phoebe was quivering, too, but with alarm at that tender side of herself which she had shown to her husband.

Edwin was going out the door.

Mor took hold of Phoebe's hand, at first meekly and then gripping it, as he felt her reluctance. With Phoebe, the most tender hold felt like a violation. The light birdlike bones, ivory-colored through her bloodless skin, were quivering.

Gideon was watching. His hands, too, were shaking as he tied a kerchief around his neck for chapel. He was trembling with anger at the threatened violation of his mother. He hesitated, unwilling to leave the house, knowing perfectly well why it had been suggested that he go to the chapel, and then he left suddenly.

Mor had not let go of Phoebe. He avoided her eyes, but understood the meaning of her reluctant hand.

"What is it, Phoebe?"

"Nothing." Her head was bowed. She frowned with irritation.

"What is it?" he repeated, as so often in the past. He felt annoyed at her refusal to talk, and as usual he struggled not to show it.

And, as always, she answered again, "Nothing."

Sixteen years before, when they were courting and he had walked her home after church or fair through dusks brimming with noises of lovers, she would merely sigh. Her heart was breaking. Why? "What is it, Phoebe?" "Nothing," she would answer. "Nothing, think nowt of it." So through the weeks, the months, and the years of their marriage she had answered him, "Nothing."

This Sunday afternoon, however, she allowed him to pluck her away, like a plant from a hedgerow, a snowdrop from a bank.

There was no weight to her body. He opened the door at the foot of the stairs and led her up. She coughed nervously, and he, one step above her, clutching her hand, turned momentarily. She looked guilty even about her own cough.

Their bedroom was at the front of the house. One wall was filled with a row of slender windows. These were not for the sake of the view, but to light that huge, ancient, inherited loom, on which Mor had learned his trade. His half-finished piece of weaving, abandoned the previous day, hung accusingly upon it. On the struts and nearby, Mor had pinned lists of wild herbs and flowers. Their common names were matched with their Latin ones, so that he could learn them. There was also a tiny library—Plato, Rousseau, Tom Paine, a Latin grammar, and Goldsmith's *History of the Earth and Animated Nature*. Always, a book was propped open, so he could read a page and digest it as he worked.

The room was quiet, dusty, brightened with shafts of light breaking among the loom strings and piercing the whitewashed corners. This whole area, which was the major part of the room, was an emblem of his nature. He felt there like a scholar in his quiet study, or a monk in his cell, or like one of the Old Testament prophets working out his thoughts in a cave in the wilderness.

The bed was forced into a corner. Near it, on a rough table, Phoebe's bridal things were displayed. Clean and undisturbed, preserved under a polished glass bell jar that had been given to her by the apothecary as a wedding present, this was her emblem of herself. Mor observed bitterly that she enoyed the preserved fact that she was married more than the act of marriage itself, meager and rare though it was.

Phoebe was out of breath, and it was not merely from climbing a flight of stairs. She was terrified because her marriage had brought a baby every two years, and by this reckoning she was due to conceive now. Despite her fear, Phoebe, like all other women, had helplessly conceived, thinking as little of it as possible, because it was what everybody did. Pregnancy at least was a period when she could rely on her husband not touching her.

She feared that another birth would kill her. And so, when she was with child two years before, she had "sent it back," using the abortionist, Rose Gledhill, who was the wife of Nathaniel Gledhill, the overseer of Horsfalls'. Mor was led to believe that she had miscarried.

She spat quietly into a rag. It was a nervous habit. Also out of habit she began to tidy the room, until Mor grew impatient. Finally resigning herself, for the sake of her husband, whom she did, after all, love, Phoebe collapsed onto the bed, removing her shoes but otherwise without disrobing herself. She had no wish to display her coarsened skin, her limbs marked with the scars of mill accidents, her stomach ridged with stretch marks from childbearing: the working man's wife, on the working man's bed stained with tears, menstrual blood, sweat and semen.

Then there came a commotion and shouts from the street, so Mor had to see what it was. Before he reached the window, he heard the noise of a stone striking a door. He expected to see soldiers, perhaps an arrest. It could be that they had come for him.

There were no soldiers in view. What he saw was a procession of strange, frightened, silent children. They were those whom he had met a few days before being brought in a cart, and now in the charge of that same Nathaniel Gledhill who was husband of the abortionist and overseer of the Sunday School, as well as of the mill.

Mor's neighbors were throwing stones and laughing at the children.

He remembered how, when he was a child, they had chased the strange witch-woman Anne Wylde through the streets. *Why did we do it? I still feel too ashamed to tell anyone, even now. "Man's inhumanity to man," as Burns the plowman put it. There they are, still throwing stones at their fellow sufferers. How can they enjoy mocking them? If instead we declared our brotherhood, the rights of man, stayed together, let none get between us, and kept to our highest, not our lowest aspirations, the earth would be ours, and no one could oppose or oppress us.*

Mor was relieved to see that the apprentices were at least fairly clean and well dressed, and he tried to convince himself that things were not as bad as he had feared. The girls were in new, blue pauper's uniforms because it was the Lord's Day, and the boys were in breeches which were also new, intended for Sunday only, and, like the prayer books which they carried but could not read, articles resentfully provided by contract from the Hackney Workhouse.

Gledhill marched in front, swinging his notorious bryony stick with its sharp-eared devil carved out of the knob. He never glanced to his rear but took it for granted that all were obedient and orderly behind.

Mor turned away from this sight that he could do nothing about, and glanced at Phoebe. He caught her in a moment of relief that he had, for the time being, abandoned her. When she met her husband's eye, her expression changed. She showed her usual torment, of wanting to give love, yet dreading the touch of his hands.

He walked toward her along the flank of windows. Not saying anything about the noises outside, he stripped to his underclothes and settled against her side. Gently, with one finger, he stroked her thigh, at first over, and then under, his favorite, flower-patterned dress.

If only she would respond! How much he longed for hands, female hands, and how vulnerable he was to them!

Having been an orphan, a baby found on the workhouse steps with nothing but the name "Greave" stitched on his shirt to identify him, he, especially, had suffered from the lack of being touched that all boys suffered. Girls were fondled by relatives but boys were not, lest it "spoil" them, and he had grown up knowing that his only hope must come from a wife. Hence his lack of judgment. The need for caressing hands had overcome other considerations, hence his ill-judged, over-eager devotion in courting unrewarding Phoebe. In his rush for hands, he had been enslaved by the first ones to touch him . . . they were hers. Her failure to satisfy him had increased his desperation and his eagerness to marry, ironically and tragically, this one person least likely to satisfy him. He had never dared admit even to himself what he most wanted. He became ashamed of it. Oh, to be caressed, held, stroked, fondled, stroked, held . . .

He was torn in the jaws of a trap. One set of teeth rending his flesh was his desire for passionate touching. The other jaw was his guilty conscience telling him to evade and deny it—anything to stop his wicked desires from surfacing.

"I'm tired," Phoebe said, frightened. "I'm so tired, Mor. Do we need to . . ."

Because of those five births and the abortion, sex caused her pain. She had sores and scabs where the apothecary had cauterized infections. She had wounds caused by the burning chemicals that had been sold to her by him, or by itinerant barbers and peddlers, to use as post-coital contraceptives. Heaven only knew what compounds they were, and because she never saw the itinerants again, she could not ask them.

They pained her, these wanderers, if not through the medicaments they sold, then with the interested look in their eyes. Some of the peddlers were also preachers, holding forth beneath an ash tree at a crossroads, with wonderful ideas that she had never thought of, before they described Hell and Redemption in such vivid images.

Mor fumbled hurriedly under her dress. It was either that or madness. Slack as her breasts were, he lifted and stroked them. Even now, she was most concerned to occupy her own hands with straightening her dress and tidying the bedclothes, not with touching him. She desperately stretched her hands out sideways, as though she was pinned down and drowning.

She had once heard a ballad about a maiden chained to a rock as the tide came in. That was how she felt.

She choked under his mouth. But then, when that cruel horrible business she dared not think about grew inevitable, she felt some pleasure . . . she dared not think of it . . . how could she dare tell him . . . ? from the submission. Anyway, she felt sorry for her husband. She started to moan, restlessly turning her face away. She closed her legs one minute, but in the next moment she was clutching him, gripping the curls at his neck, suffering the bristles of his chin and the saliva of his half-parted, hopeful mouth, as she desperately embraced that which, anyway, she could not avoid.

She did what she believed all women did . . . she pretended to be happy. As friends had told her, "It won't last long. It won't hurt much. Pretend you're enjoying it. They like that and it keeps 'em quiet later. They go to work wi' their minds rested."

Mor, in the midst of the act, heard her muttering. He picked out, scattered among other words, "pray," "altar," and "soul." She was confusing love with churchgoing.

He entered her. Usually the greater part of the animal pleasure was taken from him, because he dared not forget himself. He knew that he must pull out fast, or have a child. By this method they had unintentionally conceived six times during their marriage. He hung tormented on the edge of forgetfulness, thinking: *Coitus interruptus, at least I know the Latin for it. I'm not ignorant.*

They were his last thoughts before oblivion. He had waited for such a long time and today it was not to be taken from him.

"My gown," she muttered. "My gown."

She felt Mor's semen in her womb, a river loosed into the sea. The tide was coming. She was terrified. Tears stung her eyes.

Mor fell heavy and slack beside her. He felt desolate. It was a desolation that might now be filled with another unwanted child.

He thought that perhaps Phoebe would rather have been in chapel. If only she could love him for himself, and not for some Christ Saviour that she was looking for, through him!

While for Mor, the sense of something, someone, being absent was like confinement within a prison.

The entire world was a prison. The universe was a confinement. It was a place that he could not escape. Oh, to be with the love whom he could imagine! Oh, yes, he had imagined her, imagined it. He would rather clutch a stone than have nothing more than this. Yet if the beloved had existed, a single squalid room would have seemed bigger than the universe and all the spaces of the stars.

Singing burst from the children in the chapel; or maybe it had burst once already, but he had not heard it.

He slipped his arm around Phoebe's shoulders.

"Did you like it?" she asked.

"Yes."

"You feel spent now? Men need to spend themselves or they'd be tempted . . ."

"Yes. Thank you."

"It's all right, Mor, my love. You need it. I know what men are. You can do it if . . ."

"Thank you."

She placed her face upon his chest, at last with some acceptance of lovemaking, now that it didn't threaten her. But if a child should come of it . . .

Mor slept. A membrane was stretched between his inner and outer worlds. Shadows were cast on the membrane. Dreams.

He had a dream that had come to him several times before. A female, without precise lineaments yet he was sure she was the same woman each time, held a dark red flower, a rose, out to him. She beckoned him to take it, but when he put his hand out, he woke up.

Always after the dream he would lie for a long time, just as he did today, wondering about the significance of the woman, the flower, and the redness of it.

He would think about it later when he struggled to recall the woman's features. Always she remained faceless, though the flow of her shape was clear to him. Each time, he thought she had said something, but he could not recall what it was. He could not quite remember what the flower was, either, even though he was a botanist. He was certain only of its redness. Mor felt sure that the flower, whatever it was the symbol of, was something that he must search for and grasp. Or it would find him, some day.

CHAPTER THREE

April 16th

very weekday morning, between five and half past five, the bell rang on the tower of Horsfall's spinning mill to call the women and children. Families hurried through the town or down from the hills, across wastelands, between enclosures, and by the sides of the woods.

It was still dark in the mornings. The lamps over the countryside formed a huge star, or was it a quivering crocus-colored flower, reflected upon the bright whiteness of a late frost. The lamps were necessary mostly under the trees, for the clearest of moons hung above.

Along the Greaves' street, lamps were moving behind the shutters, points of brightness escaping through the chinks.

Everywhere in the village there was the noise of clogs and the crying of children.

"Look!" Mor exclaimed as he stepped out of doors with his family.

"Aye, it's cold," Gideon said.

"No . . . the moon. Edwin, look! Clear as a baby's eye! Don't you like to see the moon, Gideon?"

"No! It's cold! My leg aches!"

"Y'ave to look upwards sometimes."

"Not if it makes you stumble on t' ground, you don't. No one else's doing it," Gideon replied.

"No," Mor had to say.

"*I* am," Edwin answered.

"You're always staring at something," Gideon said. "Curiosity killed the cat."

Phoebe and her sons, like other families, carried, as well as lamps, their "baggin," their food for the day. Phoebe had a basket, Gideon and Edwin had bags made of rabbit skins. The food was usually oatcakes and ale. This morning, Edwin's baggin held a leg of rabbit that he had filched from his father's poachings. It was a secret—like his bottle of ale already hidden in a basket of waste wool in the mill.

Gideon limped along, his pale, clenched features still turned toward the spillings of lamplight on the ground.

The few women who did not go to the mill but still spun at home were busy raking their morning fires. They hardly spoke to the mill women. They behaved remotely, in the manner one adopted to those who belonged to a different sect of church or chapel. Phoebe still felt guilty before their eyes. The first women to go to work in the new factory had had their windows broken.

The *bang bang* of handlooms was beginning through the town. Soldiers quartered in the Adam and Eve public house were hanging around the door, where the moonlight shone off buckles and weapons.

"They say in the cropping shed that they brought down wages year by year because Mr. Pitt came up with an income tax for the masters to pay," Gideon said. " 'If you cannot pay taxes as well as adult wages, then take the children to the work,' Mr. Pitt told 'em. We're going to change all that. Beginning with the raid, we'll rise up. All will be together. The day is drawing nigh."

They passed the church. Beggars sat in the porch, many without a leg or an arm, or both, from the wars. There was a younger boy, from a hill farm, who had been crippled in a factory accident and, not being able to help with the family's livelihood, had been turned away from home.

The crowd went downhill by the vicarage. The children ran to the young eagle that had been captured by the parson when, during the winter, she had strayed out of the hills in search of food. She had swooped upon the parson's pigeon cote and he had wounded her with his blunderbuss, then staked her with a four-foot rope in his garden. As she crouched on the beaten, fouled earth where her erstwhile prey, the domestic hens and pigeons, no longer feared to come close, she was like an old, dying vulture or kite. Her unkempt feathers, in the light of the moon and the lamps, were gray as dirty, neglected pewter.

When first fastened up, the great bird was unable to believe that she could not fly. Each magnificent, confident, stately rush had been stopped by a shot of pain. She had crumpled into an undignified bundle of feathers, like a burst pillowcase in the snow. Eventually the eagle gave up, merely condescending sometimes to peck without relish at the mice thrown to her. She stared balefully at Lady Well, through her yellow, unflinching eyes. Birds do not weep.

"Anything that starts wi' foolish talk in the cropping shed will be shot and pinioned as easy as yonder brave, young eagle. There's your symbol for revolution. If we show we've got wings and brains and ideas, that's how they'll serve us," Mor said.

They hurried down the long flights of stone steps that sank through the woods. The bell was still clanging. Ewes, giving birth in the folds, were crying across the valleys. The lambs shivered on long, wide-spread tottering legs, their tails twisting in circles as they pulled at the teat.

The moon, on the frost, transformed some embankments into pale and ghostly wings. Sometimes you can feel all the weight of the moon, and see that it is no more than a cold rock heavily rolling around. Sometimes it is mysterious. But when shining high, round and bright, as it was this morning, it is like a tunnel, revealing a glimpse into a brilliant universe beyond.

Phoebe hastened along, her wiry arms moving briskly. Even from a distance, from the back, you could tell she was a troubled person, by the stoop of her shoulders, with the sharp edges of the bones thrusting through her shawl, and from the dangle of her arms.

With Edwin at her side she was holding her lamp close to the ground to search for primroses, the petals of which were shut against the dark.

Mor and Gideon caught up with them. Edwin asked his father at what time the flowers would open.

"When the sun comes up. If you slip out o' doors then, it's like entering the gates of Heaven."

"Go out o' the mill?" It was impossible!

Mor laughed. "I'll come with you! We'll all run away."

Edwin was thoughtful. "Which way is America?" He had asked this question often, but still loved to hear the answer.

Mor pointed.

Edwin stared toward the barrier of hills. "How far is it?"

"Thousands and thousands of miles."

"How long on a ship?"

"Months. A year if it gets lost."

"Where do y'ave to go first, to catch ship t'America?" Edwin knew the answer to this question too. Liverpool; his tongue savored the taste of the sweet, exotic word.

His father merely smiled, letting the boy answer for himself.

"They sail from Liverpool, don't they? Have you been t'America?"

"No, my son, I've not been to America." Just as he had answered many times before.

"Why not?" To Edwin, a place so out of reach that his father had not been there was the most fabulous of all travelers' goals.

"I suppose it'll be full of strife and trouble, same as everywhere else. They call it 'the land of promise,' though. Perhaps I'm wrong."

They had reached the bottom of the stone stairway. Bursting out of the woods, into the louder clang of the bell, they were in a moon-soaked clearing by the river. Nearby was a block of new, large houses built for the overseer, the engineer, and the clerk. It was positioned here so that they could watch over the mills and the field of tenterframes.

The workers threaded between the lines of cloth, which were guarded by soldiers. A skinny, wild-eyed factory girl shrieked at one of the guards, "What did you join the Volunteers for, Bandy Legs? Didst tha want to learn the use of a gun t'elp us win the revolution?"

But it was the girl who had the crooked legs, and who in fact envied and longed for the straight-limbed young soldier, who had no answer for her. He had joined the militia to escape the poverty of his village in southern England, and to fight Napoleon, and he was trying not to hate the work that he had been given to do. He tried to keep in mind what he had been told: that Yorkshire, too, was a frontier.

"The revolution's tomorrow, Sally," her friend joked. "Tomorrow, that never comes. Stop teasing the poor recruit. He'll be missing his mammy."

"I'm not teasing 'im! Some of the lads do join up for that, don't they, soldier? Just to find out how to use a gun."

Mor was laughing. What *he* saw was an awkward youth, armed, but unable to defend himself against a couple of girls who made him blush.

By now, a crowd had collected off the hillsides. They poured through the narrow passageway between the mill buildings and the wall at the foot of the garden which lay in front of Mr. Horsfall's house. The mansion, with its yellow stone blackening slowly from soot, sat on a steep rise, so that the master could watch over what went on below his rose gardens.

A broad-shouldered groom was posted in the millyard to try to stop the workers from waking Mr. Horsfall and his family. There were also a couple more militiamen. Nevertheless the women and children did what they usually did to make their presence felt. They began a rhythmic stomping on the cobblestones with their boots and clogs. Then they looked up, to see what effect their protest was having.

It was not for the master, nor his wife or children, that they searched. It was for the face, high up and remote in the house, of one who was locked away because of his ugliness, and who could rarely sleep. In the light of a lamp or a candle, a corroded, terrifying face would waver for a second behind the glass—frightened of being seen, yet not able to resist looking.

"There's the ghostie, there's the boggart, there's the ghost, there! There! There!" the workers chanted.

Phoebe, too, tried to glimpse that creature which the members of its own family would not go near. It was the spectral, still-living wreck, rotting from syphilis, of Nicholas Horsfall senior. *The wages of sin. The fear of Hell,* Phoebe thought. *The wounds, the tortures, the scalding pains, that the preacher selling treacle for my cough told me about.*

They all knew that food was taken in to that imprisoned wretch by a servant with a scarf drawn across her face, so as to keep her from the stench, and to hide her revulsion. Servants from the house had described to the people of Lady Well the extra details that they could not see for themselves when they looked up to the window. The skin of its face was tightly drawn back, leaving a thinly covered skull. The eyes were dead pools, although in one a little yellow twilight still lingered, to take in dim impressions of the Yorkshire it had once commanded. The nose was eaten away, flesh and bone, leaving no more than a volcanic scar. The lips were drawn back and had almost vanished. The gums were rotting, leaving the few remaining teeth standing proud. Its throat and tongue were corroded, so that it could not scream. It could barely draw breath.

The vision faded back from the window. The glass was clouded with a breath that fortunately the spectators could not smell.

After this entertainment, or chapel-like illustration of the wages of sin, or whatever it was for them, the workers turned to their right, in between large gateposts. These separated the narrow end of the main, three-story spinning mill, which was at right angles to the river, from the counting house and from a row of cloth-finishing sheds.

The gates of Paradise Mills were made of iron and brass, with a grinning yellow sun, the Horsfalls' family insignia. Overhead was the motto Labor Omnia Vincit. ("A corrupt play on 'Amor Omnia Vincit,' " Mor explained in his school.) The pillars were decorated with the carved figures of Adam and Eve. Two scenes were depicted. Facing out toward the woods, the pair were shown in Paradise, under vines. Adam grasped his spade, whilst the sensual Eve dallied with the snake, which nibbled at her lips. On the inner flanks of the posts, Adam and Eve slunk into exile—toward the mill. A joke? Another moral?

The women and children as they entered saw, ahead of them, the new house for "apprentices" built on the riverbank. On their left was the spinning mill, its farther end against the stream, powered by a waterwheel there. On their right, across the yard, was the old fulling mill built half a century before by the clothier Benjamin Greave. This was also at right angles to the stream, because of its waterwheel. The fourth side of this square was made up of a row of cloth-finishing sheds. In these the woollen pieces, brought in by the handloom weavers, had their nap raised in a gig mill, then were clipped smooth by Horsfall's own croppers, using not hand shears but shearing machines, and finally passed on to the dye house.

Paradise Mills were the grandest in the district. Having his own finishing shops meant that Horsfall did not need to depend upon Tiplady's, nor on sending woollens elsewhere, in vulnerable cartloads, to be finished.

A reservoir, or "lodge," held the water to drive the wheel. Except for the locked opening by which the engineer passed from the waterwheel housing onto the bank of the lodge, all doors faced into the millyard. The windows were barred. The main gate was locked after the workers entered and only unfastened for the passage of carts. The place was, in fact, a fortress.

Gideon did not enter between the gates, but passed on, by the mill wall, downstream fifty yards to Tiplady's cropping shop.

Mor called at the mill office, to see about obtaining credit from Horsfalls' to purchase a warp from them. Then he retraced his way up through the trees to his home and to his solitary loom.

What'll 'e do all day? wondered Phoebe, turning her back upon her husband as he climbed into the sun. *'E'll not get on wi' 'is piece. I know 'im. Books! Staring out o' t' window. Going down to t' river. Then more books!*

All over the high parts of the countryside, cocks were crowing, although it was still not daylight in the valley, and merely a yellow tinting was to be seen by the birds on the hills.

Only seconds after the first cock had alarmed the hillcrest village of Height, like the bursting of a clock spring suddenly they were all calling, on and on, through Yorkshire and Lancashire, the land ringing with them before the day began farther below.

While Mor climbed into the sunlight, at the mill the women and children entered a shadowy cave, where rows upon rows of candles were still lit.

The machines had not yet started, the door was open, the sun had risen a little more, and they could all hear the cocks over the countryside. Edwin hated the blinding plunge into the dark mill, the cloying smell, the great sizes of rooms, men and machines.

Nathaniel Gledhill, with his bryony stick, was waiting at the entrance, behind his desk. As usual, he was smiling. A man appears more fearsome when he can beam upon misery. Gledhill took out a large handkerchief. He brought it out so often and proudly, it might have been the British flag.

The overseer's desk was sloped toward the workers. It held a large Bible, with a fresh passage exposed daily. Very few of the workers were able to read it for themselves, nor did they have the time to. It was displayed for the same reasons that a Bible might be on show in a church—to impress people with the existence of a knowledge to which they had no direct access. At times, Gledhill would read a passage aloud himself. On other occasions, he would choose someone who he knew was able to read. Some beneficiary of Mor Greave's tiny school, perhaps. Among whom, of course, was numbered Edwin Greave.

"Read that," Gledhill commanded Edwin.

To reach up and read it, Edwin had to bounce on his toes. As Gledhill made a hobby of scouring the woodlands for botanical specimens, he had selected an apt passage.

" 'Consider the lilies o' the field 'ow they grow they toil not neither do they spin . . .' "

Edwin took another deep breath, and flew over commas and pauses to get it over with.

" 'And yet I say unter you that even Solomon in all 'is glory was not arrayed like one of these wherefore if God so clothe the grass o' the field which today is and tomorrow is cast into the oven . . .' "

Gledhill slammed his palm on the desk. "Enough! Not much style about thee, is there? This is an affecting passage of the Bewk, it needs some expression put into it."

"Stop now, Edwin, that's enough," Phoebe told him. "Mill's waiting. Time and tide wait for no man."

"Was it your father who taught you to read like that?"

"Aye, it was," Edwin answered snappishly.

"It could 'elp 'im advance, sir," Phoebe explained.

He speaks like his father, too, Phoebe thought. *Short wi' folk. It can be taken wrongly.*

"I 'ope so, Mrs. Greave. Too much schooling isn't always a good thing. Some get into bad ways just because of it. I've done all right for myself, wi'out schooling. The army taught me all I need to know."

The factory bell ceased to clang. It was half past five precisely, as registered by the clock on the tower, and by the watch that Gledhill portentously held in his palm.

Phoebe went straight to her spinning frame. Hers was one of the tidiest, cleanest in the factory, and she was among the first to reach her machine.

She picked up her feather duster and started to tease out bits of fluff that had settled out of the laden air during the night. The other women were idling to their work. Who was Phoebe trying to please? As Nathaniel Gledhill was not yet in sight, it must have been God.

The younger girls, in a room with the small boys present, were stripping and dressing themselves in their factory smocks, which they called "bishops." It was all done under the overseer's supervision. *The more moral a girl is, the more she suffers in this Christian place* . . . Edwin remembered his father's words as he hid under his shirt the leg of rabbit out of his baggin. The children had to put their baggins and clogs into a cupboard.

The overseer banged his stick on the floor for silence. "Praised be the Lord and God save the King!"

They all chanted after him, "Praised be the Lord and God save the King!"

From the dust, from the heat, the children's voices were as harsh as a choir of crows.

The overseer exchanged his staff for a three-foot length of leather belting, and the bare-footed children were ushered onto the floor, into the heady fumes of the rapeseed oil which bathed the drive shafts and the gears. Now Paradise Mills shook and shuddered into life.

It was at this moment that Joshua Slaughter, the engineer, went onto the lodge bank.

The setting moon, a great tired dewdrop close to the hills, swelled as it neared the horizon. In another part of the sky the sun had risen, igniting the songs of blackbirds, thrushes, and robins through the woods. A pied wagtail, in smart, new spring feathers, was scurrying and bowing along the top of the bank that separated the reservoir from the stream.

The world had been cold blue, but now the sun cast an orange light over the frosty fields; a brilliance that faded quickly, as the frost on southern slopes was warmed into breath and mist. The sun drew threads of mist off the dark, still waters of the reservoir. The higher they rose, the thinner they became and the faster they vanished. They were, fancied the engineer, being wound upward onto invisible bobbins on the spinning frames of Heaven.

Joshua, a childless widower who had lost his wife in childbirth, and who in his work, too, was a loner, looked forward to his day with pleasure, for he loved the machines. He gained satisfaction, too, from being a God-fearing man, and in the evening he planned to go ten miles to Bradford to spend an hour or so praying, debating, and looking forward to the Millennium with a group of the followers of Joanna Southcott.

He cranked up the sluice gate. An edge of water creased, folded, sucked leaves off the surface of the reservoir, twisted into braids of silver, and fell with a swift, silent glitter into the mill. A snake of water entered the factory, as secretly and quietly as a spy to do its work. Having fallen out of sight to the bottom of its stone hole, it thundered onto the blades of the wheel.

He slipped back into the wheel housing, locking the door behind him. The wheel, twenty-five feet in diameter, six feet wide across the blades, catching the flow at the top and on the downstream side, was by now turning so rapidly that he could hardly catch sight of it under its cloak of silver. The rough-fitting wooden axle groaned. The raging wheel was a god in its watery element, powering the great mill with its cargo of lives. Most of the stream fell away with a roar at the bottom of the turn, but some of the water clung and dropped later, screaming at the wheel's rise, in a glitter of rainbows like those which had recently clung around the moon. They snapped into small pieces, joined in trembling circles, broke again and darted in fragments—bright dragonflies around the turning god.

Once the wheel was in motion such a great force of water wasn't necessary to keep it running, and the engineer diverted most of it. *Wasted it,* he couldn't help thinking, although everywhere in the world it ran downhill anyway, and God Himself was wasteful. God did not appear to realize what could be done with the sleeping powers He had created. How can a man understand that? Joshua wondered.

He listened, his ear cocked, discriminating among the orchestra of sounds from the wheel housing. They all had a meaning to him. On hearing one that was not quite right, or out of his solicitous love imagining it so—like a mother with a spoiled child, and always thinking it sickly—Joshua threaded between the gears and wheels to make an adjustment. He was a slender, lithe, not very tall man, "handy for worming and diving amongst my engines," as he said.

As if he had all the time in the world, he stood transfixed, listening and marveling at this rage of energy which through the night had lain dormant and harmless in the lodge, until he fed it into the factory. Slaughter was one of the few at Horsfalls' who "labored in his vineyard," as he put it, alone, at his own pace, and had time to contemplate such things. He was in charge of the machines, not they the master of him.

The only initiate into the mystery of machinery, he was a priest and a king. He would not allow anyone else into his wheel room, his powerhouse. Good engineers being rare and essential, he could even keep Mr. Horsfall out. Oh, what an emblem of the powerful body of God was a factory for spinning worsted woollens! He felt himself like God. He found time to compose "instructive similes" comparing, for instance, a factory for mechanical weaving to the greater dynamo of the earth and the stars. He made up verses on such topics as "The Mechanical Hoist," or "The Railway to Heaven Arrived At Through Teetotalism and Methodism," or "The Railway to Hell Reached Downwards Through Drunkenness."

Slaughter put the wheel into gear and it ran more quietly.

He went into the main building, where a man was snuffing out candles, and the workers were at their stations. All over the room, coils of light, the spun threads, were unwinding down to the spindles—it was beams of light that they were spinning, not wool.

He saw something which, no matter how long he was familiar with it, touched his heart. Some machines were designed to the scale of a child, with the lowest rows of bobbins only two or three feet above the floor. With terrible irony, they were called "throstles," or thrushes, for their sweet singing sound. The machine makers—Mr. Smith of Keighley, Mr. Platt of Dob Cross—must have hard hearts! They might as well be forging slave shackles.

Slaughter felt for the women and children. Because of his difference of attitude, he and Gledhill were now hardly on speaking terms, although they lived next door to one another.

At the far end of the mill he caught sight of Phoebe Greave. "Winsome Phoebe," he whispered, with no one to hear. He admired the way she looked after her frame. She herself was as neat and gleaming a woman as you could expect to meet in such circumstances, and how she kept herself so clean, he did not know.

But he must not dwell on that tantalizing sight; others might notice him. He turned to contemplate the rows of machines, where there was no grief or despair, but only the possibility of infinite improvement. Sadly, he felt that the workers showed little appreciation for what they operated. "Just like women," they only noticed the frames when they broke down. Even Phoebe Greave did not seem to grasp the refinement of scientific principle involved, although he had stolen many opportunities to talk to her on this subject . . .

• • •

Edwin's work was as a "piecer." He had to guide the threads through the eyelets and the metal channels. When threads snapped, he had to join them up again. He also retrieved waste wool and put it in a basket. Then he had to keep his mechanical mistress supplied with raw wool, either by fetching it himself or bullying one of the apprentice girls, whose first job in the factory was to fetch and carry.

The factory ran on bullying as much as it did on water power. Gledhill walked the aisles continuously. He banged his strap on the frames, hummed, sang a hymn, or made jokes. "Idleness! Debauchery! Sluggards!" he would yell. "You'd fall asleep over your work, would you? Cheating your master of wages! When I was an apprentice I'd never dare sleep in my master's time. I'll give you something to droop your 'eads for, I will!"

The nails of his thumb and forefinger were long and curved, like hawks' beaks. With these he pinched the children's ears, sometimes tearing the flesh. As another punishment, he would dip his victims head-first into a tank of cold water. Or he would "leather" them, after he had imprisoned them in one of the big, wheeled baskets.

The spinning machines were unprotected. The children had to scramble beneath the frames next to the drive shafts, oily and unshielded. The floor was slippery with oil. It took only a moment's forgetfulness for the frames to grab their loose gowns or ragged trousers.

"Look, Gledhill," Nicholas Horsfall had complained. "It's very wasteful having children maimed, and their fingers ripped off. A great loss of money, so make 'em stay awake! How do we fight Bonaparte if we can't keep our manufactories running? And if a serious accident occurs, make sure they're buried a long way away, outside the parish. These damned factory inspectors with their philanthropy will fall heavily on you as well as me, you know."

Eight o'clock arrived. A board was turned to inform everyone that they had ten minutes in which to clean their machines. Then Mr. Gledhill swung a handbell and the children were lined up to be led out to satisfy their natural requirements. (It wasted time, but the product eked out the "night soil" used for bleaching cloth.)

The overseer and his wife, Rose, who couldn't think why she had married such a man, led them out, boys in one group and girls in another, under the blue sky of a clear day that had arisen without them. A lark rose into it, singing. It became a speck and vanished, like something thrown into a fire. A blackbird, squawking, crossed the cobbles.

The children would not receive their indentures until the age of twenty-one. How well they'd know these few yards of light by then; which paving stones had been cut by the iron tires of wagons, which were smooth; the groundsel and chickweed in corners; the purple and yellow steam from the dye house; the swearing and cursing; the dull thud of wooden hammers and tang of urine from the fulling shed; the sunlit glow of freedom through the big gates, and the square of changeable sky!

Edwin had formed a friendship during these daily visits to the yard. The little girl who had become his friend was dark with dirt and grease, thin from ill-treatment and hunger. Her hair was brutally cropped, for working amongst the machines and also so that it wouldn't harbor lice. Her eyes were extremely pale, luminous and inquisitive.

At the time when the apprentice and Edwin had first spoken, he had been gnawing a piece of dry oatcake.

"What's 'at?" the girl had demanded. "Gi'it me!"

"What's your name?" Edwin asked.

"Gi'me that!"

He gave her half, and waited for her to finish gobbling. "Go on, tell us what your name is," he repeated.

"Gi'me more," she demanded.

He asked her, a third time, "Go on, tell us your name."

The girl, though no bigger than Edwin, seemed much older than he. She looked and talked like a shriveled old woman. He felt sorry for her. He gave her the rest of his oatcake.

"They call me Numbskull and 'Ackney Cow and Little Bitch and 'Prentice and You There, and anything that comes into their 'eads. I forgot what name they wrote in a book for me," she answered at last.

"I'm going to call you Margaret." This was the name of a beautiful saint that Edwin had seen depicted on a flag in the Sunday School.

The girl was drawn to the boy who teasingly, gently, gave her both oatcake and a name, and she trusted him . . . almost. She repeated, "Morgarit, Morgarit," in a queer mixture of accents, from the north, the midlands, and the south, which intrigued him. She spoke rapidly and fluently—used to the fight for survival, to constantly adapting herself and her speech.

Soon, they were putting their minds to devising ways of meeting. Today, in the yard, Edwin pushed forward the leg of rabbit.

"What's 'at?" she demanded, grabbing it before he could answer. He explained why she mustn't eat now and she obediently hid it under her bishop.

The children were reassembled into groups, this time divided into apprentices and local children. Rose Gledhill led her batch to the apprentice house for their breakfast porridge, and Nathaniel took the others to a corner of the spinning mill, there to devour the baggin they had brought for themselves. At half past eight they were all back at work.

Margaret was a "doffer." She and her gang of girls had to climb the machines when the bobbins were full, replace them with empty ones, and put the loaded reels into a wheeled basket. When the skip was full, they pushed it out into the yard near the waterwheel, or if they worked on an upper floor, to a platform above a hoist. Then they brought back the empty skip. Edwin and Margaret had discovered that by bribing her companions she could stay hidden in the yard until the other children came with the next load, or even until the one after that.

Edwin was without such regular excuses for going outside. Yet if Margaret tipped him off that she had placed her bribe, he could not help himself from following her, to snuggle with her for a time, in a nest among old baskets, timber, bits of masonry and machinery.

At eleven o'clock, Margaret came by, one of four pushing a skip. By now, Mor's piece of rabbit had been passed on and hidden in another's bishop, soon to be concealed under a hairy, unclean blanket in the apprentice house, later to soothe some unknown hungry, sobbing misery in the dark.

The Gledhills and Joshua Slaughter were out of sight and so was the under-engineer who supervised the oiling. Edwin drew forth the flask of ale that he'd hidden in some waste wool, thrust it among Margaret's bobbins, and told her, "Don't give that to anyone! That's for us."

Eventually Edwin had to go rooting for waste wool that had dropped on the undersides of the frames. Instead of returning with a bag of scavenged wool, he peeped out the far side to make sure that Gledhill was not in sight, and then escaped to look for Margaret, where she was hidden in the yard at the foot of the hoist.

She crept out to meet him from a mass of new, oily leather belting and machinery that was piled against the wall of the wheel house. She dutifully clutched the bottle of ale.

"I've found out 'ow to sneak in by the waterwheel," Edwin told her. "In a minute, yon engineer'll go in there to check. I know 'is times, and 'e leaves the door unlocked till 'e comes out again, so we slips in behind 'im, and stays there until 'e's left."

"We'll be locked in."

"No. Slaughter comes back in an hour. So then we sneaks back to our work."

"Cor! What if 'e sees us?"

"Huh! I know 'ow to 'ide. My father showed me 'ow to 'ide from gamekeepers. Most important thing is to stay still. Remember not to move an inch, especially if 'e looks right at you."

Hidden in the corner of the yard, they listened for the engineer. In one hand clutching the ale, and with the other holding Margaret's hand, Edwin led her toward the wheel house.

All seemed safe. He tugged the terrified girl toward the shadowy, roaring wheel. Above them, there was a bright opening of sky where the water tumbled out of the lodge. He pulled her in behind him. Unable to see for a moment, they stood holding their breath. They grew used to the dark and saw that no one was there. Edwin led her farther, climbing up between the pouring wheel and the wall, onto the windowsill.

The sun illuminated and warmed the golden stone. He sat on one side and she trustfully perched on the other. He stared through the bars, and so she did the same. Looking up the valley between the trees they could see the light on the slopes, where work gangs were building walls. Long walls were already thrown like ropes over the horizon. In an enclosure filled with ewes and lambs, all the lambs together were scampering from wall to wall, running races. They turned, their noses raised, some leaping in the air, waiting for one of their number to make a decision, and then they set off again.

Nearby, little triangles of glassy light were dancing upon the water of the lodge. Margaret felt that she could scoop them up into a heap of jewels.

Inside the wheel house, dark and noisy water poured into a murky, thundering hole, the bottom of which they could not see. They were drenched by splashes from the wheel; a storm of liquid shining, of darkness, low rumblings, rainbows and soakings.

They heard the engineer enter and move around, mumbling. Sometimes they caught sight of him but, as Edwin expected, Joshua Slaughter did not look up. They watched him run his finger meditatively through the oil that smeared the gears. He put his thumb and forefinger together to feel the viscosity, then he tasted it. At last the engineer left, locking them in.

Edwin uncorked the stoneware bottle of ale. He swigged it, then passed it to Margaret. She was tugging at the stubble of her shorn hair.

"I wish it was long," she said.

"What's it like in the 'prentice 'ouse? What does Gledhill get up to?"

"What's 'e get up to? *Phee-ew!* If 'e doesn't like a gal 'e spits 'is tobacco on the floor and makes 'er lick it up. Sometimes 'e makes you open yer mouth and 'e spits into it. I've 'ad that done to me, plenty o' times. 'E makes us eat dirty bits o' candle. 'E says nasty things. 'E comes up from behind and screws 'is fingers in yer ears. 'E goes tighter and tighter inside of you. 'E watches and asks if you've wetted yourself, and doesn't stop until you tell 'im you 'ave. Every night I 'ear different ones crying themselves to sleep in the 'prentice 'ouse." She paused, and then added, "They miss their mothers, I suppose."

She paused again, and said, "My mother's still in London. I'd like to go and find 'er. I thought I'd see 'er when they sent me to 'Ackney again from Derbyshire, but I was only a few months back before they sent me up 'ere, so I never saw 'er."

"You were in Derbyshire?"

"I was apprentice there for two years, then there came a dry summer. There was no water for the wheel, and they said they couldn't afford to feed us with no work to do, so they sent us back. That place was worse than this one. We didn't even get out to Sunday School there. Mrs Gledhill's kind, but that Mrs. Newton down Monsall Dale . . .

"The night before we went up there, I'd been crying and my eyes were red. They won't take anyone with sore eyes, 'cos they get like that from the fluff and they don't want no trouble. I was frightened they wouldn't take me. I wanted to get out of 'Ackney and said I was eleven. I was nine, I think. I don't know 'ow old I am. I'd been put in the workhouse because my mother was ill and I only ever saw 'er sometimes on Sunday.

"We were taken off in the middle of the night and my mother never found out where I'd gone to for a year, but Jimmy Dawson's mother kept on at the workhouse master. My mother walked to Derbyshire to find me, and 'er ill. She ate grass on the road. She pushed 'andfuls of straw in 'er mouth to stop 'erself feeling 'ungry. She was crying when she found me, and I got all wet from 'er kissing me. Mrs. Newton washed me and give me a clean pinafore before she sent me in to 'er. I don't know what Mother would 'ave said if she'd seen me normal. She wanted to take me away, but Mrs. Newton said I couldn't go 'cos I was indet—"

"Indentured."

Margaret remembered the paper that she could not understand, but which had imprisoned her: the black gothic letters, the coat of arms wrapping the first letter, the bright red seal, the smell of hot wax, and the words that meant nothing even when some were read out to her. No one had the patience to read much, nor to explain.

"I touched a red 'orse on the bit o' paper and made an 'X' where they told me to, and they paid me a shilling. I never saw my mother after that visit. 'Er last words were to tell me not to steal—but I couldn't 'elp it. I was 'ungry.

"She never looked back as she went away. I was expecting to see 'er again in 'Ackney. She was ill. Do you think she's . . . she's . . . ?"

"She'll be all right."

Edwin, to take her mind off her worries, pointed beyond the reservoir, above the trees, to the unenclosed moors that were dark with wintry heather.

"Father takes me up there when we go trapping hares and fishing," he said.

"You go fishing and trapping?"

"Mr. Horsfall lets us," Edwin fibbed, and swigged more ale. "There's streams all over the moors, just like under the mill, only the water's not black, it's all white and brown and shining."

Edwin looked down into the murky, growling, unfathomable pit that was what became of the streams after converging from the little valleys of the moorland.

"Do you think my mother's still alive?" Margaret whispered.

"Don't worry. She'll be alive somewhere."

"I saw two girls die in Cressbrook Mill in Monsall Dale. Sarah Goodling was knocked down by Mr. Birch. He asked why 'er frame was stopped and she said she didn't know. 'I'll learn you to know,' 'e said, and when she tried to get up 'e kicked 'er down again. She was twelve. They said we 'ad to work 'ard to 'elp fight the war. She was carried up to the 'prentice 'ouse. Mr. Birch said that 'nothing ailed 'er but idleness.' The master gave 'er camomile tea and ordered 'er to go to bed, but when 'er that shared with 'er went up she found 'er dead.

"There was another girl was swinging 'er can with 'er food in it, and it 'it the doorpost. Mr. Newton kicked 'er where 'e shouldn't and she wasted away. She was always sleepy, till she wore away and died.

"I don't know what's going to 'appen to us all at 'Orsfalls'. I wish it wasn't so long. I want to finish and 'ave done."

"That'll be in ten years."

Edwin drank the last of the ale. It was having its effect. Dreamily, he looked at the sunlit hills beyond the bars.

"Sitting 'ere's like being on t' moors," he said. "Let's pretend it's Sunday."

Margaret quickly bent her head. "Our Father which art in 'Eaven, 'allowed be Thy name . . ."

"Huh! We never go to church!"

"Why not?"

"Only my brother Gideon likes going to chapel. When it's wet I get sent, if Father's feeling tired and wants to go to bed. The rest of the time, we go on the moors and roll our trousers up in the sun."

"It's not always sunny."

Margaret was envious. Thinking of Edwin on the moorlands, she lifted her smock a little and stretched her bare, skinny legs into the sun. They were oily and scarred. She imagined that the windowsill was the bank of one of those streams. She would love to see one.

Edwin looked down and saw Mr. Gledhill staring up at them, shaking his stick and unable to shout, choking with anger.

Margaret followed Edwin's gaze. She pulled down her skirt and pressed so hard into the wall that it rasped her back. The devil's head on the stick was swinging wildly, trying to deliver blows to their feet and ankles.

Edwin, after a flush of fear, hated the man. He tried to loosen a stone to smash into the overseer's face. He'd kill him, though he'd be hanged for it.

But there was no hope for it and, with Margaret, he crouched against the bars.

She was whimpering. Though tears stung Edwin's eyes, he would not cry.

Gledhill, out of breath, ceased to swing his stick. He rested his clenched fists on his waist, and said nothing—very threateningly. He simply waited for them to come down.

Edwin went first, with Margaret close behind. As if he could protect her! They were approaching a mad dog. Gledhill's long claw gripped Margaret's neck and almost went through the skin. When he slapped her face hard, she stopped screaming and went limp.

"Open your mouth," he commanded.

Margaret clamped her lips together. Her face tightened and shrank, like a little old woman's.

"Open your gob, I told you!"

She opened her mouth. All of her body was rigid except her lips and cheeks, which were trembling. Gledhill was sweating and excited. Sweat trickled down his face. He pursed his lips and formed a bead of spittle.

Margaret closed her eyes Something sticky landed and clung vilely on teeth and tongue. She did not know whether to swallow it or spit it out. Afraid of rejecting it, she swallowed, and felt sick.

Gledhill, beaming, relieved, let go of Edwin, whereupon the boy flew at him, pummeling with his fists—though they inflicted no more damage than his bare feet did, kicking.

Gledhill smiled for a moment, before he delivered a punch that sent Edwin head-first across the yard and through the open door of the spinning mill, to sprawl on the floor. Margaret was roughly dragged after him.

Before Edwin could pick himself up, Gledhill had him by the neck again. Like two dead, half-plucked hens, the wet, bedraggled children were dragged along between the rows of machines, their feet sometimes lifted off the ground. The yelling overseer said he would skewer them, drown them, tear them to pieces and have the bits spun into yarn. More realistically, he threatened to tie weights to their ears and hang them down their backs.

What he did was to tie them by their wrists and biceps, crucified upon a crossbeam above a moving spinning frame. The children had to keep lifting their legs clear of the machine's inward and outward drift, peering down into that chasm of needles and rolling metal that could slice off their feet. If they slipped out of the ropes . . .

Gledhill sauntered away.

The women worked on with their heads down, hiding from the sight of something they could neither prevent nor soothe.

"We'll run away," Edwin mouthed, over the noise. "I'll get us out."

"Where to? 'Ow?"

"Liverpool. We'll catch a boat t'America."

"I'd like to find my mother," Margaret cried softly to herself.

Phoebe, from a far part of the mill, saw her son and the other child suspended from the beam. She shrieked and, letting her spinning frame shift for itself and ravel its threads, ran headlong down the aisle, her exclamations catching with gobs of blood in her throat, the singing of throstles drowning her cries.

The rushing and the terror made her breathless. She began to cough. Clutching to her mouth her red-soaked piece of cloth, she dashed in panic around the spinning frame. She could not stop it, and no one dared to help her. Running in circles and spitting blood, she was as desperate and ineffective as a mother bird around its chicks in a trap.

She caught Edwin's eyes. She knelt upon the oil-soaked stone and prayed, but no one could hear her because of the noise of the machines.

In John Tiplady's cropping shop, downstream from the mill, they worked without an overseer and at their own pace. Although the work was hard, Gideon might sit down during the day, rest his legs, drink ale, and gossip. The croppers were an aristocracy, better paid than weavers. How manly Gideon felt, growing dreamy from the ale, and being taken seriously by the men who he believed were about to change the face of England.

But his knowledge of what happened to women and girls in the spinning mill was creating a hell of guilt for him, as if their inflictions were his own fault. The worst disgrace was his mother having to go in there. Had she, too, suffered despicably, ever since she was a girl?

She would not speak about it and he wondered why she wouldn't, when other mill women were so coarse. He did not press her, being proud of his mother's modesty. He hated his father most for not being able to keep her at home.

And what could he make of Gledhill, who attended chapel, was a good religious man, and yet did such things? He did not know. He knew that he did not know very much. Only God knew everything.

The croppers would often stroll over to the open door and look out. At midday, Arthur Crawshaw, the local "King Ludd," leaned on the doorpost, pulling angrily on his pipe. Tall and thin, he stared, like a tattered heron or a bittern eyeing a snake's egg that is about to hatch, at Paradise Mills, where the new finishing shop held a set of mechanical shears—a machine that would make the cropper's skill redundant. A month ago, the croppers had seen it brought on a cart past their workshop. It came from the forge of the blacksmith who made man-traps for the woodlands, and spinning machines with bobbin racks a child's height from the floor.

The machine, called a "cropping frame," consisted of no more than ordinary hand shears attached to a wheel to draw them over the cloth, but with it, one unskilled man could do the work previously done by three or four skilled workers.

Crawshaw wore a crepe armband. So did John Tiplady, and when Gideon had arrived that morning he, too, had been given one. It was in memory of the Halifax cropper, Samuel Hartley, killed in a Luddite raid on Mr. Cartwright's mill at Rawfolds, near Huddersfield, five days before and whose burial had taken place on the previous day. The funeral had been chaotic after the efforts by Mr. Jabez Bunting, the local Methodist superintendent, to prevent Hartley's burial in a Methodist graveyard. "Methodism hates democracy as much as sin," Mr. Bunting had announced, when he refused to conduct a service, and the gates of the chapel had been shut.

Crawshaw's latest mission was to organize a raid on Paradise Mills. It had been planned over a month before, on the heels of the Rawfolds defeat, when some had been shot and others chased until they found cover or died of their injuries in the hedgerows.

Behind King Ludd's back, John Tiplady put down his shears. They weighed thirty pounds and stood four feet high. The cloth that he had trimmed, neatly folded back and forth by Gideon, lay at the end of a long table.

John Tiplady also was angry. Crawshaw had told them that, after the soldiers had killed two Luddites and maimed others, they should use firearms themselves, and not confine themselves to sticks and stones.

Tiplady's hefty wrist had trembled. "So we too are to sink to shooting our own countrymen!"

"We should burn all 'Orsfalls' down, 'ouse and mill and everything! Burn down everything in sight and start afresh. Nothing short of a fresh start will do us any good," Crawshaw had argued.

When Arthur Crawshaw was more or less calmed by standing in the doorway, he put away his pipe and turned to face the others. He was so tall that he had to unwind himself from under the lintel.

He looked at Gideon, who was sitting on a bench against the window, resting his legs and drinking the ale which Tiplady's wife had brought into the shop. Crawshaw and Gideon formed one faction, Samuel Wrigley and Tiplady made up another.

"What's your father doing today, Gideon Greave? Reading books and thinking nobody'll take away 'is loom?" Crawshaw's Adam's apple rose and sank in his scrawny throat as he spoke. Even that seemed angry.

Gideon, although he agreed, out of loyalty to his father could do no more than scowl.

"We need our messengers and scribes too, perhaps more than we need murderers," Tiplady commented.

The master of the shop was a broad, proud, steady man who controlled both his sorrow and his anger. He would take a grip of himself by biting hard into the stem of his pipe.

King Ludd gave an angry kick at the leg of a table. "Authors! Poets!" he exclaimed, bitter and contemptuous.

He took his ale and sat next to Gideon. Crawshaw angrily touched the band of white crepe on his sleeve. " 'Ave we forgotten about 'Artley? This is no time for larking."

"Bible says . . ." Gideon began.

"Bible says everything under the sun, and contradicts itself," Tiplady interrupted. "It's time we stopped looking there so much, and making ourselves confused. You're not the only one to mourn 'Artley, but maybe we don't all want to remember 'im by piling up dead bodies."

It was Tiplady's turn to take his ale to the door and try to cool his temper. He set his tankard on the ground and relit his pipe. The smell of the smoke peacefully rising brought him great satisfaction.

He heard Crawshaw's bitter voice from behind his back. "Our Government keeps us in a poverty-stricken, out-of-work condition, so that in the end we'll submit to being dressed up like fairground dolls and sent off to fight Frenchmen or Spaniards and to enslave Negroes. So that we'll be forced to enlist—to put it simply. In a time like this we don't need authors nor dreamers. We need the revolution to start. I know that thousands are ready, and Rawfolds shall ignite the flame! There isn't a village in the north not ready to act as one man. You'd better go and talk to your father, Gideon Greave. Teach him some sense. The time to act is now, whilst men are angry and the Government still doesn't understand what we've got prepared for 'em. This is the moment to take our courage in our hands—before they send more of the army in. If we don't act now, then you for one, my lad, will be thrown out amongst the rubbish."

Tiplady came back and put down his empty jug, thus suggesting they all get back to work.

King Ludd stood up, grabbed Tiplady's wrist, and dramatically held up his "cropper's hoof"—the thickening that came from handling the shears. "What's the price of that? 'Orsfall and his like care nothing for that! So we must look after ourselves. And any who are not with us are against us. We'll know what to do with those who should be our brethren, after."

"After what?" Tiplady asked sharply, retrieving his wrist. "After the hangings?"

"I've always said we should smash Horsfall's finishing shop," Gideon muttered.

"That's because you fancy going out at night with your face blackened and carrying a pistol," Tiplady told him. "Playing at being a brave but desperate man."

"What are we going to do for our friends from Rawfolds?" Crawshaw continued. "This is a time for heroes! Either we let Mellor and Thorpe and our brave and glorious brothers be flushed out and strung up like rabbits, or we fight until we have altered the constitution of England." He paused, and added weightily, "Because of what has happened, we are called to assemble tonight and do our part by going ahead with smashing yon finishing shop."

"Who'll be defending the mill? What do you know of the forces that Horsfall can muster?" Tiplady asked.

"I have my own spies amongst the militia," Crawshaw answered. "There'll be no soldiers, not more than we can deal with—no more than on any other raid we've organized."

"Rawfolds?"

"That was defeated because some of us didn't stand true."

"Horsfall has all the military under 'is thumb," Tiplady pointed out.

Crawshaw took no notice. "Wrigley," he said, "Gideon Greave's father has deserted and we're a man short. Will you join us on this raid?"

"I'll do anything you want," Wrigley answered, genially.

"The age of King Ludd is coming!" Gideon shouted.

Lopping off heads and making a revolution looked to him as easy as clipping the nap off a piece of cloth was to a skilled cropper. He had already, one night a month before, burned cloth on a tenterframe, and he had once taken part in an ambush to smash a load of shears that were being taken to be sharpened.

"If Mr. Perceval wants us 'anged he must come and get us!" Gideon yelled.

"If you don't stop blabbering, he will," Tiplady told him.

Crawshaw gave Gideon a look that showed that he, too, thought him a fool.

Gideon blushed, stammered, and then he in his turn went to look out through the door.

Upstream, through the trees, he saw a boy's head rising on the edge of the lodge, out of the torrent that poured from the lodge into the wheel housing.

"Come and look at this!" Gideon said.

The others came to the door. They saw Gideon's brother, Edwin.

When Margaret and he had been cut down from above the spinning frame, Edwin had once more led her into the wheelhouse, this time not even considering the engineer, so tenaciously was he thinking, *Where water can get in, we can get out.*

The men at Tiplady's saw Edwin kneel on the bank and reach down to help a little girl who was following him. Both were completely drenched, their hair and clothes plastered to them after they had been nearly drowned in struggling against that powerful sluice. They ran toward the shelter of the woods.

Sauntering along the bank came Nathaniel Gledhill. He was using his midday hour to collect ferns. Suspended from his neck was his tin vasculum. With the metal box banging against his side, its lid open and trailing its specimens, he gave chase.

He caught up with Edwin at the wall. Margaret had already been pushed over, but twenty yards into the trees, she had no heart to go on alone and she returned.

In terror, she climbed the wall back to her friend, and her prison. For the second time Gledhill dragged them, fluttering weakly like two butterflies that had fallen into the water, back into the factory.

Tiplady slammed his pipe down and walked away, into a back recess of the cropping shop.

Crawshaw showed the stem of the pipe to Gideon: the deep set of angry teethmarks. "Now go and talk to your Judas father," he said.

CHAPTER FOUR

April 16th

Phoebe had been brought up with her parents at home. There her mother spun, her father wove and supervised the labor of his family. Their fire burned both peat and coals, which they dug out of the moor nearby. Their squatter's farm was a sooty, gray place, being near a coal shaft, but to Phoebe it was a lovely spot. Nowadays she remembered the hens around the open door, and beyond, in that high, lonely spot, was the ripple of distant hills. Although their room was simple—crude table, chairs, cupboard, a mere ladder to the bedroom, a linen chest, a small oak box for her father's lexicon and other volumes, a framework on pulleys to raise oatcakes above the fire—it was not bare nor cheerless. Her mother had been a servant at a clothier's house and she had brought away, as a gift for her dowry, lace mats, a set of fine crockery, knives, forks, and a Bible, which she herself could not read.

They possessed no clock. They watched the movement of light, of regular travelers on the road far below, and of birds, to register the time. Her parents worked as they willed, or thought best. The contrasting sight of travelers hurrying by brought them peace and contentment with their own lot. If the day was fine, they were in their garden, or in their two enclosures, in one of which they grew oats, and in the other grass for the pony; or they were on the open moorland, cutting rushes and peat or digging out coal. On cold, wet days they operated loom and spinning wheel indoors, or they took their cloth to Benjamin Greave's fulling mill and finishing shop.

The children had leisure to play in the stream that ran close to the door. They dabbled in the water trough. They played hide-and-seek under the sheets of white, new weaving that was hung out to dry. They never thought that the factories being built along the valley bottom would transform their lives.

Phoebe, "the sun," had an elder sister whom their father had named Selene, for the moon, and who died at the age of eighteen, after four years of a hard lump growing in her breast.

When Phoebe was six and Selene was thirteen, as they were plucking watercress out of the stream, the elder sister made a strange remark: "Wait till you play hide-and-seek with Father."

She would tell Phoebe no more. But all through that summer, she continued to suggest "things."

"What things?"

"You will see."

One day her father suggested that Phoebe stay at home, while her mother and sister took a basket of whinberries to market. They had spent a whole day of crouching to pick them from the undersides of low bushes on the moors. As soon as they had gone, Phoebe's father complained of being tired and he went to bed, as he sometimes did during the day, with one of his Greek volumes. Half an hour later he called to Phoebe.

She stood some distance from the bed. That was not good enough for him. "Come closer, by the bedside," he ordered. He touched her hair. His hands played tenderly with her. There was a smile on his lips, but the rest of his expression was angry and florid. It made her shiver.

"Don't be frightened. You're not frightened, are you?"

"No," she pretended.

"Get into bed with me, then."

She was terrified.

"Phoebe, my loved one!"

He ran his fingers under her dress and petticoat. He lay on top of her. He sweated, grunted, and closed his eyes. He seemed to forget about her. He bounced up and down. He fell asleep and let go of her.

When she crept away, she could not walk properly, and was very weak.

Although her mother on her return was perversely blind to Phoebe's distress, Selene took it all in, especially Phoebe's painful, bowlegged walk.

Her father began regularly to feel "tired" whenever Phoebe's mother and sister were visiting relatives, or away with baskets of eggs, whinberries, or other moorland produce. Phoebe grew to dread these times. When she knew that her mother and Selene were going on an errand she could think of nothing else but what was bound to happen. On the days beforehand her father would give her a sweet biscuit and wink, telling her to keep it a secret. He told Phoebe that she was his favorite daughter.

She could think only of the coming pain, and tried to resist his blandishments. He then tried to get his own way by alternating sweetness with bullying. He had a harsh tongue when opposed, so she grew weak and nervous. The more frightened she was of him, the more cruel he became.

Regularly, half an hour after he had climbed the ladder to the bedroom, he would call, "Phoebe." It was no use pretending not to hear, for he would simply shout louder, apparently angry, but then he would become quiet and tender again. He would smile at her frightened look and whisper, "Phoebe," running his fingers inside her dress.

"Do you like it?" he asked.

"Yes."

She whispered because he whispered, without knowing why. She did not know whether she liked it or not, nor what it was she liked or didn't like.

"Get into bed with me, then. It's lovely and warm."

One day her mother and Selene came home unexpectedly early.

Selene now was often in pain. She was thin, yellow-skinned, and had a wistful look, because she understood mortality. By habit she clutched herself under her breast, and they had all ceased to take any notice when she gasped. She easily grew tired, which was perhaps why they had returned so early. Perhaps.

They stood listening at the foot of the ladder. When her mother could stand no more of it, she coughed.

Phoebe's father motioned her to leave. He pretended to fall asleep, his face pushed into the mattress. Phoebe climbed shamefully down the ladder, flushed and frightened, hardly able to move, her legs spread because of the pain.

Her mother banged the pots and angrily shouted one word: "Whore!"

Phoebe had no idea what it meant, but she was certain that she had done something wrong and that the pain she felt was her punishment.

"Whore, whore, whore!" her mother repeated—holding back her tears, unable to think of anything else to say, wringing her hands with a terrible savage clasping and unclasping of her fingers.

"Will I go to Hell?" Phoebe asked.

"Yes!" her mother hissed. "Yes! Yes! Yes!"

Then she saw Phoebe's look of stricken, helpless horror, but could not take back her words. She slammed out of the house with a bucket of scraps for the hens.

Phoebe listened to the hens squawking away from her mother's agitated pacing. She sat by the fire, next to her sister. She did not know what to do with her hands. She could not look at Selene. Side by side, they were staring into the burning coals, feeling the weight of heat upon their eyes.

Selene, trying to breathe lightly to save herself from sharp stabs through her breast, was exhausted with life, so she behaved as if she understood everything.

One who was wasting away as she was would certainly die in a few years, and she'd been told that she was going to Heaven. She, who also had been enjoyed by her father, knew that she would go to Hell.

Selene threw a stick into the fire. It burst into flames.

"Look at it burning! Imagine burning like that forever, in Hell," Selene said, and then repeated slowly, "Forever."

"Is your mother there?" the father timidly called, at last. Although he made such a show of strength and anger, he was afraid of their mother.

Phoebe did not answer him, thus forcing him to shout louder. Even she could give a little pain, and enjoy doing so, sometimes. Her hands were wrapping and unwrapping themselves around one another in her apron.

"Is your mother down there? *Is your mother there?*" the father bawled, exasperated and afraid.

"No," Phoebe answered eventually. She wanted to say "yes," but to tell a lie would fan the eternal flames.

"You won't go to Hell!" he shouted. The male voice coming from above the ceiling might have been that of St. Peter.

"You will!" Selene whispered. "I have seen God, and I know."

There *were* people who had seen God, from the edge of the grave.

Selene could announce that she had seen God, as another might say he had visited Mr. Horsfall. She claimed to have looked into the pit and to know what was waiting for everyone.

Outside, Phoebe heard shed doors slammed angrily. Her mother tripped on a piece of timber, cursed and loudly blamed her husband for leaving it there. She lamented to the blank walls about his failings: a roof not mended, money wasted at markets, time idled away in reading books.

She returned indoors after half an hour. She at first said nothing, though noisy enough with crockery and furniture. Then: "You'll burn forever in Hell, you little whore!" she hissed.

"You'll burn in Hell, Phoebe," Selene repeated spitefully. She had seen the parting of the golden gates and had been given glimpses of the pastures of Heaven. Pastures which she would be denied. It did not occur to Phoebe that Selene was reassuring herself, not wanting to descend into Hell alone.

All that day her father dared not leave his bed. He was too frightened to make a sound. He did without food. Nobody went to see him. Nobody mentioned him. To them, he was dead.

Phoebe decided that she would never, never, marry a coward.

Eventually the two girls went to their own beds and waited for their mother to come up. That must have happened very late, for both daughters had fallen asleep, despite themselves.

They were woken by the row. Mother was screaming abuse. It was a clear, quiet night. The horse neighed in fright from the stable, the hens were awakened to chortle on their perches. The nearest neighbor, a quarter of a mile across the moor, came to her door with a lantern. It was all cut deep in Phoebe's memory.

Her father never touched Phoebe again—and she missed it. Although it filled her with horror, she wanted his affectionate touching, his fingering of the tabooed parts that were the cursed gift of Satan. Having tasted sin, she was shocked to find that she wanted more of it.

But it was not to be offered. Her father's reserve was now as extensive as the love he had once shown, and it was terrible. What had she done?

Her sister never relented in her spite; her mother in her coldness and suspicion.

One day, when Phoebe burned a pan of porridge, "Oh, you ungrateful . . . you ungrateful *thief!*" her mother shrieked.

Phoebe did not understand why she was called a thief. She looked into her mother's face and saw the envy and hate written there. "I'm sorry," Phoebe said, and lowered her eyes.

Her mother banged the pots. She clasped and unclasped her fingers, as she had done on that day when *it* had happened.

"You should be! Stealing him from me like that!"

"I'm sorry." She couldn't think of anything better to say.

"You're young, you've got your life before you, but me, I've only got *him* . . . and my own daughter steals him!" her mother howled.

Phoebe, her eyes still cast down, watched her mother's fingers. She was tearing at them as if she was trying to pull out the nails; as if she was plucking out of her fingers all the tension and pain in her body.

"I'm sorry."

Especially after this, Phoebe made recompense by frantically trying to please, and to become "all that a daughter should be." She made the porridge, tended the garden and animals, shoveled and dug for coals, cleaned and cooked. She did everything she could to look chaste. She wore the dullest clothes. She kept herself tightly buttoned at the neck and wrist, as a way of showing that she was willingly imprisoning her guilty body.

As her mother never relented, and her father was now afraid of showing affection, Phoebe struggled harder and harder to please, not realizing that she was doing so, until it became a habit.

"Phoebe's a good girl, a Godly daughter," it was said.

She did all that she could to nurse her burdensome sister, who would not let anyone sleep, with her nightly howls, delusions, and visions. When Phoebe was eleven, Selene died. Wherever it was that she went, she took her secret with her.

As there was now no need of an extra hand at home to take care of Selene, Phoebe was sent to earn her living in a spinning shed, where fifteen other girls were employed.

She took the greatest pains to please the overseer, as she had done for her parents. It was now his turn to play with her. He did so more than with the other girls, because she was the most biddable in the shed.

Because of his attentions, her work was spoiled, and, as he knew, Phoebe was terrified of returning to her parents with her wages cut for having been "a bad girl."

He kept the frightened little creature behind. He placed his blunt, stained, repulsive fingers down the back of her neck. He promised to say nothing about her bad spinning, if she would submit. She submitted.

Phoebe grew obsessed by terror and guilt. Those most significant events of her life were ones that she never spoke about, yet her distracted mind was always turning them over. She became virtually a mute.

She did not realize that she had become one. She froze whenever a man came near her, and she remembered the pain given by men with a certain look in their eyes.

Whenever Mor approached, it terrified her. She could not help recalling her father.

There were, indeed, some brilliantly happy moments. When Mor Laverock Greave spoke with authority of classical things and gave Latin names to flowers, for instance, she was reminded of the powerful, comforting side of her father. When in her teens she watched Mor playing "knorr and spell," knocking the wooden ball with such boldness and force, she was happy. Also, when he walked her home through the dusk. Yet she knew that her deep silences showed him that she was unhappy. It was agony not to be able to explain how she felt, and even worse when he touched her and she could not tell him how much she feared it. She could never tell him anything.

She continued to be noticeable for the prim, punitive way in which she dressed, the drab colors of her tightly buttoned clothes, and Mor could never for long get her to lighten her style of dress, or loosen a few buttons at her neck and cuffs.

Within this cell that she had created for herself, Phoebe began to believe in fantasies. She remembered Selene's sense of security, and what she described as the "glory" that she felt "in Jesus."

Through the dark's muttering and love-fumbling, Phoebe began to think that if only it were Jesus Christ who entered her, then she could give herself and be "justified," as Selene had put it. To remove the stiffness from her limbs, Phoebe would close her eyes and imagine that her Savior was entering her with His "spirit." It was in this panic and fake ecstasy that she had conceived Gideon before she was married, Edwin and the other children later.

• • •

Although she could not talk, Phoebe could pray, as she did in the spinning mill, at the foot of the frame, with the children dangling above it. Careless of the oily floor, her petticoat and apron recklessly close to the machinery, she prayed for Edwin.

Phoebe looked up and saw Nathaniel Gledhill.

Gledhill felt the eyes of one who would murder him. He smiled.

She coughed nervously and bent her head again in prayer. She was in his hands.

It was Joshua Slaughter who then ran up and stopped the spinning frame. Rarely an angry man, now he was tense and speechless with anger. So powerful was it that Gledhill, the larger man by far, stepped aside and let Slaughter cut down the children, carrying Margaret first to the ground. They would have run like frightened rabbits off among the forest of machines, but Phoebe nestled them both for a while under her bony arms.

Joshua stood looking at her. He wanted to say . . .

Joshua had once put out his hand to her. She had told him not to, and it had stopped him. It had actually stopped him! Another man would have continued trying to seduce her, but he had merely looked at her with soft, brown, devoted eyes. She had felt safe, and grateful.

Now he wanted to say . . .

For the rest of the morning Phoebe could not concentrate. Edwin was sure to get into more trouble, she thought. He'd do something else. He'd think of something. He wouldn't be stopped . . . not him.

She saw him passing by her frame, and no matter who was watching, she went to soothe his arms and shoulders.

He would hardly speak to her. He seemed unable to bear his own mother's face. He was brooding.

Shortly before the noon "sit," Phoebe went to find Joshua Slaughter in the waterwheel housing.

He turned upon her those faithful eyes.

My weasel, he thought.

"That damned Gledhill . . ." he began.

She did not respond.

"A group of us are going to Bradford tonight," he continued, hopefully. "We've hired a cart. Are you coming?"

"Bradford?"

Only ten miles away, but it was as if she had never heard of the place. She could not think what he was talking about.

"They are awaiting the Millennium there, when Christ will return to us. We know it will be soon. In the darkest hour of the night, that is when the dawn light breaks, Phoebe Greave. They know all about that."

"Who?" She knew perfectly well *who,* but could not think, having nothing else on her mind but where she might obtain ointments for Edwin.

"The followers of Joanna Southcott. Joanna has seen all in her dreams. She knows when the light will break. 'I have been led on by types, shadows, dreams and visions since 1792 to the present day.' We have it from her own mouth, Phoebe. Because people will not believe, she has to lock her prophecies in boxes, to be opened when it has been proved they have come true."

Phoebe only wanted to get out of the mill. With teasing and shifting, with smiles that were so provocative because they were rare, she made movements and gestures of a kind that Mor would not have believed she was capable of; that would have surprised anyone who knew her.

Slaughter came forward in the twilight. Was he going to touch her?

"Come with us all to Bradford," he begged.

"Let me free!" she pleaded.

He lifted his hands. "Yes! Yes! Joanna sets all her people free."

"No! Let me *free*. Let me out! Let me out!"

His fingers were brushing her apron. "She will let us all out of our darkness."

"Open the *door,* I mean!"

"The door is open, for all who seek it."

"Onto the lodge!"

"To the lodge?"

Baffled, he stopped pawing her. Was she suggesting that he go out there with her?

"I must go out to think," she said.

"Think about it, and pray, yes, yes!" He was turning the big key in the lock. "Spend an hour or two in nature's bosom, Phoebe. Think and pray. A change of heart will come. Miracles can happen."

Without a further glance at him, she slipped out into the sudden light, and to the brightness reflected off the sheet of water. She was dazzled and frightened at her own daring.

Circling the mill, Phoebe went down the yard between Horsfall's house and the finishing sheds, then past the tenter fields.

She knew that Gledhill never went home during his midday break, and she safely went to his house, knocking at the back door.

The servant girl who answered, a thirteen-year-old who slept in an outbuilding, felt that she was nonetheless better off than a female who had to work in the factory, and she was aloof.

"Master's not at 'ome," she said brusquely.

But it was Rose Gledhill whom Phoebe wanted to see.

Rose, seeing Phoebe brought into the kitchen at this odd hour, with a white, sick face and tottering footsteps, concluded that the factory woman was with child. Mrs. Gledhill assumed that her services as an abortionist were being called for. With something of a fine manner, she dismissed the servant, invited Phoebe to sit down, and set about boiling a pan of water.

Phoebe was quivering like a puppy or a kitten pulled out of a litter. On entering the cottage, she had been overcome with envy and a sense of unfairness. Rose's cottage was comfortable, warm and dry. She had the time to keep it tidy, and a servant. On a sideboard were pies, some of them only half consumed, showing that the Gledhill children were not hungry. The place smelled of comfort and cleanliness. Next to the pies on the sideboard was a glass case containing the eggs of wild birds, laid in an artificial nest.

At first, after taking a seat, Phoebe buried her face in her apron, not able to speak out her errand. Then she raised her head and began her story. Once started, she could not stop.

"Well, I don't know what to say, Mrs. Greave . . . Phoebe. I don't know what to say! To think I married him . . ."

As the story unfolded, Rose was quietly placing bread and slices of preserve pie by Phoebe's side. She took away the large pan that she had set on the flames, and in its place swung the kettle on its hook.

"Go on . . . go on, please continue, Mrs. Greave . . . I don't know what to say . . . My husband . . . I can't say I'm surprised, though. To think that I, of all people, should have married such a one. I *am* most particular, you know . . . I'm *most* ashamed. Oh, this is a barbarous place! A *barbarous* county! When will things change? Don't we learn, though! Don't we learn, Mrs. Greave! But your own man . . ."

"I don't know what to do wi' 'im, Mrs. Gledhill. 'E does nothing. 'E does nothing! A bit o' weaving, but nothing with an eye to what anybody wants, and then 'e's satisfied to be off combing the moors."

"Doesn't he bring anything back?" Rose asked cautiously.

"Well . . . maybe." Phoebe changed the subject. "But everything's in 'is own mind, Mrs. Gledhill. Reading books, that's what 'e does best. It's all in 'is mind."

"Doesn't he keep a school? Doesn't he run an academy?"

"That brings us nothing in, only a bill for coal. 'Alf of 'is pupils don't ever get round to paying for their schooling. 'Is teaching'll get 'im into trouble, too. Though 'e wouldn't 'urt a fly. It's so unfair. It's so unfair!"

Phoebe looked enviously around the room, with its polished furniture and Mr. Gledhill's botanical specimens, dried, pressed, mounted, and framed upon the walls.

"Such nice things," Phoebe said.

Rose got up and began to fill a basket with ointments and the pickings of her larder.

"Look, Mrs. Greave, I have far more than I want. Gledhill flatters me that I'm a good housekeeper. He doesn't know where the money comes from."

Rose began to laugh. So did Phoebe.

Once started, Phoebe could not stop. She doubled up, tears running from her eyes. Her mouth, too, ached with laughter. She could not understand why she was doing it. "Oh, the dirty pig!" she spluttered.

"Oh, the pig!" Rose echoed.

Phoebe stopped laughing as suddenly as she had begun. She became her usual self again, worried and ashamed.

"Don't hurry to bring the basket back. Return it any time you're passing," Rose said.

When Phoebe left, she had no intention of returning to the mill. They could dock her wages for it, she didn't care.

Climbing the stone stairway up to Lady Well, she had from time to time to brush away tears that were now less of sorrow than of amazement at the world's kindness.

• • •

Mor, working his loom alone before the window, watched the cycle of light and shade across hills and valleys. Wearing his weaver's faded, coarse blue apron, he pulled the string to drive the shuttle from left to right, pressed down with his foot to change the lines of the warp, and pulled back the drawer bar with his right hand. *Clack clack,* all day. *Clack clack.* The sound of any working day in Lady Well. In the old days his assistant would have been Edwin. Whilst the child was with him, he could have taught him. *Clack clack, bang bang.*

Across the warp, his shuttle threaded the colors of a sunrise—a broad band of saffron yellow that faded into red. The market called for somber cloths, but he was symbolizing revolution. True to his symbol, everything around it was dark and shadowy: both the room and the country beyond, out of the roots and stems of which his rose-and-yellow, unsaleable tints had been distilled.

Clack clack, bang bang. He sat all day like a crow perched in a forest of strings and bits of wood.

Mor's worries over matters that he could do nothing about built up the tension of a coiled spring in his chest. He could never catch up with his work. Horsfall, like other masters, had doubled the standard length for a piece of cloth, and also had cut the payment to half of what it had been, so that in effect he was paying quarter wages. "I've a warehouse full of the stuff because of the wars! Until they lift the trade embargo and we can export again, it'd suit me best to take none at all," his manager declared, in his office with its roaring fire, leather armchair, stepladder resting against racks of ledgers and order books, watercolors of "scenery," a portrait of Mr. Horsfall senior in his younger days, and brass scales for weighing money and letters.

There Mor, seated on a wooden bench, had often been kept waiting like a naughty schoolboy. He had no choice but to deal on Mr. Horsfall's terms because it was Horsfall who supplied the warps, on credit.

Mor never stopped looking for some small opportunity for food or money. If he went out, he was poaching. If he caught nothing, he was thinking up lessons for his school. At home, he was weaving. He could only weave what he was able to do: what his imagination prompted, what he felt good about. Phoebe thought that his life, unlike hers, was without humiliation! *Someday I'll tell her. Stop being so soft-spoken. Tell her what's really on my mind.*

Sometimes Mor would pause in order to write down the ideas that drifted through his brain. His own loom being silenced then, he became aware of the loneliness of the Lady Well afternoon. Other looms that were banging in the town only accentuated his loneliness. He soon rushed back to his work, in hope of its noise driving away his thoughts. But his mind continued to rage. He was a boiler full of steam.

He returned again to his book, which he had entitled "The Beggar's Complaint":

> The ~~suferings~~ sufferings of the Poor are not the effects of Divine dispensation. They are the offspring of wicked men and notorius systems.
>
> The slaves of the West Indies have little reason to envy the Poor of Great Britain.
>
> ~~Phesants~~ Pheasants, Hares, Partridges, Snipes, Woodcocks, Moorhens and Trouts, being protected by Laws and Gamekeepers, are a PRIVILEGED ORDER compared with the Poor of this Realm. THERE IS NO MORAL OR POLITICAL EVIL IN THE WORLD WHICH MEN MAY NOT REMEDY IF THEY CHOOSE.

Beneath his window, as he wrote, Mor saw the pretty Horsfall children, a boy and a girl, walking through Lady Well with Lydia Horsfall. Flounces and frills decorated the little daughter, who was like a doll brought fresh from a London store. There was an open lightness about her dress and about Mrs. Horsfall's fashionable clothes, too, that anticipated the spring which they were so at liberty to enjoy. The boy was in a velvet suit; one that would never come near machine oil. Loaded baskets on their arms, they were entering houses, with tight smiles upon their faces. They accepted thanks and curtsies from all around, because they were distributing charity.

Lydia Horsfall was on her dignity, behaving formally, shutting out the town which clearly horrified her. It angered Mor that she tried to appease Lady Well with gifts. *Who does she think we are? A colony of Africans, to quell with guns one minute, pacify with gifts the next? "Cold as charity," as they say . . .*

Mor hated charity. Though he'd have appreciated a slice of beef or pie, he flashed down the stairs and slid the bolts to. He was back upstairs again by the time they tried the door, expecting all in Lady Well to be open for them. They knocked but to no avail.

As Mor peeped and watched them go away, he thought of Gideon and Edwin, crippled. The confident footsteps, erect carriage, clean skin, but most of all the sight of the straight legs of the Horsfall children overwhelmed him. Why? Why? Why should it be so?

He watched them until they were out of sight. Before she disappeared, Mrs. Horsfall turned, with an expression that he did not expect to see—presumably unguarded, because she did not know that she was observed. It was the yearning, inward, poignant look of an exile.

Then she turned to her daughter, with a relaxed smile; a happiness that she was preserving, just as Mor preserved something, against the outer barbarity.

Soon Phoebe was hammering at the door, which she, too, was amazed to find locked. Not to trust one's neighbors was unheard of in Lady Well.

Mor heard her shout. Because of her coming home during the day like this, he was consumed with the fear that there had been an accident. His boots clattered so fast and heavily down the steep and narrow stone stairs that he almost fell.

His eyes asked her "Why?" even before he got out a word.

Her arms were full of amazing gifts.

"You met them?" he asked.

"Who?" It was still an effort for Phoebe to collect her thoughts.

"You met the Horsfalls and you let them give you all those?"

She could see how angry he was. She believed that his anger, which he put into no more than talk and books, was more important to him than what happened to her every day in the mill.

"Nay, I 'ave not met them. At least, not to take anything from them. I saw them doing their rounds, and only 'ad the chance to drop them a respectful curtsy, as I should," she answered tartly, in order to offend her democratic husband. "I've been to Mrs. Gledhill's."

"Gledhill's—of all people! You take charity from them?"

"Aye, and for your part, the Horsfalls 'ave been 'ere, and you turned them away," Phoebe said coldly. "You starve us for no reason. You, who . . . you . . . If you'd show a little Christian 'umility and respect for your masters we might get somewhere! It was Mr. Slaughter who 'elped me in the end! Not you! It was *Mr. Slaughter!* Where were you? You don't know what I 'ave to put up with!"

They faced one another, both brittle with anger.

"*I* don't know? Oh, yes, I do! You've been telling me all your life. What about me? What I 'ave to put up with?"

"Books," she said contemptuously.

"What's Slaughter done? Why are you back at this time? Slaughter! You . . . with 'im! I'll kill 'im!"

She flushed. She hadn't thought that he could take it that way. She was angry that he could think her capable of such a thing.

She was also pleased to have the power to make him jealous. "The things I 'ave to do to get us food," she said.

"*What* 'ave you done?"

He, too, became flushed and tense, at the thought of what she might have done, behind a wall, as some other mill women did.

"What 'ave I done? What do you think I've 'ad to do all day? And then you won't take food when it's given to you. All because you might be expected to say 'thank you' for it. Because you're afraid to bend your knee. Yes, afraid! Who do you think you are? If the Good Lord 'ad wanted you to be a master 'e'd have made you one."

He was ready to strike her. "What 'ave you done? *What?* Tell me!"

She did not answer.

"No, not you!"

" 'Ave you finished your piece, husband? I know the answer . . . writing books instead!"

She leaned upon him and collapsed. She was crying, with love, with shame.

People in Lady Well paused in their work to watch Mor dashing through the town, not speaking to anyone and hardly seeing them. His face was crimson with anger.

Slipping twice on the downward flight of stones, he rushed to the mill. All that he felt was his anger, needing to be spent. He had no plan beyond the sullen, hammering determination: *No longer will a child of mine slave in a factory! We'll do without bread first! I'll go to the House of Correction first!*

In sight of the bastion of the gray mill, with jets of livid yellow steam bursting out of chinks in the dye house and the waterwheel clanking in the stream, he realized that there was nothing he *could* do. They would all starve if he did not send his children to labor. Edwin's pennies filled the tiny gap between starvation and subsistence.

Phoebe thought that he did nothing. Well, it was true. Not anything that was any use. Mor's helplessness was rotting his soul. What authority could he appeal to? Upon what or whom could he revenge himself?

Impotence and breathlessness turned his raging face to ash-gray. His legs were quivering. Coming to a standstill in the field of tenterframes, he stared at the mill, clenching and unclenching his fists with one thought in his mind: *Smash it, smash it! Join that raid on the mill tonight after all!*

Why, in truth, had he withdrawn? Perhaps his objections to Crawshaw had in fact been an excuse to avoid learning what sort of man he, Mor Laverock Greave, was; for whether one was a hero or a coward could not be known until tested. Maybe he feared self-knowledge.

Maybe it was always this fear that kept people impotent. Crawshaw, who hated bullying so much because he himself was innately a bully, was at least a man of action.

The first trickle of workers was coming homeward, through the gates. There was a lot of respect for Mor in Lady Well, and those who knew him saw at once that this was no time to greet him. He himself noticed hardly anyone.

When Mor found his child, dragging his feet, his empty bag dangling from his shoulder, he wordlessly scooped him up in his arms, put him on his shoulders, and carried him up the hill.

Edwin was crying into Mor's neck. Yes: at last, the child cried.

Mor said nothing. Did Edwin think him a coward? he wondered. Mor knew that his silence was turning his soul into a rotten quagmire, but it would not last! He would soon be doing something! But he would not tell the child.

Mor, in his impatience to get home, hardly looked at his son until he set him down in the house. One of the boy's eyes was closed and his mouth so swollen that he could barely speak. He was soaked and cold.

Again Mor wondered, did Edwin blame him because he could do nothing?

By now Phoebe, calmed down, had cleaned the room and laid the table. On seeing her son, she was once more in tears. How could she bear her agony of a mother who has been separated from her child in pain? There was nothing any of them could do, except endure their suffering. Neither her husband nor anyone else in Lady Well, that cursed town, would ever do anything about it, no matter how they talked!

There would be no solace until Heaven—if Heaven was deserved, and who could know that?

She would have liked to talk to her husband, now, in the fire of suffering, about her hope of Heaven. But she was afraid to speak of it to him, a disbeliever—already, she felt that Mor's waves of anger were directed against herself. She wanted to say, *It's not my fault. Don't 'urt me. I 'aven't done anything wrong. Not with Joshua nor anyone*. But, afraid of adding to his fury or provoking him to recklessness, she kept silent. She feared that Mor was brooding over the revenge he would take on Gledhill, and which would get him imprisoned or transported. Then she would be husbandless and utterly defenseless. Oh, what a thought.

Before they ate, Phoebe went outside to take water from the pump, then heated it over the fire. She used up the last of the soap to wash Edwin's wounds, and put ointment on the cuts and lash marks. She examined his swollen eye.

Edwin tightened his jaw, determined not to wince. Edwin, like Gideon, was learning to endure by means of righteous anger. It was in silence today—but the hour for justice would come.

Mor sat at the head of the table in his armchair. The children were on stools at either side. Phoebe was on one at the foot, sometimes reaching out and fidgeting with the platters, and getting up from time to time to put something to rights—her ornaments, the spotted dog and the huntsman. Mor could see that she was angry, from the way she gripped and banged things down, but said nothing.

At the first mouthful of food Edwin turned white. His lips lost their color and he vomited. Phoebe enfolded the child, pressing his tearful face into her apron.

Neither father nor mother spoke.

Gideon pointed his spoon at Edwin. "What do you say to that?" he demanded of his father.

Mor made no reply.

"What do *you* think we should do, Mother?" Gideon spoke tersely, and clearly contemptuous of his father.

Phoebe was crying again. She brushed the tears away. She could not say what they should do. She could only mumble excuses for her tears. "It's nothing . . ." she said. "It isn't anything . . ."

Phoebe had a hundred ways of saying "nothing." Sometimes it was tense or angry, and sometimes, as on this occasion, there emerged a quiet sound, that just managed to rise out of the well of her misery.

Gideon, still smarting under the tongues of Crawshaw and Tiplady, turned on his mother.

"*Nothing!* All you say is 'nothing'! Look what doing nothing's got for us! I'd rather be 'anged than go on doing nothing."

"Don't speak like that to your mother," Mor commanded.

"Don't!"

"No, *don't.*"

"We're slaves in Egypt and you do nothing about it, neither. Nothing! What Mother 'as to submit to . . . Doing nothing'll get us starved, even if we're not 'ung!"

Goaded too far, Mor, rather than strike his son, pushed back his chair and left the room.

"I'll be there on your raid," he whispered, so quietly that he could hardly be heard. He banged the door and went into the next room.

Phoebe had heard what he said, though. She turned white. Her hands were shaking. *If they catch him, they'll hang him, because he's the clever one. He can write and read books. He has a school.*

"What did 'e say?" Gideon demanded. "What did 'e say?"

"I don't know," Phoebe answered. "Nothing. I couldn't 'ear."

Edwin lifted his eyes. "My father's not angry with me, is 'e?"

While Mor was roaring at a group of village children in his schoolroom, and after Phoebe had gone to the pump once again, Gideon winked at Edwin and said, "Come with us tonight, lad. We'll do some work that'll make you feel better."

"What work?"

Edwin drew the back of his hand across his damp cheeks, as if it would wipe away his pain.

"Something, that's what. You'll see!"

“Are you going to set fire to the mill?” His fear was for Margaret, locked into the apprentice house.

Gideon did not answer.

“Is our father going with us?” He believed that in that case they would not fire the apprentice house. His father would stop them.

“Maybe. You never know with ’im. Our father changes ’is mind, doesn’t ’e? ’E’s as inconstant as the wind. No faith. ‘Faith that can remove the mountain to the plain.’ ”

“I’ll go if our father’s coming.”

“First of all you must be twisted in.”

“What’s that?”

“Wait and see!”

Edwin winced from being shouted at.

“Don’t be frightened. Being twisted in is only an oath that you must take not to betray the brotherhood.”

Gideon picked up a scrap of thread dropped from Mor’s weaving. He held it before Edwin’s eyes and gave a few sharp tugs at either end.

“Watch, now. Watch carefully! This is strong because all the fibers are twisted together into one bond. Thus we are strengthened through belonging together. Don’t forget it! Twisted in with one another, we will smash the machines in Horsfalls’ mill, to start the revolution in England.”

“Conspiracies and all that sort of work’s an ’anging matter.”

“How did you learn that?”

“I’ve ’eard ’em talking, ’aven’t I?”

“Nobody today knows what’s an ’anging matter and what isn’t. Only judges and them sort o’ folk know about that, and they won’t ’ang us, because there’ll be fresh judges in England after next May Day.”

“You’re not going to fire the mill! There’s children in there who can’t get out!”

Gideon looked at his brother with contempt.

When Phoebe entered, Gideon told her, “Mother, we’ve serious business to attend to tonight and we’re taking Edwin.”

She was weary. She put down her pail. “You can’t take Edwin.”

“ ’E must come with us, so as to grow up. Women can’t interfere with men’s work when it comes to politics.”

“After that business today! No . . . ’e’s too young.”

“You can’t grow up too soon in the times we’re living through.”

"They'll not stop short at 'anging children, if they want to."

Mor was standing at the door. "I'll come on the raid with you, but we're not taking Edwin. It's not for children."

"He can be twisted in. Samuel Wrigley's to be twisted in by King Ludd tonight."

"I want to go!" Edwin cried.

"He's not going to be twisted in, and he's not coming with us. There's no question of it. Twisting in children! Is this what Crawshaw's been telling you? Your mother's right. They'll not stop short at 'anging kids."

"I want to go to the mill!" Edwin repeated. "I want to get my own back on 'em."

"You're not going," Mor repeated once again.

"You'll not be setting fire to it . . . ?" Edwin asked.

"We're not going to fire it," Mor answered.

"Some 'ave been fired," Edwin insisted. "Mr. Crawshaw'd fire it, to make 'imself famous."

After dark, when the "Watch and Ward" partrol might arrest suspects in the streets, Mor shoved a book in his pocket and slipped out with Gideon, heading first to Samuel Wrigley's house.

Mor rapped on the door, one sharp knock followed by two slow ones, and Samuel opened it a crack. He was already halfway into his coat, and smiling as if he was going to a picnic.

Gideon grimly announced the password: "The Loyal Georgian Society, and the Lord protect us."

Wrigley turned to his new wife. "Your oatcakes are burning," he told her, to get her out of the room.

"Who's that at the door?" she asked, peering; not that she cared, it was merely to show that she was not stupid.

"The schoolmaster," Samuel answered.

Satisfied now to do as she was bid and to pretend she did not know that they were trying to get rid of her, nor why, she went to haul a rack of oatcakes down from the ceiling in the back room, her hands and apron dusty with flour. Mor and his son continued to watch from the doorstep.

"Repeat the password," Gideon demanded.

"You know who I am, lad!" Wrigley teased.

Mor was laughing.

"Answer!" Gideon hissed. "Say, 'The Lord protect us.' "

Wrigley, too, was laughing. Leaving his visitors standing on the step, he retreated into the house and shouted goodbye to his wife.

Then he was on the street with the other two. He was game for anything, healthy, rakish, and strong.

" 'Ow does married life suit you, Samuel Wrigley?" Mor asked.

"I didn't know I *was* married until I woke up and found myself in bed with someone. It's better than doing everything for myself . . ." Wrigley turned to Gideon. "You're in a bit of a state, my young comrade! 'Appen it's because our King Ludd and John Tiplady gave you a rough time this afternoon?"

"That's nothing to do with it," Gideon snarled.

"Isn't it?"

"No."

"Well, you shouldn't take any notice of Crawshaw. He's too fond of his own voice, that one. It's nothing more than that."

Skirting the Adam and Eve public house because of the soldiers billeted in it, they came to the back door of the radicals' pub, the Old Tup. It was on the edge of town, and there seemed to be no sign of life. The shutters were drawn and showed no chinks of light.

Edwin lurked fifty yards away. Because he was following a Luddite band, all his aches seemed worth bearing. He prepared himself for a long wait before they would emerge from the Old Tup. They always did take a long time over their meetings in there. He rubbed at his wrists, which were almost pulled out of joint. He entertained himself by making one fanciful plan after another. From time to time he attended to his kicked shins, or to his eye.

Gideon knocked at the door of the Old Tup; the same rapping that had been delivered upon Wrigley's.

"Who's there?" answered Arthur Crawshaw's voice, although one would not have dreamed that there was a soul in the building.

"The Lord protect us!" Gideon called out.

Wooden bolts were slid back. The door opened into a primitive, cavelike room with a stone floor, and the ceiling made of great stone pavings, too. Shadows flickered over the scarred, whitewashed walls. There was a large fire in the grate. A pot of rabbit stew was cooking for a celebration after the raid. Other poached contributions were laid out on a sideboard, with whisky and ale, for after the attack. In the light of the hearth, and of ignited ropes dipped in pitch, men were already gathered around a Bible and a huge hammer, placed in the center of the room. There were also firearms. One gun was fitted with a bayonet.

"You've been on a raid already, then," Mor remarked.

"And you were not with us," Crawshaw replied tartly.

"Well, there wasn't much to it," Tiplady added. "We'd only to climb through a stable window at the back o' the Adam and Eve. There wasn't a guard in sight. You wouldn't know about that, Mr. Crawshaw. You were at the front door."

"Nonetheless, Greave wasn't with us! Now he wants to be one of us." Crawshaw looked around for support. "So then there'll be thirteen on the raid. Is someone else to drop out, or what?"

"I don't mind not going," Wrigley answered. "It's all the same to me whether I join in the fun or not."

"It won't be no fun," Crawshaw told him.

"Not with you around, it won't," Mor said.

"They'll call you a coward, Samuel," Tiplady warned.

"Nobody'll ever call me a coward, not if I come to hear of it!"

"We know why you have decided at last to join us, Mor Greave," Crawshaw said. "You had no intention of it until something 'appened to your own child in the factory. You've come for personal reasons, and not for the greater cause that inspires the rest of us. You've proved a backslider before, Mor Greave."

"*You* say that to me! *You!*"

"Steady on," Tiplady warned.

"You, Crawshaw! You're the one looking out for yourself—for a bit o' private glory!"

"Let's get on without quarrels, for God's sake," Tiplady said, as he filled his pipe.

"*You!* The pot calling the kettle black!" Mor, angry, would not be stopped.

"We're all going," Tiplady said, taking command of the fireplace, with more authority than King Ludd himself. He touched a long taper to the flames and sucked at his pipe. "We need every man, and who in the future would want to admit that 'e'd been left behind?"

"Then there'll be thirteen of us," Crawshaw said.

Tiplady stared hard at Crawshaw. "Yes," he answered. "It's time to break wi' superstitions."

So Wrigley allowed himself to be sworn in, his hands upon the Bible, and repeating after Crawshaw the Luddite oath.

"I, Samuel Wrigley, of my own free voluntary will, do declare and solemnly swear that I will never reveal to any person or persons under the Canopy of Heaven the names of those who comprise the secret committee, their proceedings, meetings, places of abode, dress, features, complexion, under the penalty of being sent out of the world by the first brother who shall meet me. And further do I swear to use my best endeavors to punish by death any traitor should one rise up amongst us, wherever I can find him and though he should fly to the ends of the earth I will pursue him with unceasing vengeance. So help me God and bless me, to keep this my oath inviolate."

"You're twisted in now, Samuel Wrigley. You're one with us, and you cannot break it without breaking with us all," Crawshaw announced.

Crawshaw then made a speech to the whole company: "Since the last week of February our brothers have attacked the dressing shop of Joseph Hurst and destroyed a cropping machine. They've destroyed all the machinery that was put in at William Hinchcliffe's on Ley Moor. They've smashed shearing frames at Linthwaite, Slaithwaite, Golcar, Honley, and Holmfirth. So our defeat at Rawfolds was not a defeat, instead it 'as inspired us. It was sent by God, not to crush us but to refresh our justified anger, like water from Heaven upon the spring grass . . ."

Before the speech was finished, the machine breakers were disguising themselves and smudging lampblack over their features. Along with the firearms, picks and iron bars were distributed. The hammer that was symbol as well as tool of the machine-breakers' mission was given to Wrigley, in honor of his strength and skill. Crawshaw tucked a pistol into his belt. Tiplady took the gun with the bayonet. Others rummaged in a cupboard that was filled with women's clothes, and dressed themselves in petticoats, cotton dresses, and bonnets.

Sad amateurs of conspiracy and revolution, the men in female dress crossed back and forth through the shadows and the firelight, like weird priests.

All except Crawshaw welcomed Mor. They broke into the ale and toasted him back into the fold. He warmed in the glow of companionship.

King Ludd briskly divided his men into two parties. The youngest and strongest were to enter and smash the cropping frame, the eldest and weakest were to keep watch. He drilled them for a few minutes; the maneuvers were difficult for men dressed to the ankles in women's frocks, and who were making do with a farm rake, a collier's pick, and a poker.

At last, Tiplady became impatient. He shook the ashes out of his pipe.

"Are we to stay drilling like toy soldiers until the moon rises and the countryside is alive wi' soldiers?" he said. "Well, you are the captain, not I!"

At last King Ludd was satisfied. Boots rang to attention for the last time on the stone floor. Through the door they took a quick look up and down, and stepped out on their mission.

It was a cool night, faintly gray and silver, the moon not yet up. One man was sent ahead to look for soldiers and for the Watch and Ward patrol. He was to give a signal at each corner. Apart from that, as they knew that no neighbor would betray them, the band showed little caution. It was almost impossible to recruit a Watch and Ward patrol in Lady Well, anyway. Crawshaw was at the front, muttering but making his peace with Tiplady. Samuel Wrigley strode at the rear, carrying the hammer easily on his shoulder. The others, in between, were trying to save their skirts from tangling with their heavy boots.

A hundred yards to the rear Edwin followed, not able to recognize which one of these weird shadowy figures was his father.

As they reached the top of the stairway that dropped down to the mill, the moon rose. With its leering, steadily brightening face, it transformed the whole of Yorkshire. Hill was folded upon hill, like gray, soft cloth folded in the cropping shop. It was so bright that the tightly shut daisies opened and turned toward it. To hide from the light, and also because there might be a guard on the stairway, the machine breakers climbed the wall and cut through the woods. Edwin followed, tingling with fear of mantraps.

Eventually, ahead of him, Crawshaw hissed for silence. The band had broken out of the trees. A sheet of bright moonlight, like silver-gray icy water, lay upon the mill's tenter field. A guard was sitting by a fire with his musket on his knees—looking out, not for Luddites, but for rabbits.

King Ludd felt it was safe to go forward, as the soldier was so absorbed. He led his men to the wall of the apprentices' building. This was the simplest place from which to break in. It was the farthest from Mr. Horsfall's house, and the most difficult to patrol because of the tangled woods nearby, and because it was close to the river. The noise of the water would also cover the sounds of the picks, and this spot was the most unlikely, therefore the least suspected, way in. It was remarkably easy; mill owners and soldiers were such fools.

The Luddites posted their guards, and Crawshaw started to swing a pick at the mortar below a windowsill. This led into the girls' dormitory, where the children were already out of their beds, watching and shrieking.

"Be quiet!" Crawshaw ordered, frightened. "Be quiet!"

Dust from his pick sifted downward through the moonlight. Mor and others inserted crowbars and eased out the sill. Crawshaw climbed a tree, in order to hack at the lintel. Finally, sill, bars, and bits of masonry dropped in a cloud of dust onto the riverbank. The larger stones toppled heavily into the water. The raiders were ready to go into the mill, demolish it, and change the world.

Like a nestful of happy starlings, the ragged little girls were putting their heads through the hole in their prison wall, out into the cloud of dust. Yet the girls who had longed so much for freedom were afraid to take it, and only a couple dared clamber through the gap. The others ran into the darkest corner of their prison, huddling together.

The raiders did not have time to spare for persuading them. Tiplady lifted out the two little girls who were brave enough for it. With a smile, he put his hand in his pocket and gave them two pence each. Not even pausing to look at this amazing gift, they ran off into the darkness.

Margaret was not one of them. Edwin, some yards away, painfully watched.

Finally, he could restrain himself no longer. He rushed to that window through which King Ludd's men had been swallowed.

"Margaret! Margaret!"

Soon her head was peeping through.

"Margaret, take my hand! Let's away!"

"I can't . . ."

He pulled her out. She slithered down the wall with a scream of pain.

"I can't do it, I hurt so!"

But she was out of the mill now, crouching against the wall, frightened both of going with Edwin, and of returning. Her flesh was burning wherever it was touched. Her hand, which Edwin grasped, was in pain. In the creamy light of the moon, now high in the sky, he made her run even faster, careless of mantraps, ditches, and brambles.

"I hurt!" she repeated, but she still kept going. "My feet! I can't go so fast!"

They heard the factory bell tolling. They listened to shots fired, and thought that they were hunted. They struggled on, on, out of sound and sight of Luddites, soldiers, factory bells, apprentice houses, and spinning machines, looking for London and Margaret's mother; for Liverpool and America.

Mor stumbled away from the mill, crashing into bogs and tangles of bramble. Inside Horsfalls' they had come across soldiers waiting to ambush them among the frames. Crawshaw had fired off his pistol, killing a private. Because everyone fled in panic, Mor had little idea of the fate of his companions. All had happened, indeed, as he might have foretold.

Hungry, tired, afraid, not daring to return to the appetizing rabbit stew at the Old Tup, Mor came by a place known as Lower Laithes. It was a derelict group of buildings, with much of its stone removed to build the Horsfalls' mansion.

He went under the precarious archway, into the eerie courtyard, telling himself that he was looking for a place to rest in and hide, in case he was pursued to his home; but in fact he felt compelled. He was overcome with awe. This thrust him forward through the dark and he found himself walking amid the tumbled stones, dilapidated barns, holes that had once been the cellars of buildings, doors hanging from hinges, collapsed floors, suspended lintels, old carts and stone troughs, broken chunks of classical carvings and hunks of plaster daubed with fragmentary depictions of the Muses—all the fashionable rubbish of a previous age—with an unseen hand guiding him. Though he possessed a poacher's skill at not stumbling in the dark, even so the ease with which he moved around these death traps was extraordinary. He would not have collided with anything even if he had behaved carelessly.

He was searching for something, though he did not know for what. He felt a sense of beauty, one that overrode the bestiality, the cruelty, the smoky ugliness and the poverty that soured the spirit and the flesh in Yorkshire.

It was very dark between the buildings, and Mor leaned his head back, looking for stars. The whole of the heavens was rearranged in a symmetrical pattern of great loveliness. The stars had formed themselves into a wheel, the hub of which was over this courtyard. Some incredible crown was fixed over this place. Yet it seemed at the moment quite a normal event.

Moving on, he found himself in a covered passageway, and at the other end a garden door, which, feeling his way, he discovered was locked. He was compelled to turn back.

At the mouth of the starlit courtyard he was unable to stir. His feet were locked into the ground, his hands fastened to the walls where he reached out to steady himself. The empty courtyard had the potent feeling of a stage upon which the curtain has risen yet it is still empty of characters; when the gentlemen and ladies have become motionless and silent in their boxes and all are waiting for the great tragic actress to appear.

Mor began to shake, in violent waves from his head down to his feet. A cry took possession of him and gripped his throat. It was not his own cry, for he had no control over it and it was not even his own voice. It was an inhumanly savage call, torn out of some unsuspected, deep well within him. It began quietly but with each successive wave grew louder. At each attack he felt he could bear no more, yet still they came. His throat was strained, yet though he was longing for peace, he shook the universe with his cries. His body was being rattled to pieces. He did not know which frightened him most—the uncontrollable yells that tore him, or the silences that followed each spasm; his violent shaking, or his feet being locked into the ground.

Then something compelled him to move again. Like the voice, it was regardless of his personal desires, and he had no more control of his motions than he had possessed over his previous rootedness. His usual limp was suddenly, miraculously, eased. He began to dash about the courtyard at great speed, with some invisible force pushing or pulling him; his only light, the marvelous coronet of stars above.

He found himself banging pitifully on the long-abandoned doors, and he had no idea why he had chosen them, nor what ghosts were summoning him. He begged, begged, to be let in and freed of the exhausting, frightening exhilaration. Then he was off again, dashing about the courtyard.

He was shrieking and screaming. What control he kept of himself, he used for a terrified pleading to be released from the awful suffering, especially in his throat, and from the tearing pain at his inner organs. He was being skewered in pain, possessed by a frightful purpose, clinging to the hope that he could survive. Yet before he completed his pleas, that rival cry was rising out of him.

He was confronted by a small ash tree growing in a crack of masonry, and found himself pulling branches from it. The first twigs that came to hand did not satisfy his occupying spirit, or whatever it was, and it made him tear desperately at others. He crushed the branches and leaves onto his head until he was soaked in their cool moistness.

Now calm and happiness possessed him. He was laughing. Holding the branches aloft, he began to pace up and down the yard. He lifted his head back and laughed at the marvelous, transformed sky. He was overflowing with ecstasy, roaring with delight because he knew that he had survived. He was certain that something wonderful was about to happen.

Tiredness overcame him and he sank upon the cobblestones, still crushing the branches to his head. Leaves hung over his temples, down his neck, over his shoulders and breast. He was silent now, spent and trembling.

Out of the darkness, a stone seemed to come forward, and he found himself gripping it tight, as something to be cherished. It was as smooth as a bird's egg, a perfect oval, untypical of any local stones. He clutched it to his breast, and it seemed to anchor him to the world.

Mor returned to consciousness. Although exhausted, he was also illuminated. He was glowing like a hot coal.

The moment that he thought of rising, he became stiff with fear of the objects among which he had been dashing. The yard was littered with the torn branches of his madness, as well as with pitfalls. Whereabouts was the well? It must be waiting somewhere to swallow him up.

At last, tentatively, he made his way to the yard's exit. All the stars had disappeared and the darkness made his head spin.

Some hours before dawn, Lydia Horsfall was awakened by the raid. She was not sure whether the gunshots, the shouts, and the tolling bell had been part of a nightmare; but the bell continued to ring after she awoke. Men were running and yelling outside the house. Inside, she heard a scream and a curse, in its intensity quite different from the usual cries of whores or of the officers billeted with the Horsfalls.

Lydia Horsfall slept alone. She chose a remote room so as to be away from such sounds in the night. However, her bedroom was beneath the even more distant room where the elder Nicholas Horsfall was kept. Every now and then she would hear him above her ceiling. She knew that as soon as dawn arrived, he would be inspired, like some form of slime life, to respond to the light. She supposed that at such a time he could not but feel some hope, yet Lydia, if woken early, would lie in dread of the coming sounds. His noises as he scratched at the window were not loud, for he had neither breath nor energy for it, but were frighteningly inhuman, as if he had been changed into a reptile or a toad. The mill owner's wife hated to awake early, to be condemned as she now was to spend yet more time with her thoughts, with her hatred for this house, and its whores, and its drunken officers, and its terrible specter: the barely fleshed ghost of a syphilitic old man. These were the horrors that drove her out, night or day, whenever she could find excuses and the weather was not impossibly inclement.

On each return, Lydia had to pause before re-entering. She chose the same spot at a hundred yards' distance to breathe deeply and recreate the composure she must feel, and the features she must bear, in order to go into this abominable house. How many of the finest mansions in England were haunted by a syphilitic old man in an attic, and perhaps also a daughter languishing more poetically from consumption in the drawing room? Lydia wondered, in the darkness. A great many; she knew that. There were more revolting creatures in the sealed-off rooms and attics of Britain than were admitted to. She tried to think that she should not be so sorry for herself, then; but she had additional afflictions. Her husband's trips to London and Brussels . . . she knew what he went for. Reasoning that his deflowering of twelve-year-olds in a brothel was because of his terror of catching from an older whore the disease that rotted his father did not make it easier for her to hide (as for society's sake she must) her revulsion and disgust.

She also had the problem of being a woman from the south having to put up with "the barbaric north." Her home looked over a crowded industrial valley, on the edge of the growing town of Lady Well, yet it was to her a place where "nobody" lived; that is, no one of her own class. She felt only charity, and deep sorrow, for those who lived there. She never went into the factory, and the nearest she came to her husband's employees was in church, or when distributing charity in the village, where the people kept a respectful distance. Nevertheless, she made it her business to know a great deal about them—their names, trades, and misfortunes. She had gifts delivered secretly to "the most deserving cases": some money to be picked up on the doorstep, a pie supposedly sent by a distant relative.

Though she had little direct contact with the workpeople, she heard them, all right. Every morning, and for much of the year in the dark, they tramped down that long gully, the yard at the bottom of her garden, with a savage noise like that of mutinous prisoners. She was sure that it was on purpose, to awaken her. If she dared to look out, she would see them jeering and pointing, it seemed in her direction, though she knew that it was actually at the monster in the room above.

At last, the gray daylight was seeping into her bedroom. She felt the tiredness that would make her ugly forming creases around her eyes and across her forehead, even before the commencement of the day that would exhaust her with its emptiness. What, what was she doing here? At the age of thirty, a cast-off, rejected woman, young enough to count herself still beautiful, yet too old to satisfy her husband's passions! A woman without friends, or a purpose!

She heard the old man scraping and wheezing above her room. She remembered the stages of his disease. A handsome, confident man, like his son was today, he had formed a habit of picking his nose. Though people remarked on it, he could not help himself, even in company. There had next formed an incrustation inside his nostril, and a little pus mixed with blood began to run. His mouth and throat were sore.

One day, she overheard from behind a closed door the kind of conversation a lady was not supposed to hear.

"Pray, sir, what is the matter with me?" Horsfall asked the surgeon.

"The matter? Why, sir, you are poxed up to the eyes."

In any case, Lydia would have soon guessed the diagnosis, because of the cure. He was treated with the notorious "blue pills": a combination of mercury with a quarter-grain of opium, taken in a concoction of sarsaparilla. Eventually, it was tacitly assumed throughout the household that she knew what the disease was, without the word "pox" or "syphilis" ever having been mentioned in her presence.

The blue pills did not improve things, so mercury was applied as an ointment. The pimples on Horsfall's face exuded a watery discharge, and his cheeks became covered with a yellow crust. He had difficulty in breathing, and they tried steaming his nostrils over a bowl of hot water. That gave him some relief, but the decay continued. Because of his embarrassment, he gave up going into society and he abandoned his business.

His family finally locked this wreck of a man away. They and their servants were unable to hide their disgust any longer.

Now, at last, the light changed from gray to yellow in Lydia's room. She watched it tinting the painting by her father's protégé, Thomas Gould: a misty morning evaporating over fields. In her room were several other paintings, including her portrait, by the same artist. *If there were not something beautiful in my life,* she thought, *I could not bear it.*

Her maid knocked, but instead of waiting to be called, she hurried in, distraught, and put an end to Lydia's painful thoughts. The girl's apron was awry and bits of hair were escaping from her cap. Lydia, recalling her proper role, reprimanded the servant, who could hardly hear for her panic, and did nothing to tidy up her appearance, as she curtsied nervously around the bed, her eyes full of tears. At last, she did pull herself together sufficiently to push back some of the hairs dangling untidily from the edges of her cap.

"They have tried to break down the mill, ma'am, but the soldiers were waiting. A man was shot. A soldier. Three children have run away, Mr. Gledhill says. He says they're spies for Luddites, fearful of being apprehended for telling secrets to the French."

"Nonsense."

"Please, ma'am, didn't you hear the bell ringing all night? We all, the servants I mean, couldn't sleep for it."

"I heard the bell, yes, and the soldiers. Do straighten your appearance."

"Yes, ma'am."

The servant, selected as a devoted member of the lower classes, collected herself and pulled at her apron, retying the strings.

A roar of pain rose out of the depths of the house.

"I take it that these desperate persons did not succeed in breaking down our mill?" Lydia said, more urgently now.

"Thanks be to God, ma'am! Two of the men are injured and crying for a surgeon downstairs, but Mr. Horsfall will not give them any help."

"Why not?"

The girl's eyes filled again. "Until they tell on their comrades."

"Which men are they?"

"Wrigley, ma'am, and John Tiplady."

"Help me to dress and I will go to see."

Attired in sable slippers and a Chinese silk gown, Lydia suppressed her deeper thoughts and sent forth her other self, Mrs. Horsfall, to do her female duty of quelling disputatious men.

In the great passageway, the width of a carriage drive, that ran the whole length of the house, a knot of servants was preparing cleaning equipment, ready to enter a room as if to make a military invasion. Halfway along the passage she spied a stranger—a messenger, it seemed—hovering with his hat in his hands. Girls in coarse work clothes were polishing stair rails, doorknobs, the wood and tiles of the floor. A boy in a green apron was bringing in coals. All these were perfectly usual sights, when the servants returned, after cockcrow, from their wings of the house; but although their brisk attitude had always shown that they had no greater wish than to spend the whole of eternity in polishing her floors and bringing her coals, sly and shifty looks met her this morning. The girl at the banister rail looked boldly at her mistress, making no effort to hide her face and her squalid apron, as she had been trained to do. The messenger twisted his hat in his hands as if they were around the throat of a despot. The boy with the coals banged them down outside the library door and stared at her. Lydia was still angry from these disturbing encounters when she went into her husband's study.

Moaning upon stretchers on the floor were John Tiplady and Samuel Wrigley. A whimpering servant girl was trying to soothe them. Nearby was a captain, a sergeant, two privates, Nathaniel Gledhill with a bottle in his hand, Mor Greave, and a gentleman whom Lydia did not recognize.

"What is happening? Revolution?" Lydia demanded. "The servants stare at me like Jacobins at Marie Antoinette."

"My dear Lydia, do leave us. This isn't a place for a woman."

But Nicholas realized, wearily, that she would not go away. She could be a most determined woman.

Bracing herself against the sight, Lydia peered down at the bodies. She was able to see so deeply into the wound at Tiplady's shoulder that she perceived pieces of bone floating in blood. She pulled back, turned white and sickened, but managed to hold back the vomit.

Men, for Lydia, were normally cruel, perverse, obscene beings. They ruled and they crushed. They rotted vilely in hidden rooms, for their sins. If they were of a lower class, they might murder one in one's bed . . . so she had been told, and told, and told. But here she saw a being equal to herself, vulnerable, weak, and feeling pain. She had seen, not a Luddite, but a man . . . one for whom she felt not fear or contempt but sorrow. She stared bleakly at the gray hairs curling on Tiplady's neck, at his freckled hand, at the pale, harrowed features and the torn shoulder. His eyes were closing and opening in pain, like the gills of a desperate fish dragged out of water, taking in only veiled shaky glimpses of the books, the people, the paintings.

"Stop this cruelty! Stop it, for the love of charity!" She spoke in a firm, strange voice hardly recognizable as her own.

"Lydia, don't you think it would be better for you to return upstairs?" her husband said, in the tone, not of a suggestion, but of an order.

"It isn't charity we want, Mrs. Horsfall," said Mor Geave. "It's our rights. We need beef and pie as a right for the work we do, not as a gift to those that suit you. We want our work and fair payment for it, and if you intend changing things, we want to be consulted."

She stared at him, trying to comprehend his speech. He spoke so deliberately, as if it was something he had prepared for this meeting.

“ ‘Needs,’ ‘wants,’ what’s all this?” Horsfall said. “You are members of a conspiracy! That is the truth of it. We must face up to the facts. Are you also in Napoleon’s pay?”

“For God’s sake, shoot me now and put me out of misery,” Tiplady whispered.

“May I bring some warm milk for Mr. Tiplady, ma’am? Look at ’im . . .” The maid was struggling with rag and bucket to prevent blood from reaching the carpet.

“Of course. And bring some brandy,” Lydia replied, sharply, as a way to cope with her own tears.

“Lydia, my dear, are you well? I should go upstairs, if I were you,” Nicholas repeated, this time with even more menace.

The servant left hurriedly, before the order was countermanded.

“They are the traitorous followers of King Ludd, Mrs. Horsfall,” the stranger explained patiently. “They were armed, and they shot a man. Fortunately, we foiled their plans in advance.”

“Who is this person?” Lydia asked with contempt.

“A spy,” Mor, just as contemptuously, told her.

“I was guarding the woods for Mr. Horsfall at the time that I saw the rebels. They drilled like soldiers, and were armed against the King. ’Tis certain they will not stop at this, but are aiming to overthrow their betters.”

“We drill so as not to be the rabble you think us to be,” Tiplady whispered.

“You drill to overthrow your country!” Gledhill knelt down at Tiplady’s side. “You shot a man!”

Tiplady screamed. Gledhill had poured aquafortis on the wound.

“Damn you, damn you . . .” Mor could think of no other expression. “Damn you.”

Wrigley tried to swing a blow. A gentle pluck at his arm from the maid, returned with the milk, restrained him. Lydia winced and pushed her sleeve in her mouth.

“What do *you* know of Luddites?” Horsfall demanded of Mor.

Mor, fortunately, had not been recognized during the raid. Crawshaw, who had killed the soldier, had disappeared. Only the two men on the floor and Mor had been arrested, so far; though God only knew who they were still looking for. Mor wondered where Gideon was. He himself, shortly after leaving Lower Laithes, had been stopped on the edge of Lady Well for being abroad in boots caked with mud "at an unreasonable hour." As Gledhill, the Watch and Ward captain, had remarked, "If he has not been at the mill, then he's been poaching." Fortunately, he had been able to drop the stone by the roadside, where he could retrieve it later, and they had not seen it. Otherwise, presumably, they would have assumed it to be a weapon raised against them.

It was as he was being brought to Horsfall's that Mor had put his hand in his pocket and realized he had lost his book, *The Rights of Man*. The chances were that it was in or near the mill, and his name was written on the flyleaf.

"Nothing," Mor answered. "I know nothing about Luddites."

"You have associated with murderers. You're a schoolmaster and, they tell me, an educated man. You should know better."

"I know what Socrates knew. That he was the wisest of men because he knew that he knew nothing."

Horsfall was impatient of philosophy. "Tell us who King Ludd is, and it might earn you a pardon from transportation."

" 'Tis fair wages that will cure this illness, not magistrates and transportations. If there's right wages, King Ludd will die."

For Lydia, Greave's words were like Tiplady's wound: gaping with pain, yet they opened new worlds of understanding and feeling for her. In this room of her own house, wounded upon the carpet was John Tiplady, a thoughtful, honest craftsman, and Samuel Wrigley, a cheerful, lusty young man who had recently married. There, threatened with hanging or transportation, was the village schoolmaster. On the other side, two of the worst men she had ever known, her husband and the awful Gledhill, with the help of that slimy spy (evidently some kind of decayed gentleman), triumphed over them.

The world was upside down, and Lydia knew that she could bear no more of this place.

"You seem faint, Lydia. I think you should leave us."

She was not going to leave.

While Mor was held by the sergeant, Gledhill waved the aquafortis bottle under his nose. "You are the King's prisoner! A poacher, a writer of sedition, and a traitor, too!"

Mor aimed a kick at the overseer's leg, which landed home.

Gledhill was about to return the blow, when Lydia shouted, "Stop that, Gledhill! What sort of man are you?"

Nicholas had never known her to speak in this unladylike fashion in front of the lower orders. Yet everyone was looking, not at her, but at him. Like himself, they thought that Mrs. Horsfall, who wandered the moors at night, was a lunatic, and they were wondering what he would do about it. Have her put away? Only Mor Greave stared at her with a different kind of expression. He apparently realized what she was thinking. Her husband, smiling, put an arm around her shoulder and dug his nails into the back of her neck as he repeated, with great menace, "My dear, I think you ought to leave us."

He was diverted from his intention of expelling her, if she would not go willingly, by the scuffle taking place between Mor, Gledhill, and the sergeant who restrained him. It was clear that the soldier liked fair play, and didn't like the overseer.

"He'll be swinging on the gallows tomorrow, sir. Let justice take its course."

" 'Anging's too good for seditious Paineites," Gledhill spat out. "Do you know that he teaches sedition in that cellar school of his? They're the ones we have to catch. Catch the ones who do the reading and writing and the filling of minds with sedition, and you'll kill stone-dead the fear of revolution."

"I haven't done anything more than take a walk in the moonlight," Mor said.

"Very poetical, I'm sure," sneered Horsfall.

"A great deal may be perceived by the light of the moon," Lydia remarked icily. "Unfortunately! Around this house! And I'm not leaving. Not yet!" She knew that in the last resort she could defy her husband simply because of what she knew about him.

"Is your wife all right, sir?" the captain asked.

"My wife is ill," Horsfall allowed, bluntly.

Rubbing his shin, Gledhill knelt by Samuel Wrigley. "Tell us who King Ludd is!"

With great effort John Tiplady turned to face his friend. "Can you keep a secret?"

"Yes," said Wrigley.

Tiplady motioned to Horsfall. "Can you keep a secret?"

"Yes."

"Come closer."

Horsfall, though he hated to come close to malodorous working people, bent down.

"Closer."

Close enough for Tiplady to observe the twitching of a man who could not help but show his repulsion.

"So can I," Tiplady whispered, and then he died.

Lydia returned to her room. She had seen too much. And now her husband had grasped that she was not merely indifferent; he understood that she had become his enemy. Because of what she knew, she could destroy him. She realized what he would do about that. Hadn't he already threatened to have her certified as a lunatic for her strolls in the moonlight?

Lydia knew what she herself would do about it, too. She knew her resources. Her father, distrusting "the Horsfall tribe," before her marriage had placed her money, inherited from her mother, in trust.

Her first act was to write to tell her father that she wished to endow an "improved" hospital as an annex to the workhouse. "Lady Well will then be the better for at least one Horsfall," she wrote.

Next, she composed a letter to the artist Thomas Gould. "This house has been for too long the theater of my exploits and the boundary of my view and prospects," she wrote, cautiously, sedately—the manner was really a sort of code. "All my affections have been too much hidden inside my nature. I am leaving Lady Well and bringing my daughter with me. My son, I will leave behind; he is too like his father for me to be able to bear it. May we escape to the Continent? You have often said that we could."

Finally, she wrote a letter advising the Factory Commission to visit Paradise Mills. She suggested that the inspectors hold interviews with the workpeople individually and without any witnesses present, so that they would dare to speak their minds.

She would not trust her letters to a servant but, at around ten o'clock in the morning, took them herself to the post office. Even on this day that was seething with revolution, most of the villagers made way for her, doffing their hats or curtsying. She felt grateful for it, and secure, for this was how things should be, but she wished that the Horsfalls had earned the respect. That was what made the difference.

She met Mor Greave. He carried a roll of cloth under his arm.

"There's no one'll buy your piece today, Mr. Greave. All business is stopped. The office is closed," she said. "May I see it?"

He unrolled the piece over the roadside wall, where the smoke-blackened tones heightened its bright colors. He stood back, with a mixture of diffidence and pride. He was not at all humble before her and, strangely, she did not mind.

"It's dyed in the wool," he announced proudly.

His eyes were looking anxiously up the street or over the hills.

"But everyone else is weaving soldiers' cloth!" Lydia said.

"That's what my wife says, Mrs. Horsfall. That no one'll buy what I make. I know it's not any use, but I wanted to . . ."

She had opened her purse, and was taking out sovereigns.

"I don't want any charity, Mrs. Horsfall."

"It's not charity. I'll buy it from you."

"I haven't change for a sovereign."

"Will you sell it to me?"

"Yes. But I've no change, and I need the money now. Today."

"I know you do. I know."

As they looked at one another, each knew that the other planned to leave. This was one reason why she did not resent his insolence. Their society was falling apart anyway, and there were no longer any appearances to be kept up.

"I want it to remind me of Lady Well—after I leave," she said.

"I thought you didn't like us much, Mrs. Horsfall."

"Does your piece mean anything?" she asked, abruptly, for the weaver was now going a little too far with the directness of his speech.

"Mean anything?"

"Hope, perhaps. The bright colors."

"No, it doesn't mean anything," he answered cautiously. "Why should it?"

She didn't answer this, either.

"Does two sovereigns seem a fair price?"

"Two sovereigns!" He laughed and then grew annoyed. "I don't want charity!" He stared across the valley. "I don't want charity, Mrs. Horsfall."

"It's not charity. It's worth all of that to me. It will be something to remind me of the best of this place, instead of the worst."

"Do you know what a weaver's paid for his cloth, Mrs. Horsfall? I'd do well to get ten shillings for it. I don't want you to think I've made a fool of you by charging too much."

"I know the value of things perfectly well, Mr. Greave. I've told you, it's worth two sovereigns to me."

He was still hesitating. Lydia found herself doing something quite extraordinary. She took his hand and prised apart his thick, stubborn fingers. She had not held a man's hand like that since . . . well, since she last met Thomas Gould. She pressed the two coins in between his fingers. He looked away from her as he ran his hand across his cheek, brushing off a tear and clutching the sovereigns.

"Bless you," he said.

"I'm on my way to the post office. Will you carry it there for me?"

He walked behind her, humble now, out of a real respect that he felt. Though it was also because he could not keep up with her, being both laden and crippled. She stayed ahead, strangely not ashamed at the moment of the grand role that had been thrust upon her for so many years. It was, she thought, because at last she had enjoyed some honest intercourse; because of this, she felt, she could accept this tribute from a man.

At the door of the post office, she waited for him. "I've been wanting all the time to know why my husband did not detain you," she said.

Mor smiled. "Because I'm the schoolmaster," he answered. "There was no evidence against me, other than that I had been found wandering the countryside, but I wasn't anywhere near the mill. I know that in another man's case, that might be sufficient to condemn him. But a schoolmaster has a little influence in his community. Knowledge is power."

Mor followed her into the post office. In front of the postmaster, they could not exchange any more words. With her letters, she left the roll of cloth to be delivered to her house later.

Once they were outside again, Mor went in one direction and she in the other.

"Lady Hell," she muttered, as she returned to Horsfall's house. "Lady Hell, Lady Hell . . ."

CHAPTER FIVE

April 17th

Edwin knew which way to run, where lay east and west, because he had drawn all those maps, asked so many questions, taken notice of where the carts came from and where they went to.

By contrast, it had never occurred to Margaret to consider that there *was* a direction in which to search for what one wanted. She had never been allowed to decide; she had always been taken to her destinations. It was other things that were active with purpose. Men. Birds. Swallows, or a stray gull or a lark that she had watched, flying through the rectangles of sky above her various prison yards, in Hackney, in Derbyshire, in Yorkshire, and over the stopping places in between.

Now Edwin dragged her by the hand along the course of the brook through Blood Wood. So, once again, she was being taken, just as she had been led to the workhouse, and as the carters had taken her to and from London. Edwin was leading her, not toward another misery, she was sure, but toward happiness; something that for her was associated with nothing else but, once upon a time, comforting folds of motherly flesh, though she could hardly remember . . .

They heard more gunshots. They listened to the mill bell ringing through the darkness. In hillside farms and cottages, lights appeared, hanging on immense walls of darkness. This must mean that people were hunting for them, but Margaret did not dwell on this thought. She was like a shipwrecked voyager, whose attention is fixed not on the engulfing ocean but on some small and solid point of the shore; no matter what her suffering, she must cling to her point of hope, and her exclusive worry was to save herself from drifting away from that other child's hand. It was wrinkled, bony, and like her own soaked deep in the oil of wool and machines—although his surface dirt, she noticed, had been recently washed away.

They clambered onto a bridge, then scrambled up a hill toward the moor. On the climb, Edwin let go of her. She quickly took his hand again.

The bare slope exposed them in the full light of the moon. They were upon the great east-west route, which was so busy during the day, but was now empty. A double line of moon-blue paving stones, long grooves worn in them by cart wheels, the edges chipped and scratched by slipping hooves, stretched upward before them. Here were cuts in the wall where a runaway cart had crashed against it; over there, tiny clouds of wool had been left clinging to thorns and brambles.

"What's your mother like," he asked her.

Margaret took some time before answering, pretending to save her breath to climb the last bit of the hill.

"She 'as long fair 'air all the way down 'er back, wi' curls at the end an' ribbons. You'll see what she's like when we meet 'er. She 'as dresses of silk reaching to the ground and lives in London where the King lives. 'E's going mad. 'E 'as to be strapped in a chair like they do to mad people in the Bedlam."

"Your 'air isn't fair. It's black."

"It wasn't, till I came 'ere. It's only black because it's dirty."

"The King is called George."

"Yes," she answered, matter-of-fact.

"Who told you 'e's mad?"

"Everyone in the workhouse knows. I saw a girl in Derbyshire go mad. Caroline Thompson at Cressbrook was beaten so much that she went out of 'er mind. They could do nothing with 'er and sent for 'er mother in London. 'Er mother got some paper signed and Mrs. Newton give Caroline back to 'er. But when she got to London she 'ad to 'ave the straitjacket on, and she died."

"My father says that England is a country all gone mad, wi' desperation and lust. Perhaps it's because something's driving the King mad, who's at the top of it."

"What's lust?"

"Ssh!" commanded Edwin.

They had breasted the hill and were in the small weaving hamlet of Height. Normally it was silent and dark as a grave at this hour, except at the inn where the carters stayed. Tonight, people carried lanterns through passageways and gardens and were arguing noisily. Some said they knew why the mill bell was ringing down in the valley and why cavalry were chasing around the countryside, some pretended that they knew, and others were inquiring about it.

Margaret would not be quiet.

"Betsy Watnough once threw away some bread that was bad. When Mrs. Newton found it was missing, she said that if no one owned up to where it 'ad gone, we'd all 'ave our 'eads shaved. We 'ated 'aving our 'air cut, let alone shaved. So Betsy was found out and Mr. Newton brought in to beat 'er. 'E did it until she couldn't see out of 'er eyes, they were so swelled up. 'E swore 'e'd still make 'er work, though.

"One day she crept out to get some water. There was a big fish pond at Cressbrook, and she fell in it 'cos she couldn't see what she was doing. She was wrapped up and put on an 'ot bake-stone and 'ad 'ot liquor poured into 'er, they were so scared, but she was dead sure enough."

Margaret's tale had taken them through Height, and they found themselves on a ridge of level, bare moorland. Two cavernous valleys tilted off its edges at either side. Other valleys and ranks of slate-blue hills creased the distance. The hills seemed transparent in the moonlight. A long, straight road stretched over the hillcrest before them. Sometimes there came the sound of water overflowing a bank, through a broken wall, and down a gully or into a trough erected for a weaver's horse, or for him to wash his cloth in. Sheep and lambs were crying with clear voices all over the distance, and they heard the plaintive, repeated call of an unseen, mysterious bird. It was all a strange and fascinating world to Margaret, though less so to Edwin, who had roamed the hills at night with his father.

"Where'll we stay tonight?" Margaret asked.

"Huh! Ne'er you mind that."

They walked on for a quarter of a mile. Then Edwin helped Margaret climb over a wall. He obviously knew where he was going, but did not bother to explain. Margaret found that she had been led to the edge of a quarry. Ten yards away was a shed, with its door open.

Margaret was the first to go forward and step into the dark opening, stretching her arms out in front of her for fear of what she might stumble upon. But all that she found was the smell of a pony that must normally live there. They felt their way to separate corners of the shed and it was Margaret who found—yes!—a pile of straw. Edwin heard her flopping down happily upon it.

Looking back from her bed, Margaret surveyed the peaceful moonlight framed by the door, which illuminated a patch of moorland, a thin strip of wall, and the quarry.

Edwin came to lie beside her. He, too, stared out, entranced. She watched him removing his clogs. In a moment, he was asleep. A moment later Margaret also fell asleep.

They were both awoken at the same moment by sunlight pouring over them. The old, bleached straw of the pony's shed was changed into a bed of gold. Neither of the children had ever known what it was to sleep so late. Margaret had never been given the opportunity, and Edwin, though granted his Sundays, had always risen early to enjoy them. Having spent their previous hours in such a deep, restful stupor, it took them a moment or two to recollect where they were.

Covering their eyes from the fierce light, they heard the clatter of hammers rising from the quarry, and a fall of stone. Edwin, the first to stand up, noticed a leather bag on the floor. A quarryman, in the early morning, had left it, and failed to notice anything amiss, even two children asleep on the straw. Edwin opened the bag and pulled out cheese, bread . . .

"Gi'it me!" Margaret was at his side in a flash, grabbing at the food. "Gi'me some!"

They were both cramming cheese into their mouths. "We'll sell the bag," Margaret said when they had finished eating.

"No."

He left the bag on the ground, open to make it look as though rats had got at it.

"We must 'ide our trail," he explained.

"Would they 'ang us?" she asked.

Edwin saw the soldiers chasing them, the prison, a boy and a girl dangling on a gibbet. He saw his mother, his bed at home, and the kitchen fire. He smelled drying oatcakes. Almost his mother's last words were about their "not stopping at 'anging children."

"Nobody'll 'ang us," he answered bravely.

"Not after what we've done?"

"We'll be all right."

He choked on his words, and turned away from her to put on his clogs.

He led her outside. Below them they could see men with the pony, which must have spent the night grazing the moor. It was hauling a laden sledge on a shelf across the face of the quarry.

Above the roadside wall could be seen the heads of carters and horses, the hats of merchants, and the tops of high loads of wool traveling the road. Then came a line of packhorses, led by one magnificent swaying animal, its harness decorated with brass studs and badges, its head bearing a plume and on its shoulders the elaborate arch of a collar with a bell at its peak, like the flagship of an armada.

Edwin ducked down and Margaret followed his example. They scrambled, crouching, regardless of the nettles, spring-new yet already coated with stone dust, along the foot of the wall, to where it turned at right angles, marking the boundary between the moor and the quarry. There they climbed the wall and ran up to the crest of the hill, over the small bright flowers of the common land, the thyme and turf that had knitted itself into a tight pile an inch deep, cropped by sheep. As they climbed higher, the vegetation changed to sparser clumps of heather, old and dry, with sharp new spears thrusting brightly up among it. There were more and more stones, then there followed barren stretches of peat and dark, sour pools of lifeless water.

"All the 'ills are black," Margaret remarked.

"Well?" He had never thought that they could be any other color.

"In Derbyshire there were great, white rocks. You could never get past 'em. We were put away at the end of a long valley, so that nobody would come near us."

Edwin looked for a hidden but sunny place where they might rest again, after the climb. He made for a huge, purple-black boulder—a swollen, pregnant belly, glittering with silica. There were lots of such huge stones in a line along the moortop. This one hid them from the busy road, yet from its other side it gave them a view of the countryside, and it was warmed by the sun. He knew what he was doing, all right. He was as sure of himself as if he had spent his life, not in a factory, but upon the moors. Even though he had been up here only on Sundays.

In the shelter of the stones, they sat side by side and looked over the panorama of moorland and woods. It was a vast amphitheater, filled with spectacle. Larks hung with their tails fanned to the limits and their wings beating so fast that they became invisible, except as small clouds around their throbbing bodies. First Edwin and then Margaret lay back in the sun that poured upon the rock, closed their eyes, and listened. A man in an enclosure far, far away was angry with a horse. A blackbird startled them as it alit close by in a rowan tree, where it called mellow and loud.

Life before had not offered either of them much peace in which to be contemplative in this way. They were drugged by it. With eyes closed, they felt themselves float through the vast space.

A smile upon her face, Margaret opened her eyes, plucked a stalk of grass, and tickled Edwin's cheek. "What are we going t'eat next?"

He kept his eyes closed and did not answer. He was in ecstasy, but could not tell her so, because he did not know the word "ecstasy."

"You said you was a poacher, so are you going to find deer for us?"

No reply.

"And fish? And 'ares? And where are we going to sleep tonight, as you're so clever?"

He rolled over, put his arm around her neck, as he would if playing with a boy but more gently, and pushed her face into the soft earth. She gave in willingly, because she had never been happy like this before.

A large bee came bumpily over the thyme and everywhere else was so quiet that its noise filled the universe. Margaret watched it burying its head into a flower, like a baby snuggling at a breast. Its rear legs were kicking with happy abandonment in the air while the head tugged and sucked the nectar.

"Which way is the Blackstone Edge road?"

Edwin, dozing in the scent of thyme, again did not answer.

"Does the road go to Liverpool?"

"Yes."

"My mother's in London," Margaret said wistfully, foreseeing the inevitable parting from Edwin. Do ships go from Liverpool to London? she wondered. Once, traveling by in a cart, she had seen the masts stretched along the wharfs at Greenwich; certainly some of the ships must have come from Liverpool.

Edwin got to his feet and set off. As Margaret followed, her attention was caught by a track shining upon the far slope, and busy with figures. In between was a deep valley.

"Is that the Blackstone Edge road?"

"Yes. My mother lived over there," he said.

Girls were always asking questions. Edwin decided that it was time he asked her something. "What was it like in the work'ouse in London?"

They were now descending into the valley, which was deep and wide. To hide themselves, they passed down dry gullies and kept behind walls or at the sides of hillocks from which no habitation was in view. They were making for a point far below, where Edwin had marked that the route crossed another river. He reckoned that after they passed over the bridge and started the ascent to Blackstone Edge, which was the high, dark boundary between Yorkshire and Lancashire, they would finally be out of reach of Mr. Horsfall and of Lady Well, and no one, other than the occasional village constable, would be interested in two traveling children.

"We couldn't leave the 'Ackney workhouse, no more'n Cressbrook nor 'Orsfalls' mill. The windows were barred in the same way. I saw beggar girls standing outside and I wanted to change places with them, though they were in the rain with nowhere to shelter. Every few months, someone would turn up to select one or two of us for work. We'd be glad to go to anything—except to be chimney sweeps, and they always picked boys for that. A lady came every year from an agency and chose the best of us for servants. We stood in a line and she'd feel us and look at our teeth. She squeezed our arms and looked in our eyes and made us take deep breaths. I was never well enough to become a lady's servant. I thought I'd never get out of 'Ackney. Sometimes I used to be sick, because I was so sad. Then they came from Cressbrook for us. I thought it was a nice name. They told us that when we got to the north, we'd be able to ride 'orses, and be paid money."

They were descending into a net of small lanes that threaded the enclosures. Handloom weavers' cottages were scattered over the slopes. They were bleak little places of dark stone and mostly without trees, unless they had a token ash or rowan planted by a spring. Tenterframes radiated from every cottage's walls.

"Why are the 'ouses spread all over the fields?" she asked.

"They 'ave to be like that, to 'ave their own springs."

"Why?"

"For the weavers to wash their cloth and such."

They came to a roadside trough and knelt by it. Margaret drank with sumptuous pleasure. "I like Yorkshire," she said.

Edwin cupped the water in his hands. "Drink to liberty!" he commanded.

"What d'yer mean?"

"You drink, and then say 'To liberty.' "

"To liberty!" Margaret shouted at the top of her voice.

"To the downfall of tyranny!"

"To the downfall of tyranny!" She swallowed her drink quickly. "What's tyranny?"

"It's what 'appens in Lady Well."

The water also washed Margaret's grimy cheeks, patchily, so that she looked as if she had been splattered with dark paint. Edwin, too, was beginning to look as dirty as he had been before his mother washed him on the previous day.

"There's going to be a revolution," Edwin announced.

"A revolution? What's that?"

"It means there'll be a change in the Government and nobody'll want to catch us for running away. There was a comet last autumn, did you see it?"

"No. What's a comet?"

"It's a sign of revolution. A great blaze right across the sky. Everyone in Lady Well went out to look at it, and we all said there'd be a change."

Edwin lay on the grass at the side of the overflowing trough of clear water, wiped his nearly shut, purple eye, and smeared the dirt from around his mouth with the back of his hand. She did likewise, as she rested by him. They closed their eyes against the sun. How delicious it was to walk, rest, walk, rest, and not be driven by a machine.

"Tell me more about the workhouse."

"Why do you want to know?"

"Because it's interesting. It's different."

"The first time we set off from 'Ackney, it was like going on a picnic, all of us laughing. They washed us and gave us new clothes and some gingerbread. We were eight days on the road, shut in the cart. No, five days—I forgot 'ow long it was, 'cos I was sick. We were all sick, wi' that yellow stuff that comes up when you've 'ad nothing to eat. The carter 'ardly spoke to us, except when he let us out every now and then. We never 'ad a wash, but we were given soup at public 'ouses. A lady brought us soup when we were sitting against a wall whilst the boys swilled the wagon and changed the straw.

"Two 'ad died, without making a sound, so no one knew until we were all turned out and two didn't come. They were buried secretly in the dark at a small chapel on the top of an 'ill and the carter got drunk with the sexton. We were scared. We didn't know what 'e'd do when 'e was drunk. 'E came back to where we were in the cart, banging the sides and laughing. 'E called us 'animals.'

"When we got to Lady Well, the people came to watch us unloaded. That Mr. Gledhill took us in. I could see straightaway we were going to be shut inside the 'prentice house. From then on, the girls were separated from the boys. It was cold. There weren't any fires, and we 'adn't ever seen any in Derbyshire, either. They always said we might set fire to the mill. We were fed on porridge and some sticky bread and we 'ad to eat in silence. Then we went to bed. Two of us 'ad to share. We didn't say prayers like in the workhouse, so I prayed under my breath and asked to be with my mother."

She closed her eyes. She felt the press of the hot sun on her face. Behind her eyelids yellow circles spread rapidly outward, as when a stone is thrown into a pool.

When she opened her eyes, rubbing at her tears, Edwin was squatting over a patch of gravelly sand in which he was absorbedly drawing with a stick.

"What's that?"

He did not answer.

"It's a fish!"

He leapt up and ran down the hill. Lower down the lane, he waited for her and, panting, they happily descended into the village by the bridge.

They need not have passed through Ripponden, but it was the easiest route to travel, and they believed they'd be safe now.

Passing down the street they met an old man, a cobbler, sitting outside his shop, repairing shoes and offering his bald head to the gentle spring sun. He stopped work, with his hammer poised, and aimed a shining smile at them.

"God bless you, you look tired!" he said. "Where have you two darlings come from? What's happened to your eye, young man?"

They could not answer such questions, but fortunately he did not insist.

"Martha! Martha!" he shouted over his shoulder, as joyfully as the Prodigal's father whose own son had come home.

Martha came running out of the house, which was next to the shop. She did not look pleased, until she saw the children. She was a gaunt woman with deep-set features.

"Would you like a bite to eat?" she asked.

"Gi'us food, ma'am!" Margaret thrust herself forward, on her toes, clutching, as always, at any kind offer.

The woman retreated into her house and could be heard drawing from a barrel. She was soon at the door again, still smiling, with ale in a deep jug and two hunks of cheese.

The children gobbled it all without speaking.

"I thought you were hungry," remarked the cobbler. "If you'll not say where you're from, will you tell me where you're going?"

"Over Blackstone Edge," Edwin answered. He took a swig at the cool ale.

"What, *now?* At this time of day?"

"Huh! It's nothing."

"Nothing!"

The cobbler touched his fingers together, and his wife did likewise. "I pray to the Lord for all the lost sheep of this desperate countryside," he said. "You look as though you've had a few accidents already. We can't let you go on at this hour. That would not be charitable."

"I think nothing of it."

"Brave words! Then will you step inside and have some decent repast before you go on? You have not eaten nearly enough, yet."

"Aye. Thank you," answered Edwin, but still proud.

"And maybe my good lady'll wash you. You're factory children, I can see that."

Edwin gave a start. "What of it?"

The cobbler stood up and put his arms around them, hugging them so closely that they could smell his greasy leather apron. He led them gently into the shadowy house.

"Nothing of it, young man, nothing of it. You're a bold one, I must say. Has no one taught you to walk humbly before God? Perhaps it's true what they say about Godlessness in the factories? Poor children, denied the wisdom of the Holy Book!"

The home of the cobbler and his wife was that of a pious, modest couple. The musty smell, coming from ancient leather, and the shadows were those of a church. A steel engraving of St. Jerome hung upon one wall. He had a venerable, bald crown like the cobbler himself, and perhaps that was why the picture had been chosen. A crucified Christ was on another wall. There were half a dozen hand-stitched texts. A large black Bible with gold clasps was placed to catch the light from the window. The earthenware jugs for water and ale, the wooden platters for bread and cheese, seemed objects on an altar table: they were so carefully placed, it was as if they could be removed only by a sacred edict. The couple put down every object with deliberation, and they performed their little duties for one another with the slow, mournful self-consciousness of officiating priests. Even the sense of the sparse clean room having received few visitors suggested, not that the couple were shunned by their neighbors, but that they had chosen to be holy hermits.

It was Edwin who noticed the chapel-like atmosphere. Margaret's eyes were darting about, seeing a loaf of bread on the sideboard, some coins on the mantelpiece, and a cupboard where the door had been left open a crack.

The cobbler's wife began working the pump in the back room. Soon she was beckoning them.

Edwin, as he went forward, held Margaret's hand. She wanted never, never to let go of it. But she must do so, being chosen as the first to be washed, because she was by far the dirtier. With haste, suggesting that there would have been an indecency in lingering, the woman stripped her.

"My goodness, you've had a fall! Or maybe it was a beating somewhere?" she inquired.

Neither of the children answered.

"But you, young man, look as if you might 'ave a mother," remarked the cobbler's wife, because Edwin was not quite so dirty. "But your eye!"

The woman was smiling. Edwin winked and grimaced at Margaret. Despite the fact that every touch hurt them, they were happy.

After washing them, the woman tried rigging them up in the couple's cast-offs; but the effect was ludicrous, and the children had to climb back into their own dirty clothes. Dressed once more, they sat on a bench in the workroom, where the cobbler read passages from Proverbs to them while his wife prepared a meal.

" 'The name of the Lord is a strong tower: the righteous runneth into it, and is safe . . .' "

Beefsteak and potatoes!

Before they had finished dining with this God-sent couple, Margaret and Edwin fell asleep at the table, almost at the same moment. They had to be carried up the stairs.

There the cobbler's wife had prepared two cots. She had to awaken the children to strip them of their clothes, before setting them into her clean bedding. Through the window, they could see the setting sun biting into Blackstone Edge. They were asleep again almost before their guardian angel had left the room, being just able to register the fact that the woman locked the door behind her.

Downstairs, the cobbler went outside again to enjoy the last of the sun. He took with him a heavy volume, in which, with his tongue curled out of the corner of his mouth, he wrote:

> A fare Day tho will no doubt turn out less gude tomorrow. Planted tatties in the small enclosure. Sat outside my Shop an hour mynding my own busyness when there came by two children, evidently run from a Public Mill. Will return the runaways to their Ritefull gude master, Mr. Horsfall I'm sure it is, tomorrow, and pay the shilling Mr. Gledhill gives for such services into our Chapel fund. So ends a gude day with some gude work done on the Lord's gude Busyness.

He continued writing until, in the last light of the day, he saw another stranger, with a pack and a fiddle upon his back, coming down the road from the direction of Lady Well.

The man, who had a slight limp, was small and dark. He carried his hat in his hand, so that the cobbler could see his long, greasy locks reaching to his shoulders.

CHAPTER SIX

April 17th

ll his life, Mor had nurtured dreams of escape. Now they were being fulfilled, unintentionally. There was no point in staying in Lady Well only to become part of a chain gang to the colonies, or to be hanged. At the moment they were hunting for Crawshaw. Mor had a day, at least, before they searched the factory and found his book.

When he reached home, he had found that Edwin was not, as he had supposed, tucked up in bed, but had sneaked out of the house and not come back. Mor guessed that the boy had followed the Luddite band, had been recognized by soldiers, and had fled. He remembered the two children whom John Tiplady had helped out of the apprentice house. Was one of them Edwin's little friend? That would explain it all.

Mor had to find his younger son. He convinced himself that he had only to stay away until May 1st, when the revolution would commence. From the combing shops, the public houses, and the meeting places of illegal debating societies in Yorkshire, Cheshire, Lancashire, and Nottinghamshire would flow a mighty river southward to overthrow the Government. Then Mor would be able to return to Phoebe, having found Edwin. He would bring him home to enjoy a new England.

Perhaps Mor, like other men, believed in such things that were contrary to his reason because circumstances gave him no other choice, nor hope.

This morning, Mor, after meeting Lydia Horsfall, had been to the cobbler's shop to get his boots resoled and some rotted stitching replaced.

"Do you think you'll return to us? Do you believe in this 'revolution'?" asked the cobbler, Abraham Binns, a rotund, happy man, who had a wooden leg from the wars.

" 'One who suffers, hopes, and one who hopes, believes,' as the saying has it, Mr. Binns."

"Don't worry, old friend! You'll not be a wanderer all your days, will you?" He looked Mor straight in the face. "You'll come back to us?"

"I'll come back."

Mor next completed his third errand. He collected the Lower Laithes stone from where he had dropped it when he was arrested by the Watch and Ward patrol. Then he returned home, to press one of Mrs. Horsfall's sovereigns into Phoebe's hand. He did not explain. He wanted to see her delight.

She did not ask him where he had sold his cloth, on a day when every mill office was closed and every clothier occupied. She said not a word, but merely gasped. Who could tell what she was thinking? Did she think perhaps that her husband was a thief, and was she shrugging her shoulders to it? Even as she locked the coin in a drawer, she seemed bitter, and hurtfully saying nothing. She didn't want to be pleased, not by anything, anymore, Mor thought.

"So why must you go? Why must you leave us?" she asked.

Although she spoke bitterly, she was preparing food for him to take. While he had been dashing around Lady Well trying to sell his piece, she had been collecting together preserves, oat bread, and a flask of whisky. She had appealed to neighbors, who had sacrificed what they could—one cooked meats, another some cheese—for Mor's flight.

"Edwin'll come back when he's tired. Why must you go?" she repeated.

He stood for a time against the fire. She had her back to him, and he could see neither her tears nor how she occupied her hands. He would have been surprised to see the thoughtful, delicate, loving way in which she cut and wrapped the food.

"Edwin's not the only one who's run off. That girl 'e likes, the one 'e calls Margaret, she's gone too. Another pair got away, but they've been caught. Edwin'll not come back without my fetching him, wife. Besides . . . I've dropped my book somewhere. My *Rights of Man*. I think I left it in the factory. My name's inside the cover. They'll want to 'ang someone for killing the soldier. It'll either be Crawshaw or me, because I keep a school and can read. Gledhill told them that I was teaching sedition. They'll not be looking until tomorrow, though. I've time to get away."

"Maybe Mr. Gledhill's right . . ." Then Phoebe fell silent.

Gledhill right! What Mor wanted at a time like this was affection! He didn't want to hear her justifying Gledhill! Where were her arms and her lips?

He could hear the sound of the spoon as she scraped it inside a jar. She said, slowly, quietly, "Why did you 'ave a book in there? *Why?* And why did you leave it behind?"

He gestured desperately in the air. His lordly stance before the fire collapsed. He sat down and put one hand on his knee, the other to his forehead, hopelessly

"You'll be all right," he said. "I've given you the sovereign. I've spoken to our Secretary. The Loyal Georgian Society will pay you something each week. There was a lot o' rabbit stew. Your share will reach you. You have Mrs. Horsfall's sovereign."

"Mrs. Horsfall?"

"She gave it to me."

Phoebe drew her breath in sharply. *I might have guessed! He'll beg when he thinks he can't get away from me without it!*

"You *would* be reading a book, wouldn't you?" she muttered. "That's what you *would* do—read a book! When Edwin was hung over that machine, you had your nose in a book, I'm sure of it. I know you! My God, I know you by now! All sins are known in the end. You're a bas—You're a Greave, all right . . . What *am* I doing? I can't think!"

She tossed aside the cloth she was using to wrap the cheese, and out of her dress she took a different rag. She held it to her mouth, trying not to cough. He could hear only a little of what she muttered.

At last she let her thoughts run, like pus out of a wound. "You're a true bastard son of that Oliver Greave, all right! God knows who your mother was, probably some whore, but it's clear enough who your father was. Gideon might 'ave been a bastard too if I 'adn't . . . Oh, I've seen too much! Begging for food, I am, and *you* turn it away, when it's for your children! Today, though, you've been begging from Mrs. Horsfall when it's for yourself."

"What did you say?"

She took the rag away from her mouth and sighed. "Nothing. Nothing at all. Nothing that matters."

Again she turned her back, so that he could not see her wrapping food. He was glad she had not taken up his challenge. He had heard enough to make him realize that he could not bear it.

"I know what you said. I heard."

At this moment, Gideon burst into the house. He threw himself into a chair, rubbing his knees, sheepishly looking away from his parents.

"Where've you been?" Mor demanded.

"On Black Hill. I was thinking. No one saw me. I've decided . . . We'll not let ourselves be defeated! If Crawshaw's gone, they'll need another to take 'is place."

"You?!" Mor's tone was bitter and sarcastic.

"Why not? Someone must show determination. If the place is vacant at the table, why should I not be the one to fill it? King Ludd will not be put down! We'll go and set fire to Horsfalls' properly, and 'ave done with it, and show 'em what we're made of! They'll not expect us to come again so soon. We'll take them by surprise."

"Lead a raid! You can't even walk, lad. You're made of nothing but wind and air. For God's sake, rest at 'ome for a while. For God's sake!"

Mor spoke more with pity than sarcasm, but it was the sarcasm that hurt. Gideon's hands, shoulders, and face were twitching and shaking. He turned white.

He leaned forward and picked up a wooden platter from the table, gripping it tightly with both hands as if he would tear lumps out of it. He threw it across the room. Bang, against the meal barrel.

Mor simply stared. He seemed calmed by it; in fact he was chilled. His face too, like Gideon's, was white.

Phoebe turned her back, showing those humped shoulders that made one want to hit her.

Perhaps they had that effect upon her son. He stood up. His body still shaking, he picked up the next thing within reach. Phoebe's Staffordshire-ware huntsman.

"King Ludd'll not be crushed! He'll not!" Blind to what he was doing, he smashed the ornament against the wall.

Phoebe whipped around, with her apron to her face. "Oh, God! Oh, my God!"

She knelt among the pieces, cupping the smallest fragments within the bigger ones, and hunting with screwed-up eyes for the smallest bits; exhibiting those tempting, humble shoulders and bowed back.

Gideon next slammed an earthenware pot containing ale down on the table. The ale bounced high enough to leave a brown stain on the ceiling.

Mor wrapped his arms, from behind, around the boy's shoulders. Gideon's fit collapsed as suddenly as it had arisen. He became weak as a trembling puppy, and sobbing.

His mother continued to fumble for the pieces. "Oh, my God, my 'untsman . . . my 'untsman."

Gideon, returned to his senses, caught sight of her face. "I'm sorry, Mother! Sorry! Mother, what a pass! *Mother!*"

"It's not your fault," Mor soothed, letting go of Gideon. "It's not any of our faults."

"Oh, my little 'untsman, so 'andsome 'e was! My gentleman so 'andsome! Gideon! Gideon!"

"Don't blame yourself," Mor repeated.

If the boy went over and held her it would help, he thought. Surely she'd let him.

"It'll mend," Mor comforted, going to help Phoebe with the pieces on the table.

"No, it won't!" she howled. "Nothing'll mend! Nothing! *Nothing!* Nothing'll mend!"

"It will! It will!"

"It won't! Nothing'll mend, ever! God doesn't want it to!"

Though it was a fine spring morning, Mor left home wearing his thick leather jerkin, tightly belted. Already, he had adopted a tramp's way of wearing everything he possessed. Under the jerkin, he wore a double layer of woollens. It being a warm day, he carried his hat in his hand. Over one shoulder went his fiddle. Hanging upon his other hip was a leather bag holding a change of shirt, his unfinished manuscript, the stone from Lower Laithes which had anchored him in his madness, and the food Phoebe had packed for him.

Phoebe walked with him a little of the way.

"I'll be back soon," he said.

"Where'll you go to? Where, where'll you go?"

"I don't know, but I'll be back. I have to go. You must see there's no help for it. You'd not ever get over the disgrace of a hanged man for a husband , would you? You must see that. But I'll be back. I *will*."

"What'll *I* do?"

Mor made no reply.

As usual, he had no answer that really helped, Phoebe thought. "The 'untsman!" she whimpered, and started to cry again.

At the edge of Lady Well, before the road in the London direction dropped into the gorge of boulders, tangled trees, and the white torrent frothing out of the mill, was an ash tree that was famous in many corners of the world. It was imprinted upon the memories of soldiers, seamen, men and women being transported or imprisoned, and those hopefully leaving to seek their fortunes; for it was the last point from which it was possible to wave and still be seen from the town. There were few families that had not received their last sight of a relative there. The tree was old, gnarled, sacred and dreaded. A fearful spirit, soaked in memories, lived within it. The earth was worn bare under the tree, from people standing beneath it.

Phoebe, her own turn come around at last, accompanied Mor this far.

"You called me 'wife,' " she remarked. "This morning."

He kissed her on the mouth, moved away a few yards, and turned for the brief moment which was all that those passing into exile dared allow themselves if they were to keep to their resolve.

When Mor kissed her, Phoebe had at last taken away the handkerchief that she had been clutching to her mouth as she walked. With it in her hand, she now pointed at the sky and, losing control, screamed, "*There is One above who sees it all!*"

Mor turned away, cowering from the mad, accusing scream, as from a hail of stones. He hurried off, stumbling down the hill, hearing her sobs for a long way. No more words followed him.

When he was out of reach of her cries, he turned and looked for her. He waved at the distant figure of his wife, who was standing quite still, except for the stained bloody rag fluttering at her face once more.

He knew what she would do now. She would hurry home, staring down at the street. (Would Gideon have stayed in the house?) She would slam the door and, to save herself from sitting in tears, knowing that she would find it hard to rise again, she would make herself busy tidying, cleaning, struggling to forget her huntsman; to forget that, for some absurd reason, at the very point of leaving her he had called her "wife" for the first time in years; trying to get that stain off the ceiling and unable to stop herself thinking all the time that it would please and placate the husband who had left.

Eventually she would lean against something, absently brushing strings of hair from her eyes, and, so long as Gideon was not present, she would allow herself to cry.

As Mor left his home village, everywhere the children were playing, amazed and excited because the mill was closed. A group of young women, though dressed in their work clothes and aprons, had found a sunny bank to lie upon and were laughing. If the Luddites had managed to shut the mill for even a day, that was something!

Mor turned, not in the direction of the London turnpike, but westward toward the cover offered by the moorlands. He guessed that would be Edwin's route, also, heading toward Liverpool.

Mor reached the bridge. He still did not dare look back at Lady Well. He lingered a moment, staring at the water. It was so quiet today, spinning delicate white threads among the stones. During the recent fine weather it had cleared from a dark brown, peaty color to a light, transparent chestnut, glazing the weeds on the bottom.

He pricked his ears to the shouts of soldiers, downstream, outside the mill. All Mor's sensitivities were alert now. He remembered the polecat that had peered at him from the darkness when he had gone out with Edwin to get rid of the fish offal. Fearful and hunted in the territory it had owned for centuries, yet because of its exile, because it was dispossessed, it had sniffed the air with the full faculty of being alive. This was Mor's condition. He, too, was a fugitive creature on its way to extinction—a handloom weaver.

Before he climbed to the crest at Height, Mor finally could not resist taking a last melancholy look back at Lady Well—as a person will do even if leaving a prison. In honor of the view, he plucked a white saxifrage from the bank and placed it upon the wall. He left it there as a fleeting memorial of his thoughts—of alleyways full of memories, the sweet water running from the springs and troughs below the church, his little school, Gideon . . . Phoebe . . . Tiplady . . .

Enough of that! He climbed the hill. From Height, he walked where

Edwin and Margaret had previously gone along the level moortop. How, suddenly, he hated hills! Nature, he realized, is beautiful only when she harmonizes with creative thoughts. At other times, her majestic aloofness is terrifying. The hills, today, seemed silent oppressors.

He could not bring himself to pass the time of day with anyone. This was especially so because many whom he met, such as a young man enjoying the spring lanes with his arm stealing toward the breast of a girl from Horsfalls' mill, enjoyed their holiday without knowing that he who hobbled past them on the road had so much to do with bringing about their unexpected freedom. He felt a dumb detachment from every human, beast, bird, and flower.

He walked onward, feeling a cavern inside himself. It was in place of a cry that might tear the universe.

I'll be back. I'll be back. I'll not ever leave Lady Well. No one, nothing, will drive me away.

The day wore on. Evening came with yellowing light and spring bird song, bubbling up out of the valleys, overflowing. Every day, steadily now, the bird song was growing louder and longer.

Mor descended to Ripponden, which also seemed busy with happy and active young people. Perhaps this struck him because of the contrast to his own mood, for they were actually doing no more than going about their business. His worries made him feel old.

The only one with whom he passed the time of day was a cobbler, sitting outside his shop in the last light of the evening and smoking his pipe. At his feet was a large volume like a ledger, and in which he had evidently been writing, for the ink pot and quill were balanced on it.

"A fair day, thanks be to God!" the cobbler said in greeting. "Though it'll no doubt turn out less good tomorrow."

"It's a fine day," Mor agreed. He was grateful to find himself chatting with someone, at last. He settled himself nearby, opening his bag to eat his bread and cheese.

"One to make the hills and mountains rejoice," the cobbler continued.

"Have you seen a child, a stranger, running this way?"

"A factory child?"

"Yes." Mor was alert with hope. "Or maybe two children together?"

"You're not an officer from a manufactory, are you?"

"I'm a weaver. I've come from Lady Well. One of them's my own child."

"I thought you were not a gentleman, by your boots. Those have been mended recently for walking some distance, I'd say. Factory children do come this way, sir, when they run away. This is the road a few have taken from different mills. I haven't seen any from Mr. Horsfall's. I don't like to see the poor sad runaways. I think we should all persevere in the duty to which God calls us, instead of running away."

"Yet God calls some to very unpleasant duties."

"I do not believe it is for us to question what God does, if that is His wisdom. You said you were from Lady Well. From what I was told, you have seen there the damage that is done by those who evade their duty to God. Machinery was destroyed and a man shot dead in Mr. Horsfall's mill, I'm told. Poor Mr. Horsfall!"

Mor discovered more of the food which he had not known Phoebe had slipped into his bag. He felt her love expressed in the way she had wrapped cheese and a stoneware jar of preserved blackberries in scraps of waste cotton. In this way she had shown the love which she had been unable to give to him directly. Each neat fold of the cotton was speaking for her.

But Mor's immediate problem was to find somewhere to stay for the night. A deep red sun was throbbing and biting a slice out of the crest of Blackstone Edge; the evening bird song had finished, and the air was filling with the coolness that suggests to birds, animals, and humans that it is time to find shelter.

"Is there an inn at which I could stay in Ripponden?"

The cobbler thoughtfully sucked at his pipe. "We have several houses. There is yonder splendid inn that you can see by the bridge. It has meat, vegetables, tea, and coffee for respectable travelers, and some splendid oak stabling for your horse, if you happen to have one."

The cobbler fixed his expert eye suspiciously on Mor's boots. "Pardon my saying so, but I doubt your being made welcome there, amongst the merchants, you being shod for traveling a good way on foot, I see. Such attire doesn't make you welcome amongst gentlemen. I have never set foot inside there myself, except by the back gate for custom, repairing boots for gentlemen, ladies, and their servants."

He looked Mor unflinchingly in the eye. "You said that you have come from Lady Well. In any case, they would suspect that such a man as you arriving on foot might be a fugitive from justice. We are living through dreadful times. There is so much sedition abroad. We are in need of a gibbet at every crossroads, these days. Life has declined so much."

From a room only a few feet above Mor's head, so near that he could almost have leapt up to the window, there came the cry of a child, awakened, it seemed, from a dream.

"You have a granddaughter?" Mor interrupted, looking for a safer subject of conversation.

"A granddaughter, yes, sir . . . Then we have an inn of the second rank," the cobbler continued hurriedly. "That one is mostly used by packhorse drivers, for though it has no stabling, it has some rough pasture fit for mules. Then there is also . . ."

Mor next heard the cry of a small boy.

"Martha!" the cobbler shouted.

His wife came out. She was thin and bony, like Phoebe. Mor already felt envious of this domestic scene—the biddable wife; hearth and home.

"We haven't seen any factory children running this way, have we?" the cobbler asked her. "This gentleman is from Lady Well . . . nothing to do, he assures me, with the trouble there." The cobbler nevertheless lifted his eyebrows in an expression full of suspicion. "He says he is looking for a factory child."

"You've lost an apprentice?" Martha asked.

"No, it is my own child."

"Your own child! Was it a boy or a girl, sir?"

"A boy, answering to the name of Edwin. There might 'ave been a girl with 'im, called Margaret."

"No, we haven't seen any. None have passed this way. Generally this is the way they run, but there haven't been any at all. It's sad when the masters lose one, isn't it, sir, after they have gone to the expense of clothing them and teaching them their trades? You must have seen some terrible sights when those murderers attacked the mill in Lady Well last night. We heard about it."

"Stop your chattering now! Go down to Mrs. Rawdon's inn, Martha, and say to her, 'I have a suitable occupant for her accommodation.' "

"That's kind of you, sir."

"Think nothing of it, sir," replied the cobbler.

Martha disappeared over the bridge. The sky had grown quite dark, and her dress was caught every now and again in the light of lanterns.

"My wife will only be a moment away. She is a good woman. Have you ever heard Mr. Saville preach, sir?"

"I don't go in for listening to preachers."

"That must be sad for you, sir—to be so preoccupied with worldly matters that you have no time to listen to a preacher. I would willingly walk a hundred miles to hear a good one."

"I don't like the lack of debate at religious meetings."

"I think you would soon be terrified for your immortal soul if you listened to our Mr. Saville. I am sobered for a week by hearing him. He can depict the fiery pit better than most men could describe their own hearths. Through the words of the Lord."

"I do not accept any lords."

"Not accept any lords! Every man and dog must have a master."

To get away from this difficult conversation, Mor rose from the ground, which in any case had grown uncomfortable, and lost himself in the darkness on the riverbank. For some reason he did not even trust his pack and fiddle with the pious cobbler, and took them with him. He stared restlessly for a while at the water.

Martha returned breathlessly from over the bridge. Mor walked back to the cobbler's shop to hear her report.

" 'Tis all right, husband. Mrs. Rawdon says she has accommodation."

Mor was relieved. "Well, thank you, sir, for your help."

The cobbler waved his hand dismissively. "I would think it a disgrace, sir, to accept thanks for so small a service. Mrs. Rawdon is a good woman, though she has been only a short time amongst us, coming from London. I believe she often attended chapel there. They call her 'the Abbess.' I do not like the Popery of it, but they say she has earned the title for her good works. She is well thought of."

Mor crossed the bridge. The inn took a little finding, and turned out to be a dwelling in a back alley. It was a rambling decayed edifice, with many outbuildings, where Mrs. Rawdon—"un unhappy widow, come into the north to drown her grief," or so Mor was told while he was asking his way there—brewed ale and ran a slaughterhouse in the back yard.

The crowded, smoky room into which Mor burst was filled with a surprising company of men and women to be recommended by a Wesleyan cobbler. The majority were soldiers of the lowest rank: militiamen from another county, under the command of an aggressive sergeant. The remainder of the patrons consisted of that flotsam of life which gathers in a hamlet near the crossing point of a river, as the rubbish carried by the water swirls around the bridge's piers. They were an exotic crowd of teasel collectors, leech gatherers, weed pickers, wall builders, moor guides, and "broggers," who scavenged bits of wool from fences and out of the litter of markets. Several fiddlers added to the din.

There was also a dirty-looking apothecary, his table spread with pills and cosmetics that he sold to the several extraordinary women in the room. He sold white lead—used to blanch the skin and make a lady look as if she did not have to labor outdoors—and mercuric sulphide, to redden lips and heighten the color of cheeks. The white lead caused, first, an irritation of the skin and, after prolonged use, paralysis. The mercuric sulphide brought tremors of the limbs, and eventually madness, but the apothecary did not advertise these facts.

No one could have kept such a crowd in order other than such a person as Mrs. Rawdon. She was a narrow-lipped, severe woman, the only one there who could possibly have met with the cobbler's approval. She was dressed entirely in black, which distinguished her in a dramatic fashion from the other women. Her overdone but quality mourning managed to be both exotic and authoritarian. The lace was plentiful and expensive; the cloth was heavily starched. So clearly the proprietor, she was ostentatiously busy, yet doing nothing with her own hands, except from time to time showing off her privilege of poking the fire. Some of her customers called her "Abbess," others addressed her as "Mother" or "Mother Superior."

Mor spent some time over taking all this in, before he approached her.

"So you are the 'suitable occupant for accommodation'?" she said, and he nodded.

She was one whom you would never expect to laugh, yet there was mockery in her eyes, which she hid behind a black fan.

"Sit you down and you'll be attended to," she commanded. "I hear you have walked from Lady Well?"

She did not wait for an answer, neither did she offer to show him to a room. No doubt there was some cheap corner planned for him. She went off briskly through the crowd.

Her knowing already where he came from gave Mor a shock.

Trying to minimize all that made him feel conspicuous, he settled in a corner. He tucked his bag and fiddle under the bench, where they were safely out of the way of thieves, and placed his hat on the bench beside him. He had not been able to find a corner in which he could be alone. Sitting on the other side of him was a dirty fellow whose proximity did nothing to make the alehouse any more pleasant; neither did the malodorous lady who was with him.

Apprehensively, Mor kept his eye on Mrs. Rawdon. By her gestures, it was clear that she was talking about him—to someone who looked familiar. Then he remembered: it was the man he had seen from a distance, on March 12th, when he was fleeing from Huddersfield; the one who had pointed up the hill at him. Mor wondered if he should get up and leave. On the other hand, that would attract more suspicion. Anyway, there was nowhere for him to flee to. And here, there might be compensations.

The one advantage to the common man of a town full of soldiers was the availability of prostitutes, and several were gathered at the table of the ex-member of the Society of Apothecaries or dancing with the soldiers. Chapel-goer or not, pining widow or not, Mrs. Rawdon had come from London to run an interesting and lively business. Even a poor schoolmaster-weaver might not find it impossible to enjoy, not merely a bed, but one warmed with animal comfort.

And there she soon was: a tall whore, walking toward him as direct as fate, and smiling.

She wore a cream-colored cotton dress with a high waistline tight under her breasts. It was in the French Revolution classical style, with many clinging folds which displayed the lines of her body—a fashion that was now shunned by anti-Gallic society. With one hand she kept the hem clear of the mud and spilled beer, thus displaying her neat green boots. Her hair was red, bundled in curls and ringlets. She wore glass earrings. Her face, covered with white-lead cosmetic, reflected the darting lights, orange and yellow, of the inn's fires and candles. Her lips were drawn bright red with the apothecary's mercuric sulphide. Her arm was hampered by her "indispensable"—her embroidered handbag—when she was not making gestures with her shawl, which she carried more to reveal teasing glimpses of her shoulders and breasts than to cover or warm them. A most impractical and purposeless dress, except for a whore, but she carried off her display with sedateness. Her long legs made watery folds of her garment. Her stride was sure and happy enough to take in the whole world and never tire or lose confidence. She could doubtless keep on walking forever, and in fact, in her trade of soldiers' whore, would probably do so.

She was a strange, bright flower to discover blooming out of the dark earth of Yorkshire; it made him think how the rich colors of his weaving were distilled from local somber heathers, roots, and berries. He had the time to observe quite a lot about her, because she did not make a direct line for him. But from far off, as she appeared and disappeared through the crowd, her smile so strong that it seemed to advance in front of her, Mor knew that she had marked him out.

As she reached the midpoint of the room, he caught and held her eye, and felt that something was inevitable. She got tangled in a dance around a fiddler, and she stopped for a moment to take a drag at a soldier's pipe, yet Mor did not cease to doubt that she was making her way toward him. She mouthed something to him from only a few yards away, which he could not make out because of the music and laughter.

He had just left home and wife, yet he could not help himself, when the woman disappeared briefly behind the backs of a sergeant and his companions, from trying to catch her eye again. He could not understand himself, for he had so recently been moved by the gifts of food lovingly wrapped by Phoebe.

She reappeared close by, her face intent upon the space next to Mor, which was almost the only vacant seat in the room.

His face, too, opened in a smile. They might have been old acquaintances. Some strangers can make you feel that you have known them all your life.

He found himself removing his hat from the seat and putting it under the bench, so that she could sit down.

Casually and inevitably she took her place next to him. "Soldiers! I've 'ad enough of them!"

She blew a wisp of hair from her dark eyes. She looked straight ahead, except that once or twice she took sideways glances at him and twitched her shawl. Whether she had come north with Mrs. Rawdon or not, he could tell as soon as she spoke that she had originally been a local girl.

She spread her legs and inelegantly plonked her indispensable in her lap. With her right hand, she scratched at her face. Her left hand had found its way into a slit hidden in the folds of her dress.

Mor was aware of the cleanliness of her bare arm. Covering a few inches of her shoulder was a small puffed sleeve made of transparent muslin. Her shawl had slipped away, and poised beneath Mor's face was a scented shoulder.

"More and more soldiers are coming into the north every day," he remarked.

"You're telling me! I'm tired out." Her voice was hoarse, not necessarily from smoking, but maybe from smoky atmospheres.

"I often marvel at all this distress we are put under," Mor continued.

"Distress? Is that what you call it? They've wore me out!"

"Do you know that all this trouble began in Nottinghamshire, from no better cause than that stockings have gone out of fashion among the gentry? The artisans and workers of Nottinghamshire have lost their employment, and the Government seems glad to see men thrown out of work, so that it can recruit them as soldiers. Thus from a little thing like that we are led to the destruction of machinery throughout the land. On top of that come Orders in Council, blocking foreign trade for our cloth, bringing a tenfold drop in our exports . . ."

"Eh?"

She had not ceased to survey, admiringly, the soldiers she'd "had enough of." She also continued to watch the movements of the other whores. But when she realized that she did not understand a word of what he said, she removed her hand from her face, turned, and stared at him. "You're a strange one," she said.

She had expected him to make crude fun of her and treat her with contempt, in order to save his face with a prostitute. It was an attitude that she was heartily sick of, but she expected no other.

"Myself, I like a stocking," she continued. "It makes the commonest fellow a gentleman of refinement, like the way they talk does for some, and the way they're generous with money does for others. Why don't you shout for some ale for yourself, weaver, and for me a drop of gin? They make good ale 'ere, for it's good water in the brew-house. There's iron in the 'illside, that makes it special, though it turns the beer darker brown than anywhere else—except that at Upper Spout, which is all right and good for physic, so they say. I've known all the places 'ereabouts since I was a child."

Her knees were lightly touching his, yet she continued to look straight ahead as she spoke. Sometimes she waved and smiled at the apothecary, who was basking before his pile of money. She still smiled at various soldiers around the room.

The fellow at Mor's left side apparently wanted to talk now. From the bench at his side, he brought onto the table a stoneware jar. Mor could see into it. It was filled with slimy water and leeches.

The man lifted his leg and rolled up his trousers, to show Mor and the woman who had joined him. "Look at that, sir! The leeches 'ave tore off my skin with their sucking. But we must be glad of the spring when we can work, sir . . ."

Mor, who had wanted some company when it was not on offer, now ignored the leech gatherer.

"How do you know that I'm a weaver?" he asked the woman.

"Oh, I can tell every sort of man. I'd say you was a schoolmaster, too, from the way you talk."

The leech gatherer returned his attention to his own lady, who held in her lap a basket of wool scraps gathered from fences, and had bits of wool stuck over her dress and hair.

The whore restlessly tapped the table with her fingertips. The nails marked her as either a lady or a prostitute, because they were unbroken and clean. With the other hand she again scratched nervously at her cheek.

"There's oil and fluff on you, even though you do talk like a schoolmaster. And do you play the fiddle as well, dear? They say you come from Lady Well, where they attacked a mill last night."

Mor jumped. He glanced at the leech gatherer, who was, however, still occupied with his own companion.

"You don't have to tell me if you don't want to. I don't care what you are. Not many tell the truth to a whore. They said over there that you are a—never mind. You're a strange one. I'd describe you as innocent, sitting 'ere as if nothing could 'arm you. What about that gin, master?"

She moved her knees an inch away. He could see that there'd be no more touching until her gin was on the table.

Mor went to the kitchen door, where the "Abbess" confronted him as if this shyest of her customers was the most troublesome. "Well, my young cock?" she asked truculently.

"Ale for me and a gin for the lady."

Not caring that she insulted him, Mrs. Rawdon held her palm out for money before she would serve him. He put some coins in her hand, and she snapped her fingers together like the jaws of a trap.

"Sit you down with the lady, and my girl will bring you what you want. We'll find you your room later."

When he returned, the woman, making a display, opened the silver clasp of her indispensable to produce an orange-scented perfume, which she daubed on her neck. Her manner was the ostentatious one of a peddler displaying wares. The aroma pushed back the fog of smoke, the smell of ale, tobacco, and urine, and made the two people intimate, wrapping them in their own invisible cloud.

"I'll tell you something for nothing, shall I? When you were over there with Mrs. Rawdon, I was thinking, 'I've never met a gentleman like that one before.' No, truly! I expect you think that's what I always say, but I don't. Usually I have to take 'em down a peg or two. But you . . . I wish I knew what it was."

But she knew what it was. It was the seriousness with which he had treated her, as if she were any other woman, and more than a whore.

"You're very innocent, sir. You want to be more careful than what you are." Her voice had become tender and motherly. "Haven't you come my way before?" she asked.

He didn't answer.

"No, I don't suppose you could 'ave, or you'd 'ave remembered me. They don't forget me. I just 'ave a feeling that I know you. Do you think we might 'ave met in a previous life? Do you take an interest in things like that?"

"I've never thought about it."

"You ought to. It can be an entertaining subject."

Mor took the edge of her shawl between two fingers and carefully felt it, just as he was always tempted to judge the feel of woollens.

"And you think no one can tell you're a weaver of wool! I wonder what else you are, master."

"That's fine wool, is that, very fine, smooth as silk," he mumbled, embarrassed.

"Glad you like it. It was a present from an aristocratic gentleman. From one of my 'erostocrats,' as I sometimes call 'em. Tell me about yourself. Left 'ome, 'ave you? How long 'ave you been away? You look tired. Been awake all night? You're not the only one, neither. Tell me about yourself."

He did not answer.

"I could tell you lots of things about yourself, that I'd bet even you don't know. Just from looking at you. Just from the way you sit and walk across the room and set your face. You don't need to say anything to me. You can trust me, darling, but there's no need to say a word if you don't want to. Not even your name. I'll wager you're an interesting gentleman. Oh, I mean it, my love. I'd wager an 'ouse and lands. I could tell at a glance you're something out of the usual."

She waved to some acquaintances, who quickly looked away. The customers couldn't care less whether Mor was a Luddite or not; all they cared about was his business with the whore, about which they were tactful. The leech gatherer and his woman had now turned their backs, too. The apothecary was packing up his stall. She knew everyone there, and it made him feel ill at ease. He himself knew no one. Yorkshire nowadays was full of strangers.

Mor realized that he and the prostitute were locked in a transaction. The roomful of turned backs was telling him that he had made a claim on her and he'd better go through with what he had begun. Common sense cautioned him not to be carried into indiscretions with a whore, yet she excited him, more than he had ever felt with Phoebe.

The ale and the gin were brought by the skivvy. Their knees were touching again. The whore was no longer glancing around the room while they spoke. He was foolish with sudden, forgetful happiness.

"Tell me your name," she demanded.

"Mor Greave."

"More Grief? I like that!" She slapped her thigh and laughed. "That should 'ave been my name! I've come across every name there is, but not that one. Do you know 'ow many Georges there are? More than there are stars in the 'eavens. And I've counted the stars, I can tell you, for I've 'ad to lay out many a time with a weight of sadness on my chest. I'm sick of Georges. I'll throw up if another man tells me 'is name is George, so you can thank your God, if you 'ave one, that yours isn't, I can tell you. And Thomas. I used to know a good one o' them in Bristol, said 'e was a sea captain, but they all say that in that town. I wonder where 'e is now? Probably manning a slaver to America. William's another name that's sown like stars in the 'eavens. But More Grief—I like that. I'm called Mary. Mary Wylde. Some call me 'Mary the Scar' because of a mark on my face . . . I've always been called Mary. Honest, that's my name! You can believe it. Without the word of a lie, it's true."

"I believe you. Why shouldn't I?"

"Mary, Mother of Jesus, Mother of the Immaculate Birth. I've seen a few girls 'ave those—not a father in sight, when it came to it. But I've never 'ad a baby myself, except for one, that's managed to live for long. Thank goodness, too, in my profession."

"A child gone back is a poor man's blessing, so they say."

"No man knows 'ow it breaks a woman's 'eart, More Grief. I'll tell you a secret, shall I? I do 'ave one daughter. She's been adopted by a gentleman who's rearing 'er to something more than I've managed to become. Her name's 'Arriet . . . You see 'ow you can trust me? 'Ere I am telling you all about myself. You can tell me all about yourself, dearie love, don't worry about it. I'm . . ."

She paused, with a moment's powerful, unexpected emotion. "I'm going to see 'er soon, over the 'ills. I've no time to waste. I'm warning you. I'll be off soon, over the 'ills."

Mor wondered how old the prostitute was. The cosmetics, intended to make her seem gay and young, made her appear sad and old. He wondered why she applied the white powder so thickly and kept scratching it. She looked nearly as old as himself, but then a prostitute would wear out quickly. He felt she was tired and at the end of her career. He liked her. He told himself to be cautious.

They had finished the ale and the gin. This time the maidservant was hovering near, looking him over. He carefully fingered the sovereign and the few other coins in his pocket.

"Aren't we getting sad!" Mary said, because they had fallen awkwardly silent after the servant left. "Now go on, tell me about yourself, you promised you would. Tell me about your mother. Who was she? Pretty, was she? Affectionate? Loving? Do you miss 'er?"

Mor laughed. "Why should I tell you about my mother? I didn't promise anything."

She pressed her knees tight against his and brushed her face upon his shoulder. "I've hardly ever known a man who doesn't start off by telling me about 'is mother, 'ow 'e's lost 'er, 'ow 'e wants to find 'er again. That's a fact of nature I could tell you about, but I won't. One that even the French 'aven't put in their encyclopædia yet—so that scholar of Oxford said, coming to me regular so he can wear his dead mother's dresses in bed. Wants nothing else except to spend the night by my side in 'is mother's nightgown."

"I don't have a mother."

"There's one thing all men 'ave, More Grief. A mother. If you miss her, it's my speciality. I can be a gentleman's nanny, too. Would you like that?"

"I mean, I never knew mine. I was orphaned early."

"Then I'm sure you're still looking for 'er. A lot of them are. Wanting to know 'ow she looked, 'ow she behaved, whether she was like this woman they meet or like that one. What she smelled of. Roses, mimosa, kitchen wells. What she wore."

Not getting an answer, she said impatiently. "You can tell *me*."

"I'll tell you then! My mother left me in the church porch at Lady Well. All I 'ad was the name 'Greave' stitched to my shirt. She must 'ave done that because my father, it is said, was Oliver Greave."

My Gawd, Oliver Greave! Mary could barely contain her shock.

"He used to be an important man in these parts, before he went bankrupt," Mor continued. "He was of a 'wayward disposition,' they say, fathering children here and there. It was our present Mr. Horsfall's father that cheated 'im of his inheritance, they say. So perhaps what Horsfall has should be mine. So now I've told you the truth . . . Are you all right?"

"Yes, I'm all right, my love. Thanks for asking. Stranger things 'ave 'appened, More Grief. You don't know who your mother was, then?"

"No."

"No memories at all? Don't you remember the color of 'er 'air? Was it black?"

"I don't know."

"How old are you?"

He looked sad, even shamefaced. "I'm . . . turned thirty."

"I'm always being told some sad tale like yours by my gentlemen. I 'eard about them Greaves when I was a child. Peculiar things 'appen . . . There are so many interesting categories of 'uman nature, aren't there? Are you interested in anything special, dear?"

"Goldsmith's *History of Animated Nature* was my constant companion at my loom."

"My Gawd!" She laughed, and sighed. "Well, then. It's not your mother, your interest? That's a pity, I'm good at that. What is it, then?" She put forth her toe. "Do you like my boots?"

He didn't answer.

"They're green."

"I can see."

"Are you slow or something?" She laughed at him. "You can say anything you like to me, my dear. You won't be able to tell me anything new. I know everything. If I can't satisfy you myself, someone else 'ere will. You interested in widows and funerals? You seem on the melancholic side. That's Mrs. Rawdon's line . . ."

He wasn't answering.

"What *do* you like?"

"A short while ago I was reading Goldsmith on the origin of rivers . . ."

"My Gawd!" She slapped her hand to her cheek and screamed with laughter.

Once again ale and gin were on the table, and Mary winked at the servant.

Mor found himself getting drunk. He was very tired and he didn't often take alcohol. He also drank faster because he didn't like the feeling of being out-talked by a woman.

Mary gently stroked the back of his neck. " 'Ave you been a bad boy, by any chance? Is there anything you think nanny should do for you? There, there . . ."

But he did not respond to that, either. She quickened her voice, as if she were losing interest in this performance and wanted to get it over with.

"Then tell me what was that about 'stockings out of fashion' and 'destruction of machinery' and 'distress we are put under'? That's what you said. Tell me about that. I'm a very patient listener."

He foolishly raised his voice. "I'll tell you, all right! By God, I'll tell you a story, if you want one! In York I saw a judge put on 'is black cap to pass sentence of death on a dozen wretches, telling them they should be 'ung by the neck and their bodies given to surgeons. One 'ad stolen only a pair of old shoes that 'ad been left to be mended and 'e put them on 'is own feet because 'e needed them. So that they could 'ang 'im, they were valued at one shilling. I saw those shoes and thought they were not worth fourpence. The shoemaker at first said they were not worth threepence, then someone 'igh up told 'im to say otherwise, because you can't be 'ung for stealing less than a shilling's worth. What a cursed world, where little knaves are 'ung or transported, but great ones swim in wealth and pleasure and are flattered with titles and dignities."

"Don't shout so loud! For Gawd's sake, not so loud, More Grief!"

It was her turn to cast worried glances around the room, and at the leech gatherer, who was busy with one hand inside his lady's bosom. Nonetheless he had picked up what Mor had said. "That's right, sir, that's right! They allus 'ang the wrong ones. You tell the lady!"

The drink and the encouragement were affecting Mor. He shouted even louder. "Pheasants, hares, trouts, partridges are privileged, compared wi' the poor and distressed like us." He waved his hand toward the smiling leech gatherer. "They are protected by gamekeepers and laws and fed without stint to make 'em fat. Truly, Mary, you are not to be blamed for what 'as 'appened to you."

"Thanks very much. You talk like an educated aristocrat, More Grief, only they don't usually shout their business for all to 'ear. I can't puzzle you out."

"I keep a school."

"Yes, you teach writing and Latin, but you know nothing about life. Say some Latin to me, then."

"Sic transit gloria mundi."

"Gawd help me, just like a parson. What's a weaver doing keeping a school?"

"If I don't teach my neighbors what I've learned from going short . . . short . . ."

"Your speech is slurred."

He pulled himself together. "Short-sighted by candlelight, they'll be taught something else by the vicar, in the grammar school."

"Goodnight, sir, goodnight," said the leech gatherer, and led his cheerful woman away.

"God bless 'em, I 'ope they 'ave a roof," Mary said.

Mor looked at her intently. She returned his look. There was something between them that, like her perfume, pushed the smoke and smell of the room into the background.

"You're sorry for people like that?" he asked.

"Oh, More Grief . . ."

She appeared to him quite differently now, after what she had said, and after the way she had looked at him. Her restless glances and movements had ceased. An essence of closeness, of familiarity, surrounded them.

"Our vicar in Lady Well says our life is an heroic labor in darkness and ignorance, in order to earn an eternity of bliss and ease. He never talks about what should be a parson's concerns—love and duty to our neighbors, and forgiveness. Instead, 'e tells us we might be snatched away into eternal fire between this sermon and the next if we don't keep our noses to the grindstone. So I've stopped going to the church. People only listen because they like to watch his Adam's apple going up and down in the pulpit."

"Don't talk so loud, More Grief! Please."

Apparently she was crying. Mor did not know that whores could cry so easily. "Tell me about yourself," he said softly. "How did you come to . . ."

"To be a whore?"

"Yes."

She wiped away a tear and smiled. "I don't mind my profession. We are what we make of what 'as been done to us, I say. I've made the best of my fate. What I was born with is just something to make a living with. It's only men think women 'ave got a temple between their legs. None of us females gives a pig's fart for it. Not even ladies. Especially them, in fact. They'll drop their drawers in a wink for the sake of a fortune and a marriage and a chance to pretend to 'ave 'eadaches whenever they like.

"I'll tell you what 'appened to me, if you really want to know, More Grief. When I was fourteen I was turned out of 'is house by my father because I'd gone behind 'is 'aystack with a lad, and that's 'ow I came to follow my trade. 'E wasn't my real father. I was adopted, like you. I was taken to him secretly when I was a baby, and not even my own mother was supposed to 'ave known I'd live. I know why they adopted me. They wanted a slave, but they'd picked the wrong one. They thought I'd be afraid to raise my 'ead because of my birth mark . . .

"I was thrown out with nothing but my trunk. I wasn't sorry to leave. He once nearly kicked my eye out with the tip of 'is boot 'cos 'is dinner was cold. Called me a 'bastard' and said even my natural mother couldn't bear the sight of me, 'cos I shouldn't 'ave been born. So there I was, thrown out o' the farm, which I didn't mind at all, for I've never been in love with pig sheds and rainy weather.

"Then along comes a young man and picks me up, just the same as you've done today, but 'e was younger and in them days I was more worth 'aving . . . ' 'Ullo,' I thinks, ' 'ere's my fortune coming.' I wasn't no green fruit, I can tell you, that could find a Mother Superior easy. I'd lost my virgo intacta behind that 'aystack, which was foolish because if I'd gone whole I'd 'ave been worth twenty pounds and that would 'ave bought me a bride's trousseau fit for an aristocrat, wouldn't it?

" 'E took me in his phaeton to an 'ostelry, no expense to myself, just like in a novel. We stayed there for a week, as I'd nowhere to go. 'E said 'e was a lord and I believed 'im, for 'e behaved like one. I was waiting for 'im to take me to 'is family or introduce me to a lady who'd employ me as 'er maid. He talked about 'love' and 'I wish you were mine.' Then 'e stuck me in a whore'ouse. 'E said it was to pay off my bill for gin. I ended up in London.

"Just listen to me talking! What about you? You told me as far as being left in the church porch. When was that? Where'd your mother live? . . . Oh, my Gawd!"

"What is it?"

"Oh, nothing. Just the sergeant there . . . Mad Dick. I 'ave to watch 'im. Go on with your story. Your father was Oliver Greave, you said?"

"Yes. I was put in the workhouse, then I was sent out to a weaver and 'is wife. They brought me up well. I was lucky. ' 'E shall grow up imbued with bewk knowledge, and 'e shall be learned to write a good 'and.' " Mor began to mimic the weaver's high-pitched voice. He had not made fun like this since the days when he had courted Phoebe. "He taught me the principles of science and he said the verses of Mr. Wesley were better than Shakespeare's. He taught me about the miraculous varieties of nature, through Oliver Goldsmith's book . . ."

They were interrupted by the drunken sergeant stumbling against their table. He was a huge, wild fellow, with a Tyneside accent.

"You're talking deep, Mary the Scar! Let's play games. Let's go upstairs."

"Fuck off," Mary answered. "Go on, Mad Dick! Fuck off. I don't want yer, Sergeant Chadwick."

"What's up with yer?"

The soldier spread his arms, lost his balance, and reeled backward into his companions, who, having nothing to fear from his size because of his drunkenness, pushed him back to the whore's table, as if he was a sack of wheat.

"For Gawd's sake, why don't the King take you lot off to fight Napoleon and stop you pestering honest English whores?" Mary yelled.

"I hate Napoleon," said the soldier, addressing Mor. "But don't think I'm not a democrat. I hate Napoleon, 'cos o' this: 'e's spilt more blood to find crowns for 'is own brothers than the revolution in France spilt to institute the liberty of man. Isn't that so, friend?"

"Don't answer him," Mary commanded fiercely.

But Mor had to nod his agreement.

"Now there's an honest gentleman!" the soldier smirked. "Are you the one that's being talked about? You don't look the type. Tell me what you think."

"For Gawd's sake, keep your mouth shut! You're a fool, More Grief. You're a babe in arms."

The sentimental sergeant turned as vicious toward Mary as previously he had been soft.

"That's a democratic sentiment that wouldn't be understood by a whore, Mary the Scar! When I was in the coal pit . . . when I was in the Newcastle pit . . . Ah, what's the use? There's nothing that the common man can do, is there, sir? You know what 'appens in 'Is Majesty's armies when you dare to complain? Ah, what's the use? No wonder the army's on the edge of revolt. Tell you what, Mary the Scar, come and play wi' me, 'tis better, I'm sure, than thrusting on this kind gen'leman 'ere your ugly face. Do you know, sir, what she's 'iding under that . . . that . . ."

Mary threw her gin at the soldier. She amazed Mor with her quickness to defend herself. Mad Dick did not retaliate. He staggered away. Mary was only a little flustered, as if she were used to this kind of scene with the sergeant.

"You've dropped your bag," Mor said. He picked it up and put it in her lap—taking the opportunity to brush her thigh.

The sergeant, restored to his companions, was meek again. "I love her. I love her . . ." he whined. He was in tears. But he did not come back.

"You never know with 'im," Mary said. "One moment 'e's crying on my shoulder, the next 'e's a brute."

"We suffer from what Byron in the House termed 'a double affliction of an idle military and a starving population.' "

"No peace for the wicked, you might say. Who's Byron?"

"The owner of coal pits near Rochdale and a grand house near Nottingham. But he speaks for the common people in Parliament. A good man, though a lord."

"Oh, my Gawd, an aristocrat! There's one or two of them come to me regular. 'Appen 'e's one of them. They generally don't give their proper names. I'll tell you something else about the respectable classes, More Grief. They all marry unhappily, and that's because they can afford to be unhappy. The poor 'as to select with greater sense and make the most of what they gets."

Mor gulped.

" 'Ave you ever 'eard of a poet called the Earl of Rochester?" she asked suddenly.

"No."

"I can't read a book nor anything writ down myself, but a gentleman of mine sometimes reads his verses to me out from a book. 'Ave you really never 'eard of 'im?"

"No," Mor repeated, irritated at having a gap in his learning discovered.

"I'm surprised at you. I was told 'e was 'profligate.' What does 'profligate' mean?"

"It means he threw his money around."

"I wish I'd met 'im. I was taught one of 'is poems by 'eart. There was nothing else to do in bed with my friend. Get us another gin, sweetheart."

While Mor was away, he thought of what he would tell her when he got back.

The ale and the gin slopped out of the pots. He set them down, leaned comfortably next to her, and announced, "I'm looking for a red flower. I saw it in a dream."

She touched his arm and left her fingers lingering there. "What sort of red flower, More Grief?"

He closed his eyes. "A splendid deep red rose, like nothing on earth."

"I can see it! I can just see it! I can bring a man a flower, redder than any sunset . . ."

Watch it, Mary, she told herself. *Not with this one. Habit of a lifetime.*

"Do you believe that Christ will come again?" she asked.

He wouldn't answer.

"There's lots who do. There must be a reason for it. Miracles 'appen. You'd be surprised at what 'appens." She removed her gaze from him and stared at the floor. His violin poked from under the seat. "If a fiddler plays right, you can feel Christ is in the room with you," she said.

When she looked up she saw that several more soldiers had gathered around the sergeant and the man whom Mor had recognized as pointing him out in March.

"Oh, my Gawd, that's 'B.' Come on upstairs now!"

Mary was already standing. Mor felt in his pocket.

"Never mind your money!" She had hold of his hand, while she looked around in all directions.

She tugged him to his feet. Drunk as he was, he remembered to pick up his bag and his fiddle. In her haste, dragging him off, she abandoned the elegant holding of her dress.

"You don't know how your fortune's changed, because I've changed my mind about you!" she shouted over her shoulder.

Phoebe might have been in another country; Phoebe who kept her bridal trinkets under a bell jar.

Laughter followed the tall whore and the crippled weaver as she dragged him toward a battered oak door, which looked as though it led to a coal cellar or a place for animals rather than to the pleasure chamber of a lady. It opened to a dirty staircase.

"You 'aven't any idea 'ow to look after yourself, 'ave you, More Grief?"

The staircase was so steep that as they climbed, the hem of her dress dangled above his eyes. Halfway up, on a tiny landing, they had to press themselves against the wall for the skivvy carrying a bucket of coals to pass by.

Mary gave the girl some money and Mor turned away. Through the window he saw the moon beaming upon stagnant blood and water in the yard. He could hear low slaughterhouse moans, and from the head of the stairs, the similar cries of a whorehouse.

They reached the top landing. Mary led him on and opened a door a short distance along the passageway. They went in and she shot the wooden bolt.

Her room, in contrast to the barren stoniness downstairs, was a warm red color. It was invitingly lit by a newly stoked fire. As Mor expected of a whore's room, the double bed was the most striking thing in it—an antiquated four-poster of black oak, with curtains and carvings of fruit and flowers. There was a chaise longue, which to Mor looked to be a valuable piece of furniture, although it was scratched and scuffed. There were mirrors; more than he had ever seen before, except at Mr. Horsfall's. There were large cupboards and wardrobes, so cavernous that for a moment he feared a spy might be hidden in one of them; then he dismissed this idea as ridiculous. Most of the items appeared as unloved and impersonal as the furnishings of any coaching inn, and were evidently not Mary's own. They contrasted with some of her own decorative touches: a few pieces of lace, a blue cloak arranged over a chair, and a silk scarf dropped, as if casually, to transform a large and very battered leather trunk. A blue Chinese jar for biscuits decorated the windowsill. There was a ewer of water, and a bowl with forget-me-nots painted on the rim.

"Never let yourself again be led by the nose by somebody describing you as 'a suitable occupant for accommodation.' "

"Why not?"

"Gawd, you're a child, you're a babe in arms! You need me to take care of you! Didn't you notice the way it was said, solemn like in a church? It's what they always say, meaning you're suspected as a fugitive, that's why. It's a code. The cobbler over the bridge is a spy for the military, and 'e sent you into a trap. They know you're from Lady Well 'cos you told them yourself. They sent me over to find out about you because they 'ope to get out of you what you've done, for a reward. What *'ave* you done? 'B' thinks you might 'ave been in Huddersfield . . . My Gawd, don't start telling me! I'm not going to inform on you, and I don't want to know!"

Mor put his bag and fiddle down, removed his scratched, greasy leather jerkin, and ran his fingers around his neck where he had sweated with fear.

Mary placed her indispensable and shawl upon the chest. The adventure had not put *her* out.

He fumbled in his pocket. He had never been with a prostitute and did not know whether to pay her before accepting her services or afterward. He felt that a sovereign was too much, but his small change amounted to too little. He did not know where his sovereign would be safe, or whether he could really trust her; though trust, indeed, was what he felt.

"I don't want money," she said. "No, don't, I don't want it! Anyway, you'll 'ave to stay, now you're 'ere. There's nowhere else for you to go. You can choose your own side of the bed. Look at whatever side of me you want. I don't always do that, because there's some Georges and Thomases I don't like. You're gentle, but they don't know 'ow to treat a lady and so I don't give them privileges. Anyway, I expect you'll sleep."

She herself seemed quite sober. She sat on the edge of the bed and lifted the hem of her dress to give him his first glimpse of her ankles.

"Tell me about your wife."

He did not answer.

"Go on, tell me about her. You can do. I won't be jealous. You promised to tell me."

"I didn't promise!"

"Tell me anyway. Please."

"Nothing."

"What do you mean, 'nothing'?"

"Phoebe—that's what she always said to me: 'Nothing.' Even when we were courting. I'd walk her home through the dusk and she'd sigh. 'What are you sighing about?' 'Nothing,' she'd say. 'Nothing.' "

"Poor dear! I bet she 'ad 'er problems."

Mary lifted her dress higher. She wore a petticoat which was also cream-colored. An absurd thought of it as virginal and bridal crossed Mor's mind. After all, she was virginal and bridal to him. Certainly she was without shame.

She had another little purse hung from a cord around her waist. She rolled petticoat and dress higher. Above her stockings she wore a pair of men's woollen drawers, worn back to front. Thus she could easily get at the strings of the waist, normally worn at the rear.

She untied the strings and peered. "Damn!" she said loudly. "The blood's come. I've got the flowers."

His disappointment thudded like a lead cudgel.

"I felt something, downstairs. I thought it was . . ." She laughed.

She untied the string that held her purse and slid it under her pillow. She slipped off the bed and stood erect, so that her clothes fell into place again, her dress flowing around her, a crumpled flower. She turned her back to him and bent her neck. She was expecting him to unfasten the ties and buttons, but he was unused to such delights.

"Are you going to do it, or must I call the servant girl?"

He didn't know how to. He fumbled and eventually succeeded. She struggled to her commode. She looked so awkward that he went to help there, too. He could hardly believe that he was doing such a thing. He removed her boots and moved to the garter at her knee, while she was pulling down her drawers.

"Careful," she warned.

Some solid objects were caught in the garter. A silver watch and a spoon.

"What's this?"

"What's what?"

"This . . . these . . ."

"One's for telling the time, the other's for dipping in your dinner, if you're lucky enough to have one. A lady has nowhere to keep nothing, but I expect you've never realized that. I'm sure you must be glad not to be a member of our unfortunate society."

She got up off the commode and took the watch and spoon to bury them deep in her trunk. "No need for you to wear a sheep's bladder tonight. But I'd wager an 'ouse and lands on it, that you'll sleep. Anyway, we ought to behave, you and I. I'm not very religious but still . . ."

He was looking at her in amazement.

"You don't know what I'm talking about, do you?"

"No."

Out of the trunk she took some rags, washed but lightly stained, and positioned them between her legs. She put on a nightgown and slipped into bed, sitting upright. Her fingers scratched at her face. She did not seem to realize that she was doing it.

Removing his layers of coarse, oily woollens, Mor felt rough and unpleasant. He peeled off his shirt, then his canvas underclothes. He was more conscious of his body than he had been in years.

He made use of her chamber pot in a hearty gush.

"Don't be surprised that I know gentlemen, More Grief. There's types from every level of the land comes after me. I can talk to 'em all, bishops and dukes and Members of Parliament and military officers, 'cos I've learned their way of speaking. You must have noticed. The aristocracy of England 'as been my downfall, More Grief."

"Mine, too."

"Come and lie down, love." She spoke softly.

"Why do you like me?" he asked.

"Oh, if you knew what I've seen and put up with! Oh, dear . . ."

He did not care anymore about an answer. Lying next to him, him, Mor Laverock Greave, on a clean and sheeted bed, was the flesh of a woman who smelled of a jungle of perfumes. He kissed her shoulder. Avoiding her lips and cheeks because of the paint, he kissed her neck.

Her flesh tasted not of rank machine oils but of tingling, erotic essences. He was longing to try the olfactory excitements of her body, to do what he had never done but only imagined: to bury his face between her breasts, under her armpits, between her legs; to kiss her toes. He had never in his life lain with any woman except Phoebe. He was amazed, charmed, by the variegated red streaks of her hair, by her still wearing her glass earrings in bed, by her perfumed cleanliness which made him feel ashamed of his own dirt.

"Do you believe that Christ will come again?" she asked a second time.

"No."

"I do," she said. " 'E promised, and Christ is one who'd never break a promise. 'E's the only one who'd never do that."

He could not continue the conversation. For the first time in two days he was able to relax. Mary pressed his head onto her breast, and he was asleep. Mary was awake much longer.

What she most wanted was for promises to be kept. When, in her girlhood, she had seen cottagers, with their battered carts and tattered baggage, cleared off newly enclosed lands, hoping to make new homes on the moorlands, she had thought: *They were promised homes to live in peace and have been given nothing.* All earthly people, she had found, broke their promises in the end. All lovers had failed her. She preferred to be a whore, play-acting brief fantasies, with contracts that had only to be kept for a night. In fantasies she could be a goddess in her own Garden of Eden, where there were no promises to be broken.

Once in Halifax, when she was a girl, she had heard Joanna Southcott speak to a thousand people. Christ had promised to come again, Joanna said, bringing eternal rest for the poor, starting at the coming Millennium.

Mary heard this message not from a parson, but from a woman like herself. He-who-would-keep-his-promise would be born, as before, to some humble earthly woman, Mary was told.

An immaculate conception. No men. Save a lot of trouble.

Mor was woken in the night by the noises of the whorehouse. His mouth was sticky and would hardly open. His head was thick and buzzing. The fire had died down, and the moon patterned the floor with light. He felt he could pick it up and give pieces of blue silk to the woman at his side. He looked upon her sleeping face as at an awesome miracle.

His staring at her so intently woke her.

"Won't you go inside me, More Grief?" she whispered. "Never mind the flowers."

Before he climbed onto her, she removed her protective cloth, dropping it to the floor beside the bed and he thought of Phoebe's blood-stained rags, the ones she had held to her mouth; she never let him see the other kind of rags, hiding them as if they were obscene.

Mor came quickly, excited by abstinence and by the expert manner in which Mary entwined her arms around his neck, violently yet also tenderly, and by the way she stroked his shoulders. Her painted face, with the heightened red patches of lips and cheeks as if they had been stung, had the tranced look of a death mask. Perhaps it was only in moments of death and love that character was so extinguished.

"Kiss me on the mouth," she begged softly.

He brushed and lingered over her lips, which had a strange bitter taste like poison.

"I'll tell you something about whores, More Grief," she whispered. "We all keep one place that none of our clients are allowed to touch. For some it's the breast, for some it's the 'ollow of the neck. That place is for their true love's sake, and is kept so that they have something special for 'im only. It's to keep love pure. With me it's the lips. They can all go into me down there, anyone that pays for it, but you're the only one that's kissed me on the lips for years. No one else'll be doing it, ever. Ever. I can promise you."

They felt together the influx of the most revolutionary feeling in the world, the force that breaks up everything else, and reconstitutes it to center on itself . . . He did not dare mention love, lest something so insecurely planted should vanish.

They felt that they had both tumbled into a conspiracy.

Part 2

April - May 1812

CHAPTER SEVEN

April 18th

or awoke with Mary still sleeping beside him; red hair tangled out of control, the earring closest to him broken into glassy fractures as it caught the morning light, tossed like a buoy in the henna-red sea. During much of the night she had not slept, from protecting this babe in her arms, realizing how much he needed rest. Asleep now, she had a defenseless, naïve look, which made her seem young.

Rosy dawn was over and the whitened light showed that it was late into the morning. This felt like the days of his youth, before the factories, when a man could rise as early or as late as he chose, if he would pay the price. He had slept as unconsciously trusting as a baby. Several times she had called him "baby," he remembered. They had twice made love, despite the blood.

"You might say we're 'blood relatives,' " she whispered.

After the second time, he had fallen gently asleep while resting inside her, her arm around his shoulder.

He tried to feel guilty about this association he had so surprisingly formed, but was unable to do so. He turned over thoughts of Phoebe, of the children, of Lady Well. He was on the run, having to learn the new skills of watching his back all the time, yet paradoxically it was now that he felt he was, at last, his own man, free. The coiled spring of anxiety that had always been in his chest had vanished.

Mary awoke and, in her nightgown, used the chamber pot after him. She unfastened the window and emptied the pot into a space that was blasted by the smell and moaning of cattle. The wild colors of her face met the light. Idly scratching her cheek, she laughed and shouted to some men in the yard.

She turned her face, smeared with rouge but still lit with pleasure, to Mor. He was lifted on a pang of love, just from seeing her like that. He went to join her at the window and looped his arm around her waist.

"Kiss me," she said.

They stood cuddling each other and staring out the window. It promised to be a stormy day. Strong sunlight fell momentarily upon Ripponden, yet above the hills there gathered heavy clouds, of a most threatening, greenish tinge. The slopes were shadowed with rain.

They could also see a busy street, and workshops and factories along a rapidly flowing stream. There was a large mill, its beam engine rocking with gigantic strength on its horizontal shaft. It put forth steam, smoke, and a dirty smell of coal.

"Dies irae, dies illa, solvet saclum in favilla. Gawd, I don't like the morning."

"You're a Catholic?"

"I pick up bits of knowledge, like you do. 'Day of anger, day of mourning.' It's their Mass. 'When to ashes all is burning.' You're not the only one with a bit of Latin."

She moved away from the window and he closed it. She dressed in the same clothes as the day before. Mor noticed that the slits on either side of her petticoat were lined up with two slits cleverly hidden in the folds of her dress at the hips, so that she could get at both the purse hung around her waist and into the gap in the front of her drawers.

Out of her trunk she lifted a small wooden box and, taking it to the table that held the ewer of water, opened the lid. It had a padded red silk lining. Inside were several small bottles, some sable brushes, a piece of sponge, small porcelain palettes, a bar of palm-oil soap, and a silver-backed mirror.

She washed and dried her arms, the top of her breasts, her neck, and some of her face. Mor felt that he himself was one who liked to be clean, yet this interest in, he presumed, daily washing amazed him.

Then she renewed her old layer of face paint, mixing some white lead and using the sponge to apply it from chin to hairline. She heightened her cheeks and lips with the mercuric sulfide rouge. She smoothed her eyebrows with a finger, before using one of the brushes to paint them. Her face when she had finished made him think of the hectic colors of autumn when the leaves are dying.

"I'll wager you can't tell I was brought up on a farm," she said.

She turned back to her trunk for the silver-backed hairbrush, and worked at her hair.

All this took a long time and he continued happy to watch. *Like a married man,* he thought.

"More Grief, why don't you wash yourself too, before I throw the water away?"

He had been considering that very thing. He washed himself and dressed at last.

"We should get you some shirts . . ." She let this unintended hint that there was a future for them together hang in the air. She replaced the cosmetic box in her trunk and pulled out napkins and a tea-service. Taking the service downstairs, she said she was going to order a breakfast. She was some time away. After she returned, a fine breakfast was brought to her room.

When they were alone again, " 'E said 'e was a lord of some place that I found out later never existed," Mary said.

"Who?"

"The one who gave me this china, o' course. Who d'yer think I was talking about? St. Paul? 'E was a one, I can tell you. I was glad to be rid of 'im. 'E used to bring his dog with 'im. Dirty beast."

The white lead that was still on her fingers left smears on her oatcakes.

Mor, who had never in his life had fine china in his hands, did not know how to hold it. He touched it gingerly, frightened of breaking it, as if it was a wild bird's egg.

"I need to get some change," he said.

"I don't want you to pay me. Don't insult me any more . . ."

Mor's heart jumped with fear, for a man stood at the door, an open razor in his hand; a sinister fellow who smiled and said nothing. He turned to beckon someone in from the landing.

The servant girl came in, this time with a bowl of warm water and a towel. Mary, during her absence, had arranged for the services of a barber.

The girl left, her face stiff.

Mor sat on the trunk. He realized how jumpy he had become. He had to calm himself for the barber, who snipped at his hair as well as shaved him, for half an hour. The house was still quiet. Against one wall, he could hear the soft banging of a broom.

"They told me last night before I came over and spoke to you that you are a 'desperate man,'" Mary said, after the barber had left.

"Yes, I'm desperate. Magistrates think the only cure for it is a noose at the end of a rope. It is not only the feckless who starve. Families in full employment, who can do no more, are also starving and they will become desperate, too."

"You don't have to make excuses to me, More Grief. I don't care what anyone's called. Think 'ow often I must put up with being called 'whore.' I've never wanted to be anything but an honest woman. Just because I enjoy life, such as it is, they don't understand it. I judge by what I find out for myself about a man."

She asked him to go with her to the slaughter yard. She would not say what for. Judging by her familiarity with the place when they reached it, and her manner with the workmen, it was a regular errand.

She collected a supply of sheep's intestines, already dried for her, cut into short lengths, knotted at one end and hung in a shed, where they were causing amusement.

"What are those for?"

"Where've you been all your life, schoolmaster? Spare my blushes! The lads over there know what they're for and they don't 'ave no Latin. They're for me to 'and out for my gentlemen to wear."

As they stood in the yard, surrounded by the brutal shouting of slaughtermen and the defeated lowing of cattle, Mary said, "I don't care what we are, the two of us. I mean, if we're whore and . . . whatever . . . so what? Will you promise never to leave me, More Grief?"

It seemed the most inevitable and natural thing for her to say, and for him to answer, without a pause, "Yes."

They walked silently for a while, feeling stupid because they said no more about it. The world had changed. He had meant what he said, but found out that he meant it only after he had spoken. Then he understood the implications for a woman who had explained to him how heartily she believed in people keeping promises.

They maintained their silence, their every step seeming to echo with meaning.

They returned past the tethered bullocks, catching their warm smell.

From a barn, they heard scampering, slipping hooves, and the heavy fall of the pole-ax.

"You said you were forced to have your daughter adopted?"

"That's right, More Grief."

"I've lost a child, also," Mor confided. "My boy ran away two days ago from the factory."

"Oh, my dear."

Mor, in a rush, described Edwin. His curiosity, his desire to learn, his longing not to be crushed, and his interest in distant places. Mor was finding himself articulate as he had never been before. He told her about Phoebe and Gideon.

"Edwin's my boy. Gideon's much more 'is mother's. 'E'll turn into a preacher . . . something o' that sort."

"Which way do you think Edwin 'as run?"

"Liverpool. 'E was always asking where Liverpool was. 'E will 'ave gone into Lancashire, either along the turnpike road to Oldham or over Blackstone Edge to Rochdale."

"I've business to attend to in Oldham," Mary announced. "I told you I 'ad to go somewhere—well, that's where it is. We'll go together and maybe find news of your child. Even if 'e's going by Rochdale, I've friends there who would 'ave news of 'im."

"It might take a long time."

She smiled. "You'll be away a long time, all right. I'm told you killed a man on your raid on Horsfalls'."

"No!"

She put a calming hand on his shoulder. "They don't say it's you for certain, but they're looking for people who were there, right enough. You'd best all scatter and lose yourselves. There's a fellow called 'B' on the trail . . ."

"I'm not going on trial! I killed no one. I'll gain nothing for anyone by getting myself transported."

"We'll both be away lying low for a long time together."

"What about your business with Mrs. Rawdon?"

"I pay a nightly rent to 'er for the room and I give 'er some of my earnings. I'll arrange things with our Abbess. Someone else'll use the room and properties whilst I'm gone."

"Properties?"

"Theatrical devices. You'll learn, schoolmaster! It's all pretend. Mrs.

Rawdon does the widow-taken-in-grief. I do nanny. I've a friend who does the ravaged bride. We find out what our client wants and then we make it real for 'im.

"I'm known for my wanderings, More Grief. It'll surprise no one that I go. There's people in 'igh places who will cover up for me and say to Mrs. Rawdon, 'She 'as business to attend to, don't you worry about 'er, if you know what's good for you.' I'm known for knowing what's going on all over the counties. I'll pack my trunk and 'ave it sent to Oldham, in charge of my friends. We'll meet it there. You with your fiddle, and me with my own instrument for playing, as you might say, we'll get by. There's a good living to be made on the roads out of the soldiers, and there's masons and navvies with money in their pockets from building factories. We might be lucky, and I might 'ave the opportunity to introduce you to one of my aristocrats. Lord Byron up 'ere to inspect 'is coal pits and estates.

"I know generals, too, who will talk in their sleep about what they're planning. I know General Maitland, who's to be in charge of the whole operation against the Luddites in the north." She laughed. "I'll introduce you to 'im. It's often republicans like you who turn out best in a gentleman's service. A general's bedchamber'd be the best place of all in which to 'ide a fugitive. 'Ow'd you like to be intimate servant of General Maitland? 'E'll be needing one when 'e gets 'ere. You'd 'ear everything then, Mr. Machine Breaker."

There was evidently nothing she would not do for Mor so long as she believed his promise to love her.

Love, instant, total, and inexplicable as this, frightened him. It also made him feel more daringly a man.

And Mary could not resist the feeling that she was inspiring daring in a man.

It was soon called for. When they returned to the inn, the soldiers had been alerted to find and arrest the "Ludd" who had been trailed from Lady Well.

Under Sergeant Chadwick's direction, they wrenched open cupboards, poked their noses under tables and chairs, and one even sifted through a pack of cards, apparently to find their quarry.

"Get into our room, quick!" Mary said.

He made for the stairs. Mary lingered behind.

"No time for whores this morning," one soldier said to her, and she blew him a kiss.

"Our progress is remorseless," Mad Dick Chadwick boasted. "The place is surrounded. Whoever 'e is, 'e's trapped."

Before Mary went up, she spoke to the skivvy. The girl followed soon after, carrying past the unobservant soldiery a bundle of her own spare clothing.

Soon, a private searching the passageway outside Mary's room imagined that he heard the sounds of unspeakable morning pleasures. It was laughter from Mor being dressed by Mary in the clothes of a servant girl; a cheap, black cotton dress, a baggy apron smelling of oatmeal, and a wig from Mary's cupboard.

A scrambling outside the window told them that the soldiers were combing the slaughterhouse. They had turned the cattle loose into the yard, which a sudden heavy shower of rain had made into a mudhole. The frightened beasts were sliding and bellowing.

Then the soldiers could be heard outside Mary's door.

"You'd better get some practice to make it convincing before they break in. 'Ere, fasten this on my leg for my business in Oldham. And don't say anything when they come in. Pretend you're dumb."

She sat on the bed, waiting for him to tie a scarlet garter around her thigh. It was while he was doing this that Mad Dick burst in with two privates.

"Sergeant Chadwick of the Cumberland militia!" he announced as he led his soldiers to hunt a "desperate fugitive" among Mary's clothes, scent bottles, and underwear. " 'Ave you got a tall thin fellow with a long thin neck 'idden in 'ere, Mary the Scar?"

So it was Crawshaw they were looking for!

Mary did not bother with the question. Coyly, she stared down at her feet. "I like my little boots," she said. "They were made for me by a cobbler. He fitted out a cottage so I'd stay in 'is nest, but to be a cobbler's bird in a cage was never what I wanted. 'E wanted me to be 'is *awl* but it would never 'ave *lasted!*"

"Our orders are to hunt down a tall thin fellow who may or may not spell 'notorious' in a clownish fashion. You seen 'im? If you 'aven't, you ought to look out for 'im. There's an 'andsome reward. It's gone up to five hundred guineas. That'd set you up with a decent retirement. That's what you want, isn't it? You could buy a country estate and keep a dozen servants with that."

Mary turned her eyes, bovinely wide and placid, upon the soldiers. "My cobbler was a gentleman at 'eart, though, not like a common soldier."

"Listen to me, you fucking whore!" shouted Mad Dick, who seemed to have forgotten that he had approached her with drunken endearments the night before. " 'Ave you opened up your sewer to a machine breaker? If you 'ave, you'd better tell us who, or we'll 'ave you transported with 'im and the rest o' the mobs from the Rawfolds and Lady Well jobs."

"Why would I do that? Who do you think I'm working for?"

"Because you might be working for them a well as for us, that's why! Knowing you. Who was that with you last night? 'E'd come in from Lady Well. Where's 'e gone to?"

"Left. He gave me the slip in the night. Went out the window, 'cos it was the wrong time of the month. You want proof? Look at that." She picked up the rag from the floor.

"Don't be disgusting. 'Ere, you," the sergeant said to Mor. " 'Ave you seen anything? What are you? Where've you come from all of a sudden?"

"I'll thank you not to use foul language before my new maid, soldier!"

Sergeant Chadwick laughed. "Maid, my arse. The things that go on in this whore'ouse! They're disgusting. Well, Vicar, or Doctor, or whatever you are, tell me what you've seen."

"She can't tell you," Mary said. " 'Cos she's dumb. She's never been able to speak a word since she was a baby. A born idiot, that's what, aren't you, love? It's a good job I took you in. She's just arrived today, a gentle girl brought into service because 'er father died for 'is country in Spain. 'E gave up 'is life by impaling 'imself upon the spikes at the fortress so that 'is comrades could climb upon 'is back to their glorious victory, as is mentioned in the dispatch of the Duke of Wellington. A general 'imself told me of the 'eroic deed. It makes me weep to think of it. But true bravery is a stranger to you scum who are only fit to 'unt your own unarmed countrymen."

"I hate Napoleon as much as any man!" protested Mad Dick once again, but more soberly, as he disappeared in and out of cupboards, tipping petticoats and dresses onto the floor and getting his boots entangled. "I'd be as glad as any to cut off 'is tail in Spain, 'cos 'e's spilt more blood in finding crowns for 'is own brothers than the revolution in France did to institute the liberty of man. Isn't that so, Vicar?"

Mor had to nod his agreement, as he had done the night before.

"I don't know anything about politics," Mary said. "I can't read newspapers, can I?"

Playing the lady, she lay back upon the coverlet and let Mor perform his duties. He picked up the underwear soiled by the soldiers' boots, folded and replaced it.

One of the privates came to Mor to show him his tattoos. On one arm a snake wreathed around a sword, and on the other an eagle hovered in a sunset which might have been painted by Turner. The tattoos were new and raw, and the recruit stroked his flesh admiringly, trying to pretend that it wasn't painful.

"You'll get the pox off the old whore, if you 'aven't contracted it already. She's got a scar from being bitten by the Devil, under all her powder and paint," the soldier teased.

"Fuck off," said Mary.

"All right then, scrape it off and show the Vicar. We'll see then where the Devil bit you. Everyone knows. Don't they, Sergeant? 'E knows. She's got the Devil's 'oof on 'er cheek."

"That's right. That's got under your skin, as you might say, 'asn't it?" Mary was clearly stung by the ridicule.

Sergeant Chadwick continued to play at hunting for fugitive Luddites. He even tried to smell them out, holding the prostitute's most intimate clothing under his nose.

"We'll get the bastard! Come on, let's 'ave 'em—where's your love letters?"

"Love letters to a whore? You must be joking. *And* I can't read."

"Let's 'ave 'em! They're evidence. We're looking for a tall thin one who spells 'notorious' in a comical fashion."

"You couldn't read spelling if you saw it, Sergeant Chadwick."

"Yes, I can. I've written letters myself. And to the newspaper."

"No, you 'aven't. You got someone else to write it down. I know you, Mad Dick."

"So?"

"So what's the point of you seeing my letters, then? Go out and fight your battles like a man, instead of spying in a lady's correspondence."

The second private, a shy young man who was laughing to himself, searched quietly but more usefully through Mary's cupboards and wardrobes.

Sergeant Chadwick threw Mary's cloak onto the floor and began to dig into the chest. "Now, just look at this!" he said, dangling the watch. "What do you know about this, Vicar? How did you come by this, Mary the Scar? Not honestly, I'm sure o' that." He put it into his pocket. "Evidence! You might get 'ung for it, we never know our luck, do we?

"Your mind's nothing but a farmyard drain, Mary the Scar. A fuckin' sewer, in common parlance. If you don't want to go to Australia, you fuckin' Devil's spawn, I must warn you it'll go better with the judge if you 'and over all the evidence, and all your letters—"

The sergeant stopped dead. The shy private had found, hanging on the wardrobe rail, what appeared to be the leather tail of a giant mouse. He began to pull it out into the room. Sergeant Chadwick blushed and lost his words, then he began to shout. But before the private could be countermanded, he had dragged the whip, handle and all, onto the floor. The private began to crack the whip on the furniture and Mary, laughing, rolled on the bed.

"Look at our sarge! His face is as red as his tunic!" shouted the soldier.

"Attention, Company! It ain't no use looking for Luddites in a whore's room! They 'aven't enough spunk to know what to do with 'em. Out of 'ere, quick march! Quick, I said! Quick march!"

"That was a scare," Mor said.

"No, it wasn't. They were only clowning because they were in a whore'ouse. Trying to get what fun they can out of a dirty job that they 'ate as much as any Ludd does. If I'd said you were a parson, they wouldn't 'ave believed me. Mad Dick wouldn't arrest anyone. 'E's not on that side. They 'ad to pretend to be working, with 'B' in the 'ouse. 'E's the one to be careful of. Better keep out of 'is way. It's a good job 'e's looking for someone tall and thin. You'd never pass as a woman. We'd better get out of 'ere fast, though."

Mary left him to change, while she went to see Mrs. Rawdon.

"So the Lady Well one gave you the slip?" Mrs. Rawdon said. "Out of the window, Chadwick told me. He wasn't the thin one. But you shouldn't have let that happen. They were going to arrest him, more than once last night, only you took him off."

"I thought I'd give 'im 'is last rites. 'E said 'e'd die for 'em."

"What?"

" 'Is rights."

"You should have kept tight hold of him. He might have been in the raid. He could have been anything."

" 'E 'asn't got away, Mother! I've got 'im in my room right now. Don't you worry about that business. I've 'ad a message. I 'ave to see a senior officer in Oldham right now. This morning. I'll take 'im with me. 'And 'im over on a plate. Leave it to me, Mrs. Rawdon. I'll be away a while. Just send my trunk over. Make sure we leave without any trouble, so 'e won't suspect nothing."

Mary's trunk, laden with her clothes, silk throws, teapot, et cetera—the objects that were intended to transform the temporary rooms into which she was endlessly moving—and one or two of her "theatrical instruments" were to be sent later by traveler's cart. When she returned to the room, she placed her personal belongings, such as her cosmetics box, hairbrush, small leather purse for sheeps' bladders, and a tiny mirror, in Mor's bag. Their sharing of one bag struck him as being very intimate, like sharing a bed.

They left the whorehouse. Once out of its garish theatrical atmosphere, it was obvious how acclimatised Mary was to the artificial world she had left, and what an oddity she was in any other. But she was a confident oddity, despite the catcalls of the street. Mary understood herself perfectly, and had reconciled herself long ago. Born with a birthmark that made everyone regard her as a diabolical freak from the start of her life, and having to live out her beginnings in a narrow-minded, puritanical corner of Yorkshire, she could hardly have avoided some introspection. Her answer to her problems had been to escape and throw herself into strange ways of life as soon as she could, and to make herself at home among them. She would appear a slightly mad freak everywhere, except in a whorehouse—or a madhouse.

Mor, too, felt an oddity; his sense of freakishness springing from being in her company—he with his working-man-cum-schoolmaster appearance that was perfectly suited to walking out with a woman of Phoebe's sober appearance, but not with a fantasy such as Mary.

Dashing between showers, they climbed to the moorland that divided Yorkshire from Lancashire. Mor carried the bundle and Mary took the violin, sometimes sheltering it beneath her flapping cloak.

The stony, wet road shone before them like pewter as it crossed the open stretches of heather and whinberry, under the swiftly flying sky. Here they sheltered against a boulder, and there under a rowan that was tucked into a cleft formed by a stream. During the spells of fine weather, they dashed forward, laughing.

After an hour or two, when they had reached the watershed between the counties, the weather changed entirely. The storm showers were over. As they looked down a broad saddle of the hills, the meadows and enclosures of the Lancashire plain lay sunlit before them. One could even say that it was hot, where the slopes faced the sun. Yet the peaks had become touched with snow. Mor wondered where, in that plain, Edwin might be.

"What about that watch Sergeant Chadwick found?" he asked.

"Well, what about it?"

"He said you could be arrested."

"Poof! They'll not arrest me. That matter won't get any further, 'cos Chadwick'll want to sell it 'imself. I know Chadwick."

They had walked a further distance, when suddenly Mary stopped in the road and turned her face to him. She looked garish in the open air. It was so strikingly not her element.

"Kiss me!" she demanded.

There was no one around. As she was taller than he, he had to reach up. He closed his eyes and delivered a long, careful kiss. He did what he had never done with Phoebe: He searched with his tongue inside her mouth.

He opened his eyes to look into hers, as wide and expressionless as moons shining upon him. She had given herself in such a wholehearted fashion that her features had become blank in their entrancement. She had emptied herself into him, thrown herself into a well, lost her personality.

"What do you think of when you kiss me?" she asked.

He could not think how to answer her. He did not know how to express his deeper thoughts. Nor could he say how they were mixed with a dislike for the taste of the lip rouge left upon his tongue.

"You do love me, don't you?" she said.

"Yes."

"I want to tell you about my child," she said. "Not 'Arriet. Another one. It didn't die naturally. I 'ad to bury it in a well, for it was born without eyes, as well as without a father. It could never 'ave survived, especially in my way of life. Poor thing just screamed, so I 'ad to put earth in its mouth to stop it. What else could I do, More Grief? I was going mad with it. What do you think I could do with a blind baby? It was a girl as well. Couldn't 'ave been born with less fortune.

"So now you know my story that could get me 'ung. I 'ad to tell you about it. We can't betray one another now. We're like brother and sister . . . aren't we? It's a pact."

They walked on again, in silence. On all the hills, larks were rising, singing, and swooping.

"There's no bird builds so low, flies so high, and sings so sweetly," Mor said.

"Eh?"

"As a lark. My middle name's after them, 'Laverock.' The workhouse master called me that, because I loved to lie in the grass and heather watching them."

"That's what we are, More Grief. Building in the muck, but we can fly high and sing about it, can't we?

"There's something that draws us upwards,
There's something drags us down,
And that is what always keeps us
Between muck and a golden crown."

"Laverocklaverocklaverocklaverock . . ." Mor trilled, imitating the bird. "A lark can save its young threatened in the nest by carrying them to

safety in its claws. I've seen it 'appen. Imagine if I could do that for mine."

Soon, smiling both to themselves and at one another, safe in the possession of each other's secrets, they were descending to the village of Denshaw, which lay in a valley before Oldham.

They took ale at the inn near the church. The first dandelions of the year were in flower—not dents-de-lions, but powerful manes of lions; golden suns.

Here they shared the last of the salted beef and oat bread that Phoebe had sacrificed. The bread which Phoebe had shaped on the kitchen table, and which bore the impress of her hands, stunned him into silence. He tore off her handprints and pushed them down his throat. Piece by piece, he was swallowing his marriage.

"What's wrong?" Mary asked.

He hesitated before speaking. " 'Ow did you bury a child in a well? Did you drown it?"

"That would 'ave poisoned the water and they'd 'ave found me out . . . Oh, don't ask me, I can't bear to think of it."

"Tell me. Please."

"After I choked it, I climbed down a ladder and hid the body in a cavity in the wall. A mason that 'ad repaired the well 'ad left the space on purpose for 'iding things. He was a clever fellow and wanted a secret or two 'e could blackmail us whores with in return for our services. 'E knew that every now and then one or other of us'd want to be rid of a baby. Oh, 'e ruled the roost, all right, just by putting a cavity in a well and telling a whore'ouse about it. Cock o' the yard with it. Slimy. It was a decent burial, though. I did bury 'er decently, Mor, honest I did! Six feet below the ground, but no signs to show . . . Worse things 'appen."

Mary's eyes glistened with tears.

They climbed one last hill, to Grain's Bar. Mor could taste the smoke rising up from the town beyond.

To reach Oldham, they dropped through Greenacres, where the land was being enclosed for building mills. Unfinished walls were stretching upward onto the moorland. Groups of men were working at their far ends.

Spread in the other direction was a dirty landscape of cotton-spinning mills, made of brick, on the Lancashire side of the hills. Most of them were driven by steam engines, and had tall, slender chimneys, which even on a Saturday afternoon were spouting little twists of smoke. The beam engines *tump-tumped* like so many frogs. Collieries and slag heaps were scattered amongst them. The old gray-stone church and the brick or stone buildings of the old town rose in their midst, with Oldham Edge behind.

They passed through the tollgate at Water Sheddings. By the time they reached Mumps, the great brick mills of Oldham were towering over them. The smoke was now bitter in their throats.

"That's Mr. Lees' mill," Mary informed him. "Over there, that's Mr. Hilton's factory."

She knew the owners of all the factories and entertained him, not with information about their beam engines, but about their mistresses.

They climbed up Yorkshire Street, toward the church. At the side of the churchyard was a three-story inn, the George. Today was market day, and the brightly tented stalls, cream-colored or striped, spilled down the cramped road, up to the door of the George, like a flotilla of small sailing craft around a mother vessel.

Mary led Mor straight into the George, through the grand doors. Under the fanlight, which had the "red rose of Lancashire" etched on it, they entered a lobby full of merchants. They were dressed in tall hats, finest-quality woollen suits, and shining top boots. The yard, visible through a large polished window to the rear, was busy with grooms, well-brushed horses, and shining equipages.

"Why, there's Mr. Sam Lees!" Mary exclaimed. "He turned the old corn mill at Water'ead into a cotton mill and made a fortune out of it. The way 'e spends it! Oh, dearie me!"

Mary was no more shy about her exotic appearance than an actress would have been on braving the candlelight of a stage. Things altered when she came into a room. People left one group and went to another. They halted their conversations to take account of her, struggling for anchorages in an unexpected storm.

The couple had no sooner left their hand luggage with the porter than a gentleman made his way toward them. He was small and plump—no doubt from a lifetime of feeding on beef, Mor thought enviously. The man was himself like a rare-cooked steak, red, juicy, and tender. Everything about him was baby-like—his gurgling laugh, his bobbing head, and his glances of apprehensive dependence, like a child with an unreliable mother or nanny, toward Mary. For no reason that Mor could understand the man was in a nervous sweat, which glistened upon his forehead and cheeks like warm grease. His dark thinning hair, and his palms when he waved them excitedly, shone with perspiration. His eyes were continually shifting, not only over Mary but also over the whole room, in a hungry fashion, and with an appetite, whatever it was for, that could never be satisfied. His eyes seemed shaped by this nervous habit. They were narrow and elongated, as though the pupils from so much swiveling from side to side had stretched their sockets.

"Nibbles!" Mary exclaimed.

Although Mor was so repelled by Mary's acquaintance, she, seemingly unable to wait a moment for her gratification, held her arms out to clasp and hug him. He rolled into her embrace. In the press of the crowd, she bent his head to her bosom. From within the dark wool valleys of her cloak, between her breast and her armpit, he mumbled, "We're in luck, my dear."

"My naughty little boy! What have you been up to?"

So this, then, was her business in Oldham! Nothing more than a vulgar assignation with a factory owner! He had been deceived—betrayed with lies. It had taken her only a second to throw herself into the man's arms, and Mor had never seen a woman behave so passionately. Her whole mind and body were absorbed. She shut him out completely, as she gave away the riveted attention of her eyes and the swaying of her hips. Her long arms wrapped around the man's body. For a moment she seemed even to be offering the possibility of her pursed lips, despite what she had said in bed about never being kissed on the mouth.

The man was struggling to be free, lest he choke; lest he look too undignified before his colleagues.

"Look, Mary . . ."

"My child, my babe in arms! There, there . . ."

The very words she said to me! Mor felt himself thrown into a horrible pit. This was what it meant to associate with a whore: inconstancy, betrayal, and lies! He had not allowed for this and he could not bear it. He hated this stranger. He loathed him.

"Nibbles" removed his head from the folds of Mary's clothes and was caressing her shoulder, first with his pudgy butterfly of a hand, then with his lips, possessively and familiarly.

At last, she turned to Mor. "Nibbles, this is Oliver. Call him Oli."

Both Nibbles and Mor gave her a surprised look.

"But we've urgent matters to talk about," Nibbles said. "We must be private."

"It's all right. Oli's my brother. You can trust 'im same as me, no different. Oliver Wylde. Oli's in trading. 'E's taking 'is piece to sell in Manchester 'cos there's no business left in Yorkshire. It's the fault o' them dreadful Luddites. Oli, this is my friend, Mr. Emanuel Burton."

Mor offered his hand, but Nibbles wasn't interested.

"Are we to take tea?" Mary asked lightly.

Nibbles led them to a table, one that was neither too public nor too private to attract attention. He bounced ahead like a child in front of its mother, adventurous but staying within reach of protective arms, and every now and again looking back for approval.

Once they were seated, Nibbles must have felt more secure. He put on the display of a worldly man, and called the servant.

"We'll have our tea, and then we must retire privately to talk business," he said briskly.

"Nibbles," she answered softly. Then to Mor: "Oliver, Mr. Burton is a most eminent cotton goods manufacturer of Middleton, who 'as installed steam-driven machinery to drive 'is looms, despite the opposition of obstinate workmen. That takes bravery, p'raps more bravery than fighting in the Duke of Wellington's wars, Oli!"

"Oh, I hardly think so."

Nibbles was blushing.

"Don't be modest," she said.

When the servant had left, Mary confidently poured the tea and said, "I'll tell you something, Oli, about Mr. Burton if it won't make 'im blush. 'E's the best boy, I mean the best man, I ever 'ad. Honest, Oli, 'e was the one who taught me what love can mean."

"Oh, come, Mary. You can't really say . . . I always thought . . ."

Mr. Burton's shifting eyes, Mor noticed with pain, drifted constantly toward Mary's legs, which she was displaying beyond the edge of the table.

"Ah, but you're so sensitive. You're not a brute like some, and it does charm a lady." Her voice turned gentle. "Oh, the words you say! I don't know where you learned 'em all. You're a poet."

Mary was speaking loudly—too loud, at least for Mr. Burton, who was already embarrassed by Mor's presence. She could be heard at the next table.

"Oli, this is the gentleman who I told you could read out the Earl of Rochester's poems, reciting 'em beautiful. Beautiful!"

"You're interested in verses, sir?" Mor asked.

Mr. Burton failed to get a word in.

"You see 'ow I have to talk about you, Nibbles? You're my favorite of all my naughty boys, as I've always said. It's because you're a poet yourself. You say things lovely and it shows in the way you treat a lady and make her feel. And the things you can do with your 'ands . . . Oh, my!" Mary cooed, with doting eyes.

"You can't mean it?"

"Oh, I do, I do!"

Mr. Burton's blush deepened.

"So 'ow's 'Arriet, then?" Mary asked sharply.

"Harriet?"

"Now then, Nibbles, you naughty boy. My daughter, 'Arriet."

"Yes, of course! Your daughter."

" 'Ow is she? Still getting good reports for 'er 'arpsichord, is she? . . . Ooh, are we 'aving cakes as well? Sweetmeats! That's what I call a tea." Mary started gobbling and Mor followed suit.

Mr. Burton waited for the servant to leave before speaking. "Her studies are expensive, you know, and my fortune is not so great as all that."

"We can't allow ourselves to be 'indered by the malicious opponents of progress, can we, Nibbles? Look at Oli and me. I told you 'e's in the weaving business. Fleeing from those same insubordinate workers, them desperate men, who 'ave destroyed the trade in Yorkshire. We 'ave walked all over the moors to see you, for nothing'd stop us. If I was you I'd get the soldiers to bayonet them Luddites. Where's my brave boy, then? 'Bang bang bang,' them naughty boys is dead! A brave boy like you can do anything 'e wants. It's poor Nanny who's 'elpless. But a big boy like you . . ." She paused. "I'm thinking of taking 'Arriet away with me to Bristol.

"*Bristol,*" she repeated.

"An education's expensive . . . ," he murmured.

"To *Bristol.* I'll come to your 'ouse at Park Mount in Middleton and get 'er. A tobacco dealer who lives on White Ladies Row in Bristol wants me, wants us. What could please a mother's 'eart more? It's a long way to Bristol. 'E won't let me come back to give Nibbles what only I can give 'im, I know that. Thomas is that kind of man. Determined. 'E knows 'is own mind."

"There's no need to decide precipitately," he said. "If we could talk this matter through?"

"My gentleman's taking ship for Africa on the spring tide. Only waiting for the new moon, 'e tells me. What else can I do than go with 'im? What other chances does a poor woman 'ave? If 'Arriet and me go with 'im, 'e might decide not to bring us back to these shores again."

"I'm sure we can arrange something."

"I'll 'ave to come round for 'er, to Park Mount. I can't be sure when I can come, so if your wife's at 'ome . . ."

Mr. Burton was sweating. "I think that we should . . ."

" 'Ow's 'er French?"

"Capital, I believe."

"I think nothing's more important than French and the 'arpsichord, for seeing a lady through life. It'll open all doors. Shouldn't I know?"

Mr. Burton found himself once more enjoying Mary's hands. Perhaps he was forgiven. But, also, because of her silence he did not know if he was forgiven . . .

Mary left with Mr. Burton for another part of the inn.

"I'll only be an hour, Oli. You take a look at the market if you get bored. I'll find you there. Don't worry."

How could Mor not worry? He was suddenly alone with his thoughts, his apparent betrayal by the woman with whom he had fallen in love, with his bewilderment at where to look for Edwin, and his fear of what might be the outcome of his running away. He was worried about what he took to be suspicious eyes from all over the inn.

On a table nearby were newspapers and Mor grasped the opportunity to read his favorite, the *Leeds Mercury*. The April 11th issue reported the execution of nine food rioters at Caen in Normandy, with a comment that it demonstrated "the leniency shown under the British Constitution towards food rioters and machine-breakers, compared with the sanguinary courts of France." In a later edition, Mor read of riots in Manchester, where a baker's shop was raided; in Barnsley, against the high price of potatoes; in Sheffield, where workmen "came in a body" to the corn market and attacked the potato dealers before destroying "fire-locks, drums, uniforms and banners at the local militia's armaments depository"; in Stockport, where machinery for making calico shirting was destroyed and the manufacturer's house set on fire; in the market at Carlisle, where a pregnant young woman "was shot dead on the spot" by soldiers; in Cornwall, where the miners at Truro had risen up and compelled the market traders to sign an agreement to sell wheat at no more than 30 shillings per bushel; and in Ireland, where in County Cork three thousand people assembled to burn down a starch factory because it made use of potatoes that they, who were starving, could have eaten.

So Crawshaw had been right about this, at least—twenty or thirty places in the north had risen since the Rawfolds raid.

Where was there not a state of riot? Before he returned to Lady Well, the revolution would have occurred. He would go back to his home on a triumphal cart!

He read in the *Mercury* that the reward for the capture of machine breakers had risen since March from one hundred to one thousand guineas. But it would be ministers, generals, and judges who would be hanged! Somewhere, sometime, in the next few days, Mor would look through a window, down a street, or from the top of a hill and see the revolutionary people of England on the move. Who would be their leader? Sir Francis Burdett, perhaps? George Mellor, the cropper from Huddersfield? Henry Brougham? Someone would appear. Some final, all-powerful King Ludd.

Mor felt eyes piercing the news sheet. He looked up to find a soldier staring at him as if he had been doing so for quite a while.

"What are you reading about?" the soldier asked bluntly.

Before Mor could answer "I cannot read," the soldier boasted, "I don't need to, because I can see with my own eyes what's going on. You see that mud on my boots? That's from my ride from Huddersfield today, bringing intelligence. I was on duty at the court-martial of the soldier, I cannot name him 'comrade,' who refused to defend the Rawfolds mill. The coward refused to use 'is musket, 'because I might hit some of my brothers,' says the miserable traitor. I ask you! 'E 'ad been tampered with by the Ludds, o' course—a common weakness of our soldiery, so it 'as to be punished 'eavy, don't it? Three 'undred lashes!

'E won't survive the 'alf of it; which is as well, for the sentence is to be carried out in public at the scene of the crime itself, Tuesday next, because of the disgrace. Scum of the earth is Ludds and revolutionaries, ain't they? What do you think? They did a raid at Horsfalls in Lady Well on Thursday night. That's before it gets in your newspaper. Did you know about that?"

"I'm not interested in politics."

"Not interested in politics but you're reading a newspaper . . . ? You look scared, sir. If you're fearful at what we do to them Ludds, you should learn of 'ow we treated 'em in Spain! I'm freshly posted back from there. I've traveled, I can tell you. Seen all sorts. They're just like Ludds, them diegos—nothing but a load of scum. I've seen 'ow they live. O' course, we soldiers dwell in mud 'alf the time, but that's different. We're building an empire. But them diegos! Them Jimmies! Well, I tell you! Me and my mates strung one up on a tree. I've seen 'em garrotting priests for being Papists. I've seen more than once the corpses of a whole village piled on the ground. They paint the 'ouses white down there, and the blood was splashed red as roses on the walls. It's what they should do to these Luddites."

CHAPTER EIGHT

April 18th–20th

Mary had been led by Mr. Burton down a passage guarded by two privates with muskets, and into a wing of the inn that was entirely occupied by soldiers. He took her into a room as bare and unloved as a cell, with no more than a scratched table, several rickety chairs, a pack of cards on the windowsill, and the soldiers' counters for gambling. Tobacco smoke staled the atmosphere. Its bareness was ominous.

"Why did you bring your brother with you?"

"I told you, 'e's going to Manchester with 'is cloth."

"He hardly said a word."

"I'm the noisy one in our family."

"You get up to some strange business, Mary."

"Am I the only one? What's this new treat you've brought me to Oldham for, Nibbles? A friend of yours to be initiated into the Mysteries? I'm not interested. I want to know 'ow 'Arriet is."

"There's to be a meeting of radicals and machine breakers at Dean Moor near Manchester tomorrow."

"You mean they're not going to church? I'm surprised at 'em."

"I'd like you to be present at that meeting."

"And report to you what's going on? It'd be more than my life's worth."

"I already know what's 'going on,' as you so felicitously express it."

"Eh?"

"They'll be discussing their plans to destroy my mill and machinery, and if they should succeed in doing so I would not be insured against the loss, it being an act of 'riot and civil commotion.' I'd be reduced to beggary, Mary. Think what would happen to Harriet then—not to mention all your little presents. I want to take no chances. I want you firstly to discover what their plans are, but, much more important than that, I want you to use your fullest charms on the general. General Maitland has arrived to make a secret reconnoiter before he takes up his posting here. I'm going to introduce you to him. Use your wiles on him, this evening if possible and certainly not later than tomorrow after the Dean Moor meeting, and persuade him to take steps to forestall an attack upon my mills. That's what I want you to accomplish for me."

"General Maitland? Oh, no, I couldn't go before 'im! Who is 'e? Where's my indispensable? I'm leaving! That's more than I dare . . ." She paused, examining him. "What's it worth?"

"It's worth, to you, ten pounds."

She shivered. "This is a cold shop, this place. It gives me the shivers. Twenty, Nibbles. Not a penny less than twenty. It's a dirty business and I don't know as I'd enjoy this General Maitland's peculiarities. What's 'e like? 'E might want to do something that'll end me in the Rochdale Canal, and I've my daughter to think of."

"I'll give you ten pounds now and ten when the military effectively forestalls any risk to my mill and machinery. There's no need to be afraid. The general has already expressed his interest in meeting you."

"What's 'e like?"

"I can assure you there's nothing unusual . . ."

"Come on, you can't fool me. An officer wouldn't be looking for an old scarred hag like me unless I satisfied 'is peculiarities. He'd 'ave a virgin. What's 'e want?"

"Nothing you can't satisfy. You'll soften him, I'm sure. He's a stern man, regarded by his colleagues as eccentric, but if you do as he wishes I know he'll treat you kindly."

"And if I don't, I'll end up in a sack at the bottom of the canal. And maybe also if I do. I know 'is sort, the 'eccentric' kind. Give me the ten pounds now, then."

Mr. Burton was opening his purse.

"If I end up in the canal, I'll go down shouting lots of things about you, Nibbles, so you be careful, too. And I'll need my coiffure attended to."

"How did you guess?" asked Mr. Burton, surprised.

She didn't answer that. "I'm too cheap with my prices, that's my trouble," she said.

He had closed his purse, and the money lay on the table. At least with him she did not need to count it, and she scooped it up.

Mr. Burton was already prepared. He went to the door and called, whereupon a hairdresser appeared in minutes with his equipment. He busied himself with his art, while Mary and Mr. Burton argued; he wanted her hair done one way, she insisted it be raised under a headband, to display curls at the nape of her neck.

"I know what I'm talking about, Nibbles."

She was very insistent, and Mr. Burton, growing sweaty again as he anticipated his interview with the general, gave way.

A cavalry sergeant interrupted them. "You ready for King Tom, sir?"

He conducted them up a flight of stairs, along corridors, to a remote room on the top floor.

"Oh, I don't think I can face up to a general, Nibbles. I'm only a poor timid woman. I'm scared. If 'e's new 'ere, who knows what 'e'll be like? I'd got used to old Chippendale, I could manage 'im."

"Don't worry, my dear."

"Don't worry, don't worry!" she mimicked. "They've been telling me 'Don't worry' since I was born. They'll be saying it when I mount the scaffold."

" 'E's a character, is King Tom Maitland," interrupted the sergeant. "Full of surprises. After the French Revolution 'e led a secret expedition for the Royalists that somehow ended up in America and the West Indies. He was in Santo Domingo and surrendered Port-au-Prince to the black slave leader, Toussaint-Louverture. Don't remind 'im of that, by the way. A sore spot. Served on both sides of the world, 'as King Tom. Calcutta and Madras, Commander of Ceylon, then in the West Indies."

The sergeant clicked his heels, swung open a door, and stepped aside as Burton and Mary entered. The door was shut behind them.

Thick wood paneling and a layer of green baize over the door sealed off the noises of the inn. This room, too, was bare of ornament. The only thing on the walls was a mirror, positioned opposite the leather armchair in which General Maitland awaited them. Even during interviews and meetings, he liked to observe his resemblance to the Duke of Wellington. Around his jaw there was the same relaxed droop of flesh, like the haunches of a contented bull in a field—the Taurean features of a commander who has occupied his territory; similarly, too, in his upper face was the expression of big, dark, alert eyes, raised eyebrows, and a brisk haircut, signifying the other half of a soldier's nature—the readiness to be up and off, to take advantage and show initiative.

Mary could see that the course of the interview had been fixed before they came in. Mr. Burton collapsed into the only chair available, mopping his brow, leaving her standing where she could be surveyed and embarrassed on center stage.

Maitland paid no attention to either of them. He was one who made tactical use of remaining mute. When speech might be expected of him, he would maintain a silence of such unnerving power that people looked at him as if he had in fact spoken and said something profound, or alarming. Through awesome silences he communicated threats that were deeper than words.

Mary did not dare to speak, as she stood unconsciously scratching her face. Mr. Burton mopped his brow, afraid even to pant and bow in his usual manner. From outside could be heard the calls of the market: obscenities and jokes the general's guests dared not pay attention to.

The general at last looked up. "Have a brandy," he snapped at Mr. Burton, waving toward a sideboard to indicate he was to fetch brandy and glasses himself. "I'll have one, too."

He stared at Mr. Burton's soft hands around the glass, then turned his gaze on Mary. He did not return her smile. She was still scratching herself.

"You should have that face of yours attended to by an apothecary."

"It's nothing, sir. It's an itch that all the ladies get."

"It'll land you in the surgeon's hands. You use lead, don't you?"

"Yes, sir."

"Come here."

She stepped forward.

"Kneel down and open your mouth."

She did so.

With his fingers he pushed back her lips. "There's a blue line on your gum. You know what that means, don't you? Do you know what lead poisoning does to you?"

"No, sir."

"Paralysis. Can't digest. Bowels closed. Your skin'll go gray. You'll die a terrible death. And do you know what comes of that mercury rouge that you use?"

"No, sir. We can't afford to care, sir." She stood up again and moved away.

"Stomatitis. No one'll go near you because of your bad breath, and that'll be a blessing for my men, won't it? Madness. Every woman who uses mercuric sulfide goes a bit strange—it's the coming madness. Like the hatters of this drab and lunatic town. It's the mercury they use in their trade. You're a bit of a strange case already, aren't you? You'll get the tremors. Your hands are shaking now."

"No, sir, that's because I'm . . ."

"You women would be well advised to pay a visit to a dispensary, before you commence your business. Why don't you use natural cosmetics? That's what the ladies of London and Edinburgh are turning to these days. Sour milk or horseradish makes a fair skin, I believe. Lemon is good, too. You could use chalk as a whitener instead of lead, and cochineal for a rouge. That's the safe thing for a lady to do."

"They're expensive. We can't get them. We don't think they're as good as the old ways, sir."

"The only cure for you now, madam, is to drink sulphuric acid, two and a half ounces to a gallon of water, like they give to the lead miners of Derbyshire. Otherwise you can count yourself a dead woman.

"You see what I have to concern myself with, Burton? I have to be a whore doctor as well as a commander and a spy on behalf of the Government and who knows what else, otherwise my men are riddled with disease. Sedition is as rife amongst them as disease, already.

"Which brings us to the subject of your letter, doesn't it? Our men are, as you say, 'singularly ineffective in arresting the troublemakers' in your mill. Something is going wrong, as you say. What is it, then? Now I'm here, and about to bring another seven thousand men along with me, what shall I do? Do you think, for instance, that we might become more effective through erecting communal barracks for the soldiers, instead of quartering them around the inns of the countryside? In barracks they would be safely away from the attention of disaffected radicals and diseased whores. Perhaps Mr. Pitt, in not giving Oldham a barracks, made a mistake."

Mary smiled, but dared not laugh openly.

"Lodged in public houses, my soldiers come into daily contact with the populace. Are you aware of what happened recently in the defense of Mr. Cartwright's mill at Rawfolds in Huddersfield? A disaffected private refused to 'fire upon my countrymen,' as he put it, and he has perforce to be delivered up to an exemplary sentence. To a vicious flogging. None of us wants to hand out that sort of punishment anymore, but one has to put an end to this business. It is most distasteful, Burton, to be firing at one's own countrymen when there are enemies abroad to be shot at."

"It seems to me, General, that rather than putting ourselves to the expense of erecting permanent buildings for a temporary force—"

"Temporary force!" The general slapped his palm upon the table. "I wish it was, but it seems to me that as usual in these circumstances we bring in a few soldiers for a week but are soon compelled to pour in more and more troops and establish a garrison for a lifetime. Look what we have to do in India. In Ireland. In the West Indies. As if you manufacturers don't know we've a war to fight overseas. What will happen to your Lancashire if we lose our battles against Napoleon? You are sapping our strength."

"We are threatened with revolution, General. There will be no point in fighting Napoleon, if we are to have a Bastille Day at home."

"I'm most annoyed with you, Burton. You and all your kind. But never mind! Never mind!" He clapped his hands impatiently and it sounded like gunshots. "Tell me more about your proposal. It sounds most interesting. You suggest that this woman inform us about the forthcoming meeting at Dean Moor?"

"Dean Moor is near Manchester . . ."

"I know where Dean Moor is," General Maitland said testily.

Mr. Burton had to screw up his courage to continue. "I'd like to learn the scale and date of the planned attack, an estimate of how much military assistance will therefore be necessary, and how much can be counted on, to support my own tiny band of sixteen defenders of my mills. Chippendale, our captain of militia, suggested I put it to you."

"Ah, yes, at least you are trying. I'll give you credit for that, instead of always shouting for cavalry—you who have never seen what a cavalry charge does to its victims. Someone ought to show you mill masters over the field after a battle. Show you what you propose we do to your own countrymen. And you want this woman to apprise herself of the situation and persuade me to take the action you would like to see taken? Because I am fresh to Lancashire, you intend to be the first of the mill-owning brethren to come to me with your complaints? To influence me? That's what's in your mind, isn't it?

"I'll tell you what the root of this matter is, Mr. Burton. The price of food has trebled, whilst wages have fallen in the same ratio to that in which provisions have risen. What would you expect a weaver to do for his starving children? Lie down and die?

"Pay decent wages, Burton. You can afford it, and your devil, King Ludd, will be dead tomorrow. What you have done by bringing us into the northern counties is to leave us with the fear of an army rebellion on our hands, dammit!

"When my new force arrives there will be twelve thousand regular soldiers in the north. Plus militia. Wellington took only ten thousand to Spain. Yet what arrests do we make? The villages are tight, they will tell us nothing. Children spit at the cavalry. We offer large rewards to starving people, but no one collects them.

"Pay proper wages, Burton, and you'll have no need of soldiery. It doesn't need a philosopher to see that. I speak only as a man of practical affairs, not as a democrat. For, by God, if I have to put a revolution down, I will."

"In cases of civil commotion we have no insurance for our properties, that is why we need defense . . . cavalry," Mr. Burton said.

"You didn't take in a thing I told you. Why don't you steady yourself with a drink downstairs, Burton, whilst I talk to the woman?"

Mary wanted to cheer.

The general behaved as if the lowly man of commerce had already left, and he concentrated upon pouring, for himself only, another glass of brandy.

When Burton had gone from the room, the general rested his hands behind his head and smiled at Mary, who now lost all of her apparent timidity.

" 'E's not much of a man, is 'e, that Burton?" she said, smiling back. "Give us a drink! I've walked 'ere all the way."

"A wet and dismal journey too, I'll be bound. This is a dreary country. I'm used to hot places. I'd die of rheumatism if I stayed here for long, so I intend it to be a short posting. You mark my words, we'll be hanging them for Christmas. Where's the nearest spa?"

"That at Upper Spout's quite good."

"Where?"

"On second thought, I don't suppose it'll do for a gentleman such as yourself. It's just a sulphur spring coming out o' the ground."

"That they decorate with flowers on May Day? And cast spells?"

"Yes. As a matter of fact, they do."

"This is a barbaric part of England. I want somewhere where I can dance. Where there are ladies. Decent young men, too. It'll have to be Buxton or Harrogate, I suppose. I'll take up my headquarters in Manchester, I think. If this business takes more than a month, I'll move to Buxton. I'll be damned if I'm staying long in this wild, wet place. It'd kill me."

Mary boldly helped herself to a drink, using Mr. Burton's empty glass. Then she went around the table and sat on the general's knee, giving him the opportunity to fondle the curls at the base of her neck.

"King Tom!" she murmured.

"How's Mrs. Rawdon? Has she brought all of her establishment northward with her?"

"Only a few of the girls, and not all of our implements. Imagine them dropping off a cart."

King Tom laughed.

"Not 'er 'arpsichord, neither. I remember 'ow you used to play Clem- . . . Clem- . . ."

"Clementi. Mozart, too."

"When you came to us in London."

"Delightful pieces, some of 'em."

"All the girls loved it. Loved your coming. We all remember."

King Tom smiled at himself in the mirror. Mary filled his glass, while he hung on to her curls, sipped and relaxed.

"I'm glad you sent us up 'ere. Back 'ome," she said.

"All part of the grand plan. My force will soon be here for you. Have you found anything out for us yet?"

"I've only 'ad a few weeks, General! I 'eard that someone 'ad damned the King. The Ludds threw a corporal into the Rochdale Canal, 'cos 'e wouldn't join with machine breakers. I don't think 'e 'ad any more of a mind to join 'em when 'e came out than when they threw 'im in."

"You have reported the matter?"

"I think 'is officer already knew."

"These Luddites travel. Our intelligence is that a great deal of trouble spread outward from Yorkshire. That's why you're based there. You should have found something out by now."

"I'm trying."

"Well, you can forget about going to Dean Moor to satisfy Burton. I don't want you there, attracting attention, Mary the Scar. I've my own men amongst the rebels to play their part in their decision-making. I want you for something that I know you're good at. Causing trouble. You are to provoke a few scenes when they raid Burton's mill. They'll probably decide to go there on Monday. It'll certainly be next week. No matter what Burton expects, there won't be any soldiers to defend it, but we'll turn up afterward. These damned machine breakers have had it their own way for six months now, it's worth sacrificing Burton's to catch them. If they put it out of commission, we might even find the working folk themselves turning against the machine wreckers, for taking away their employment. We'll come along afterward and have an excuse to hang a few of the ringleaders. Then we can all go home. My commission will be over before it's properly started. That's my plan. Your business is to provoke 'em to as much damage as you can make 'em do. Make sure they do enough damage . . ."

"Or I'll end up in a sack in the canal."

"We could hang you."

When she didn't laugh, "Forgive me my humor," he added. "But I *shall* have my own way, Mary, and quickly! You know that. As well as a report on you from a mason about a child buried in a well, there's your thieving. The cutlery, watches, and clothing you've stolen over the years. You'll go too far with it one of these days, you lunatic woman! The civil authorities will catch you, and it'll be too much for us to save you. You'll be swinging outside Lancaster Castle, and not even have the good fortune to die of paralysis and insanity in a bed in the Bethlehem Hospital. Mrs. Rawdon's not expecting you back, is she?"

"I've cleared it with 'er already. I knew you'd want me for something. But I need a safe and secret place to live in 'ereabouts, General. With my brother. I can't be a 'Luddite' and live in a soldiers' whore'ouse, can I? I need a place, and my things delivered there tonight. They're with the porter at the moment. Also my trunk will be arriving 'ere soon. I'd be obliged if you'll send it on with a big strong lad."

"Leave your face alone, madam! I tell you, that face of yours will land you on a surgeon's dissecting table. According to our reports, you're twenty-four years of age. You look thirty already."

She left off scratching her cheek and looked at the general with moist eyes. "Please promise me 'e'll be safe."

"Who?"

"My brother."

"Why? What side of the law is your brother on? Thief? Pimp? Poacher? Murderer?"

"It's not that. We need to stay together. 'E's ill, and needs me. The surgeon says 'e 'asn't long to live. 'Is 'eart is suffering. We can't be parted. Promise me we'll be left safely together." She knelt and rested her cheek against his thigh. "Promise me!"

The general filled Mary's glass to the brim. "Bottoms up," he said, and watched her raise the glass. He wanted to see if her hand was shaking. It was not.

"I promise. We're not interested in him, but in how you behave yourself. We'll find you a hovel to hide in. But mismanage things and I promise you that your brother won't be safe, either. We'll have the pair of you on the gallows."

His thick fingers were raking through her curls. They began to reach into her clothing. "Mmm . . ."

"You're a man, King Tom. So when are you wanting me to come to you again?"

"After the raid. Make sure you keep in touch. We don't want any of your disappearing tricks. You keep going at your business. Make sure you sleep with as many as you can. Non-commissioned officers especially. Or rather, make sure you don't sleep." He chuckled at his joke. "This is an important time. Do you understand me? We'll pay you next time we see you."

"Promise me another thing," she said.

"Something else?"

"If your soldiers find a child, a boy of nine, wandering the hills or towns, saying 'e's looking for Liverpool, will you tell me? Name of Edwin Greave. From Lady Well."

Mor left the inn and wandered around the market for a time, until he was brought up suddenly.

Twenty yards away, head and shoulders above the crowd, was Mary, alone, her back to him as she strolled among the stalls, the baskets, and the litter of the market.

Her hair had been fashioned into a high pile of ringlets. For him? He lost all the anger he had been storing up against her. Gratitude and joy made him want to rush up and kiss her.

But he saw her take an apple from a stall without paying for it and calmly slip it into her dress. His impulse to kiss her vanished and his eyes darted from her to the stall-holder. Fortunately, this person was staring, with simple-minded engrossment and pleasure, her hands lapped comfortably under her apron, at a scene on the other side of the street.

Mor secretively, with fear and shame, followed ten yards behind. The next stall at which Mary paused was one selling lace. Mats and handkerchiefs were strung under an awning and displayed on tables. The stall-holder was occupied in packing away his goods. Mary took a lace mat and slipped this, too, into her clothes. It was only Mor who looked anxiously toward the stall-holder—Mary did not bother to glance at him. Farther on, she collected a pair of shoes.

She also surveyed the passing men, showing a bold interest in the bulges of their trousers. A professional habit? Surely, after what she had said about love, it must be no more than that. Some of them gave her a brief touch as they went by. They were still laughing and making jokes about the harlot as they passed Mor.

In fear and panic he ran toward her, wanting to say so much and yet speechless, his mouth stopped by the vision of the pair of them swinging on a gallows.

When he caught up with her, she smiled and gave him the apple. He could not eat it. He felt that it would choke him. She did not seem to notice.

"I found a room," she told him sweetly.

"Stolen?" he said viciously. "Or is it a gift from Mr. Burton?"

Her manner changed completely. She behaved as one who has been needlessly hurt. And she was flustered, for once. Irrationally angry. "Stolen from no one! People owe me favors! I'm not a—" She was drowning, struggling to explain the inexplicable, with tears in her eyes "—filthy Luddite!"

It was too late to bite her tongue.

It numbed him. He even lost interest in looking out for pursuers. "I thought you believed in our cause," he said desolately.

She tossed her head of new curls. They walked on in silence. She had hardened herself within a shell of self-righteousness. She had that cutting, confident smile of a woman who is used to getting the better of men, with her sharp tongue and the situations she creates.

Excited, noisy deals were taking place on either hand. Pigs were squealing, hens squawking, people laughing, yet Mor's and Mary's seemed the only, lonely, steps in an emptied universe. He longed to take a leap off this sterile, cold planet they now inhabited and join those others, but their argument stuck to them like shipwright's glue. She longed to remove the stain of her words.

Mary tried to placate him. "It's a nice little room in a cellar. It belongs to a cobbler who must leave it, if you must know, because 'e's been spying for 'Is Majesty's forces and 'as now been found out by some radicals who will send 'im to 'is Maker when they catch 'im. It 'asn't anything to do with Mr. Burton, More Grief. It 'as entrances on different streets, so we'll be safe, and not get trapped."

He wondered how he would ever disentangle her lies from the truth.

She stopped in her tracks so suddenly that a boy with a tray of loaves ran into her. "I believe you're jealous! You can't be jealous with a whore!" She pulled a sheet of paper from the caverns of her underclothes. "Read it! Go on! It's a letter from Emanuel Burton."

I dream of when I shall draw your shift from the snowy mounds of your breasts! he read. *From your skin softer than the down of swans and scented like the spices of India! Your eyes that dart a million piercing arrows! I think of you as a being of another order. As a goddess! I worship you with every breath! As the living sun!* He could read no further.

"That's what Mr. Burton thinks of me."

"You told me that you couldn't read."

"I didn't need to. 'E sat on my bed and read it aloud to me, a dozen times, then 'e give it to me to keep. It means nothing, nothing at all. Listen! 'E carries everywhere with 'im a pocket guide to the pleasure gardens and gin palaces of London. It 'as a condom tucked into the flyleaf, and a whole chapter on 'ow to avoid syphilis and paralysis of the insane. But that means nothing either. Why? 'Cos 'e never comes anywhere near me. 'E can't get it up! 'E can't do nothing at all, so you've nothing to fear from 'im. But if you don't like using 'is money, of which 'e's got too much and, as you said yourself, 'as taken it from the sweat of the poor, then you can fuck off and get yourself 'ung instead. You should be grateful for what I do for you." Tears stung her eyes. "I want a man with some boldness in his nature. It's a pity you was never a soldier."

After all she had said about the military! He looked at her in amazement. "All right! But I was watching you at the farmer's stall—what about that?"

"Have a bite of apple, sweetheart," she said softly.

"I don't want it."

"Why not?"

"It would. . ." It would choke him.

"Why not?" she repeated in a maddening, victorious tone.

He wanted to believe that she was not a thief.

"Why were you hiding it?"

"I wasn't 'iding it."

"Then why was it inside your clothes?"

"It wasn't in my clothes."

"Then where've I seen you bring it out from, then?" he shouted.

His exasperation had the effect of calming her. "A lady 'as to put her things somewhere, doesn't she?"

"You've a lace mat in there as well, and a pair of shoes."

"What nonsense you talk."

"Well, show me and prove your case."

"Don't talk to me like a judge accusing a common whore."

She was trying to sulk, but it wasn't natural or easy for her.

Her grip of her gown loosened and the pair of shoes fell to the ground. She snatched them up and slipped them under her arm.

"Where are those from?"

"Is it any business of yours what I do with my earnings? I'm nothing but a common whore anyway, why do you care?"

She was crying, but he didn't know whether to believe in her tears or not.

"You stole them," he said grimly.

"I'm not a thief!"

"Can't you see how you're risking bringing us before the magistrates? That you're deliberately courting the gallows?"

"Leave me to my whoring, then, if you don't have no stomach for nothing."

He remembered how earlier they had loved one another. "You stole those shoes."

"I didn't."

"You did."

"And you told me you were going to catch 'ares and trouts for us. So what's the difference? Left to you, I think we'd starve."

"The difference is, to be secretive, not ask for the hangman to come and fetch us."

A pause. "I don't want the fucking shoes anyway. I don't need them. I've plenty of money!"

A pair of new shoes flashed through the last light of the afternoon, as Mary flung them high across the market, anywhere so that they'd be away from her. Sailing over the heads of the crowd, one shoe hit a pyramid of turnips, which tumbled and destroyed some carefully built piles of potatoes, carrots, onions, and leeks; the other struck a fishmonger on the shoulder.

"It's a riot! Lady Ludd's coming! It's a food riot!"

To the women who had been arguing with the stall-holders about their prices, to the poor and hungry females who likely enough would be beaten by their husbands if they came home empty-handed, the flying shoes were the signal to commence battle.

A housewife with the physique of an Irish navvy flung one of the turnips. It, too, struck the fishmonger, this time on the forehead. Frightened, he crouched behind his stall.

His cowardice inspired the women further. Mary, grasping the opportunity of this diversion, sprang to the head of the mob, leading them to tip offal and a barrel of salted herring onto the fishmonger. None of the other stall-holders helped their comrade, in case it drew the fury of the women upon themselves. But, as with the fishmonger, cowardice did not help them. When one tried to sneak away to rouse the authorities, the women tipped him into his barrel of oats, nearly suffocating him.

More and more women joined in the havoc. Mary and Mor in the lead, they advanced between the stalls. Cottons and calicoes were ripped into shreds. The women filled their baskets. One stuffed a couple of fish into her bosom.

To add to the chaos, Mary let a crate of hens loose. She released some geese and sent them flapping through the street. Finally she unfastened the cages of wild birds, letting surprised goldfinches and larks escape toward Oldham Edge and the moors, their wings, as they escaped over the housetops, glittering like shattered glass in the last of the sun.

At last a sniggering band of Oldham Volunteers arrived, but they could not take fighting a marketful of women seriously. The soldiers were smiling, blowing kisses, and wishing that their own women would start riots and get vegetables, meat, and fish, instead of "robbing" their pay to feed themselves and bring up babies. Eventually, they made a brisk but good-humored charge. "Whoops!" "Ooh!" "Oh, dear!" the soldiers yelled, trying to frighten the rioters but not harming or arresting anyone.

"*Don't worry!*" Mary found the breath to say, as they all ran away. "Don't worry, Mor! Trust me!"

Out of the dispersing crowd, she led him uphill, through the back ways where the handlooms clattered on the north side of the market, up to Oldham Edge. Eventually she paused at a Baptist chapel which had a grandiose front facing south across the valley. To the rear of the chapel was a narrow yard set against an earthen bank; here was the spring that filled the Baptists' tank. It was a hidden place, and indeed somewhere to be ashamed of, dark, muddy, and filled with rubbish. It was shortly before nightfall and already darkness had gathered there, among the dripping ferns.

"I'm sorry for what I said about . . . about . . . I can't say it again . . . about the Luddites, More Grief."

They embraced, then they washed themselves and drank from the baptismal water.

Her hair fell out of its band as she stooped, and Mor noticed that where the henna was wearing away it showed black patches.

The spring also filled a trough for a row of cottages lower down the hill. They slipped out of the yard and made their way toward the houses. The cellars were built into the wet bank, reached by stone stairs also cut out of the bank. At the foot of the stairs, they came to a patched door that had a piece of rope dangling through a hole, to raise the latch.

The dark cellar smelled of moistness and wet cinders. Their eyes were drawn to the only source of light, a window at the far side, through which, in the last silver gleam of evening, a view of a lane was still distinguishable. Eventually they were able to pick out the sight of a straw bed and rough blankets, a few chairs, and a fireplace with an untidy litter of damp kindling and logs beside it. The floor and ceiling were made of large flagstones, and the walls constructed of brick.

There Mor saw his fiddle and his bundle waiting for him. "But how . . . ?"

"I told you, I can arrange things. I can, if you'll only trust me! And I'll find your child for you, don't worry. Forget what I said, please, More Grief. Promise me you can love a whore, promise me! I'm sorry about the market, and I've no need to thieve. I'll not do it anymore. It was only out of 'abit. I'll stop now, I promise. I couldn't admit the truth then, because you confused me."

"*I* confused *you?*"

She seemed unaware of the lies she told about herself; the confusion about what she was really doing with Mr. Burton; the lie which was her whole appearance. Her red hair was in fact black. She really seemed to believe that lies were truth. Was she as mad as that?

"Yes, I was thrown off my balance. But I've found us this 'ome, 'aven't I? People are in my debt. Don't worry about it, and the next thing my friends'll find is your Edwin."

What was the point of worrying? What choices did he have?

He set about lighting a fire with the kindling, taking tinder and flint from his bag. Of course she wouldn't find Edwin.

"What is it you're up to with Mr. Burton?" he asked.

" 'E's useful to me, that's all. I've got 'im where I want 'im. 'E's frightened of me turning up at his 'ome to claim 'Arriet. O' course, I wouldn't do such a thing. 'Ow could she be better off with me, than where she is? But 'e's scared of me turning up, 'cos 'is wife 'as adopted 'Arriet, and 'e thinks I don't know. What a row there'd be if 'is Lisette found a whore trying to claim 'er daughter! Burton's scared stiff of 'is wife. The funny thing is, Burton thinks 'e 'as an 'old on me. You shouldn't inquire into these things—just leave it all to me."

"What color is your hair?" he asked.

"Red. Why?"

"Oh, nothing."

"Why do you ask?"

"It doesn't matter. It's nothing . . . nothing at all."

The flames played upon the black chimney, and, full of pattern and life, upon the crumbling, blistered, cracked walls of the chimney, while darkness settled outside.

From out of his bag, Mor took his stone and placed it on the hearth. The oval pebble glittered with small stars which changed as it moved. It was like the twinkling of a whole universe at night.

"What's that?"

"Something I like to carry with me."

"You're mad, More Grief."

They both fell asleep instantly on the damp straw bed.

During the night Mor awoke to the delight of finding, not the leaden thoughts of wrong, injustice, and misery that usually woke him, but the presence of a naked woman.

His wakefulness awoke her. In fact the mere stirring of his eyelids seemed to awake her—she was as responsive as that to his body. Her hands and legs gently explored him. They cuddled, she burrowing her head in the nest of his shoulders. They kissed and called each other "love." To be happy was . . .

"A flower growing on a dung heap," he whispered.

"What's that, More Grief?"

"I said we've grown a flower upon a dung heap."

"I'd like to be with you, all the time, anywhere, oh anywhere on earth, just to touch you from time to time. To be with you. 'Ow's this 'appened? 'Ow on earth's it 'appened?"

He comes into me so shy, thinks he's no right to a woman, she thought. *I'll cure that. It's charming. I'm grateful. But* . . .

She was determined that there would be more.

"Forget all about it's me here, More Grief. I'm just a woman. I'm just *your* woman. Think of yourself, only yourself. Forget me! Forget me!"

It made him even more self-conscious.

"Kiss me!"

He felt all her body opening to him. She was showing him how to explore her. For the first time, he discovered his own body. Her movements drowned him. She was all over him, in a light net of surprises, showing him fresh things, leaping at him with little bites, digging her nails into his shoulder blades. She was searching for anything that he had not yet expressed. Things which she sprang upon him as her own caprices were responses to gratify what he had shown her about himself, unknowingly. Tempting words flew by, randomly, like migrating birds. He found himself calling out to her from his deepest, most inaccessible part, from the pit of his throat. He had never done such a thing before. It was a sound he had never made. He let out several such calls, hardly knowing that he was doing it, each progressively louder. Lifting his head back, he was an ecstatic animal baying.

No client had ever done this to her. When they had finished, she lay on her side, humming with contentment, Mor curled against her back. Inside her, she felt a warm bath of semen. The heat ran all through her body, right up to her heart.

He knew that her body belonged to him. He had never known until now how a woman's contentment could ooze through her every touch.

They slept, but awoke quite soon. The ashes had ceased to glow in the grate. A single, huge star bejeweled the window, and as Mor turned his head, the metallic blue planet changed its shape in the warped glass, ran quick as mercury, then twisted off in the other direction.

In the half-conscious seconds before he was properly awake, he called out, "Phoebe." The two whispered syllables sounded like the weak calls of a small bird in a hedge at twilight, so he hoped she had not heard him, or that she had even mistaken what he said for "Mary." He felt ashamed.

Mary heard him, but did not reply. She was used to men calling her by the names of other women.

The dampness of the bed had caused an ache in his back. He turned on his side to ease it, and felt Mary's limbs. He ran his fingers over a thigh as smoothly cold as marble, and he tried to warm her legs between his own; worried about her; but she kept on sleeping. Or half-sleeping. She was muttering something, out of a dream, before she disappeared into it again.

It was still dark, yet he heard a cock crowing, on a roof or a hilltop where it caught the rising light.

Then a robin was singing and people were stirring.

The sun hit the lane. Shadows were passing by the window. Boots and clogs, some tipped with iron, rang upon the stones, not with that clockwork sound of workers forcing themselves to the factory, but with the more haphazard noises of people in the enjoyable hours before they had to go to church. "It is Sunday, it is Sunday!" the clogs were singing.

Mor rose, shivering. He wiped a patch of dirt from the window and took a look out. The villagers were going forth for a jug of milk, to relieve their bladders after last night's drinking, or to release their hens and collect the eggs from the little crofts that still survived among the mills and collieries.

The family that lived above the cellar was making a happy noise, too. A man was clattering bits of wood. Cheerful and un-Sabbathlike, he was presumably knocking together something for his family, on his holiday.

Mor returned to the bed. The lovers dozed once more, back to back. Yet they awoke in each other's arms, not to make love, but to enjoy the feeling of being fulfilled.

Mary knew what he was thinking. "What color are 'is eyes?" she asked.

Mor smiled. "Blue."

"I'll tell all my friends, don't worry. The soldiers'll find him."

"Soldiers!"

"There's nothing to be frightened of. I pretended it was me who 'ad lost a child that was making for Liverpool, not you. A mother'd know what color 'er son's eyes are, wouldn't she? So I'll tell them, they're as blue as a thrush's egg."

"No, they're blue-green, more like a blackbird's. Not a piercing color, but a more thoughtful gray-blue."

"I'll tell them all that. What I can understand of it. I can talk most poetical when I choose, you must have noticed?"

He kissed her.

"You don't believe me, I can see," she challenged him, laughing.

"I do. I must find him and take him home."

They slept again, their mouths lightly touching.

Mor had never in his life been able to indulge this lovers' pleasure of waking and sleeping, on and off through the night. When he finally arose, it was late into the morning, and to the sound of church bells. Outside in the lane, shadowy figures, like wind-blown leaves, were weaving their own familiar patterns, to which the two fugitives were strangers. It made Mor feel bound more closely to Mary. He lit a fire in the grate.

"There's a chaffinch singing!" he told her. He pointed it out as he would have done for Edwin, or anyone else he was fond of.

"That bird, you mean?" She turned to sleep again.

"No, listen! Listen to it. Listen to its music! More coarse than the willow warbler, but similar, and still beautiful, in a different way."

"I thought it was just a bird."

But she listened; and also to the crackle of Mor's newly lit fire.

"When I was a boy, I used to wander the moors on Sunday, listening to the bells in the valleys. All the people were down below, bowing and whining in church, and there I was, picking whinberries, catching trout, reading a book if I 'ad one. I used to lie in 'ollows where no one could see me. I feel just the same now. I've escaped! Though Monday'll come, I know. I'll 'ave to go back in the end."

" 'Ow do you know that?"

"You always end up back at your work."

"Oh, do you now?"

There was a stone sink and a bucket of water, brackish but it would do for washing.

When he looked at her again after washing himself, she seemed to be sulking. He had forgotten what he had just said.

"What's wrong?"

"Nothing."

As he could not guess, he ignored it.

Outside, people were going to their various churches. Girls in their best dresses were in hope of making passes at the lads. The boys were ogling the girls, whom they only saw on Sundays. Old ladies thought of meeting a sister, a son or a daughter from over the hill, and men of a deal to make en route to the church. But they were isolated in their sects. Methodists would not speak to Baptists, who would not murmur a word to Anglicans, who would impale or burn Papists if they could. The members of one denomination would not so much as pass the time of day with another, even if they lived next door. They moved through a place that was filling up with mills and smokestacks. This was transforming their lives, yet they were more interested in the trivial points of doctrine that divided them.

Mary rose at last, shaking herself like a bird in a dust bath. She hunted through Mor's bag for her belongings. She lifted out her cosmetic box, hairbrush, and hand mirror. She renewed her appearance, smearing on the white paint with her sponge, touching up her cheeks and lips with a sable brush dipped in a porcelain bowl of mercuric sulphide. She plucked her eyebrows.

She saw him watching her, and was annoyed. "You always end up back at your work—as you said."

She took the bucket of water in which they had washed and, as self-assured as a housewife in her own home, she ascended the steps near the chapel. She flung the water into the street, narrowly missing the chapel-goers, who were already disgusted because she was emptying her slops on a Sunday, and because of her appearance. She went to the spring and refilled the bucket. She heard them singing hymns.

"Me, I live for the day," she said to Mor, back in the cellar. She spoke bitterly.

He still hadn't realized what he had said to anger her. The sight of the water, its surface glittering as it sloshed about in the bucket, made him happy. On this day, just as simple a thing as that made him happy.

Mary, from that other well, the deep recesses of her clothes, produced ham, beef, eggs, a rabbit, and a loaf of bread—all saved from the market on the previous day. She hunted through the cupboards and found cooking pots to set over the fire. Here for the first time in her life she was creating, not that display of illusions, a whore's stage set, but a home, a shelter for a man, though frugal and temporary. The birds and animals at this season were doing the same thing; the chaffinch at the window paused in its song to pick up a straw in its beak.

Mary was herself building a nest. This was the only way to keep him close to her. She would warm the egg until a new life chipped its way through the shell and flourished. No matter what she had said earlier, she would pay with any amount of thieving, lying, spying; any degree of compromise with the circumstances that were thrust upon her; and keep all that unshared in her heart, for the sake of the peace and happiness of a lover who had promised to love her forever, who had promised to keep his promise.

After they had eaten they leaned against each other, staring at the fire.

"Gawd, this is peaceful," she said. "I'm happy. Gawd, I'm happy."

Mor got up and was pacing about restlessly. "I wish I could look for Edwin."

She smiled. "Just sit here with me and stop worrying for a time. Do you think you'll find 'im? All you'll do is get yourself arrested. The soldiers are looking for the boy. They'll do much better than you, and they'll tell me when they've found 'im. Stay by the fire. Enjoy the peace."

"I don't know what I think of soldiers looking for 'im. What *are* you up to?"

"If it wasn't for me, you'd be in custody by now."

He became restless again.

"What are *you* doing?" she asked.

From the bottom of his bag Mor had produced his notebook and an ink bottle. He sharpened a quill, tipped the bottle on its side because it was nearly empty, and began to write with the notebook on his knee.

"What are you writing?"

"My thoughts, as they come to me."

She stood up to survey his busy scrawl in "The Beggar's Complaint." It reminded her of rows of black trees on a distant horizon, or of the shapes of hedgerows racing across the landscape, as she had seen them when traveling with the girls from London in that big, old-fashioned coach. She watched the quill entering the bottle, leaving it, and touching the paper. The people whom she had seen writing had mostly been magistrates, clerks, clergymen, and majors, who made a great display of it and who were mostly copying formulas. A handloom weaver—schoolmaster—author was a new phenomenon. She moved around the room in silence. She kept looking at him and biting her lip.

"Read me what you've written, then."

" 'These poor creatures whom God made and Christ redeemed were sent in multitudes to Spain and Portugal. Why is it, oh why is it, that all this slaughter should go on and no one show compassion for his fellow creatures, taken in their youth, led away in their simplicity and inexperience to be slaughtered with more cruelty than was ever practiced by butchers in a slaughterhouse . . .' "

"For Gawd's sake, stop! Is that what you've written? It'll get us 'ung. Do you know 'ow little you can get yourself 'ung for? And you worry about an apple from a market. You don't know nothing, More Grief. I would 'ave 'andled any soldiers that 'ad come along, but if that gets into the 'ands of a magistrate . . ."

"It's no more than people are saying, all the time, everywhere."

"They don't write it down! They can get away with things in an alehouse. Look at it from a general's point of view. What they're scared of is of *anyone taking any notice*. But suppose thousands of people get to read that? Suppose when they're all gathered together someone reads it out to them?"

He smiled. "There'd be a revolution."

"And you've got it all written down in words as evidence! You're a child, a babe in arms." After thinking for a moment, "It sounds like a sermon," she added. "If you make it sound enough like a sermon, you could say you was practicing to be a Methodist preacher."

"You don't understand. My thoughts are only for myself—for the time being. This manuscript is what I want to leave behind. It's all that I will be able to leave. Can you understand that, Mary?"

"At any rate we'll be saved the worst when you run out of ink. You 'aven't much left, 'ave you?"

He went back to his work. He felt refreshed by his writing. It was like dipping into a river on a hot day.

Mary crept out of the room. There was no place for her in it. It was full of silent thoughts.

The street Mary entered was nearly empty, except for two soldiers pinning a notice on a tree. Their horses were tethered to the tree—a couple of nags that had doubtless been requisitioned from a farmer.

"Oh, my Gawd . . . Mad Dick!"

"So what can we do for you, now you've turned up in Oldham again, my fair maid? Private, this is Mary the Scar. She's someone every recruit 'as to meet before 'e can call 'imself a soldier."

"I want a bottle of ink, Mad Dick. Where did you steal your old nags from? The field of some poor weaver? They're true infantry nags, is them. You'd 'ave to walk all the way with 'em."

"They're first-class cavalry 'orses, just a bit short in the leg for me, and not 'ad enough oats to liven 'em up. They brought us from Manchester, anyway. What do you want ink for? You can't write."

"Maybe I know someone who can."

"Is 'e another clergyman, or a fucking aristocrat again, Mary the Scar? Tell the private 'ere. Who's your latest fucking aristocrat?"

" 'E's an aristocrat amongst men, with more refinement of feeling in 'is little finger than you lot will ever know. Fucking militia! You can't even read what you're pinning on a tree. You're animals. Nothing but animals."

"Oh, yes, I can read. And I can write, too. What's your fancy man going to write for you? Love letters? A complaint on your behalf to a Member of Parliament?"

"The chapel'll 'ave some ink, sarge," the private said quietly, frightened of Mad Dick's size and truculence.

"You can do some mighty things through a bottle of ink, so I'm told," the sergeant said at last—looking at Mary, not at the private. "Write down all sorts of acts of Parliament. Very well, soldier, go and see what you can find."

The soldier set off, running in order to appear breathless at the Baptists' door, to convince them of the military emergency necessitating the requisitioning of a bottle of ink.

After he had left, the sergeant squatted against the base of the tree, in the sun. He unfastened his tunic, a fine display being better than words. But Mary was staring over his head reading the notice.

ABSCONDED

WHEREAS the weaver MOR LAVEROCK GREAVE has absconded from LADY WELL, YORKSHIRE, following a raid upon a

MANUFACTORY

and left his family chargeable to the town:

NOTICE IS HEREBY GIVEN

That whoever will apprehend the said MOR LAVEROCK GREAVE and lodge him in any of His Majesty's gaols, the person or persons, so apprehending him, shall be HANDSOMELY REWARDED: or if any Constable, Bailiff, or Press Gang will seize him and put him in His Majesty's Service, they will oblige the Churchwardens and Overseers of Lady Well.

THE PERSON IN QUESTION is 5 feet 5 inches in height, dark complexion with a limp, writes a fair hand and expresses himself in flowery fashion, having once kept a school.

"You can't read it," the sergeant challenged. "What are you looking at?"

"What's it say, then?"

"It's about some poor runaway Ludd they're going to 'ang, poor sod. Now what are you going to do for me in exchange for a bottle of ink?"

"I 'aven't seen no ink yet."

"You should be careful of bottles of ink. They're like gunpowder. I ran away from the Newcastle pits and landed in the Cumberland militia because of a bottle of ink I'd dipped my pen into. It was to write to the paper about the slavery of the pit men under contract to the mine owners."

"You've already told me all about it. You didn't write it, neither. You bullied someone else into setting it down for you. 'E's the one who got transported, you said. Because 'e could write, they 'ad to deal with him severe, you said, so let that be a warning. I remember it all."

"I 'aven't told you I've been playing my bagpipes most nights at the Eagle Inn at the corner of Manchester Street, 'ave I? You should come along."

The private now returned, with a little stoneware jar. He pressed the ink upon Mary as if it were a valentine.

" 'Ave you got any more of them notices, Mad Dick?" Mary asked. "I've some errands in Oldham today. If you give them to me, I'll pin them up around town for you, and you can go to the public 'ouse. I bet I know better than you the sort of place where a Ludd'd be 'iding."

The sergeant looked at the private and winked. "Where're you going to put them up for us?"

"I'll put one up against Mr. Lees' mill, for I knows 'im, and one by the Unitarians' chapel and . . ."

"Ain't we got something better to do on a Sunday than hunting poor Ludds?" the sergeant interrupted. "We could be going to church."

"Give 'em to 'er, Sarge!"

"Might as well be 'ung for giving the King's messages away to a whore, as for anything else. A kiss on the cheek for 'em, then."

Mad Dick gave her a bundle of half a dozen notices and she kissed him on the cheek.

" 'Oh, I am slain by the darts of a fair, cruel maid,' as the song goes. Give the private one too, for his trouble."

• • •

Mary re-entered the cellar on tiptoe, the notices hidden in her clothes. She hovered, hardly breathing, then put the ink beside him. He made a sound of surprise and pleasure, then returned to his writing.

She could hardly bear this desert of silence into which he had flung her.

And he had said he would go back to Lady Well.

She stood behind him, leaning over so that he felt her chin on his head, and she locked her arms around his shoulder. He continued writing. She hummed quietly, swaying her body to make him dance with her, as she secretly read what he had written:

> England has been in friendship and enmity, at war and peace with Spain several times in the past twenty years. If we were to see one man hit another and spit in his face, then caress him and hug him and kiss him and call him dearly beloved brother, and then again pick his pocket and kick him and brake his head and spit in his face, and again embrace him and call him most nobel friend and the bravest and best of men and so forth, we shuld see the relatif picture of England and Spain.

"What do you get from reading and writing books?"

"I survive my pain because of it."

She did not understand what he was talking about. If he had drunk the ink, she might have understood just as well.

"I know a street, Holywell Street in London, where you can buy and sell all sorts of books, in plain covers. About murders. The infidelities of the Prince Regent with ladies of pleasure. Mind you, you can be misled. A gentleman paid a guinea for Mr. Wesley's sermons because they were wrapped inside a plain envelope. Those who can write them make a good living from it. Novels, I mean, not sermons. There's some take them round selling them to the servants at the back doors of 'ouses. Why don't you write a novel, instead of sedition, and make us some money? My friends'll publish it for you in Holywell Street."

Because of her chatter he had to give up, at last. In any case, he was cramped from sitting. Putting his manuscript on the floor by the bed, he got up to stretch his legs. He walked around the room, ending by staring through the window.

Mary had gone to the fire, stooping over the flames. "If you're short of ideas, More Grief, I can give you a few," she said. "I can talk for hours the way men like to 'ear. 'She was wide open waiting for 'im' (the Turk, that is) 'and she was powerless. "Oh, no," she said. "No," she whimpered.' They like that best. ' "Oh, yes," she whimpered. "Oh, oh . . ." ' If I say it for you, you could write it down. It comes to me as easy as spitting."

She wondered whether or not to tell Mor why it came so easily to her. During her childhood in her stepfather's moorland farm, without playmates, regarded as a freak even by her stepparents and their relatives, how else could a clever girl console herself but by learning to read? Which she did, firstly by perusing gravestones where the names were known to her, next by casting her eye over familiar passages of the Bible, but most of all by stealing away with a volume from her stepfather's library of pornography.

Mary's fantasy life was fed on riches, and she was well prepared for a career in a whorehouse long before she was booted out of her home at the age of fourteen. But if she told Mor about it now, he would also learn how well she was able to read. It was a little too soon for that, she judged. She did not know whether or not that secret might still be useful to her.

He had turned from the window. "What's that you're putting into the fire?"

"Nothing . . . just some bits of paper."

"It's my—" He rushed across the room and grabbed hold of her wrist.

"No! No! It isn't . . . Let go!"

"You're lying! Thief and liar, you've burnt my . . ."

"You're hurting me!"

She stood up, her arm twisted in his grasp. His grip was tighter than he realized. They were glaring at each other in fury. He could have been looking into the burning fire itself. He did not care what anger he showed. He did not care about anything but his lost manuscript. She had burned "The Beggar's Complaint." It meant that all trust, everything, was gone. He could not stay a moment longer with her, because not for a second ever again would he feel secure. There would be nothing at all to show for his life if his manuscript was destroyed. He let go of her and tried to rescue the charred bits of paper.

"Look, look, it's all there," she said.

Of course it was; all there, on the floor by the bed. He hadn't even looked.

"You've hurt me!"

She rubbed her wrist. She sat on a chair with her back to him, her head in her hands. Her shoulders were heaving.

She looked haggard and frail. He remembered seeing Phoebe with her shoulder blades poking through her dress like that.

Outside, the townspeople were returning from the churches. A few faces glanced in through the window.

"What was it, then, that you were burning?"

"Filth. Just some filth."

"Filth? Like you've just been describing and wanting me to write down?"

"Filth, yes, filth! Ordure, vile muck, shit, fucking filth! I hate it, I hate it, I hate it! Don't you think a whore hates filth and muck more than any clergyman, More Grief? 'Aven't you ever thought of that? I only do it because men like it, not for myself. Why do they blame me? The judges? The parsons? How I 'ate their . . . Do you think I like their . . . After I've been . . . After they've been . . . I've been the one that's 'ad to climb down a well shaft in the dark alone, burying my own baby that I've been forced to murder, and soldiers looking to 'ang me when I come out. That's what I've done for someone's moment of pleasure . . .

"Oh, More Grief, don't let anything happen to you . . . please . . . I'm sick . . . sick . . . sick . . . of . . . *themmmm!*" She ended in a howl.

Early on Monday morning, while still in bed, they heard the footsteps of yet another band of men and women. They glimpsed colliers carrying their picks like weapons upon their shoulders. Four or five passed by and, following a gap, some more.

Then came other trades, bearing their implements with a threatening swing. Masons or builders with hammers, carpenters with heavy steel yardsticks, a fishmonger with a knife. There were flurries of white, as bands of women passed. It was snowing aprons. The women were carrying heavy rolling pins. Another group was singing "The Oldham Weaver":

I'm a poor cotton weaver, as many a one knows,
I've nowt t'ate in th'ouse and I've wore out my clothes.
You'd hardly give sixpence for all I've got on,
My clogs are worn out, and stockings I've none.
You'd think it were hard to be sent into th' world
To starve and do th' best as you can . . .

"They are going to Middleton to destroy Mr. Burton's mill," Mary announced, calm as an oracle.

"How do you know that?"

"Why do you think I wouldn't know? 'Cos I'm a woman? I know the secrets of generals. I've seen all of Mr. Burton's letters from 'is workmen, when 'e thought they'd fill in the boredom of a night and 'e read them to me. 'E's trained sixteen of 'is own men in firearms to defend 'is steam looms. That's no secret to anyone. 'E boasts about it as loud as 'e can, to frighten people. They 'ear 'em drilling inside the mill. Poor devils, them traitors, says I, when the mob turns up. 'Ow do I know? 'Cos whilst you were writing yesterday, I was on the street, asking questions. There'll be thousands'll turn up today, from all over the north."

Mor was hastily pulling on his boots and grabbing his woollens and jerkin, hardly listening or trying to make sense of the event as yet. One word lit up his brain—REVOLUTION—one which somehow would resolve both his new love for Mary and his more dutiful regard for Phoebe. Edwin would return from hiding, Gideon would be granted a straightening of his legs, and the fish would leap out of the streams into the hands of the common man. Mor would no longer have to run for his life, and machine breakers would be regarded as heroes. Tomorrow.

In a moment he was outside, the light of a bright spring morning on his face. He knew that such riots were occurring in towns, villages, and cities everywhere in the north of England.

A few dozen people had already passed down the street. Others were still coming. The crowd consisted largely of boys and young men. They blew kisses at the women and girls who formed an aisle of flickering white cotton for them. Young colliers, weavers, blacksmiths, farriers, and joiners were hammering on doors, as they went along, calling for recruits. One weaver, ashamed of himself, shoved some money through his door, which he opened a crack, and slammed again. But others came out with the clubs which they used on the moors for clouting rabbits, or with scythes and sickles.

"We're going to smash the mill! We're going to smash the mill!"

The wife from the house above the cellar, who possessed—or rather, was possessed by—a large family, descended her long flight of stairs into the road. She leaned against the wall with her two smallest children, who one minute buried their faces in her apron and the next peeped out.

"I've sent *'im* to join them!" she shouted to Mor above the noise of the crowd, and pointed her thumb toward the upper window.

Curious about her new neighbor, she came closer.

"These young fellows'll need the steadying of an older man, won't they?" she said. "My master's too old for jumping through 'oops, so I 'ope they don't bring out the soldiers. I'd go myself if it wasn't for the children, and the next one on the way. If they bring out the soldiers, I don't know what I'll do. Well, we'll 'ave to see. Some say the soldiers'll be on our side. They were kind enough in the market on Saturday. Did you see what 'appened in the market?"

"No. What happened?"

"I've never 'ad so much food come my way in my life before. Lady Ludd appeared. You know Lady Ludd? She came by. Nobody knows where she comes from but she comes, and finds food for us all. Those farmers from Cheshire, the devils, could do nothing and 'ad for once to take a fair price. If women can do that, perhaps men can do even better, when they try. We 'ad beef and cheese such as we 'aven't seen for years. The soldiers just stood by, laughing and playing games. After finding 'ow Lady Ludd tore up the market, the men met at the Eagle public 'ouse, and now they're after Burton's Mill in Middleton. But they are coming from everywhere today. So there must be leaders somewhere, even if we don't see 'em. There's that man in the Parliament . . . What's 'is name? . . . Burdett?"

Was there a leader? Mor wondered. Was Sir Francis Burdett or Major John Cartwright or William Cobbett really waiting to stand at the head, ready to set up a new Parliament? Some said they were, and some that they weren't. Or was there nothing better than a lot of Crawshaws scurrying about, with no substance to them? Was the army ready to revolt? Or, as many others said, had all the radical spirits been sent already to the front lines against Napoleon?

These youths, behaving with such certainty, knew no answers to these questions. Mor thought of how many countless times through the ages young men have set off down this and all the other streets of the world, to wars and revolutions, singing with joy as they went, only to return, if they returned at all, with maimed limbs.

"We're going to smash the mill!" they were yelling. "We're going to change the world."

Mor returned to the cellar.

"We're going to the mill!" Mary echoed the shout of the street, and laughed.

"This is the moment, is it?" he said, with some sarcasm.

"They're coming from all over the north."

"Why?"

"What do you mean, 'why'?"

"Who's told them to?"

" 'Ow do I know that? Somebody must 'ave done. I thought this was the day you've been waiting for."

"Maybe. Maybe not. I thought so, even 'alf an 'our ago. But just look at 'em."

"What do you mean? There's some lovely young men there."

"Some are hardly more than children! Just look at 'em. If they stay together, perhaps the army will join in. And if they scatter over the countryside, they'll be hunted down. If the army and the people stay together, perhaps they'll march to London—if someone turns up to lead them. Perhaps Sir Francis Burdett's on his way now. If 'e's not, or someone else like 'im, then a hangman's waiting."

"*If! Perhaps!* You said you'd march with us. You promised!"

"*I* said I would?"

"Yes. You said you would love me forever." She hung her head and said quietly, "I don't want to think of you as a coward."

"No, I'm not a coward!"

Well, why not go, then? Mor thought. *Some fool of a Crawshaw will probably step to the head and collect the glory for himself while the rest of us are killed, and the innocent young step into the trap, just like a thousand times before; but why not go and have a try?*

There isn't any wisdom in my love for her, either. One foolhardy adventure or another is what lies before us, or we die anyway.

Mary sealed her victory by the simple means of assuming that she had already won it.

"Burton's the guardian of my daughter, 'Arriet. I must go to see what 'appens. Just in case."

She carefully tied up her hair, opened her cosmetic box to take a last look at herself, then gathered up her cloak.

CHAPTER NINE

April 20th–21st

It had been an incongruously peaceful Sunday at Park Mount, the mansion in Middleton of Emanuel Burton. The sleepy hour of three in the afternoon arrived. The meal had been demolished to a filthy chaos of carcasses, fatty bones, and the inedible slime of greens, and the servants had melted away with it to distant kitchens. The ladies retired to one room, the men to another. Emanuel's father, Daniel, a bombastic gentleman whose main pleasures were to drink brandy, bully people, and tell smutty stories, was going a little too far with them, as a way of getting the clergyman who was his guest to make for the door.

Emanuel Burton, rescuing the clergyman from the attentions of his father, took him by the arm and led him to the window. He pointed out, below the slope of the garden, and standing at the foot of Wood Street near the market at the center of the town, the "famously progressive" mill of Messrs. Daniel Burton and Son.

It being Sunday, all was quiet except for the movements of the workmen trained to defend the place. The clergyman was able, from Park Mount, to peer over the top of the recently built wall that surrounded the factory. The engine, the focus of the working people's anger, stood at the end of the mill, its big awkward limbs awry, resting. The horizontal pine beam, fifteen feet long, was pivoted at an angle, with the pistons at either extremity. One piston was a vertical pillar of steel, shining like a silver fall of water; the other, at the lower end of the beam, was sunk into its iron casing. The three brass balls of the governors, which whirled through the air when the machine was in motion, now hung quiet and still.

So *that*—that soulless contraption—was the cause of all the late troubles in the parish!

For host and guest looking out from a warm, comfortable room, through polished windows, over sheltered lawns and shrubberies, to the carefully constructed vista of the mill—itself artistically dressed to appear like a gentleman's country residence—it was more natural and easy to dwell upon loftier matters of the soul. Nature displayed a majestic prospect all around, and Park Mount on its smooth hillock seemed the axle of God's creation. Within their view were six or seven miles of wooded dells, tucked into the folds of green enclosures. Here was a small peaceful town or village made of red brick; there, a church tower or a spire; over there were one or two other factories, built in the same delightful style of architecture as Messrs. Burtons'. The whole was contained in the magnificent semicircle of the Yorkshire moors.

Looking the other way from Park Mount one could see an older residence, Alkrington Hall, and beyond it the plain spreading toward Manchester and Liverpool. This was a less tidy view (which was the reason why Park Mount faced the other way), yet it was still impossible to imagine that only a few miles in that direction, on this same Sabbath day, was being discussed, planned, and already betrayed, the working men's meeting at Dean Moor.

Before dawn on Monday morning, Burton's Mill came into life. Three rows of lights glowed along its flanks, so that it was like a great house lit for a ball.

Emanuel Burton was up early, shortly after dawn. Before six o'clock, he could see through his bedroom window that, already, the beam of the engine rocked majestically up, down, up, down, on its pivot, *cch! . . . bump . . . cch! . . . bump . . . bump!* in the fierce light of the furnace that heated the boilers. It was a savage idol dancing in the flames. Its metal gleamed, obscured sometimes in billows of rosy steam. On the ground floor, it worked frames for spinning cotton. On the second and third floors were the mechanical looms, of the type that had already been destroyed by Luddites.

The workers had entered Burton's at half past five. Today, judging from what Burton could observe of them moving about in the yard, the work force was only slightly smaller than usual and was behaving peacefully—despite what had been rumored and threatened. They must have heard a little, at least, of what had been declared at Dean Moor. Evidently, most in Middleton were more concerned to keep, not destroy, their means of employment. They treated the cannon situated in the yard with impertinent familiarity, rather than with resentment. As Burton knew, most of the trouble was engendered, not by his own workers, but by artisans scattered around the town and countryside—by the employees and owners of small craftshops and by the home workers in the villages, who were the ones who suffered from competition with power looms. Abetting the foment were Lancashire's cells of literate Jacobins and Republicans.

Emanuel Burton, dressed by his valet, went down to his mill at seven o'clock, anticipating that the morning would progress almost in its usual fashion, after all. The lack of restiveness amongst the employees, and the fact that there were no soldiers present in Middleton, soothed him into believing that there was little to fear. There were no signs that anything untoward was about to happen. His private force of defenders bore themselves with a brisk, martial air, making a fuss with their firearms and cannon.

Burton nevertheless showed himself to be irritable and nervous, leaving his work in his office in order to scurry around the machines and in the yard, then returning to stare at his bills and papers, or to snap at his clerks. That was the only sign of apprehension.

Life seemed to grow even calmer as the morning progressed. But at two o'clock a report came that several thousand armed young men, and women too, were "converging upon Middleton from every point of the compass." They were marching down the roads from Bolton, Bury, Rochdale, Oldham, and Manchester.

The report claimed that the hungry men were breaking into stores, helping themselves to bread, cheese, bacon, sugar, and other provisions. After they had fed themselves, they were willfully wrecking the shops.

The crowd swept Mor and Mary onward. Through Oldham, it filtered along the alleyways and then into the Middleton road. More and more groups were joining in, and the march filled the width of the street. Those behind were pushing forward those in front. Going past mill owners' residences on the outskirts of town and shaking their fists, eventually they broke out into the countryside, with roadside cottages and the occasional colliery visible. In every house, the looms were silent.

The county of Lancashire was gently rolling country, but seemed flat to Mor after West Yorkshire. The villages were of brick, or of black and white timbered houses. The enclosures, surrounded by hawthorn hedges, were bright green, for here spring was more advanced than on the hills.

Spring had finally come on an irresistible wave rising from the south, and the plants and trees were responding as lovers to caresses. The trees of Chadderton Park were brushed at their tips with opening buds. Chestnut trees were coming into leaf, the clusters of great leaves hanging down, it seemed, with weariness at the effort of being born. Struggling in his limping fashion to keep up with the fast, youthful crowd, Mor the naturalist observed the spears and buttons of plants thrusting through the dross of dead grass, twigs, and wrinkled leaves. By the time they reached Chadderton, he had noted several summer migrant birds—a willow warbler, a chiffchaff, a swallow, and a whitethroat. For a hundred yards, a hedge bottom was thick with violets, their color suggesting distant, misty valleys down in the thorns and grass.

For the purpose of changing the world, Mor felt he had to turn his eyes from such sights. Were his bookish concerns, his guilt, his desire for change, merely because he was not big enough to take into his soul a hedge bottom dense with violets, larks skating across gaps of blue on a spring day, or the song of a whitethroat?

He plucked a violet and gave it to a comrade, who did not understand why he had received the gift, but crushed it roughly through his buttonhole.

There should be either a bright sun or a fierce thunderstorm to herald a revolution, Mor thought. Today, the sun was behind a gauze. Though sometimes it broke into small patches of blue, it never became more than a soft delicious promise of itself. It was not strong enough to evaporate the fecund sweat that bloomed from the trees and plants. This was one of those misty spring days when even the hills seemed to turn into light clouds. Within that mist was a sleepy promise of growth, of new life. If anyone was to die today, it would be especially cruel.

But in the midst of these jolly young men, singing their ballads, showing no more concern for bayonet and gunshot than they did for larks and violets, you would not guess that anyone could possibly be killed. At the roadside, women with trays slung around their necks were selling red paper roses, the symbol of Lancashire. On other roads, no doubt, the white roses of Yorkshire were being sold.

But it was for his lusty singing of the "Marseillaise," his hat pushed to the back of his head so that he could look up for bright gaps in the sky, that David Knott, a twenty-year-old glazier, was given a loaf of bread by a servant girl who had run out from Chadderton Hall. Hearing of the young men coming, she had boldly crossed the estate's park with the loaf in her hands. She was no kitchen slattern, but neat in a starched white pinafore, and she reminded David, a grubby and desperately hungry young man, of an immaculate white dove, come to the door of its dovecote.

Though cheeky enough to brave the eyes watching from the house, and full of determination to make a gift to these heroes even if dismissed from her post for it, yet the girl was shy when she confronted the tattered young men marching along the road. She became self-conscious, blushing and sweeping back strands of hair. She could not decide whom to choose. Then she spotted the young glazier and made up her mind, even though, to reach him, she had to elbow her way through the crowd, thus getting smutty, greasy stains on her clothes.

After a moment's attention to the girl's shining face, David Knott turned to the loaf that she was pushing forward. He was much more hungry for that than he was for embraces. By the time he had got over staring at the bread, he had passed her by. "I'll be back later," David remembered to shout over his shoulder.

The crowd dragged the girl a few yards in its wake, until discarding her at the end of the park wall. When David turned to take another look, and note where she lived so that he might call there on his victorious return, he saw her wave and smile, promisingly. He lost her when he plunged into the crowd that was pouring in at the junction with the Chadderton road, just before the bridge over the Rochdale Canal.

The river of people was gathering tributaries at every junction. On the canal bridge there were handshakes, embraces, and hats thrown into the air, while orators termed the murky little canal "the Rubicon."

They spoke of Cicero and of Roman republics. It was declared that a "ring of revolutionaries was tightening around Middleton."

The more they closed in on the town, the more they were emboldened by their numbers to raid shops on the way. At first they entered only food stores. Then they began to break into the premises of every shopkeeper who was notorious for meanness, for unwillingness to give credit, or for cheating: the shop belonging to Lizzie Hargreaves, known for resting her finger upon the pan of the scales and diverting her customer's attention with her slander; that of Mr. Wrigley, whose packets of tea and sugar contained short measure; that of Fry the draper, who was forever creeping off to tell tales to the vicar or the magistrate.

As the crowd grew larger and larger, it was the most destructive members who joined last of all. More of the women who lived along the route thought that they "might as well be hung for a sheep as a lamb"; they decided that it was better to raid a shop than be beaten by a husband for having no food in the house. Shopkeepers ahead were boarding their premises, and that stimulated the mob to greater destruction.

Two or three thousand people finally came to a halt in the Middleton marketplace—excited, ravenously devouring their thievings, perhaps saving some for their families. They stood or squatted on their heels while listening to their orators, who were mostly the older men. Kings Ludd, Harry, and Arthur, and "the Constitution of England," were evoked; so were Greece, Rome, and France, and those emotive words "bread," "corn," and "obnoxious frames."

An empty stall tempted Mor to stand upon it. He had never made a public speech before, but when his eyes alighted upon the empty space, he was drawn ineluctably forward. He left Mary's side and scrambled up, pushing through a few men who were sitting on its edges and laughing as they ate their stolen apples; one also had some crockery, another held a stolen clock, to take home to their wives.

"Friends! Friends!"

His mouth went dry and he believed it would refuse to deliver another word. His throat tightened. He felt himself to be the loneliest man on earth. His heart pounded. One of the men on the planks at his feet turned and laughed, spitting out apple pips, waving the core at him, telling him to shut up.

"Confederates in the fight for bread and justice!" Mor shouted. "Less than twenty years ago, a meeting was held amongst the Oldham weavers to petition King George the Third for a reform of Parliament. It led to nothing better than fighting amongst the spectators. Or were they government agents provoking trouble? Anyway, the meeting was broken up.

"And all of us have seen ignorant Church-and-King mobs burning effigies of that light to liberty, Tom Paine, so as to crush our few hard-won freedoms."

At last, he found himself attracting interested eyes. One or two, then three or four, then five or six attentive faces were blooming in the crowd. His words swelled with pride and confidence.

"Now that we are here, the only thing that will save us is our staying together. Refuse to be scattered, friends, no matter what! If the army is prevented from picking us off one by one, the disaffected amongst the soldiers will join us, too. If a few of the military come with us, the many will follow. If the army is with us, we will win over the whole of England. All the working people everywhere will follow. It is only by this means that, this time, we will be able to march on London and secure Parliament for ourselves."

Silence spread through the crowd. Someone quietly placed a quart of ale at his feet. He was gathering the largest audience in the market. They were drifting away from others to listen. But now what was to be done? They had been swept by minor currents into the body of a river, but it had flowed into a lake, swirling, unsure. Speechmaking and calls to action were fine, but facing the mill, the crowd realized how impregnable it was. On the other hand, they had not come to Middleton to listen to speeches. They began collecting bricks and cobblestones. A few were lobbing missiles in the direction of Burton's, without reaching it. Before the walls of the factory, the march had drifted into anticlimax, and everyone was dithering.

It was then that Mary climbed up on some boxes, pointed her arm and shrieked, "There is the mill!"

They thought it a great laugh to hear a woman, especially such an "artful doxie" with her red hair and painted face. But her shout was simple and dramatic, and it was because of it that, at last, they moved forward.

Once again they stood helplessly, seeping around the building like water eddying before a dam, undecided and confused. Through the barred windows were poked guns and the faces of the sixteen defenders. These were the only workers left inside. Emanuel Burton had dismissed the others—some of whom had joined the marchers.

Burton's defending army seemed afraid of the weapons in their own hands. They had discovered that both they and their fellow workers in the street had been tempted into the same trap, which could be sprung by their own guns. They had realized, too late, that they had been placed, unwittingly, on opposite sides in a battle.

Desultorily, the crowd broke the ground-floor windows. Then someone loaded a pistol and fired a signal. The shot, the smashing of glass, the missiles, and the shout "We're smashing Burton's Mill!" brought about panic inside the building, and the cannon blazed in the yard. There was an acrid smell, with a thin blue column of smoke rising in the still air, to drift away gently when it reached the roofline. Some screamed. Mostly, the crowd fell silent, surprised not to find themselves dead.

When they saw that there had been no casualties, "They're firing only powder! They daren't use bullets!" the crowd shouted. They thought that victory was theirs, and a hail of stones poured into the upper windows. They hacked at the stonework. They prised the hinges and padlock off the gates.

Then the first real shots were indeed fired from the mill. Mor saw Joseph Jackson, a baker's lad with a gift for oratory, receive a ball in the groin. A look of incredulity swept over his features. He let go of the chisel with which he had been stabbing at the mortar and cried out to God; but it was to his companions that he turned, with an unforgettable look of surprise that lingered upon his chalk-white face. A friend threw a coat over his mangled groin, hoping Joseph would not realize what had happened to it.

David Knott, the glazier, was smashing windows at the rear of the building. "We came to Middleton to find bread and work, and by God, there will be plenty for us glaziers when this day is done!" he shouted. The next moment, he was staring at the slippery tangle of his intestines that were spilling over his hands. He looked at them as if what he saw was not part of his own body but an alien creature, an animal with a life of its own. He tried to bundle the snaking mass into his stomach. Then he fainted.

The crowd, especially the workers from Burton's, could not believe that their own fellows had fired upon them. Frightened, many of them began to disperse.

"No! No! Stay with it! Don't go!" Mor shouted.

But finally, a little later, they all fled in panic when they heard that a cavalry troop of the Scots Greys was approaching from Manchester.

In the late afternoon, a servant girl in Chadderton left her work and crossed the park to stand in the road for a clear view toward Middleton. She met impatient, angry men approaching from the town, without songs on their lips this time, and who could tell her only that four of their number had been killed, but the steam looms had remained invincible.

She tried not to be impatient while the crowd kept coming, until it thinned to a trickle. Perhaps the young glazier was returning along a different route and would come by Chadderton Hall on another day?

The bird song of a spring evening simmered in the woods and bushes of the park, at first so quietly that it wasn't noticed. She waited until the songs of blackbirds, robins, and thrushes rose to a crescendo, then died away, and there was no one left on the road.

George Albinson, a nineteen-year-old weaver, bled to death two miles from Middleton, which was as far as his wounds would allow him to travel. With his last scraps of breath, he urged his companions to return on the following day and burn to the ground Burton's mansion and the houses of the mill's defenders.

That was George's last wish. He could not go another yard without the help of a surgeon, and there were none who would help machine breakers. His friends who had carried him, and who were soaked in his blood, could do nothing more for him, other than lay him in a roadside copse and promise to fulfill his last wish, vowing curses upon themselves if they failed.

George had imagined that his life would be an obscure one, measured out in the ale that he drank in the Eagle or the Roe Buck Inn; a life without a thought of immortality. He had come along because of his friends, and he did not care a fig whether he weaved by power loom or hand. He would marry that Sarah who worked in a dairy and he would rear a family. It was his being shot at "as if on a foreign battlefield" that had turned him into a revengeful beast.

That evening, at a meeting in the Eagle, in Oldham, they decided to return to Middleton in the morning, to fulfill Albinson's last wish. If anyone wondered why neither militia nor cavalry had appeared in Oldham to arrest them, they did not raise the matter. Such was their hubris that nobody considered it extraordinary. They believed that the soldiers were intimidated by their numbers. Even the Forfarshire militia, stationed in the town, and the Oldham Volunteers were lying low.

The only soldier around was Mad Dick. The sergeant of the Cumberland militia had deserted from Manchester. His tunic was unbuttoned and stained with ale as he talked in the Eagle of "cutting the throats of bastard officers and mill owners." He seemed eager to be rid of his money, and was aflame to seek martyrdom.

"The army will follow my example," he swore, tottering with drink. "There's not a man that is content. I've seen recruits crying with hunger. If you step out of line they flog you. The officers are terrified of revolution! If the army deserts, they know they've lost the day. Well, I tell you, they have lost the day already. The army's had enough."

The army was won over to the revolution! To Mor, as to the others, Mad Dick's defection was the most exciting news, and the real victory of the day.

Mor and Mary did not sleep in their cellar that night. In the yard of the Eagle they helped to make a six-foot-high figure out of sacks stuffed with straw. Pinned to its chest was a card saying KING LUDD. The innkeeper provided the straw, his wife gave a giant turnip for its head, and an old weaver who lived in bachelor retirement at the inn, haunting the taproom with memories of France during the Revolution, contributed a pair of his white corduroy trousers and his most precious memento, his blue liberty cap. Mary cheered on the work by kissing the weaver on his bald crown and miming obscenities at the effigy. With a large carrot between his legs, she made him truly a king. Dressed and ready, King Ludd was set up on the innkeeper's donkey cart.

At ten in the evening, Mor slipped out, going down Domingo Street, past the Methodist chapel, to retrieve his violin from the cellar. The army was deserting! he kept thinking excitedly.

Meetings like the one at the Eagle were taking place all over town. He called in at several public houses, and told them his good news. The kind of people whose greatest pleasure it is to run from door to door with tales were scurrying around Oldham, in effect keeping the meetings united.

By the time Mor returned to the Eagle, he had done his bit to rebuild the confidence of the whole town. The now-famous public house was crowded with people come to ogle the deserter and celebrate his defection. Mor played his fiddle, Mad Dick blew his Northumbrian bagpipes, and the others danced and sang. Who cared about anything tonight? The whore moved through the company, appearing willing to give herself to the bravest. Under the influence of music, dancing, alcohol, and the baleful King of Straw, which was especially frightening in the light of swaying lamps, curses were uttered against mill owners, machine makers, deer parks, enclosures, the King, and finally against God, "the greatest manufacturer and most murderous king of all," declared Mor Greave.

Around midnight, Mad Dick led a drunken raiding party to the armory of the Volunteers. The local militia, too, were so drunk that it could only have been the luck that cares for fools and babies that brought success to the raid. Yet Mad Dick returned with guns, swords, and bayonets, which, as he knew, had been stored at the rear of the factory owned by their colonel, John Lees.

There was a light in Mad Dick's eyes that caused others to grow silent, to give way to him and treat him with awe. He again played his pipes, swaying upon the cart with his arms around the straw effigy of King Ludd, pausing to kiss the figure that, through the effects of drink and of the unsteady lights, seemed to be stirring with life.

It was four in the morning before most were asleep. Only half the revelers reached their homes or the bedrooms of the inn. The others collapsed in corners of the yard, the stable, or the woodshed. Mor found himself a corner, lined it with straw from the stable, and dozed peacefully, waiting for Mary.

She took some time to join him because, when she was on her way, Mad Dick saw his chance and pinned her against a wall.

"Who's the one with the fiddle—your 'brother,' as you call him? 'E ain't your brother, is 'e? I can tell by the way you look at 'im. And you were touching 'im, when you thought no one'd see. What sort o' rascal is 'e, that you're 'iding and disguising?"

She tried to push him away.

"Don't think you can make a fool of me," Mad Dick warned. "I've seen 'im before. 'E was with you at Mrs. Rawdon's, wasn't 'e? I remember 'im. 'E comes from Lady Well. You're a one, Mary the Scar! They call *me* mad! 'E's the one you wanted the ink for, then? Isn't 'e?"

She was still struggling to get away, and he took it for a game.

"Isn't 'e? 'E's the one doing the writing? 'E's the one we were pinning a notice up about, isn't 'e? Mor Laverock Greave? Kept a school? Wrote a fair hand?"

She pulled even harder away from him, but he easily held her.

"Absconded from 'is family, the bastard! You choose 'im, and you could 'ave a *man*."

Their faces were inches away from each other. Mary looked ready to spit.

"Why did you run away from the army, Mad Dick?"

"For love of my fellow man—my fellow soldier."

"What 'ad you done? Fucked one? . . . Ow! You're 'urting me!"

"Don't say that to me! I'm not *unnatural!* I wrote a letter on behalf of my fellow soldiers."

"Not that story again! You can't write, Mad Dick. And you're jealous of Mor Greave, because 'e can."

"All right, then! All right! Shut up, Mary the Scar! Someone else wrote it down, but I thought it up. I was the brains. I can be a scholar too, but it's all in my 'ead. It was me who composed it. It was to the newspaper, and all about flogging in the army."

"I'd 'ave thought you'd enjoy that, Mad Dick. OW!"

He hit her so hard that she was quivering, and spitting out her hate.

"But you were both drunk when you sent it, Mad Dick. When you come to, sober, you realized they'd tear the army apart to find out who sent such a stupid letter, and when they found 'im they'd flog 'im to death, in front of 'is comrades. So you thought you'd best join the revolution instead. I know you!"

"Yes," he said simply. "That's it. I'm like you, then. I'm 'ere looking after myself. So we should stick together, shouldn't we? Really tight. As tight as two people can be."

"No, Mad Dick! No! So fuck off."

She bit him and fled.

"I'll get you!" he shouted. "In the end. The pair of you!"

Mor, feeling the soft rub of her flesh, opened his arms to her. He noticed that she was breathless but otherwise realized nothing of what had happened.

At around eight o'clock, the chill of a spring morning as sharp as a lemon woke them all. The word was passed around to muster in the yard. They straightened and remembered, piecemeal, what they had promised and threatened during the previous night. Minute by minute, they remembered more.

Mad Dick realized that the day would end in a cavalry charge. He knew that most of the others, dozily rubbing their eyes, holding their aching heads, dousing themselves at the pump, could not imagine what that would be like. He was not going to tell them, or they'd turn tail and run. The cavalry wouldn't hack limbs off all of them, he consoled himself.

The important thing was to get a huge crowd confronting the militiamen at the mill, who were more pliable than the cavalry who would arrive later. They would be persuaded to desert, and he then would be the leader of a gang of desperados—not an isolated, hunted fugitive. There'd be half a chance, then. Revolutions *did* occur, by such means.

In the yard, the men were fingering their weapons, afraid of the pieces sprung into their unsoldierly hands: the heavy gleaming metal, the bolts and springs, the weighty wooden stocks. To be in possession of weapons was probably sufficient in itself to get one hanged. Fortunately, there were not enough to go around and most (though they pretended otherwise) were glad to find sabers and muskets snatched from them by those who had been in the army and knew how to use them.

Mad Dick, the only skilled soldier, took command. He was an awesome sight in his tattered uniform of a non-commissioned officer. He showed a lust for blood that was as pure as an animal's.

He led them off along the road to Middleton. As before, the crowd was joined from streets all over the town. They poured out of public houses, shaking their fists at windows which the occupants dared not unshutter, and defiantly singing Luddite songs.

Come cropper lads of high renown
Who love to drink good ale that's brown

And strike each haughty tyrant down
With hatchet, pike and gun . . .

As on the previous day, groups from surrounding villages joined at every junction. The decision to return to Middleton had swept across the countryside from public house to public house, like a fire through a warehouse. Mary, who had become their mascot, was given the red flag to carry. She and Mor were at the head of the Oldham contingent, with King Ludd on his cart, and Mad Dick.

At midday, when they arrived at Burton's Mill, a silence fell upon them. The Cumberland militia were camped inside the yard, waiting for them. They had been sent from Manchester late the previous evening, after Mad Dick deserted, and were now roasting meat over a campfire. The smell of food, and of burning, oily wood that had been scavenged from the back of the mill, hung in the air. Few of the mob had enjoyed a breakfast, other than a handful of currants or a piece of bread given to them along the way, or something stolen from a shop. They realized that the hungry and the fed do not belong to the same species.

As the crowd, keeping out of range of gunfire behind the walls, set King Ludd up near the gates, adjusted the lettered board, and set to rights the awry liberty cap on his head, one of the militiamen shouted, "My God, it's Mad Dick!"

"We'll be along to watch you swinging, Sergeant Chadwick!" yelled another.

Mad Dick put himself boldly in view. "Come and join the revolution! Here's your chance to change the army. Either that, or come out and fight your battle like men."

"Not likely. We're safe 'ere. We'll leave you lot to the cavalry. You'll run fast enough then."

"Come out, damn you!"

Mad Dick knew that the militiamen would not abandon the safety of the mill, except to desert.

He roared to his own men, "Divide yourselves into three forces! You, and you—you're officers, one for each group. You watch me, 'ow to do it. All them on this side o' the post, line up! Form ranks, damn you! Right? See 'ow it's done? Now you two, choose your men!"

Mad Dick's section shuffled into something like lines. The other commands formed into loose groups.

Mad Dick marched before his battalions. "Now then! You lot can stay 'ere to keep the militia busy. Say whatever you like to them. Call them bastards, cowards, or unnatural. They won't do anything about it. I know them. Country bumpkins all of 'em, never seen nothing but the back of an 'orse and plow. My section's off to the 'omes of them damned blacklegs that fired on our comrades yesterday. They're not going to get away with that! You others get off to Burton's 'ouse and flush them out o' there."

"Oh, no, not that! Not there!" Mary shouted.

"Why not that, Mary the Scar? You've been keen enough on the battle so far."

"My daughter, Mad Dick! My daughter's in there!"

"Your daughter, eh? So what sort of a mother are *you,* talking about your daughter?"

"Stop that," Mor threatened.

Mad Dick laughed at him. "What do you think you can do about it, runt?"

"You can't, Mad Dick! You mustn't go to Burton's. Please!" Mary appealed.

"Mustn't I, Mary the Scar? I don't think I know the meaning of 'mustn't.' I've never 'eard the term. I'll do as I like. Don't you worry. Do you think the Burtons'll stay in there? They and all their dependents'll be gone before anyone gets near."

He turned to the troops. "What were you lot doing before you joined a rebel army? Asleep every day in a public 'ouse? Quick, march! Off you go to Burton's 'ouse!"

"We'll go with them," Mor said. "Come on."

Mary's red flag was left in the crook of King Ludd's arm before the factory gate, and off they went.

Mr. Burton, his French wife, Lisette, and the servants who remained loyal watched from the elevation of Park Mount. They believed that the factory was safely in the hands of the Cumberland militia, with the cavalry on its way to back them up. They did not worry unduly as they saw the mob converge and gather at the foot of the park, before the mill gates. Yet none of the militia opened fire. Burton glimpsed, outside the gates, the rebel sergeant, but still did not worry too much.

Then he saw Mary the Scar. And wasn't that her brother with her?

Next he saw workmen with picks, shovels, fourteen-pound hammers, and axes set off toward the residences built for the mill's most valued artisans, and for the clerks, managers, and engineers. These were fine houses with flower gardens in the front and kitchen gardens in the rear, bow windows, alabaster fireplaces in their main rooms and, in their back yards, rows of brick kennels where the poorest, most unfortunate breed of maidservant lived in proximity to washhouses and sculleries.

The Burtons were forced to watch the destruction of these civilized amenities. They crumbled under blows from the expert hands of the very men who had built them. Dainty rows of peas and other sprouting vegetables were being trampled into the earth.

The mob set fire to the chief engineer's shed, where he experimented with steam boilers and turned bits of brass on a lathe. They threw all his brass turnings onto a tip.

From four of the houses, they pulled out the furniture and made a bonfire. On every side, men and women were fleeing and screaming.

For Emanuel Burton, it was the end of civilization.

He spotted the party that was making its way toward his own house, and realized that his family must either be burned up themselves or flee.

Lisette, fussing noisily all over the house like a canary in a panic at the loss of its familiar cage, was creating chaos. The servants, who should have been ordered to saddle horses, were being sent to check on a Chinese powder box or a silver candlestick. Lisette was behaving in the same distracted fashion as she did when they were going to a ball or a party, even though at the foot of the park there pressed a rebel army; one so violent that twenty yards of iron railings collapsed beneath them. The crowd was swarming over the low foundation wall, and their boots were churning up the splendid lawn.

At last, the Burtons got into a carriage drawn up under the portico. Emanuel now grew impatient with Lisette because she was fussing over their adopted child, Harriet—a pudding-faced creature, slow, stupid, bovine, ugly and always waiting for something to be done for her. As a matter of fact, he hated her; but he had to provide his wife with a child from somewhere. He had thought he could bribe the whore who was her mother into silence by taking the girl under his wing—kill two birds with one stone.

Lisette's personal possessions so obsessed her that she could not spare a thought for the mill. Emanuel did not know whether it was from her egoism or her bravery, but next she was delaying because she did not like the shoes she was wearing. She was leaning out the window and, against the murderous howling of the workmen pouring across the park, was instructing the coachman to look for another pair in the trunk.

Emanuel Burton leaned out the other carriage window. He saw that some of their servants were scattering across the park, while some were welcoming the mob.

"Coachman, drive on!" he yelled.

"Darling, I must have my shoes!"

"Drive on! Drive on!"

The Burtons finally made their escape as the wildest of the band flooded under the colonnaded porch and went boldly in at the front doors. They did not care whether anyone was inside or not. Other attackers entered through the kitchens. Mor and Mary, hanging back, hoping not to be seen by the Burtons, went to the front of the house as soon as the carriage was out of sight.

On the steps Mor came eye to eye with Crawshaw, who had a white paper rose of Yorkshire in his lapel.

"Dragging your feet again, poet? Last to arrive, as usual."

Crawshaw vanished into the house.

The crowd was divided into those who garrulously evoked the storming of the Bastille and those determined to find something to eat.

The ones with a penchant for oratory made straight for the drawing room. Before the ornate mirrors, they prepared to make their victory speeches. They had been savoring this moment of revenge. In heavy boots, they clambered up on exquisite tables as if they were apple crates.

But when they looked around for audiences, few were there to listen. Most had imagined, not the pleasure of smashing drawing rooms or making speeches, but of gorging on the food that was stored in the cellars. They had visualized preserve jars full of plums and raspberries, joints of cold meat, finely matured cheeses, and bottles of spirits. They had made straight for the cellars.

Never at Park Mount had food been devoured with such gusto. What was not eaten was wasted through the excitement of being surrounded by plenty. Heaps of cheeses were knocked to the floor and trampled on, slabs of meat were soaked with spilled wine. They returned upstairs only later, to satisfy their appetite for destruction.

Mor would have expected to number himself with the orators, but when he saw how useless that was, he went for something to eat. He stole only one thing apart from food—a length of fishing line.

With amazement, he watched others smashing furniture, mirrors, crockery, and could see no point to it.

Then he came upon Crawshaw, with his maddening smile as if to say, "Well, poet, I'm all right. What about you?" How Mor blamed this "King Ludd" for the fates of Tiplady and Wrigley, for the flight of his son, and for his own fate as a fugitive!

The elegant drawing room temptingly waited to be smashed, like a still pool asking for a stone. Mor, without knowing whether it was Burton or Crawshaw whom he was attacking, picked up a figurine and threw it at a mirror.

Carpenters were taking pleasure in prising apart the elaborate joints of furniture which they themselves might have made and been proud of, and in kicking through door panels. What would have horrified and filled them with incomprehension to have merely heard of yesterday thrilled them today.

The havoc came to a climax when someone relieved himself on the carpet, and another into the fireplace. When the destruction of the drawing room was complete, some of the women drifted upstairs into the bedrooms, tittering as they sniffed at fine linen sheets before they tore them from the beds and ripped them apart. They howled with laughter as they held before their bodies the fine gowns and feathered hats, then cast them aside. One poured the contents of a chamber pot over a mattress.

They grew tired of this orgy as rapidly as it had arisen. When most of the house had been wrecked, the destruction took on a weary, commonplace cast. Trampling through a mess of broken furniture, they drifted, like people come to the end of a genteel party, out onto the terraces and lawns.

Mary ate little of the food, except a few delicacies that she grabbed as she was rushing by. She hunted in panic through room after room, in case Harriet had been left behind. She was still searching attics and remote corners after everyone else had left. When she was satisfied that Harriet was safe, she tore down one of the curtains, lit it at the embers of the fire left in the grate, and thrust it under a sofa. This set alight the remaining curtain, and the fire soon spread to the whole house.

It was a conflagration that would surely satisfy General Maitland. Mary ran out into the garden, where everyone, stunned into silence, was watching the blaze.

Not to be outdone by a woman, a party of young ruffians went to Burton's adjacent farm and set fire to a haystack. Then they released the beasts from the barn and burned that.

Down below, they could see the furniture of the overseer, the chief engineer, and the mill mason burning.

It was a perfect day for fires. In the distance the ring of Yorkshire hills was brushed by blue shadows that were as soft as feathers. Wonderful banners of smoke stretched across the sky.

The fire they had lit might spread across the whole town, the whole country, maybe even the world, and everything be born again from ashes.

CHAPTER TEN

April 17th–23rd

After Mor had left home, every time that Phoebe tried to say something she merely cried. On her way back from the ash tree where she had parted from him, she met a neighbor and, hiding her problems, tried to speak about the weather, but at the first syllable she burst into tears. Had there been no one in the house she might have been able to get on with cleaning it, as Mor had imagined, but when Gideon greeted her with the angry words, "What are we to do, Mother?" she looked up at the stain he had made on the ceiling and again burst into tears.

"What are we to do?" All of Lady Well was asking this question of its preachers, now that the radical leaders, Tiplady, Crawshaw, and Greave, were dead or had fled. Methodists in one house, Congregationalists in a second, Baptists in a third.

It made the cynical soldiers smile. They visited Phoebe's home on the first afternoon, after they had found Mor's *Rights of Man*. They held the cursed book that had ruined her life. Before this time, she had seen the detachments of troops as genial presences who would not harm her, but in her house they turned into shocking, angry, violent men, crashing contemptuously into the furniture and cupboards. Two of them were larger than any man she had ever seen within her walls. She imagined how easily they could violate her. However, the soldiers only violated her house, taking away the works of Plutarch, Shakespeare, and Herodotus, saying that they were seditious works.

"Take 'em! Gladly! They've been no good to me. They only make folk idle, and lead weavers to think themselves gentlemen."

The soldiers left behind Goldsmith's *Animated Nature* and some other books of botanical and bird illustrations. Also, thank goodness, they did not find the sovereign she had hidden under a floorboard, where Mor used to hide his poachings and Gideon had put some seditious broadsheets. She had been on tenterhooks about that.

They told Phoebe that because of her husband's crimes, she would no longer be wanted at Horsfalls'. Gideon was out of work because Tiplady's was closed down. "You ain't even fit to sign on as a soldier, are you, young man?" one said, studying Gideon's lame walk. The family would therefore have to seek charity, said the sergeant, unless her husband was found. If he was innocent, then he could "clear himself like a man before the courts," and they could "live honestly again by handloom weaving and decent employment."

Phoebe burst into tears yet again. Her howling pained her and she spat blood. The soldiers left hurriedly then. "Ma'am, you should go to the infirmary," were their last words.

Mor, she reflected angrily, had left her with nothing but the past: his loom, his damned books, his chair, his bed, and his cottage. He had taken the future for himself, and had left her with only ashes and memories.

This shell of her body, and this house, were lifeless husks without a husband. She hardly thought it worthwhile maintaining such a poor thing as herself. She felt too ashamed to go to the churchwardens. Probably they would say she was mad with grief and put her in the workhouse, where they had terrifying facilities for "lunatics and refractory paupers." She knew how easily, once within the walls, she could become one or the other of those. She had heard their screams.

She kept her surviving ornament, the spotted dog that Gideon had not broken, but she took the Goldsmith and the other natural-history books to the bookseller in Halifax. Mr. Slaughter arranged a lift in a cart for her. Because the mill was shut, there were many people on the streets, and Lady Well was listless with defeat. People who were determined to be silent when questioned by soldiers were practicing by being moody with one another. Mostly tut-tutting and muttering followed her, although some cheered her on. But they weighed her down with their sympathy—just as they did Tiplady's widow and Mrs. Wrigley, whose husband would be transported. From within several houses, as she passed by, she heard the murmurs of prayer meetings; neighbors would gather around one person's fire, a second contributing bread, a third ale, and so forth. Occasionally the voices rose in a hymn. The "seditious" books in her hands made her burn with shame. She was glad that none of the Horsfalls were about. She would have felt even more ashamed before her superiors—rather than feeling wronged by them.

She was glad to get clear of the town, onto the hills. The sight refreshed her, with its perspective. By the time she reached the fine streets of Halifax, one would hardly guess there was so much trouble in smaller places such as Lady Well.

She tipped the volumes onto the bookseller's desk, like someone ejecting poison.

"Books 'ave never done me any good," she said. "I don't suppose they're much use to anybody else, either."

Until she said this, he had been thinking of offering her a guinea.

He murmured over the headings, suggesting reluctance by his very tone. " 'Division of Spinous Fishes, The Frog and Its Varieties, Origin of Rivers, Varieties in the Human Race, Turbinated Shell-Fish of the Snail Kind.' " He fingered the engravings of hares, larks, fishes, and snakes. "Much defaced with notes," he mumbled. "The scribbling is unfortunate. And encyclopædias aren't fashionable at the moment, anyway. Too French."

"I suppose so," she agreed.

He looked at her over his spectacles. "We've seen of late what a little learning does for the working man, haven't we? If they'd been of a theological bent I could have done better . . . Five shillings."

"No, they can't be worth so much, master! You're making a mistake!"

"I should never have been in trade," he sighed. "But I'd like to help you."

"Well, that's very kind of you. Five shillings!"

She came away laughing. Perhaps she could sell Mor's loom, too.

But by the time she had walked home, she had started to reflect that the comforts to be bought this way would not last long. She put the five shillings away with her sovereign under the floorboards.

After a further day, she went to Joshua Slaughter to offer her services as a housekeeper.

She had never before been indecent enough to visit, alone, the home of a man known to everyone as her admirer. Hurt by the reputation of factory women, Phoebe was more prudish than most. She slunk to the place, trying especially not to be seen from Gledhill's, next door.

Out of the habit of a lifetime, Phoebe knocked at the back door. The kitchen she was let into was clearly that of a bachelor, without frills. It was not dirty, because an irreproachable widow came in occasionally, but there were oily rags on shelves and in cupboards. On a sideboard, instead of Staffordshire ware and ornaments, was a small wheel-cutting machine for making brass gears. The main touch of homeliness was given by several clocks which ticked in harmony, like crickets in a summer meadow.

On the table was a bowl holding a single hen's egg.

From Phoebe's face, Joshua thought that Mor had been arrested. For several minutes he stared at her, but when she showed herself capable of saying little, he simply declared, "Let us pray," in the grand, quiet, fatherly voice of one who understands everything.

His chair scraped back from the table and he knelt on the flagstones, putting his hands together, his slender engineer's fingers touching the tip of his nose. He waited for her to kneel beside him—just as if miracles might be expected to happen every day.

When the whole town was at it, why had she not thought to pray before now? Phoebe wondered. She who had always found it difficult to speak to humans about her troubles. It was Mor who had stifled her prayers, with his opposition to church. Something else to blame him for.

She knelt. It was as if an unseen hand was forcing her shoulders down. The chill of the stones touched her like baptismal waters.

She was thrilled with silent confession, thinking of Jesus. *Lord, Lord, how weak are thy servants* . . . For the first time in her life Phoebe allowed her thoughts to rise, though she still dared not voice them. *None, save Jesus, knows me. I have done wicked things.*

Several minutes passed.

"Joshua . . ."

"I know! There's no need to say anything at all. I know."

They were silent again, hearing the ticking of clocks.

Joshua and she met, at last, in this shared silence. There was love in the air, without its being accompanied by any scandalous touching, any compromising or suggestive words. There was an unspoken complicity. Yes, a miracle was about to occur in the humble kitchen.

Phoebe closed her eyes. She saw Jesus with his slender, pale, suffering limbs descend from the cross and fill her spirit.

Joshua watched her make fists of her hands and screw them into her eyes.

"Do you feel anything?" He spoke in awe. He knew that she had seen something, although she did not reply. "It is the breath of the Holy Spirit," he continued. "I have seen God. I know."

In surprise, Phoebe opened her eyes. She recalled her sister, Selene; not only the words were identical, but also the tone. When someone spoke with that authority it was impossible to say that you doubted them.

Joshua rose from his knees. He put his hand upon her shoulder, and she almost expected him to say, "All is forgiven you."

The mill was closed and silent, and she could feel Joshua's sorrow about it. She could feel that Joshua was ready to talk to her.

With grandeur and certainty, in words as ponderous as monumental granite meant to hold down a corpse, he began.

He had spoken to God when he was in Bradford, with the followers of Joanna Southcott.

He took the egg from the bowl on the table and delicately put it into Phoebe's hand. She could see the pinpricks at the ends, where it had been blown. She was just capable of reading what was written on it, with uncertain flourishes, in royal-purple ink: CRIST IS RISEN.

"Mary Bateman's egg," Joshua said.

Phoebe did not understand.

"Her hens laid them with that already written on them. Nature's own miracle, announcing the coming of the Messiah. Only the spelling's bad. Jesus was an 'Ebrew, you see. Not one of us."

Nonetheless, He had his way of helping a poor old woman such as Mary Bateman to survive in starving times, by providing her with eggs she could sell at double the price in the Bradford market. There was the egg, cool, perfect, in Phoebe's hand, and her hope was strong.

"Do you believe in the egg?" Joshua asked.

"'One who suffers, hopes. And one who hopes, believes,'" she answered mechanically, with a common saying.

Mary Bateman, a follower of Joanna Southcott, had been hanged in York four years before as a poisoner, and Joshua told Phoebe that, like Jesus himself, she had been accused and pilloried, although innocent. She was in fact a simple, honest woman—one such as Phoebe—who had been chosen by Christ.

A servant in a great mansion thinks more of himself than one in a small house, though in either case he does no more than scrub floors, and Joshua had authority like no other man she had ever met, since he had become the servant of Christ.

"Have faith that, out of the mud of despair, flowers the rose of joy. Here, in my humble kitchen, you see the bud of that rose. You have only to shine upon it with the sun of faith."

She could believe that, too. Joshua's metaphor was quite clear to her. It was only faith in an inscrutable, all-powerful will, the kind that could write its consolations upon an egg, that could redeem joy out of misery. A moment ago Phoebe had been the unhappiest of creatures, but now that she had discovered hope and faith, she enjoyed the happiness of one at the beginning of a new life.

She believed.

Trust in God that everything happened for the best. The coincidence of the change in Joshua, and her husband leaving home, was surely intended—dare she think such a thing?—to bring them together.

"Margaret!" Edwin awoke in the dark. "Margaret! Are you awake?"

Her cot was at the other side of the room. After some moments, "Yes," she answered.

"I think she locked us in."

He got up, clasping his arms around him because of the cold, and went to the door.

She sat up in bed. "Where are you going?"

"Trying the door." He rattled the latch gently. "It's locked, all right. They want to send us back to 'Orsfalls'."

"Do you want to go 'ome?" she asked. "To your mother?"

"No," he pretended.

"Don't you miss your mother? I miss mine."

"I think we should get out of 'ere," he said brusquely, evading the painful question.

"Now?"

"Yes. I don't trust the cobbler. 'E'll turn us in."

Margaret climbed out of bed. She went to the window and tried the latch.

"We'll break the latch," Edwin said.

"There's no need." She had already swung it open. A cool breeze brought in a smell of moorland.

"What if she 'adn't left us our clothes?" Edwin said. "We'd be stuck."

"There were some girl's shoes downstairs," Margaret said wistfully, as Edwin was putting on his clothes. "I could 'ave got 'em."

"No, you couldn't. It would've been stealing."

"Everyone steals," she answered.

He left his jacket for her to wear. When he was dressed, he put his foot over the sill, onto the stone-tiled roof of a lean-to. The stone scales were silver in the moonlight.

"I'm scared," Margaret said, getting dressed.

But Edwin was already disappearing, and did not hear her.

"Wait for me!" she cried, and clambered out after him.

"Be careful wherever it's mossy," he told her. "Walk where it's dry. Keep away from the edge and don't look down, and you'll be all right."

The row of cottages was built on a hillside, with their rooftops at different levels. Edwin had climbed onto a neighboring roof by now and was standing by the chimney. She did not dare to rise from all fours but crawled cautiously.

In the moonlight they could see that the roof on the far side reached almost down to the ground. She watched him walk sideways down the slope and disappear. She heard him land in the dry grasses. Then his head popped up.

"Come on!"

She jumped. He caught her.

The moonlight shone on the church clock. "What time does it say?" Margaret asked.

"Half past six. Can't you tell the time?"

"Never been shown."

The village was almost deserted as they ran through it, but they could hear two drunken soldiers shouting in a lane.

"Militiamen!" Edwin whispered, with proper contempt.

They made their escape, not in the Oldham direction, but along the other side of the great moor, over Blackstone Edge, toward Littleborough, Rochdale, Middleton, and Manchester.

No one was interested in a couple of children. On reaching the far side of the Pennine hills, they spent a couple of nights sleeping in barns.

On Monday, as they traveled through the Lancashire towns, making their way toward Manchester, they came across confusion and violence. Near Rochdale, the churn of a farmer who charged too much for his milk had been overturned at the roadside. They were informed of the facts by the soldier who was on guard, presumably against cats, as nothing else could have licked it up.

Farther along the road, young men carrying sticks, hammers, and other tools told the children they were going to Middleton, "to see to Mr. Burton's mill." Some had white paper roses in their lapels.

When Edwin and Margaret reached the Rochdale market, fish, vegetables, and meat were scattered everywhere, and the stall-holders had been driven off. What the crowd wasn't able to either swallow or take away, it was laughingly feeding to stray dogs, to abandoned pigs and hens, or tossing into the road. So far, the children had fed themselves entirely by thieving or begging, and this was too good to be true.

Between the tumbled stalls, over the crushed fruit and vegetables, broken baskets, and smashed pottery, came a procession of women, laughing, savage, yelling obscenities, setting pigs squealing and hens squawking; throwing stones at the shuttered windows of the inn and of the grander houses where the traders were hiding. At their head came Lady Ludd, carrying a loaf of bread, soaked in blood and stuck onto a pole.

Eventually, troops arrived to read the Riot Act. They arrested a few, and drove everyone else home. The children were requisitioned to help clean up the mess. They were given a penny by a smiling sergeant, who thought the whole day a great joke.

They slept that night among the stalls. There being so much scrap food still available, and some more pennies to be earned by cleaning up, they stayed all of the next day also.

On Wednesday morning, they set off to pass through Middleton to Manchester. White blossoms of blackthorn fountained out of the hedgerows. Flowers of cow parsley, great white dishes of them, poured out of the banks.

Middleton was empty and funereal, with a smell of ashes in the air. Bolted to the railing of Burton's Mill was a notice, painted on wood and varnished; sign painting was, apparently, the only trade to survive the riot.

Edwin could almost read the notice unaided, but he asked some bystanders to help him out—not that they could read, but they knew by heart what it said:

NOTICE

D. Burton and Son have determined NOT to work their looms anymore. Dated April 11, 1812.

Along the roads to Manchester, the children passed rows of deserted cottages. Hundreds of the workers who had lost their employment had left the town. Loaded carts were on the road. Doorsteps were crowded with people discussing it. They did not talk about revolution, but about the need for law and order. They wrung their hands and worried about how they would manage. Who were the culprits? Who was going to pay?

Late at night, the children reached Manchester. They came upon the cathedral, where tramps muttered in their sleep against the walls, and this frightened them away. They continued along Mill Gate and passed the orphanage, feeling envious of the waifs in their dry beds.

It had started to rain, so they tried to find shelter among the warehouses along the banks of the River Irwell. Edwin felt like a mouse in a store. The only large buildings he had ever been inside were Lady Well church and Horsfalls' mill, and one warehouse following another amazed him.

They were not successful, so they penetrated into deeper regions of the city, beginning to give up hope of finding a refuge. Every door was locked, every passage barred, and there was hardly a crevice to serve as a hiding place. All the buildings were dark, except for an occasional office with a yellow light glowing where an ambitious clerk was toiling through the night.

They wandered along Deans Gate, until they came to the elegant houses there. They turned into John Street. Wet through, they crept hopefully under any shallow arch or leaning plank, until the wind and rain changed direction and drove them out again. Edwin was by now despairing, but Margaret felt at her most confident in a city, trying doors, never losing hope of finding one unlocked. At last she found . . .

"Edwin!"

They rushed up the stairs. There was another door, and that too was unlocked. They found themselves in a big room that was faintly lit by a huge skylight. The place was overhung by a strange smell. Most of the floor was bare, but in the middle was a gaunt wooden structure, fitted with ropes, pegs, and winding gear. It was encrusted with thick globules. Edwin touched one and penetrated a dark wrinkled skin, finding it red and sticky beneath.

"Blood!" he cried.

"It's a gallows," Margaret whispered.

They must rest here, even so. Stumbling around, they came across some rolls of fabric, very stiff but they would do for a bed.

They curled up, clutching each other. They did not undress, except for Edwin removing his clogs. He slept immediately. Margaret lay awake for a long time, staring at the rainy blackness in the skylight, watching the flowering stars before shutters of cloud were drawn over them again.

As the rain sprinkled the skylight, so tears swam across her eyes. Was she to say goodbye to Edwin tomorrow? She had to make her way to London, though she did not yet know how. Because Edwin was going to Liverpool, they had decided it was to be in Manchester that they must part company. She feared her sniveling would wake her friend, and willed herself asleep.

The gray light of a bleak dawn was breaking through the skylight when Edwin awoke. It lit up row upon row of jars of pigment—cadmium red, alizarin crimson, Prussian blue, chrome yellow, indigo.

He leaped up, thrilled at the sight.

A marble-topped table was splattered with the glowing pigments. There was a mortar and pestle, a jar stuffed with brushes, a kidney-shaped mahogany board with a hole in it and colors dabbed around the rim, an oily rag, a dirty smock, and a queer black hat, such as a judge might wear before delivering the death sentence.

Edwin went up to the "gallows." He turned a little brass handle, but when part of the structure started to squeal and slide noisily, it scared him, so he left it alone.

He turned to the palette, smelling for the first time in his life the aromas of turpentine and poppyseed oil. He put his finger into it, feeling the texture, the way his father fingered cloth.

He picked up the fattest, softest brush and dipped it into a container filled with turpentine and oil. He watched the bristles swell and droop as he brought them out. He exulted over the profusion of colors.

Margaret awoke. "What are you doing?"

"Nothing," he answered. "Nothing."

He loaded his brush with chrome yellow and knelt before a primed canvas against the wall.

He remembered the young eagle chained in the vicar's garden in Lady Well. He drew its great wings in flight, from one corner of the canvas to the other.

"What is it?"

"Nothing," he said again. "Nothing."

CHAPTER ELEVEN

April 21st–May 10th

manuel Burton's house was burning to the ground. From the end of the Park Mount garden, a crowd of vandals, with Crawshaw at their head, watched one flaming beam after another topple through a shower of roof tiles, masonry, and dust. A short distance away, a haystack was crackling and flaring. Frightened horses were rearing and cantering around a field.

Across the town, the Hollinwood colliers with Mad Dick's inspiration were smashing the gable of the mill manager's house.

"But our enemies have escaped us!" Crawshaw shouted against the roar of the fire and the crashing timbers. "The rats!" He turned this way and that, looking for a following. "The bastards have gone to Burton's father's house at Rhodes! We should go and fire it while we have the chance!"

"And which of us will be hung for murder?" Mor retorted.

Crawshaw tried to get away from him.

"Our enemies are at Rhodes—the father's house! We can burn 'em in their hideout like so much vermin."

Mor still followed. Harriet would be at Rhodes.

"And be hung for murder!"

He was hoarse from shouting as he followed Crawshaw from group to group. Now Crawshaw was trying to hide from him in the smoke, but could be heard coughing.

Crawshaw, flushed, turned on him. Already a stream of people, like hornets in flight, was humming with anger toward Rhodes, obeying Crawshaw.

"Backslider! What's wrong wi' thee? Are you a coward, poet? Prove you're not a coward."

Mor made a jump at him, and found himself hanging onto Crawshaw's lapel. He fell away, with nothing but a white paper Yorkshire rose crumpled in his fist.

"Thou'rt a coward! A short-arsed cripple wi' no stomach for the fight!" Crawshaw shouted, then turned and ran across the fields.

He disappeared amongst a cluster of tightly shut cottages, where Burton's employees were hiding, or peeping from windows.

On his long legs, he soon got to the head of his followers. Mor struggled to catch up. He still believed that he could explain their foolishness to blind, excited people.

Then a troop of Scots Greys was seen cantering from the Manchester direction. One detachment split off into the town, the other turned toward Rhodes, where some of the crowd had got into the grounds and yards. The cavalry began their charge a short distance from Mor. They had no need of their swords. Mor found himself clawing, as ruthlessly as anyone else, into a soft mass of people who were scrambling away from the hooves. He hardly saw the tunics, the sashes, the heaving muscles of the towering horses, the clods of earth flying up. He saw only what was before his face. For a second, he was thrust against the breast of a woman whose blue cotton dress was damp with milk. He had spoken to her earlier; her baby had died of starvation and cold.

The crowd, in its panic, kicked out like the horses of the cavalry. Cries tore by Mor's ear. One second he was buried in flesh, smothered in the sweaty smells of fright, and the next he was taking in a flash of open sky.

When he was able to look around again, the Greys had passed by. The great haunches of their horses were disappearing down the wide path cleared for them, and over the brow of a hill.

In the drifting smoke and confusion, there was no sign of Mary.

Mor took no interest in where the Greys had gone to, nor in what they might be doing now. What he did see was that everyone was fleeing.

He stood with tears in his eyes. How could they hope to stand their ground against cavalry? They could now be picked off one by one; grabbed on the highroads, hunted in the villages. Many would be arrested. He should save his own skin. He decided to make his way alone to Oldham.

Scraps of conversation, words of bluff, or of fear, and nervous bits of advice were scattered in the air: "Will the cavalry chaps recognize us, d'you think? Spies are everywhere." "We all must melt into the countryside." "I've an aunt who bakes cakes by a mill in Meltham. Nobody'll look for us there."

Mor knew his direction only vaguely. Like everyone else, he tried to avoid the highroad. He found himself trampling across a newly sown field of oats. Again and again on his journey, he heard from nearby, "The countryside is the only safe place." "I've a sister in service to a schoolmaster who writes pamphlets in Marsden. I'll go over there, I think." "Will they recognize us? The cavalry man looked me straight in the eye. I don't think I'll go home. He'll come looking. The women'll have to manage without me for a while." "I'll go into Yorkshire. There's no village in Yorkshire that won't take us in. That's what they're like in those hill villages . . ."

Following minor lanes, asking his way of the odd rambler or fellow fugitive threading along hedgerows, Mor continued until he saw the Oldham church upon its hill.

Hostelers came to the doors of their inns, and people were lingering at farm gates. They wanted to know why so many were lugging furniture and pictures. Two men had Mr. Burton's voluptuous "Danaë"; another pair carried a mahogany cabinet. A woman, who by the look of her had no food at home, was struggling with a gilt mirror. It seemed that her desire for beauty was what meant most to her.

Mor stole into Oldham, along Manchester Street, going right past the Eagle Inn. He had left his fiddle in charge of the proprietor there, but soldiers lounged by the door. There was little sign of them elsewhere, yet Mor felt uneasy. A fellow in a fine coat, who apparently had nothing to do, was eyeing him. Mor turned left, along Cheapside, to the cellar.

Even from the outside, he knew that Mary was not at home. But why should he expect her to return?

Although they had spent such a brief period in it, the sight of the building filled him with poignancy. He realized, then, that any place they might inhabit together would become haunted with love.

Their upstairs neighbor, with her tired and tearful children, was pacing the street, up and down, catlike, stopping everyone she could. She had heard the same story time and again, but there was no news of her husband.

" 'E's a joiner by trade. There's a new cradle inside that 'e was making. 'E never thought he'd 'ave another baby at his age. But I'm young," she lamented.

"We know nothing of 'im, Mrs. Johnson," she was told. "Seen nothing of 'im. Last we saw, 'e'd gone into the public house."

" 'E's late," she announced simply, to Mor.

From her look, he knew that the woman loved her husband. "I don't know anything about 'im."

"Did you see the soldiers—the dragoons?"

"I don't think they killed or caught anyone."

"I've 'eard that a man was shot dead at the corner of Tonge Lane. I've 'eard that from several. Those Scots Greys officers are not like us. They're not militia. They're gentlemen. They've no time for such as us—not if we so much as raise our 'eads."

Mor offered the only comfort he could. "The chance is only one in thousands that the man they shot's your husband."

"Aye, maybe. The children are crying. You didn't see anything?"

"Nothing. We all just ran."

"He can't run so well."

She was stroking the head of a little girl, absentmindedly. When she realized what she was doing, she wept again. "The children . . ."

But as Mor had no news to give her, Mrs. Johnson was already turning to others.

There was nothing to do now. They were defeated.

Mor retrieved the key from where he had hidden it under a stone.

The cold ashes, the empty bed, the tear in the straw mattress where he had hidden "The Beggar's Complaint," Mary's cosmetic box, mirror, and hairbrush all awaited him.

He sat and blubbered for half an hour. His chest ached and his throat tightened with soreness, yet the tears kept coming.

He tried to recover by reading what he himself had written: "The sufferings of the poor are not the effects of divine dispensation but the offspring of wicked men and bad systems . . ."

He thought of Edwin, Gideon, and Phoebe, until it grew dark. He laid a fire. He lit a candle. He picked up his oval stone from the hearth and fondled it, deriving comfort.

He heard the door move. He turned and there was Mary.

The look upon her features, one he had not seen before, took him so much by surprise that he didn't quite recognize her for a moment. She was transfigured by her longing to see him, and then by finding him. He had never had such an experience with a woman before.

Her dress was torn, her cosmetics smeared, her hair in disarray.

His chair fell onto its side as he jumped up to greet her. Starting with lips, they were in need of four, of six, of eight, of ten hands, wanting to touch every part of each other, all at once.

"Poor darling, your eyes are red!" she said. "But it's all right! I've found a place for us to 'ide. Talking to them along the road, I found a place where we can go. In Delph."

"Delph?"

"Six miles away. Back in Yorkshire. They'll soon come looking 'ere. It's not me that I'm scared for. They'll not bother me. It's you. We're staying with a farmer named Gartside."

"My fiddle's at the Eagle."

"We'll go for it. My trunk'll be at the George by now. I'll think of some way to get it transported. We'll go and get your fiddle. Take a stroll through the starlight. I'll leave a message about my trunk. Get someone to 'ide it for me."

"And Harriet? What'll 'appen to 'er?"

"The cavalry didn't let the crowd get near Rhodes. Burton didn't see me, so she'll be all right. She's better off with 'im and never seeing 'er mother again, than knowing she's . . . she's . . . that she's the daughter of a whore. Oh, I'm sick of it, More Grief! I'm sick of that life!"

They collected Mor's fiddle, but returned to the cellar. The danger was not immediate, and they needed a night's sleep before they left Oldham.

A lot of scurrying took place outside during the night. Mor picked up only a little of it, and then he slept. Mary was awake for a long time, her thoughts running away with her.

In my life now it's either Mor or the general. This game can't go on forever. I'm tired! I'm wore out! The men don't want me! I can feel they're laughing at me 'alf the time. The general doesn't understand that even a corporal can be choosy, and won't take risks. They don't tell me the news anymore. So as to get by, I 'ave to do more and more specialities. My schoolmaster-weaver 'ere couldn't stand it for five minutes, if 'e knew . . .

My 'alf brother! For 'is father was mine—Oliver Greave. Anne Wylde couldn't be 'is mother, as 'e's thirty. Must 'ave been from Greave's philandering before that.

'E'd be shocked, though, if 'e knew. Fancy, so I've got a family at last! That's important in life, that is. In the end, it matters. "Blood's thicker than water," I've always said.

We'll get away to the south. Give the general the slip. Take up a little farm somewhere, be like the Queen of France, Marie Antoinette.

Otherwise I'll get picked up in Oldham or somewhere, and when the general's getting no information from me, 'e'll say, "She's wore out, she is, why bother with 'er? She couldn't tell a disaffected soldier from Adam. There's been no news from 'er for a month. Chuck 'er in the canal with a stone round 'er neck."

Either that, or my poor brother—well my 'alf brother—Mor will watch me swinging at Lancaster and not even know who I am.

No, thank you, that's not for me. I've always kept a step ahead and that's the only way I've stayed alive for so long . . .

Just look at 'im sleeping, blowing bubbles like a baby. Wish I could sleep like that. Gawd, though, I love 'im.

Gartside's our answer for the time being. Why didn't I think of it before Mad Dick mentioned 'im, in 'is sneering way? "What is it you do for Gartside, Mary the Scar, you fucking whore?"

What else does he think I am but a fucking whore? It's my profession.

" 'E only likes men, doesn't 'e, that Gartside? Unless it's animals. What can you do for 'is unnatural practices? 'E lives upon the 'ills wi' nothing but the sheep for company, doesn't 'e? That's what 'e likes. 'Where sheep may safely graze.' Not in Delph, anyway, they can't. Why don't you run to 'im and 'ide? You seem to do something for 'im, I don't know what."

If only 'e knew . . .

"As a matter of fact," I says to Mad Dick, "that's where I am going—to Gartside. And as a matter of fact, Gartside doesn't like men at all," I says to Mad Dick, "because I cured 'im, good and proper. And 'e

doesn't go in for animals. 'E doesn't like nothing at all. 'E's one of them sort, if you want to know. Why don't you go to Gartside's yourself, Mad Dick, and 'ide there?"

The way 'e spat then! "Me! Near 'im! Not if I'd be 'ung for it."

You probably will, you mad deserter.

"I think you're scared of Gartside," I told 'im. "You're scared because you can't understand 'im. You're scared because 'e's not a bully like you. Yes, you're scared when 'e turns the other cheek, and doesn't do what you expect of 'im. Like they were frightened of Jesus Christ, when it came to it. 'Cos your type thinks you're men but, when it comes to it, you're scared. You wouldn't dare be like Gartside, who you think of as a coward, just because 'e'd never 'urt a fly."

As a matter of fact, Gartside'd be perfect for me and Mor. Doesn't want anything from me, except the pleasure of doing what 'e's told.

It's a mystery to me, too, why 'e likes being a servant. Can't be expected to understand everything, can I? But there were men like that who came to Mrs. Rawdon's when we were in London. Members of what Mor would call "the endless varieties of 'uman nature." Men who are delighted to serve—well, you can't say beauty, you can't say that anymore about me, but to serve something that they recognize. There's not much I can't get to the bottom of but . . .

Bottom, ho! ho! They soon drop their drawers wi' me. But 'e comes and never touches me. Scrubs the floor, washes the privy, and pays for the privilege.

Says it relaxes 'im. So long as 'e can watch me with a soldier sometimes. 'E's never jealous, 'e just likes me to be around, giving orders. Mor'll find soon enough 'e's nothing to be jealous of, neither. Nobody'll look for us in Delph.

I remember Gartside coming to me for the first time. The state 'e was in! All boastful and giggling at first, throwing 'is weight about, not that 'e 'as much to throw, talking about who 'e knew, where 'e'd traveled, as if I'd be impressed. I who've been everywhere.

Then it comes out. Nothing 'appened. I tried everything I knew. Nothing 'appened. Until I started getting angry. In a manner of speaking nothing 'appened then either, but 'e was overcome. Blissful.

"Oh, I see," I said. "I understand." 'E told me 'e couldn't do anything with a woman, 'ad suffered some terrible disasters, 'cos 'e felt too much like one 'imself.

"I bet I know what you like," I said to 'im. "Don't tell me you travel all over the place, neglecting your loom, bending the ear of a duke's footman, of staymakers and 'atters, for no reason at all." After two or three gins, 'e was rolling on the floor confessing to 'is nanny.

Things 'e knew that, if I told someone about them, they'd 'ang 'im with more contempt than for a dog. And 'e made 'imself vulnerable to all that, in my 'ands. Quite deliberate. 'Is eyes were all wet. Next thing 'e was laughing himself stupid, 'is face purple, crying 'is heart out, whimpering like a puppy, poor lamb, kissing my clothes, clutching the carpet, banging the floor. All 'e wanted was to be forgiven and then controlled. Told 'e'd been a bad boy, oh wicked, but now it was all right.

"Do you know I can do anything I like with you now you've told me all that?" I said to him. "There's only me between you and the 'angman."

And suddenly I perceived the whole design, I knew everything. That was just what 'e wanted! Me in control of things, to forgive or not to forgive. Oh, I 'ad 'im then.

I'd never 'ave believed it would turn out like that, when 'e came to me. 'E was solemn as a judge, righteous as a Methodist preacher.

And when everything was told, it turned out that 'e 'adn't after all done any of the things 'e claimed 'e 'ad with 'atters and footmen—'e'd only thought about doing them. 'E just wanted to be treated as though 'e had. The benefits of being a bad boy, without having been one.

Wonder what it's like in 'is shack in Delph?

And, after that, as soon as the roads are quiet, in a month, we'll sneak away to the south.

"Are you awake, Mary?"

"Yes, I'm awake, More Grief."

"What is it?"

"Just thinking."

"I love you."

"It's light. We'd better be going."

They were traveling east out of Oldham, toward Yorkshire again. But instead of going back to Ripponden, they followed the edge of Greenacre Moor at a different angle, toward Delph. Once again, Mor's fiddle was strung across his back, and lying the other way across his shoulders was his leather bag.

Many other travelers were on the roads—workmen carrying their bags of tools, young men and women looking frightened. The world was full of fugitives.

"You ever tried to catch a fly on a summer's day?" Mary said. "When it's never settled in one place more than a second? That's 'ow they'll never catch us. We'll melt into the countryside. They'll never find you, I promise."

"We ought all to have stayed together in Middleton. If we'd not been dispersed, we would be undefeatable. Now it'll be sport for them to hunt us down like foxes."

"We two will always be together. Some day soon, we'll take a little farm. I've got some money laid by. I could surprise you."

"I could manage a little farm. It'll get rid of the fluff in my lungs." He was laughing. Of course, he didn't believe her. "Who is this Gartside?" he asked.

" 'E's been a friend of mine for years."

"Oh? I thought you were tired of all that."

"Not that kind of friend. 'E's different. Someone on the raid mentioned 'im as asking about me, and I thought, 'That's a sign from the Almighty. That's where we go.' 'E's been coming to me with 'is problems often enough and I've solved them for 'im. It's my turn now."

"So what's different about him?"

" 'E's got something special bout 'im, this one. 'E's so kind, and grateful. Wouldn't 'arm a fly. I know 'ow to treat 'im. You don't understand yet. But don't worry, you've nothing to fear from 'im. I've never been to 'is place, it's somewhere 'idden out of the way, but we'll find it. It'll be all right. When we've done with Delph, and things 'ave gone quiet again, we'll go to 'Olywell Street in London to see about printing your writing, before we take up a farm."

"I'm not writing that sort of book. I write about history, and history's wrongs, to be its witness."

" 'A Turk in 'Is 'Arem' is 'istory. So is 'The Infidelities of the Prince Regent.' "

"You make it all up—all that sort."

"All 'istory's made up. It's just that your sort is made up in the 'eads of poets and scholars. They don't think they make it up, but they do.

How do they really know what 'appened? We're the ones who know what 'appened at Middleton. But when they come to write about Burton's raid, nobody'll mention us. It'll be all about 'mobs' and 'troops of Scots Greys.' Not unless we get tried and 'ung, then our own words might get taken down. So long as we confess, and say it all started wi' not going to church on Sunday."

Along the road, they heard more of what had happened during the previous day. A certain John Nield was shot while "trying to run away" from the Greys near Alkrington Hall. A woman, who had been watching the sight from her window, received a bullet through her arm from the Cumberland militia. And a man had, indeed, died at the end of Tonge Lane.

"Was he a joiner?" Mor asked.

"There was an old joiner shot in the churchyard, at about six o'clock in the evening. 'E'd been sitting in the public house, and walked out when 'e thought that all was quiet. Mr. Johnson. They say 'e was standing in front of a gravestone—'e 'ad something to do when no one was looking. A Cumberland militiaman decided to send a ball through 'is neck."

They crested Wall Hill. They were facing east, with the risen sun on their faces, the road branching steeply down to Dob Cross on their right, and to Delph, hidden to their left behind Knott Hill.

"We'll have roses round the door, 'erbs in the garden," Mary said.

"Where?"

"At the little farm we're going to take, of course. You can write in the evenings. We'll grow old together. We'll take different names. Nobody'll know that we're not married. We'll go to a different parish and be carefree as aristocrats. We'll be 'appy."

They had to descend into the shadow that still enveloped Delph, the great hill looming over it like a tombstone. Then they must climb beyond, toward Friar Mere.

As they looked back, the stone roof tiles reaching out of the shadow shone with light, like the glossy wings of black birds flying into the sun.

"You don't believe I could look after pigs and 'ens," Mary said. "But I was born to it."

"Oh, I believe it. I just can't imagine that anything so sweet could 'appen."

"What I've learned in life is that anything can 'appen. Anything at all."

"What I've learned is that things don't change, though they seem to."

They asked their way of a weaver who was out early in his garden, planting peas and broad beans. The sun drew warm smells from the turned earth. One would never guess that, a few miles away, a disaster had occurred.

"We call 'im 'Bachelor,' that Gartside. Lives up there like Jesus Christ 'imself," the weaver told them.

As they climbed, more and more of the enclosures were filled with rocks. Men, women, and children were carrying them to the edges of the fields, using them for heightening walls or filling gaps. In the valleys, new walls were being properly built with foundations under the instructions of masons, but here the "moor-edgers," as they were contemptuously called, simply threw up what were no more than boundary markers with the cleared stones. One way or another, lifetimes were being spent in spinning a web of thousands of miles of stone walls over the Pennine hills.

Mary cuddled up against him as they climbed. "I want a little place in the south, not here. Nothing much. Something like Marie Antoinette 'ad, the Queen of France, who kept sheep. We'll 'ave roses round the door."

"And typhus in the kitchen."

The road grew increasingly stony and like a stream bed, because of the water spilling from horse troughs or breaking through the rough walls. They reached the moortop, where the light crossed at a level angle. Fields of sapless grass mirrored the strong, morning sun.

They passed a man heading downhill, his horse so highly laden with wool that it caught and almost toppled in the strong breezes at this height, above the windless valleys. When they asked him where Gartside lived, he smiled and simply pointed over his shoulder to where more jagged, dark rocks fringed the sky. Then he spoke harshly to his horse and continued down the track. When he had descended twenty yards, he turned to stare after them, either baffled or intrigued by where they were heading.

At last, Mor and Mary arrived at their destination. It was a little cottage, built of blackened stones, with smoke torn from its chimney by the ever-present moorland breeze. At its side was a small stone shed. The place stood with a barren air of hopelessness in a nest of unattended enclosures. No weaving was stretched on tenterframes, which made one wonder what its inhabitant lived on. A few hens picking flies out of the bog, and an old ragged pony having a hard search for fodder, were the only signs of husbandry. Its occupant did not appear to be fond of being out of doors.

To Mor, it seemed an alarming spot to choose for a hideout, because it was so exposed. Anyone moving there would attract attention from the other side of the valley. In the somber landscape, the bright colors that Mary wore would flash for miles.

On second thought, he realized that anyone coming for them could be spotted from far off.

"Gartside is in for a surprise," Mary said.

There was no dog tied up to frighten away visitors, and this made the hovel seem even more deserted. The door was open: this may have been a gesture of invitation, but was more likely to be because the cottage was so damp and cold as to be on most days pleasanter for a gust of fresh air.

Mary entered first, boldly, as if it was her own home. The lintel was so low that even Mor had to duck under it. A fire was burning, and it was needed. Upon the whitewashed walls Mor saw, scrawled and corrected in a large hand:

UNIT~~Y~~E IS STRENTH

EGALIT~~Y~~E FRATERNIT~~Y~~E

ALL IS VANIT~~Y~~E

Beyond Mary's shoulder, Mor saw an apparently serene little man, thirty or forty years of age, and more like a dry little old woman in his dark, Sunday-looking clothes. He was sitting by the hearth with a large book on his knee, his white face polished by firelight. The first impression was of a sad man, waiting for something to turn up. His shyness, possibly, was what made him also look forbidding.

" 'Ullo, Mr. Gartside. So this is where you live, is it? We've come to see you. This is my friend, Oliver."

"Mary!"

Gartside put his book on the floor and got up, bustling nervously. He had entirely lost his hopeless expression.

"What a remote place this is, sir. You live by weaving?" Mor asked, but Gartside took no notice of him. It was as if he wasn't there.

"Mary! Well, well . . ."

"We have walked a long way, sir . . ." Mor began again.

Gartside still hardly noticed him. "Glad to meet you, too, friend" was all he managed to say, before returning his obsessed attention to Mary. "Sit down, Mary, do. Oh, my, fancy you coming here! Who'd have thought it?"

She had already taken his seat by the fire and pulled off her boots. Gartside picked them up. She sat calmly as Gartside fussed around his cottage. He was like a woman who was looking for something of which to be ashamed, and tidying things into cupboards; the way that Mor had often seen Phoebe behave.

"Oh, yes, please . . . do warm your feet. Oh my, oh my."

"Come and sit down, Oli. Make yourself at 'ome. Still fond of your Bible, Benjie? Ecclesiastes, is it? Miserable stuff. My friend 'ere's a radical, too, so you can trust 'im all right. Don't worry. 'E won't turn you in, Benjie! Oh, my feet. Don't put them boots too near the fire, Benjie, or I'll be cross. You 'aven't changed much, 'ave you, Benjie? To be honest, we're on the run. There's been a big raid on Middleton. 'Ave you 'eard of it?"

"Some of the fugitives were in Delph a few hours ago, talking about it and they said—"

"Don't interrupt me, Benjie! So you've met 'em coming this way already, then? Well, we want shelter for a while. We're spreading the story that Oli is my brother, so that's what you must say to anyone who asks. Where's your teapot, Benjie? You got any good blends from your grocer's? Come on, sit down, Oli. Stop 'anging around like a bad smell. Gartside'll do us the honors."

Benjamin Gartside swung the kettle over the fire and rooted in his cupboard for tea. He was not the slightest bit embarrassed or resentful at the way Mary treated him.

"Oh, Mary, Mary. You!" he muttered.

Mor sat by the hearth, not understanding what was going on, yet feeling safe because of Mary's self-assurance. Like a cat, she blinked and never once averted her gaze as she watched Gartside.

"I 'ope you've got a decent room for us, Benjie! We don't want something where the 'ens 'ave slept before us. Now, you may come and 'ave some tea with us. You sit on the floor 'ere. That's nice. Now, Benjie, what's been 'appening to you? Tell us all about everything . . ."

In late April and early May, a warm spell blanketed the moors. Gusts of fiery wind swept through the heat—blasts out of the door of an oven. They bent and stretched the grass, creating silver waves that died off listlessly in the distance. Each morning and evening, the hills were sharply defined, dancing in fire. The sky, the streams, and the bleached grass upon the moortops became pools of red.

In the valley, early every morning, weavers and farmers took advantage of the dew to scythe their crops. The hills soon turned gray with heat. During the midafternoon they disappeared into a soft mist. All day, the farmers hardly looked up. They were too absorbed in getting their grass cut, dried, and into barns, lest a wet summer set in soon.

Gartside's own farm had no grass to grow. It was too high up. Someone, with arms full of grass, might look up to see the farmhouse hung as a dark little mark on the edge of the sky. The haymaker might just be able to make out Gartside, watching him as he leaned on a gate or wall, or by a certain rock where he went sometimes to pray, calling it his "altar."

Mor would often stroll over to him. Side by side, they would stare over Friar Mere—not a mere, that is, a lake, at all, but an expanse of bog and peat gullies.

" 'Vanity of vanities, saith the preacher, all is vanity,' " Gartside held forth. "It's too bright to last. We'll be paying for it, you'll see. 'What profit hath a man for his labor under the sun? One generation passeth away . . . the earth abideth forever.' It's a good text, that. It's looking very black over Rochdale way."

Gartside was right. He knew a great deal about the sky above his rocks.

The weather broke. The storm slashed at the grass, leaving the fields broken. The black cavities among the rush beds of Friar Mere filled with water.

The sun burned through again, and the gullies on the moortop cracked. The farmers below resharpened their scythes and did their best with the wreckage.

Conversation had not at first flowed so easily. Gartside was wary. When Mor tried to break the ice with tales beginning "In my village of . . ." Gartside would interrupt. "Don't tell me! Keep to yourself where you've come from and what you've done. That way, you'll oblige me by never suspecting that I've told anybody about you. You'll find that they're all like that in these parts. They've got enough secrets of their own."

Mor could see that Gartside, the "Bachelor," pretended to be more of a hermit and an eccentric than he was, in order to inhibit questioning. The ruse was his cover.

It was guilt at his own nature that made him so pessimistic, Mor realized. He saw all of nature as unsatisfactory, transitory, fated, and so he consoled himself with the gloomy enigmas and fateful questions of Ecclesiastes.

Mary was showing herself to be surprisingly domestic, stewing the young rabbits that Mor knocked on the back of the head when he caught them in the grass.

When she'd had enough of overhearing the men, she would intrude on their discussion. "Where's my indispensable, Benjie?" she would ask. Or, "Fetch me some water, Benjie."

The day came when she needed a change of clothes, and so she was anxious to retrieve her trunk. Presumably it was still hidden wherever the friend at the George Inn in Oldham had put it. The authorities must not be able to track it to Delph. She sent Gartside to investigate and he came back with the news that a soldier had already collected it.

A soldier!

Mary refused to be upset. She was a calmer person, now that they had been granted the peace in which to explore their love. When one walked into a room and found the other, the place seemed flooded with the sensation. They touched each other constantly, creating a world between themselves that shut out all others. When they wanted to be alone, Gartside, who had also blossomed into happiness, was glad to be got rid of.

They talked again about that dream of "a little farm." It *could* happen!

They *could* escape! "What profit hath he that hath labored for the wind?" Had not Mor labored for the wind—for a revolution that never came?

Although Gartside seemingly held the world at nought, every evening at six o'clock he rode his old pony down the hills to buy a newspaper. From the Post Office, he collected the *Leeds Mercury,* or sometimes the *Manchester Mercury,* in issues that were always a few days late. Before returning home, he read them aloud to his fellow drinkers over a pint or two of ale taken in his special corner of the public house. They had grown used to him there at this hour of the day. Because of his dry humor that masked a warm disposition, no one persecuted him for his "eccentric ways." His iconoclastic radicalism made him popular, and they did not think that his special Utopia might be different from their own.

From the newspapers, and from the fugitives passing through the remote Pennine villages, they learned of what was happening. Sometimes the travelers had come from a hundred miles away, walking via secretive routes from Nottingham, Sheffield, Manchester, Stockport, or Chester. They brought rumors and news from the organizations that were euphemistically called "burial societies" or "charity clubs."

Thus they learned of the destruction of a mill holding two hundred power looms at Bolton, three days after the firing of Mr. Burton's establishment. In the Nottingham court, five boys, aged sixteen, seventeen, and twenty-one, had been sentenced to be transported for from seven to fourteen years for smashing stocking frames. On May 5th, the newspaper reported, "A woman and two men were apprehended at Middleton and safely lodged in the New Bayley prison for being concerned in the late riots there," and "Thirteen rioters have been committed to Lancaster Castle."

On May 9th, or rather May 10th when the *Leeds Mercury* reached them, they were informed that "the person known by the name of King Ludd is taken and committed to Chester Gaol. His name is Walker; he was a collier, and marched before the deluded mob in a large cocked hat."

King Ludd, despite his "arrest," remained alive and kicking, and continued to provide incidents for the newspapers. "The tranquility of the country is only imperfectly preserved even at the point of the bayonet," concluded the *Leeds Mercury.*

• • •

Mor and Mary spent two weeks in the cottage, so peacefully that it was like a marriage. One day, as they were leaning together at the door, Mor spotted a figure coming toward them from a distance.

Over the crest of the field appeared the tall, battered figure of Mad Dick, lopsided under the weight of Mary's trunk on his shoulder. He had brought it thus far on the pony of a weaver, who could be seen leading his beast away downhill.

Mad Dick disappeared into a hollow, rose again and, although stumbling, was pushing on fast. He was filthy and tattered. He had changed his military uniform for a suit of clothes; if it could be called a suit, for it was in rags and too small for him.

As he came close, Mary laughed. Mor scowled.

Mad Dick dropped the trunk into the yard. He was shaking and sweating.

"Mad Dick, you'll smash my belongings. My china and my teapot are in there, you madman! What's brought you 'ere? How did you get 'old of my trunk?"

"A tankard of water, for Christ's sake! Water, ma'am, water!"

"How did you get 'old of my trunk, you lunatic?"

"I met one o' the general's men confiscating it from the George, didn't I? It cost me a shilling. You owe me something for retrieving it, you do. You can start by giving me some water."

Mary took pity on her old tormentor, and herself fetched him water.

"Thank you, dear. You old whore, you. You're an angel—in disguise, o' course."

Mary laughed. "Who's talking about disguise, the state you're in?"

He gulped and spilled the water, then looked at Mor. "Ah, Mor Greave, if I remember rightly. The one that absconded. Five foot five, and a runaway Ludd. Escaped our clutches once, but now we've got you! 'Left 'is family chargeable to the town'—didn't you? Well, well. There's a reward offered for lodging you in the jail."

"Mad Dick, 'is name is Oli. 'E's my brother, Oliver Wylde. That's what everyone thinks, and don't you forget it. Or I'll turn *you* in."

"We're all in the same boat now, aren't we?" Mad Dick said.

"Yes, we are," Mary answered.

" 'Cos you've let Mr. Burton down, and maybe the general too, so I've 'eard," Mad Dick continued. "I wouldn't be in your shoes for anything. What a weight this trunk is! Try it, Oliver. Go on, try it."

Mor raised one end easily enough, but both ends together was a different matter. He could do it, but only just.

Mad Dick was challenging him. At last he brusquely took over. Mor did not feel in a mood for jokes or physical challenges.

"Oli, me gallows-mate Oli! We'll both lug it inside together. I've 'ad enough of managing by myself in the world. What do you think, weaver? You see, I remember everything. We should all work together. Democrats. Where's the one they call 'the Bachelor'? I want 'im. Where's 'e 'iding? I've come for 'im."

"I'm here," Gartside said from within, quietly. "Who wants me?"

"I do. They call me Mad Dick."

Mary followed the two men as they hauled the trunk into the cottage.

Gartside, wearing a weaver's apron, was washing pottery. "What do you want with me, soldier?" He was trying to be bold, but he was frightened.

"So you're 'im, are you? You're it, I should say. Benjamin Robert Abr'am Gartside, late of Diggle and of Sheffield? Call yourself a man? Then listen to what I 'ave to tell you, fancy pants. I've come to arrest you. Listen to this." He pulled from his pocket a scrap of newsprint. " 'Ere, Mr. Greave, read that. Read it aloud."

" 'Mr. D. T. Myers late of Stamford was convicted at Peterborough last week of an unnatural crime and ordered for execution on Monday next.' What of it?"

"Tell me what *you* think of that, Gartside? Your turn next, isn't it? Don't tell me you don't know what an unnatural crime is, you little beast, you crawling worm. That you've never 'eard of it. 'Ow many 'ave you committed?"

"None," Mary interrupted. " 'E 'asn't done nothing. 'E couldn't."

"I can tell you what 'is crimes are, because there's them that 'ave 'eard 'im confessing when 'e was drunk," Mad Dick continued.

"It's not true," Mary said. " 'E was only talking big. No one could witness what 'asn't 'appened."

"Once with an 'atter in Oldham, once after being drunk on Christmas Day with a silk merchant, and once with a lord's footman, so I've 'eard. He boasted of it 'imself, when 'e was drunk. I don't know what else 'e's done. Young boys too, probably. It makes me sick to think of it."

" 'E's never touched anyone, Mad Dick! I should know, for I'm the physician. I cured him of wanting it. Don't you go talking about 'im when you're drunk, either. Do you 'ear me? Do you *'ear me,* Mad Dick? You 'ave the loosest tongue in Christendom when you've 'ad a drink. 'E's done nothing. 'E *can't,* and that's the sad truth of it."

"And I know different. The truth's out now at last, ain't it, Gartside? What a bugger. If I could bear to touch you, I'd drag you off right now. But it needs a special sort to 'andle the likes o' you. I'm 'ere on behalf of the King, who will shortly send 'is prison cart for you. An open cart, so that everyone can take a look at you, see what a worm you are, see what degradation a 'uman being can descend to. What you've done is worse than being a child murderer. Don't try to tell the judge you're not guilty. Runt! Shit! They've caught your fellow blasphemers now. There's papers on you."

"You liar, Mad Dick," Mary said. "Don't be frightened of 'im, Mr. Gartside. It's 'is sick 'umor. He can't arrest no one. He's a deserter. It's 'im they're going to 'ang. I'll tell you this, Mad Dick. Open your mouth and I'll see to it that you 'ang."

Mad Dick laughed. "Frightened you then, little feller, didn't I?" he said, backing off.

Gartside laughed nervously. Mor went to help him with the crockery.

"You can get on with your needlework now," Mad Dick said. "Your sewing. Your women's skivvying. I won't touch you. Not for the time being. It might make me ill. Just be careful, that's all."

Mad Dick unfastened his belt and, without being offered it, sat in Gartside's chair by the fire. Once he got comfortable, he continued his diatribe.

"Don't try coming near me when my back's turned, that's all. Filth! If you want to save your skin, find me a bed 'ere for a day or two. For a week, for a month if I like. And don't tell no one, or I'll cut your throat and nobody'll be sorry. You're worse than any pig. Call yourself a democrat? You're worse than the filthiest pig. Do you 'ear me? If you were a man you'd do something about it. I can say anything I like to you, can't I? Filth! Shit! Piss! You'll be 'anging with your friend Myers. The sooner the better. Bring me some ale. Go on! Find me some ale. If you 'aven't any, go out and fetch some."

"Give him his ale, Mr. Gartside. Let us have some peace."

Gartside went into the lean-to at the back of the cottage. They could hear him pouring ale into a jug. He returned humbly. He was trembling.

"Don't behave to me like you was Jesus Christ," Mad Dick hissed at him. "Don't you touch me. One thing you learn in the army is 'uman nature. It stinks."

Gartside filled a tankard that Mad Dick had plucked off the mantelpiece.

"Spill any and I'll kill you, you slave. Unfasten my boots, you dog. But don't touch me. Don't you dare."

Gartside knelt on the floor and pulled off Mad Dick's filthy boots.

"Ah, that's better on."

Gartside, leaving the jug and the tankard on the floor, retreated to the back of the room, hiding his shaking hands.

"Don't threaten 'im, or 'e might 'ave the pleasure of seeing you swinging first, Mad Dick," Mary said. "We might all enjoy that. It only needs a message to General Maitland. Mr. Gartside's not scared of you. Nobody is. 'E'll give you a bed—won't you, Mr. Gartside? But only out of the kindness of 'is 'eart. Not because 'e's afraid of you, you bully, but 'cos 'e's a democrat. 'E never gets tired of 'uman nature. That's because 'e's never met you before."

Mad Dick sloppily and noisily swilled back the ale. "Right, then. I won't touch him if 'e's a good little girl. Where's my bed, worm? I've been sleeping amongst the stones and thorns for a fortnight."

"You can sleep with the loom," Mary said.

" 'Ere, are you two married or something? Who's the lady of the 'ouse, 'im or you?"

"Shut up and come with me. You're sweating with fright yourself. I can smell it on you. I can smell cowardice all over you."

"No, I'm not! It's my stockings. I've been living rough." As he stood up, his head grazed the ceiling. "This is an 'ole, this is. It's like worming about in the coal pit again. You should get your wench to do some cleaning, Gartside." He laughed at his joke as if it was the funniest one on earth.

Mary led Mad Dick, in his bare feet, upstairs.

"What are you going to do for me, Mary the Scar, for bringing you your fancy trunk? *I'm* a man, remember."

"Mind your 'ead, Mad Dick."

Too late. Mad Dick cracked his head on the lintel. From living in the open air, he had grown unused to cottages, and found himself too big for one. In a temper, he slammed the door behind him at the bottom of the stairs.

Mary was already at the top. He followed her into a creaking room with brilliant daylight pouring through a long window.

"He's a coward, your unnatural friend. That's why I 'ave to make fun of him. Keep 'im in 'is place. Who's this Ludd you've made up with? What's 'e like?"

"E's a gentleman."

"First weaver and Ludd I've met that's described as a 'gentleman.' There's no such thing. What's 'e got? It's unusual for you to travel the country for two weeks with a fellow."

"Perhaps I'm in love."

"In love! A whore in love!"

"This is your room, Mad Dick."

"Where's the bed?"

The room seemed filled with the loom, but a mattress was tucked behind it. Mad Dick spotted the mattress and fell onto it.

"Talking about cowards—why are you sweating so much?" she asked.

His quivering fingers ran nervously over his face. It was as if he was trying to rip off a mask. "Do you know what 'appened to the private who did not perform 'is duty at the Rawfolds mill?" he said quietly.

Mary sat on the window ledge, safely distant from him. "If 'e behaved anything like you, I 'ope they 'anged 'im."

"They sentenced him to three 'undred lashes."

"You'd 'ave enjoyed it."

Mad Dick buried his face in his hands. "Three 'undred!" he repeated. "Them officers are bastards."

"Did they carry them out?"

"How could they 'ave done it? 'E'd 'ave been dead long before they were finished."

He raised his face, yet looked anywhere but at Mary. To the side of her, through the window. She could not believe it, but there were tears in his eyes.

"It's pretty up 'ere," he said. "No one'd find you. You could live 'ere forever, getting Gartside to do the work."

"So what 'appened, Mad Dick? They used to give 'em a thousand. In doses. It didn't kill 'em."

"They gave him twenty-five, then 'ad to stop. It was the owner of the mill, Mr. Cartwright 'imself, who put a stop to it."

"So there you are, then! You've nothing to be afraid of, Mad Dick. Nothing you're not used to in a whore'ouse."

"Twenty-five!" He became angry again, pummeling his fist into his palm, the tears growing bigger and brighter and unashamed. "Twenty-five is enough to—I'm no coward, Mary! I'm not like that Gartside."

"Leave Mr. Gartside alone."

Mad Dick smiled for a second. " 'E could be useful, couldn't 'e? I could live up 'ere like an Oriental potentate with 'im around to do the work. We could live 'ere together. We could make 'im do anything we want, with what we've got on 'im. He's shitting 'imself with fright."

"Leave Mr. Gartside alone, I said. 'E's not *your* slave."

"I'd like to stay 'ere. I'd like to take the place over. I'm no coward, Mary. I'll accept anything they 'and out to me, but do you know what it's like to suffer twenty-five of the cat?"

"It's a long time since they whipped whores through the streets."

"It's not fun. As soon as it touches your back you feel that you're floating. The pain goes right through your body, to your toes and the ends of your fingers. It burns and it freezes, at one and the same time. That's only the first blow. After that comes the second. Then the third. Your body's already broken in two. You're gasping for breath. You feel there's a noose around your heart. You fight for air. You feel you'll never take air in again in your life. They're beating a drum, and your comrades are brought on parade to watch you, to destroy your self-respect. There's an officer standing by with a sneer on 'is face. And a surgeon, to keep check that you're still alive. You yourself wouldn't be able to say. You feel as though you're already a corpse. The fear of the next blow's worse than the actual pain of it. When it falls, it cuts you in two. If they didn't tie you down, you'd leap off the ground.

"Twenty-five times, Mary! That was just for not firing 'is musket at his downtrodden fellow Englishmen.

"They soak the cat in water. After a time they bring a fresh soldier to carry on with the flogging. One who isn't tired. That's if you're still alive. At every blow you feel you can't go on anymore, but you do go on. Your mind's not there at all.

"They brought 'im to the mill to carry out the sentence, so as to 'umiliate 'im by letting the villagers see 'im flogged. Only—the crowds thought 'e was an 'ero.

"But them dragoons escorted 'im. Sneering dragoons, Mary—officers, gentlemen! You can't imagine 'ow they look down on an ordinary militiaman—like you was the scum of the earth, and that's before you've committed any crime. Pitiless, out of Eton and Oxford and them sort o' places. That's what it turns them into. It makes your blood run cold. They're glad of the chance to flog you, because you're infantry. They say . . ."

He looked at her queerly.

"They say you 'ave peculiar feelings for the one who's doing it to you. Not 'ealthy. You feel that both of you are dancing together, and there's no one else there. Just you and the one who's flogging you exist in the world.

"It's sick!" he shouted. "They tear the flesh off you for writing the truth to the newspaper, and then you get creatures like that Gartside running around free. It makes you mad! There's no justice. Filth like 'im, getting up to 'is tricks."

"Pull yourself together, Mad Dick," Mary said. "You 'aven't been caught yet. And Gartside's no 'arm to anyone. 'E enjoys 'is life, and is meek as a mouse at it. Can't you live and let live? We'll find 'im very useful to take with us when we go, and it makes 'im 'appy."

"We?"

"Not *you*. Me and the weaver, Oli. We're going to 'ave a little farm. In the south. I've saved up the money. It's lodged with friends," she added quickly, in case Mad Dick had thoughts of stealing it.

He looked right through her. Very strange. Murderous. "You think you'll live forever, don't you?" he said.

"No, I don't. Not me." Mary nervously scratched her face, making crimson channels in the white cosmetic. She could see no way to put some spirit into him. "But I'll live long enough to see you 'anging, if you don't pull yourself together."

Gartside did not offend her, because he was consistent and at peace with himself, but she loathed Mad Dick's cowardice, after having relied upon him to be reckless and strong.

Mary swung off the windowsill, teasing him with a show of her leg. "Ah, well, if you're satisfied with your accommodation, I'll be off to find a *man*."

He leaped up from the mattress and pinned her against the wall. "What do you mean by that? Nobody's ever dared say that to me, you old whore! And you go with Gartside!"

"Ow! Let me go! I told you, no one does nothing with Gartside. Now let me go."

Mad Dick was crying.

She spat in his face. He let go then, and she ran. "A coward *deserves* a flogging!" she shouted over her shoulder.

He did not follow. Before she reached the foot of the stairs, she heard him crashing his fists into the furniture and sobbing.

How was Mor to know whether or not Edwin had returned to Lady Well already? Mary had told him that her contacts were looking out for him, but still there was no news. Perhaps the child was with Phoebe.

Mor, instead of caring for his family, was hiding on the moors with a whore. He ought to do as others did, and creep back home at night.

Suppose he sired a baby on Mary and had to stop its mouth with earth? How could he bring himself to bury a child in a well? Or, if he did not do that, then face the responsibility for the tortured, tormented life that it would probably live? What kind of mother could Mary be? He had deluded himself.

He poured his unhappiness out upon Mary. It was provoked when, one night as they lay together, he glimpsed again the black color creeping up from the roots of her hair. The truth was that this woman had made quite sure that he knew nothing whatsoever about her.

"Your hair is black," he said.

"What's that? I'm trying to sleep, More Grief."

"I said your hair is black."

"Yes. What about it?"

"Nothing. It doesn't matter. I've been thinking. Edwin might have gone back to Lady Well. I ought to see if he's there."

"Hold me," she begged.

"I can't . . . I'm afraid of . . ."

"Children." She finished his sentence for him, and turned her back.

He concentrated upon thoughts of Lady Well. The geranium in his window would be coming into bud, and Phoebe would turn it toward the sun. In the valley opposite, which he saw whenever he looked up from his loom or his books, skeins of lighter green would be traced through the old grass.

"Why do you scratch your face all the time?" he asked irritably.

"I don't realize I'm doing it." She buried her hands under the blanket, safe from annoying him.

"What's underneath all that white?"

"My skin. What do you think's underneath? Buried treasure? What is this? The Inquisition? Do you think I'm a witch?"

"What is it that you're trying to hide?"

"I'm not 'iding anything."

Only that I'm pregnant, she thought. *I'm certain of it. I don't need to wait until the next lot o' flowers. I feel different. Everything smells differently. I can smell More Grief all the time, wherever I go, all over me. My mind wanders. I'm not the same person. I keep forgetting where I am and what I'm doing. If that isn't being pregnant, then what is? But 'ow can I tell him, now?*

"What's all this talking for?" she said. "You're keeping me awake."

"You're always hiding something. Your true appearance. Your stealing."

"More Grief, don't! If I didn't steal, we'd starve."

"Even the true color of your hair."

"It's my profession. You know I 'ave to, More Grief! I couldn't survive, and tell the truth. If I did, I'd be at the bottom of the Rochdale Canal by now. In a sack. I'm hiding *you.*"

He wanted to bite off his tongue now, and yet he continued. "The lies that you invent for all those men—just so that they'll enjoy having you."

"Quite the married couple tonight, aren't we? Why don't you take a turn with me? Instead of behaving like a married man. I can't sleep now."

She spoke briskly, like a whore with a client whom she did not like. Angrily, she turned this way and that in the bed. He did not move nor speak.

"You've no need to be so frightened," she continued. "As you're so scared of 'aving children, I've a sheep's intestine for you to wear. You don't need to worry. I know all there is to know about condoms. That's because I long ago learned 'ow much trust I can put in a man's promises to love me and make an honest woman of me—especially when 'e's whispering in the dark. You don't want children, do you? I know, I know! Not with a whore. That's what's troubling you, isn't it, More Grief? Well, don't fret yourself, I don't want babies from you, either, not if you don't trust me. I tell you, I'd rather put my trust in a swab of vinegar, or sulphate of zinc, or iodine, or corrosive sublimate, or strychnine, like some girls put inside themselves."

"Strychnine? Poison?"

"Yes, strychnine. They take a chance on the poison, rather than run the risk of bringing babies into the world and trusting men that say they loves 'em. If I find myself with child, I know what to do, don't worry."

He turned his face into the pillow.

"I'll tell you this, More Grief. When it comes to 'aving children, all men go back to their wives in the end."

"Don't say that."

"It's true. No one wants a whore when she's pregnant. When it comes down to it, a whore's only for enjoying life with. For the deed of darkness, when it rears its ugly 'ead. But a *wife* is what you need for bringing up a family, isn't it?"

"No."

"Oh, yes, More Grief! Don't lie to me. That, I despise. Every whore knows that men all go back to their wives in the end. Love isn't being with a whore for the sake of all you can get out of her, More Grief. All that kissing and falling in love and passion that's in novels—anybody can put it on without effort. It's as easy as picking things up off the street, with a whore. But love—real love is the day-to-day living together, quarreling perhaps but still being 'appy, with children and the old grandparents, grandchildren perhaps as well. Love's a fight and an effort, with its light 'id under a bushel. Something I've never 'ad. Because the men always go back to their wives for that, no matter what they've been whispering to a whore. What do you think 'appens to a whore when she's old? Do you think I'm too much of a fool not to know? I'm dying of poison from the lead, as I'm often told."

She fell silent at last.

"I want you to be mine," he whispered softly.

"There's no reason why I can't be your wife—in the south. We'll take a little farm. That's my dream. Let's go, More Grief. To the south."

She collapsed into tears, her body shaking.

But he did not trust her love, and that was the trouble.

Abruptly, Mary opened her eyes. Gartside was at the bedside. His hands were trembling against his knees as he bent over her. From the other room, she heard Mad Dick moaning, punctuated by short screams.

"Benjie, what is it? What 'ave you done?"

"I think Mad Dick's ill."

"Ssh! Don't wake up Oli. 'E needs to sleep something off. 'Ave you poisoned Mad Dick? I wouldn't blame you for it if you 'ad."

"No, but I daren't go in. Perhaps he's only dreaming."

"All right, Benjie, I'll go." She did not wish Gartside to see her breasts, and so she pulled her nightgown around her as she rose. "My Gawd, 'e sounds as if 'e's being murdered. Are you sure you 'aven't poisoned him, Benjie? I won't tell on you if you 'ave."

"No, Mary. If 'e's eaten anything bad, it's not my fault."

She made for Mad Dick's room, and crept up close. His body was jerking like the last spasms of a hanged man.

"Mad Dick! Sergeant Chadwick! Wake up! It's me, Mary the Scar. You're all right."

Under the blanket, his shoulder jerked like a frightened animal in a sack.

She bent her face closer. "Mad Dick! It's all right. It's me, Mary."

Suddenly both his arms were around her neck, choking her.

"Let go!"

She tore at his hands but they were immovable. His screams and moans were in her ear. She dug fiercely into his ribs, and that awoke him.

"Mad Dick!"

"I love you, Mary. I love you."

"Let go, Mad Dick! Let me go!"

"I love you . . . Oh, Mary, I was dreaming."

"I know. Now let go!"

"I dreamed that a dwarf with iron 'ooks for 'ands 'ad them round my neck."

"That's what I feel like, so let go, Mad Dick."

Instead, his grip tightened.

Struggling to turn her face, Mary searched for Gartside. "Benjie! Do something!"

But Gartside had stood watching for a moment, and then had left.

"Let go, Mad Dick! I'll see you 'ung for this!"

He clamped his hand over her mouth, easily pulled her down, and mounted her. She tried to bite him, but he was too excited for her to dare to struggle much. The first wisdom she had been taught was not to struggle in such a situation, for strangled or ripped-apart girls were often dragged out of canals or from the bottoms of wells, murdered by some frustrated soldier. She must put up with it until he fell asleep. Meanwhile, she concentrated on keeping her lips away from his mouth.

When Mor awoke without Mary at his side, he thought that she had slipped out of doors to relieve herself. Then he heard Mad Dick's horrible moans from the other room. He rose and followed the sounds. He saw the two figures on the bed.

She talks of family? Of love?

He crept back to his room, their room. For three weeks it had been their home. Mary had contrived a pathetic little dressing table. Earlier it had held only her cosmetic box, mirror, and hairbrush, and now the bulkier contents of her trunk were added. An expert traveler, she had transformed the poor, dusty room, draping her silk scarf over the trunk, arranging her blue cloak over the chair, scattering pieces of lace so that it looked as though her maid had not yet cleared up after a visit from her dressmaker, and placing the blue jar on the windowsill, just as in Ripponden.

She lied about everything, and even the room was a fake. Her whole appearance was a lie. She lied about her stealing, her sources of money, her association with Emanuel Burton. She lied about himself. If she had saved his life, it had been only to make him party to her thieving. He could not recall anything she had said which he could believe was true. All that she had said about loving him must also be a lie.

He could still hear her love moans. He emptied his bag of her things and filled it with his own. After he had dressed, he slipped his bag and fiddle over his shoulders. He had his portable props, just as she did, and, like the characters of their respective owners, they were an incongruous mix, a farce.

He was a tramp who had stumbled into a brothel. That was all. He crept down the stairs. He put his boots on by the door. A cool breeze was stirring, smelling of rushes and water. The curlews had returned to Friar Mere from where they had wintered on coastal beaches, and one called over the sweet, newly cut grass, the loneliest of sounds; then another bubbled out of the rush beds. The boulders were bulky against a sky where stars were sweeping through fast clouds.

In the middle of the night, Mor left her.

CHAPTER TWELVE

May 9th–May 12th

Edwin and Margaret did not part company in Manchester. She could not resist traveling on with him to Liverpool. There, at last, they went their separate ways.

Margaret found herself in a coach, traveling away from Liverpool, she believed toward London. She spent two days in the fast coach, which was dark with its curtains drawn. She had peeped out at the untidy villages, the boggy land and pools of Lancashire. Long, brown, symmetrical lines of drainage ditches were cut in the marshes, marking bright green enclosures.

She was not alone. There was a strange gentleman who had said that his name was Pickles. This morning he spoke to her sharply, when he warned her yet again not to "peep out and show your face."

"Where are we going?" she asked, trying to smile. If she scowled he might beat her.

"That's none o' thy business. Thou wouldn't know, if I told thee." He spoke with a strong Yorkshire accent.

"I've been to London before, Mr. Pickles. I'd know the way."

"Would you, then? Well, don't you worry about it. You're safe now, my lass, and thank God for it. No more roaming the streets, an orphan, for thee. Thou 'as food and bed and thou's traveling like a lady. Still thou's not satisfied. At the end o' this trip, we'll 'ave a nice position for thee."

The coach was more comfortable than any bed she had ever been in, and for most of the first day's journey, when she was brought from Liverpool back to Manchester, she had slept, stretched out at full length on the upholstered seat opposite Mr. Pickles. He was most interested that she should be properly rested—a concern that had never before been shown to her. From time to time, she was awoken by shouting at a tollgate, by a noisy market, or by the coachman cursing a herdsman and his flock of sheep.

" 'Ave a rest, child. Thou needs it, poor lamb, so that tha can work for thy living. Thou'll grow up to be a fine lady's maid, I can see that. P'raps to a countess. Why, anything can 'appen when we get to London."

On the first night of her journey, she was locked into a small bedroom of a Manchester inn. Through the second day, she resigned herself to leaning back quietly, or lying curled on her side, studying the strange gentleman, small, plump, and white, who "thee'd" and "thou'd" her, with unpleasant politeness sometimes, and at other times addressed her brusquely as "you." He hid himself, covering his chin with the lapels of his coat or pulling down the brim of his hat. He hardly answered her questions. Instead, he would give her a sweetmeat to fill her mouth, tell her to rest, and not to worry.

Edwin had never stopped trying to persuade her to go to America with him, but on reaching Liverpool and seeing ships, and foreigners, rather than being excited as he was, she realized that she could not trust herself to water and to hiding in the hold of a ship. She could not leave England. She said goodbye to Edwin and went to the inn from which the coach departed for London. She had a timid hope of persuading some lady or gentleman traveling to London to take her on as a servant, or lend her the fare until she obtained a "position." She had become so used to her dirt and her smelly rags that she did not think about it putting others off.

On reaching the inn, she had not known what to do. She did realize that she was too filthy to go inside. Menials were cursing her. A dog snarled. She had arrived early in the morning and was still there at midday, when it started to rain. She cowered in a kitchen doorway, drawn by the smell of food.

She had been aware of the gentleman watching her for some time before he tapped on the dining-room window, three times slowly. She could not believe it. She saw him leave his seat, then he appeared smiling in another doorway at the far side of the inn yard. He looked up at the pouring sky, decided not to go under it himself, and beckoned to her. He was welcoming her from a door beyond which she knew there was food; she was blind to everything except that. She did not mind walking through the puddles in her bare feet. She did not resent standing before him for some time in the rain, shivering with cold on a lower step.

"Where are thou 'oping to go to, child?" he asked.

"To London, sir, where my mother is."

"Thou'rt a lucky girl. I 'appen to run a servants' registry in London. I'm always on the lookout for such a likely article as you. How old art thou?"

"Thirteen, sir." She decided to stick to that.

"Thou seems much younger. Starved, I suppose." He looked disappointed and in doubt. " 'Ave you been turned out from somewhere?"

She couldn't think of an answer.

He winked. "Well, we won't ask why you were dismissed, will we? Let's put it this way. I'll not ask questions about why you're roaming the streets of Liverpool, if you'll not ask anything of me, either. That's lucky for you, isn't it? Some employers might 'ave asked for a character reference. Do you 'ave relatives in Liverpool?"

"No, sir."

"That's good. We don't want anyone poking their noses into our business, do we? I must talk to you about one or two matters, and if everything's satisfactory, I'll take thee to London. But because I've business to attend to in Manchester, we'll 'ave to travel that way first. You wouldn't mind that, would you?"

"No, sir."

"That's a good girl. Hungry?"

She smiled. "Yes."

He touched her head, and it made him grimace. "I'm Mr. Pickles. What's your name?"

"Margaret."

"Any other name?"

"Never 'eard of any."

He led her in, out of the rain. The servants were now smiling at her. He handed her over to a woman who took her into a scullery where the pans were scrubbed. There were huge wood- and coal-fired stoves, and pans of steaming water. Two women scrubbed her face and neck. After half an hour, she was returned to the main kitchen, where she was handed a plateful of food and a fistful of cutlery. The gentleman, who was served the same food, led her to a private corner in the dining room.

"I've had my troubles in the world, too," he said. "My debts to pay. But we can only descend so far, and then the wheel of fortune must turn upwards."

She struggled with the cutlery, being used only to a wooden spoon and knife. Instead of stabbing with the fork, she tried to balance a small potato on it, but it fell into the gravy. She next used her knife to pierce a lump of mutton. She tore at it with her uneven, yellow, ratlike teeth. The meal was served on a china plate. She had never eaten from anything other than wooden bowls before. She looked up and found that the other diners were staring at her.

"My friend Edwin . . ." she began.

"Your friend? You told me you 'ad no friends. Where is 'e?"

Mr. Pickles stood up, eager to take away both plates. He was holding out his fat little hand, expecting her to politely give up her food. Margaret clung to it with one hand, and with the other hand she stabbed hurriedly with the knife. Decisively, he took hold of her plate. His thumb sank into the grease. Margaret clung more tightly, and gobbled faster.

"America," she growled, like a dog with its teeth in a bone.

"America!" Mr. Pickles laughed.

"My friend's not very old."

" 'Ow old is 'e, then?"

"Nine," she managed to say through the food that was scalding her mouth.

Mr. Pickles smiled. She continued to gobble as fast as she could, in case his mood changed yet again.

He sat down. "Let me ask you something," he said. "Something very important. Do y'ave any lady's problems yet?"

"Problems?"

Mr. Pickles was blushing.

"No." She had a whole hot potato in her mouth. Being used to a diet of oatmeal, she did not know how to cut it up. When she had got rid of it, she added, " 'Cos I'm not a lady."

"Art thou sure thou knows what I mean?"

"No."

"Do you . . . bleed?"

"Bleed? No. Where? Can I 'ave more mutton? I don't like the fat. Ugh!" She dropped a lump of fat out of her mouth onto the table and picked it up with her fingers.

He was pointing angrily at her with his knife. "Do you bleed down there? Tell me truthfully. I don't want to put it more candidly, not wanting to offend your delicacy . . . your childish . . . But I must know. Tell me the truth. Yes or no?"

He was now white with anger.

She lifted the plate and licked it. "No."

"Are you sure? Are you telling the truth?"

She eyed him suspiciously over the rim of her plate. "Yes. I don't think so. I don't understand what you mean, Mr. Pickles. Can I 'ave some more?"

"If you don't understand me, you can't 'ave started. Are you sure you're telling me the truth?"

"I don't tell lies, Mr. Pickles."

She waved her empty plate at the servant. "I want some more food!" she shouted.

The servant mouthed something back. Heads were turning at other tables, everyone sternly disapproving of a child with "tantrums."

Mr. Pickles stood up, ready to leave. He hurried her out into the yard and into his coach.

Early on Saturday morning, after she had slept in Manchester, she was again hustled into the coach. Although still forbidden to look out, after they left the city she could tell that they were climbing, more and more steeply. Mr. Pickles told her nothing, so she curled up and went over her memories of the walk to Liverpool.

The coach stopped once, so Mr. Pickles could step out for a brief lunch. He returned smelling of beer. Margaret's bread and cheese were brought to her in the coach, in which she was locked with the curtains drawn.

After a steep drop, the wheels squealing on the brakes, and then a climb upward which almost rolled Margaret off her seat, they came to a halt.

Mr. Pickles opened the door and grabbed her wrist. She could hear the horse being freed from the shafts and clomping off to its stable.

Mr. Pickles stepped down first. Then he handed her out, keeping a tight hold.

She could see she had been brought to the rear of a mansion. The stables, the carriage shed, and the kitchen entrance were nearby. Margaret was not one who expected to be told where she had been taken to, so she did not ask. As Mr. Pickles hurried her toward the house, she kept her eyes down so as not to stumble and cut her feet on the cobblestones. At the top of a flight of stone steps a door opened, without any knocking, and a stout woman pulled her hastily inside.

Margaret took a look around and screamed, then sank her teeth into the fleshy hand of the woman, who yelled and boxed her ears. Mr. Pickles, who was blocking her retreat, grabbed her by the collar. What had thrown her into such a state was her glimpse of the roofs of wool-finishing sheds, a spinning mill, an apprentice house, an old fulling mill, and beyond these, the glint of a small river and woods rising at the far side to moorlands. She was back at Lady Well, at Mr. Horsfall's.

The door was banged shut and locked behind her. The woman removed the key and pocketed it. Inside the room, lamps were lit, because the shutters were drawn. There were piles of clean, sweet-smelling linens. She had been brought to the laundry room.

Mr. Pickles let go of her. He expected her to stand still, but off she set, flashing round the room, blinded by fear, knocking over copper pots and piles of laundry. She tripped over a chair and hopped onward, holding her hurt ankle, as the woman made a grab at her. She flew at a door, but it was only to a cupboard. She wrenched at another, but it was locked. Dashing away again, she knocked over a pitcher of water that was on the floor.

It was Mr. Pickles who caught her. He bent her arms behind her back and clapped his other hand tight over her mouth, so that she could not bite him.

"Whatever's come over her?" he said to the woman. "Dashing about like a stung calf. She might 'ave seen the Devil. It's a mystery. For the Lord's sake, fetch some brandy!"

The breathless woman came with a glass bottle, holding the stopper in her hand. They could do nothing, though, until that violent look passed out of Margaret's eyes. Mr. Pickles saw that if he let go of her she would scream the place down.

"Make a sound and I'll beat the daylights out of ye, I will. Does tha understand?" He gave a warning kick on the shin. "D'ye understand me? Nod your 'ead if y'understand."

She tried to nod.

"I'm going to let go now. Make a sound and I'll kill thee."

He slowly took away his hand. Standing behind her, he slipped an arm around her shoulder and pinched her nostrils, clamping her body against his own, trapping her arms.

"Open!"

She opened her mouth and quickly closed it again. She was exhausted and could not put up a fight. She was trembling and gasping.

"Fetch me a spoon," Mr. Pickles said.

The woman, who clearly did not like her job, brought a silver spoon. Mr. Pickles took it, forced the handle between Margaret's teeth to hold down her tongue, and prised open her mouth.

"Pour it in."

The woman tilted the bottle into Margaret's mouth, gingerly, frightened of being bitten. Margaret felt it spilling off her lips, onto her chin, running down her neck. She did not dislike the taste, although she did not like it either. With her nostrils and tongue clamped, she was forced to swallow. It made her splutter and cough.

Margaret's head began to swim. They allowed her a moment's respite, then forced her to take more brandy. There was a pain behind her eyes, clouding her head. The room was expanding and contracting. Her legs felt weak. And then she collapsed.

When she came to, she was in a small room, sitting naked in a china tub filled with warm, very dirty water, in a steamy, white light. The same fat woman was soaping her body and scrubbing her with a stiff brush. It was the second scrubbing she had received in two days, and this was a really thorough one. Her flesh was tingling, and had turned an extraordinary pink.

The woman smiled. "There, you've had a shock. Mr. Pickles doesn't mean you no harm. 'E's got 'is job to do. But you took your medicine like a good girl in the end, didn't you? Why did you run around like that? Like an 'eadless cockerel. Laugh! You led us a dance."

Margaret's head was thumping. Her eyes still did not focus. The woman was working on her shoulders.

"Why are you scrubbing me?"

"You're in Mr. Horsfall's employ now. You remember that name."

"I do."

"He's master 'ere. Mr. Pickles promised you'd be found employment, didn't 'e? Well, you're Mr. Horsfall's servant now. Nothing to be frightened of."

"I'm not frightened." She was in too much of a daze. She could not gauge the distances of the steamy walls, nor even of the edges of the bath.

"I'm Mrs. Flitcroft."

"I want to see my mother!" she cried.

"You'll meet your mother someday, dear. There, there!"

Without warning, she was sick in the bath. A servant girl brought in a fresh ewer of hot water, and Mrs. Flitcroft patiently washed her again.

Mrs. Flitcroft helped her out of the bath and rubbed her hair with a towel. Her black hair had become fair.

"I want a drink of water."

"Jenny, bring some water!"

The girl returned and handed her a glass. A *glass,* for Margaret to drink out of!

"Where've you come from?" Mrs. Flitcroft asked.

"I don't know."

"Liverpool, I was told. What were you doing there?"

Margaret would not answer.

"Is your head bad?"

"Yes."

She was gently led into another room. Amazing clothes, in the colors of a sunset, lay on a bed there. An open wardrobe was filled with girls' dresses. Her extraordinary new, rosy body was dressed by Mrs. Flitcroft, first of all in loose, lace-edged pantaloons, then in a cotton petticoat edged with cream-colored lace, and over this a pale pink dress made of silk, with puffed sleeves of fine lawn, likewise ending in creamy lace. She was given white stockings and white kid slippers. A dark pink satin sash was tied around her waist, with a large bow at the back.

Meanwhile Jenny was heating curling irons in the fire. When Mrs. Flitcroft had got as far as Margaret's stockings and slippers, Jenny came forward with four irons on a sanded tray, and soon her short, thick hair was a mass of soft curls.

One servant at her feet, another at her head—and only yesterday she had declared that she was not a lady! She brushed her hand over the silk dress, she stroked her scrubbed arm; nothing would ever surprise her again.

"Am I being adopted?" she asked.

"I could kill him!" Jenny spat out. "I feel ashamed."

"It's nothing to do with us," Mrs. Flitcroft warned her.

"That Pickles is a worm! He's a slimy toad," Jenny declared. Mrs. Flitcroft answered Margaret's question, at last. "Yes, Mr. Horsfall has adopted you."

"And have you noticed him these days?" Jenny said. "He picks his nose, just like his father did, when he had one to pick. I've watched him for hours when I've been serving dinner. The dirty beast. So long as he doesn't pass it on!"

"You should mind your own business and respect your betters," Mrs. Flitcroft said.

There were tears in Mrs. Flitcroft's eyes as she put the final touches to the child's appearance.

"I don't know 'ow 'e could adopt me. When 'as 'e seen me? 'E never looked into the factory 'prentice 'ouse. Was it in chapel?"

"Her mind's rambling," Jenny said.

"When you go in to see Mr. Horsfall, he might want you to sniff something out of a cloth," Mrs. Flitcroft said. "Sniff it up, like a good girl. It's ether. It won't do you any harm. When you come round you'll be all right. Don't make a lot of noise and fight, like you did before. It'll only make 'im angry."

"The beast!" Jenny said.

"When you come round, probably you'll be found work in the kitchens. You'd like that, wouldn't you?" Mrs. Flitcroft said.

"Unspeakable beast!" Jenny wailed.

"Now aren't you a lucky girl?" concluded Mrs. Flitcroft. "You look like an angel. A proper picture by an artist." She clasped Margaret warmly for a moment. "Jenny, you'd better take her in before she spoils," she said.

"You take her in, this time," Jenny retorted. "He can tell that I don't like doing it."

"Nobody likes doing it. We all 'ave our turn. It's all quite fair."

"Then you take her, this time."

Margaret settled the matter by walking over and taking Jenny's hand.

Jenny, carrying a lamp, led her a long way through corridors and up several staircases. "They say they've passed a law in Parliament about this," Jenny said. "I don't know. Them as can read say so."

They went so far that Margaret wondered if they were lost. The house seemed deserted. On the few occasions that a servant was spied, Jenny pulled her into a side room for a moment.

Margaret was eventually taken into a gentleman's dressing room. It was small and gloomy. One wall was filled with huge cupboards. A door was open, showing trays of shirts. Jenny knocked on a carved mahogany door at the further end.

"Send her in!" It was a man's voice, no louder than it needed to be.

"Go in and curtsy," Jenny whispered. "I'll stay here." Jenny opened the door, then slipped behind it, hidden. "Good luck," she whispered, as Margaret stepped forward, a stiff doll.

Mr. Horsfall, wearing a silk dressing gown, sat by the fire picking his nose. Most striking to Margaret was not the man, but a painting that was on the wall. It depicted a little girl who looked confusingly like herself, as she was now dressed; pink silk dress, sash, pantaloons, satin bow, and curled, although longer, hair. It was Mr. Horsfall's daughter.

He turned to look at Margaret. She dropped the curtsy, clumsily for she was not trained in such manners, but he flushed at the sight.

"My rose! My perfect angel!" he said.

She was aware of a thin, swooping shadow rising out of the chair and against the fire. Then he was kneeling beside her, feeling her dress with delicate, unworn, gentleman's hands. "My angel, my rose! What innocence, what innocence!"

He was kissing her dress. His hands were feeling her thighs through it. His breath smelled of brandy—the smell of the same stuff that had been thrust down her own throat.

"Your lips are a perfect rosebud. Some bee has newly stung them. Kiss me!"

She was as frigid as the picture of which she was a living replica, as his lips passed over hers.

"Am I being adopted?"

His hands stopped fluttering over her dress. He stood up and took her hand, leading her to the bed.

"Are you going to adopt me?"

"Of course I am."

"When?"

"Afterwards. Lie down there. Let's lift you up!"

"It'll spoil my dress. Are you my father?"

"Yes."

"No. You're not!"

She tried to squirm away from him as he flopped upon the bed beside her.

"For the time being, I am. Lie still! Lie still, damn! There. You are a young filly!"

"Will there be no more Mr. Gledhill?"

"Gledhill?"

"In the mill."

"You know about him?"

" 'E does what you're doing to girls."

"Does he? We'll have to report him to the factory inspectors, then."

"Don't tell 'im I told you, please!"

"I'll deal with Gledhill, if you're a good girl."

"You'll spoil my dress."

"I'll buy you a new one. Lots of them. Hundreds of them."

"Shall I be a lady then?"

"Yes, you'll be a lady. And Gledhill's days are numbered, I can tell you."

"I don't believe you."

"It's true."

She tried to escape him by turning onto her side. "You're heavy!" she complained.

"Stop talking! Don't make a sound. Shh . . . don't say a word, my rosebud, my angel."

"Oh, don't do that! Edwin will kill you."

He stopped abruptly. "Edwin?"

" 'E'll cut your throat. 'E's my friend. 'E's in America."

Horsfall laughed.

His mocking tone made her angry and indignant. "But 'e'll come back. 'E'll cut your throat. 'E told me about you."

"Did he?"

"Yes, 'e did. Mor Greave's 'is father."

"The schoolmaster? The one who kept a seditious school and deserted his family? He's a wanted man. We're going to execute him."

"Oh, no, you're not! You're a bad man!"

He put his forearm across her throat and forced her head back. She tried to scream.

"Damn you, keep still!" He forced his arm tighter under her chin. "Oh, my angel, my rosebud . . ."

At three in the morning, Pickles took Margaret away in the same light, fast coach in which she had arrived. She was dressed again in her tattered clothes, although Mrs. Flitcroft had boiled and dried them, and a blanket was thrown over her. It was all that Mrs. Flitcroft could do.

If Pickles had not taken her, Margaret could not have walked. She could hardly see him as he muttered to her in the dark. "What a man, what a monster. I'm sorry, lass. I'm no better off with 'im than you are, so don't blame me. I'd be in a debtor's prison if I didn't do my job. But thou's not alone. There's five 'undred o' your sort walking about Piccadilly every night."

He took her to the Lady Well workhouse. No one came out to them; the master and mistress did not want to know. Looking around to make sure no one was watching, Mr. Pickles lifted her out of the coach, and she was surprised at how gentle he was. He left her shivering and crying on the steps, an envelope holding five guineas clutched in her hand.

She did not much care where she was. Silk dresses? Being adopted? Such lies!

Horsfall did not see Margaret go. Yet, after he had shouted for her to be taken away, he still stayed up and about.

As Margaret departed from the rear of the mansion, Horsfall, at the front, stared absentmindedly over the garden.

He heard a carriage and realized that it had stopped at the side entrance. He heard luggage being carried in or out, or something like that. A few minutes later the carriage swept around to the front and down the drive.

A head popped out, lit by the carriage lamp and taking a last look at the house.

He smiled. Why did Lydia choose to leave secretly in the dead of night? He did not mind her going, if that was what she wanted. So long as she did it decently and took nothing away with her, he did not mind. It would save him the expense, trouble, and taint of disgrace in having to certify a lunatic.

Mary prepared to set off in pursuit of Mor, planning to leave her trunk with Gartside. She dressed in pantaloons, stockings, two petticoats, two light dresses, and her cloak. Her most important possessions were buried deep in the recesses of this clothing. Her money was separated into two pouches, so that if a thief made a grab for one, he might miss the other. These were hidden, one at the bottom of her cosmetic box, under the lining, and the other inside her pantaloons. She took with her only her hairbrush, cosmetic box, henna, and three lace handkerchiefs, in case she had to show that she was a lady. Her blue cloak hid everything. Her indispensable was the only thing visible upon her arm. In this she had only four small coins.

Her sensibilities had changed when she became pregnant, and Mary was hightly conscious of all smells—most especially that on herself. Despite Mad Dick, she was scented with Mor. It flowed from where she had been impregnated; a fountain which left a veil of scent over her body.

She was behaving oddly. She could not judge distances. Her steps were unsteady and stumbling. That morning, working the pump handle for water to wash out the filth of Mad Dick, she had absently filled the bucket to overflowing.

Gartside thought that her odd behavior was because Mor had left. She told him that she would be back—looking, however, not at him, but out through the open door, her eyes searching somewhere beyond the hills, and her expression told him that she was thinking of anything but coming back.

"What about the soldier?" he asked, with frightened eyes.

"Mad Dick'll be no trouble, Benjie. 'E'll leave today or tomorrow, I promise you. I told Dick that the authorities knew about 'im, and would be coming for 'im tomorrow."

"Dragoons are coming up here?" He was more scared than ever.

"They won't turn up. They don't know anything really. I just wanted to get rid of Mad Dick for you. 'E won't appear again. 'E 'asn't a chance. They'll easily find 'im, and 'e'll be done for. You keep the place spick an' span for when I get back, Benjie."

She walked away through the rushes, among which in drier places the tiny yellow cinquefoils were in flower. Two men, in their different ways both in love, watched her go. Mad Dick at the upstairs window, and Gartside at the door, stared after a whore who was also in love, but not with them. She did not know if she'd be back for anything more than her trunk.

She was painfully sensitive to the smells of the moor. Here it was smoke, for they were burning the old grass and heather. Farther along, she was sickened by a stagnant quagmire. In the next few yards it was thyme, then a peaty smell. Odors that by turn thrilled or nauseated her.

She followed a spidery black sheep-track that wound uphill among the stones. She burst over the moortop and Gartside's place sank out of sight behind her.

The valley of the little River Tame lay below, with mills strung along its course. Horrible dungeons. Gawd, she thought, I'd hate to be in one o' them.

On the downward slope, meeting the highest of the lanes that sprouted like starved, pale tendrils out of the valley, she set her sights toward Ogden Edge in the east.

She was single-mindedly going in search of Mor Greave, to tell him the truth, if he would believe her, about Mad Dick and the seed in her womb. She was Mor's wife, not his legal wife but, nevertheless, his wife, and his half-sister. They must leave straightaway and head south.

She must get away quickly. If soldiers picked her up she would prefer to hang, rather than give her body again for spying. Even though the thought of the gallows made her heart jump.

The fear, the possibilities, filled her imagination. They would not hang her while she was pregnant, but after being allowed a few weeks in which to nurse her baby, she'd be bound for the gallows in Lancaster or York; with her in the cart, the short ladder, the rope, and her own coffin. She would find that she, who knew everybody, did not have one friend in the world. Mr. Burton would read about her in the newspaper, maybe read it aloud to his French wife, and they would tut-tut together. If she didn't find More Grief now, would he know nothing about it, before he too read about her in the news sheet? Yet there was no one else who would care. She had not seen her foster parents in Soyland for years and didn't know if they were still alive. She hadn't given them a thought; nor did they, she was sure, ever spare one for her. And all those men; their confessions, their whispers. And what about Harriet? So long as she remained ignorant of her mother, Harriet would be all right. But she, without a husband, would have no one to be interested in her fate.

She wanted no one but More Grief to touch her, yet he did not believe her, just as no one else did. Mad Dick had thought her struggle with him was in order to excite him and that her fight was part of the game. The more she had spat and cursed, the harder he had tried, and if she had not given in, he would have torn her to pieces.

Walking toward Denshaw, scratching nervously at her cheek from time to time, her clothes and belongings heavy about her, she suffered all of Mor's pain for him. She who had played the part of mother to a thousand worldly, pompous men now truly suffered as a mother for her child.

She told herself that this pain was what she deserved for building her life on fantasies and lies; for her fake moans of joy, while her mind wandered away from the man she was with, into more entertaining thoughts.

She could not move in her ever-shifting, insecure world without the support of her web of lies. She invented stories, mixtures of truths and fantasies, about public house "cells of disaffection," and was paid according to the extremity of her tales. More often than not, the authorities acted upon her inventions but neglected the truth, and as her reward they defended her from the civil justices who would try her for murder. She was able to stay alive only because the army believed that she was useful to them. To the common soldiers, she lied so that they would tell her their thoughts and secrets, which she could pass on to their officers.

When it came to realities, no one would believe a word she said, which was why she never spoke a serious word to anyone; hardly, as yet, even to More Grief. When she had tried to do so, he too had not believed her.

Why did the color of her hair matter to him? Why did he ask her so often where she had been and what she had done? Surely he knew that it would torment her in her cage of lies?

In the one certain truth of her life, her love for him, she had not been believed. Mad Dick had roared outright at the thought of a whore in love.

What if she encountered Phoebe Greave in Lady Well? What rights had a pregnant whore over a wife, in the wife's home village?

She imagined herself, a scarred whore, not old but getting beyond the years when she could practice her profession, her red hair streaked with black, calling at the cottage of a handloom weaver, trying to tell a wife that her husband was the father of her unborn child.

Mary's reflections carried her two miles to the junction with the main turnpike at Denshaw. This was the route she had originally walked in the opposite direction with Mor. She threaded her way across hills dappled green and yellow with unmown or drying grass in the cloud-broken sunlight. It was Sunday morning and church bells were clanging. Despite her fears, she was distracted by an extraordinary happiness. She was smiling down at the ground, or was it toward her womb? She could not understand herself.

She began to climb the turnpike up into the hills, among sporadic traffic. Normally able to endure long walks in any weather, and the many hazards of the roads, today she was easily tired.

Shortly before the Ram Inn, which was the last outpost high upon the moors, she did not hear the loud grinding of a cart about to overtake her and she, usually alert to everything, wobbled into its path. The driver cursed and reined in his horse. Seeing what she so obviously was, he smirked and offered her a lift.

It was a soldiers' provision cart. A sergeant held the reins. A younger militiaman with musket and fixed bayonet sat behind him among barrels and sacks of oatmeal or wheat. Mary perched on the tailboard, huddled in her cloak, dangling her legs out of the men's sight.

"What are you doing walking the roads on a Sunday, young woman?"

"I'm a tightrope walker from a circus. I fell off my tightrope and broke myself in the fall. I can't practice no more."

The conscript tried again. "What got you up so early? You don't look the type."

"I told you—I fell off my tightrope. I 'ad a good balancing act, till I fell. You can ask anyone."

There was something about Mary which inhibited further teasing, and she was allowed to doze. She had a disturbed night to recover from, but this was still a stupid thing to do on the tail of a cart from which she might tumble; or while traveling with money on her person in the company of two soldiers.

The jolting awoke her from time to time. It seemed such a long journey to Ripponden, which was the first village on the far side of the hills.

At last, the cart came to a stop. The grinning young militiaman, who thought himself very advanced in the art of war because he had picked up a woman in a cart, pricked her bottom with his bayonet. She leaped off, less anxious for the things in her pocket than for the precious seed that she bore.

A group of idlers were hanging around the door of the forge, where they were employed on weekdays in making cropping machines and spinning frames. They were arrogant because they were well paid, and could afford to pass the time watching traffic converging at the junction of the two routes over the moorlands. If one waited long enough, it offered such excitements as, for example, the sight of Mary jumping from the cart and brushing dusty oatmeal off her fancy blue cloak.

"I wish I was a soldier, Sam, to guard a load like that one, I do!"

It was near midday. Mary was hungry and she went to Mrs. Rawdon's. Although she needed food and rest, and felt she had to get off the streets, she stayed only a little time. She had both money and appetite for a good meal, but the smell of beer made her vomit. She tried to tackle the heavily salted pork and greens that were set before her, but again she had to dash for the door. In any case it would not have been safe for her to linger. "Some men from headquarters are looking for you," Mrs. Rawdon warned.

She climbed steeply uphill, crossed a moortop, went downhill again and up. Looking over the hills, she wondered where all the things were that Mor had described so lovingly, so precisely, so many times. His memory had been triggered by almost anything, in bed or on the roads. The ash tree from which he had taken his departure. The pasture above the woods where boys looked for plovers' eggs. She herself knew the district from visiting Horsfalls' for the sake of servicing the officers quartered there, but, under orders to be discreet, she had never made herself known in the town. Flitting in at twilight, thrown out at dawn with the other whores, she'd had no attention to spare for trees, plovers, and larks.

Where, she wondered, was that bank on the curve of the river that Mor had described, the one where the current ran fast and there was always a trout to be found? Mor had described certain views to perfection. The farm buildings were there, the walled track ran down exactly so, the tower on the mill peeped through the trees. Brought up on a farm herself, it was not unnatural for her to observe the wild things and feel the seasons, and now it was coming back to her. Having for many years despised the daytime, the out-of-doors, she now loved the sunlight, the breezes, the wildflowers, the streams.

Mor had not only left his scent upon her body. She had adopted his attitude. To have him near her, she tried to see through his eyes, to see everything around Lady Well as he must have seen it.

We'll have a little farm together . . .

She descended to the bridge, with one steep rise remaining up to Lady Well, and there she rested, leaning on the parapet. She was dizzy and still nauseated. She looked down at the water. The banks of weed now grew thick, and were speckled with the white flowers of water crowfoot. She watched a trout rise. There was the tiniest flash, like the spinning of a silver coin, before the fish sank again beneath its ripples and circles. She thought of how often Mor must have leaned on this same parapet, watching the trout.

Already she could hear, through the still air, hymn singing and the ejaculations of the "saved" from the top of the hill. The raucous hymn singing from cottage and chapel was matched by the thinner, but more piercing, singing of larks. Lady Well, when she climbed up to it, was as busy as a market. Outside the chapel, one preacher was shouting among the graves. Shouts and bursts of hymns came from different parts of the town. Looking through a doorway, she saw a "hedge-preacher" kneeling in a kitchen. Others were haranguing groups along the streets.

People were out of work, had run away from home, were under the suspicion of the justices, of the occupying militia, of Gledhill and other Horsfall officers. The situation was such that married men slipped back from the hills at night to see their families, sleep an hour or two with their wives, and change their clothes. They brought in food or money if they had any; otherwise, they depended upon their families. How many sad and secret departures took place all over the town in the early hours of the morning!

Yet the Lady Well crowds believed that they sang and shouted with joy. In fact it was an animal cry of pain and anger that she heard pouring out of the village—she saw their grief in every industrial wound, in every wounded sullen face. Families that had said they were starving had been ground into the dirt for daring to speak.

A man was standing alone. He had a wooden leg, and was leaning on a stick. She asked him the whereabouts of the Greaves' house.

"Straight on, up the 'ill. That's one of the 'ouses that's taken, I believe."

"Taken?"

"You're a stranger, I see. Taken by the Lord. They make more noise about it than any battle I've seen with the French. They tell me it serves Greave right, because 'e left 'ome."

"Serves 'im right?"

"That's what they say. Some don't speak well of 'im."

"Why not? I 'eard 'e did lots of things for people in Lady Well. 'E taught school, and never did 'arm to anyone."

"You know 'im, then?"

"Aye, I know 'im. In a manner of speaking."

He gripped her arm. "People soon forget all such things as that, miss . . . ma'am."

"Ma'am."

Typical of a man, he did not bother to see if she wore a ring.

"They think differently about what's right and wrong, as soon as the Lord comes into it. As soon as folks start saying, 'There's One above who sees all.' "

"Who says that?" she asked.

"Phoebe Greave does. 'E'll not get 'is 'ouse back! It's full of righteous folk. That's an easy trick to cheat anyone of their rights. Just say God's on your side, and who can argue? You can cheat a man of 'is property easy that way."

" 'Is 'ouse can't be stolen from 'im, and it be right, not if it's 'is."

She had started to walk away, and gone a few yards up the road.

"Ma'am!"

She turned and they looked at each other. He was waving his stick. They approached each other again, like old friends, long parted.

"I just wanted to say that I knew 'im, too. And I knew John Tiplady. I'm Binns, the cobbler. I'd 'ave gone with them if it 'adn't been for my leg. I'm not one of *them*." He waved his hand at the town, more as if he was dismissing it than indicating anything.

"I've loved this place, because I was born 'ere, but it's all new now in Lady Well and they've forgotten what it was we fought for, a short time ago. Four weeks—it's nothing. But in that time . . . John Tiplady dead, and so many others run off. Ah, dear! They've lost this world and told themselves they've found the Lord instead. They've lost the present, so they can tell themselves they've found the afterlife. Who cares now about Mor Greave? No one. They kept expecting 'im back, the way they do expect 'em to come back in the night, after there's been trouble. But no sign of 'im. Nothing. Now they don't even speak of 'im. I won't forget 'im, though. 'E was writing a book. If it's printed, they probably won't even read it. If they read it, they'll 'ardly understand it. Not the pain that went into it. 'Is wife knew, o' course, but she won't tell anyone about that. All she'll talk about is 'ow 'e's wronged 'er, 'ow 'e starved 'er, 'ow 'is sins kept 'er from the Lord.

"She's a different woman now—and to be honest, I never liked 'er before. I could see all this coming. She's found 'er voice and says it's the Lord's. You can't argue with that. Mor Greave's nothing but 'evil doings' to 'er now. Bound to be true, if the Lord says so! When people get like that, they are out of their minds. They make so much noise, they cannot 'ear the truth. I'd like to . . ." He began to whisper. "Do you 'ave any news of Mor Greave, then?"

" 'E's well, don't worry, Mr. Binns. But 'e should be 'ere, in Lady Well. 'E was coming 'ere."

"I've not seen 'im."

" 'E wouldn't make it public, would 'e?"

"Well, 'e wouldn't be welcome in his own 'ouse, not now. You might be, though." Binns laughed. "They'd set about reforming you . . . I don't mean to insult you, ma'am. Phoebe Greave's turned it into a meeting place for the Methodists, so that they can rant and scream in 'is schoolroom. 'Is little front room is a bedroom for visiting preachers. Gideon . . . you know about Gideon? I was never too keen on 'im, neither. 'E reminds me of 'is mother's sister, Selene, who died young. The boy always took 'imself too seriously . . . 'E sleeps upstairs. 'E's a seven days' wonder, is Gideon."

" 'E's a preacher?"

" 'E 'as 'acquired the gift of tongues,' as they put it. 'Ow did you know?"

" 'Is father always said that would happen."

Mr. Binns grasped her hand.

"Where does his wife live?" she asked.

"She's moved in with Mr. Slaughter, the engineer, to be 'is 'ouse-keeper. Nothing improper about it, you understand."

"There wouldn't be, with 'er."

"There wouldn't be, no. She's got born with religion, out of a fake egg . . . do you follow my meaning?"

"No."

"You will, when you've been up there. *Eee,* I'm glad to talk to you, ma'am! Whoever you are, welcome! A lark on a murky day. You've made my day. Come round to see me sometime. I live in the last 'ouse by the church. Welcome! I live alone. I'd be glad of something 'appening to upset 'em all."

"If I find Mor Greave, I'll come to see you."

"I mended Mr. Greave's boots for 'im, the day 'e left."

She was stepping away. "Good day, Mr. Binns."

"Good luck, then, ma'am."

Mor had never said that his home was a place of charm or comfort, but the details that he gave had created a picture of something very sweet. The rose he had tried to grow, but which had failed because it was a hothouse plant from Mr. Horsfall's, unable to survive in the open air; the view, painfully drawn upon his memory; his books, described exactly in the order in which he had kept them, title by title along the shelf.

When she found Mor's home, the sight gave Mary a shock. There was a crowd pushing in at the door and spilling over the flight of steps; yet, despite the crowd, it appeared gray, derelict and unloved.

She felt that these people, Phoebe Greave's friends, defiled it. As she stood on the edge of the mass of people, she was horrified by the air of stale unhappiness. Whoever used the house that had now become

Phoebe Greave's chapel was refusing to live. There was an odor of stubborn unhappiness in there.

Mary had once known a woman who, after her husband died, would not change or clean anything, letting curtains and bedclothes rot with dirt; leaving platters and knives uncleaned where he had left them at his last meal; letting mice and spiders run everywhere, over a memory that was slowly rotting.

Mor Greave's house was permeated with that same atmosphere, and the lugubrious crowd made it even worse.

It shocked Mary especially, because, if anything characterized her, it was her refusal—against the odds—to die.

CHAPTER THIRTEEN

May 9th–May 12th

Mary climbed the stairs, hesitating at the doorway. The crowd within, with backs turned to her, was quiet at that moment, listening to a young, confident male voice that was chanting emotionally.

"For behold, the day cometh that shall burn as an oven, and all the proud, yes, and all that do wickedly, shall be stubble . . ."

One or two turned to look at her. Her ears picked up the word "Jezebel." A way was made for her. When she did not move, a hand irritably waved her forward. Another firmly advised "a prayerful attitude and modesty." A hand touched her, probably by accident, but it felt obscene. Eyes were searching her for evidence of a miracle occurring to change her. It would happen if they wanted it. People could talk themselves into anything. She went where hands forced her to go. She entered the house, into the presence of more eyes gleaming inquisitorially at the stranger, under the low ceiling. The sweaty smell of the crowded room made her want to vomit. She felt giddy and faint.

"What's all this?" she began boldly.

"Shh!"

"And ye shall tread down the wicked; for they shall be ashes under the soles of your feet . . ."

"Gideon Greave's a miracle," someone whispered to her. "Only fifteen but he has the gift of tongues. The way he talks, the way he says the Bible . . ."

The room held a ring of darkly clad, standing figures. Within this were others, kneeling. By the unlit fire, a boy, with an expression of pain transcended, was leaning on the back of a spindled chair. Gideon's eyes turned upon Mary—the blue cloak, the pile of red and black hair, the painted red cheeks—but he carried on until he reached the last line of the Old Testament:

"And he shall turn the heart of the fathers to the children, and the heart of the children to their fathers, lest I come and smite the earth with a curse."

The room sighed.

A bony, mad-looking woman sat on a stool beside Gideon. Mary knew that she must be Phoebe—she looked up at Gideon with such amazed admiration, and sometimes she coughed and hid her mouth in a handkerchief. Mor had described her as "letting folk walk all over her like a doormat," but she did not look downtrodden now. Mr. Slaughter's housekeeper wore new, well-made shoes, and had on a gray woollen dress with a large pocket for her handkerchiefs. She was a servant respected by all, and comforted by them in her "misfortune." Even Mr. Gledhill sat in the cottage with her, listening to the marvelous words that came out of the mouth of her son. Now that Gledhill and she were together in the Lord, she had forgotten her hatred and her horror at what he had done to her family. Forgiveness was at the very heart of the Gospel.

Gideon, calm as a born preacher who feels the crowd malleable under his spell, turned his attention to the stranger. "Step forward, woman! Yea, even at the last moment, before the final casting down, all might be forgiven you, daughter of Eve. Step forward into forgiveness and eternal life, or stay forever in darkness, and alone. Come, come."

"Step forward!" his mother shrieked. "Step forward into eternal life!"

"No!"

Mary shrank into her cloak. She lifted her arm across her face.

Phoebe was pointing into the air, her stiff fingers stretched in a show of reaching up. "There is One above who sees all!" she shrilled with her inviolable conviction. "Do not be afraid! You can be forgiven!"

"No!" But Mary was frightened.

"What sort of woman are you that you have no need for forgiveness?" Gideon asked. "You who come to us a painted and gilded lily."

"Come forward into eternal salvation!" Phoebe beckoned. "All can be saved. Alleluia!"

Cries of "Alleluia!" went up from the crowd.

"It's Mary the Scar," said Gledhill.

"Mary the Scar?" Gideon echoed. He had heard of her.

The crowd closed in on Mary.

"Jezebel!" Phoebe shrieked. "Abomination!"

Mary fainted.

"The Lord's taken 'er!" Joshua Slaughter said.

"She's not dead yet. Take 'er into the fresh air, ne'er mind the Lord's bosom," someone suggested. "She'll come round. She's hot and tired, that's all. She's pregnant, maybe. Well, why not? There's something wrong with her. Who is this Mary the Scar, Nathaniel?"

"A Jezebel, like Phoebe Greave said," Gledhill answered. "Not that I know much about 'er. But I've 'eard. She's a bad one. Mr. Horsfall knows 'er. 'E's 'ad to boot 'er out many a time, for 'anging round the door. That's why I know who she is. The world'd be well rid of 'er, in my 'umble opinion."

"Mutton dressed as lamb," a woman hissed, as they took Mary outside into the open air. Because of her cosmetics, it was impossible to tell whether the color had returned to her cheeks and lips or not. Nobody was bold enough to loosen her dress; something might be made of their being so familiar. Even the women would not dare to touch such a person.

"She should be cleansed and redeemed," Gideon said. "Forgiven, to mark this day of our Love Feast, and brought back into the fold."

Although he talked of forgiveness, repulsion caused the skin to shrink on Gideon's face. Tight reins pulled at the corners of his mouth and narrowed his eyes. At the age of fifteen, he could not understand what had produced such a female.

"It would be a memorial to this special day of prayer if we were to cleanse the fallen woman," Slaughter echoed. "Let's take 'er to the bath in the workhouse."

Mary was coming round. Her eyes were open and she moved her hand to her forehead. "Oh, Gawd, what's 'appened?"

"She's speaking."

"Nay, she's calling on God," Slaughter said. "What a sight."

Someone gripped her shoulders and raised her to a sitting position. Someone else was helping her up. She could see over the iron railings at Mor's door. There was the sunlit valley.

They were helping her down the worn stone stairs, and pushing her up the street.

"Where are you taking me?"

"To the workhouse. You called on God yourself . . . to be cleansed."

As Gideon gingerly supported Mary's arm, he was staring at her face. He wanted to know what lay beneath the leathery cosmetic, and beneath the nickname Mary the Scar. Horror had begot fascination; fascination begat guilt. Guilt was as familiar to him as clothing warmed through by his own smell and shaped by his own body.

Still faint and confused, Mary was brought to the workhouse door. How could she escape them all? She must bend with the wind.

The commotion brought the workhouse mistress to the door even before they knocked. Her name was Queen Elizabeth Farrer, or sometimes she was known as plain "Queen Bess." She was big, with bones rather than with fat, and plenty of muscle. She had a loud voice to match her size, severe starched clothes, hair pulled back so as to thrust her face aggressively forward, and a scrubbed look, yellow from spending her time in badly lit, damp interiors.

"What do you want? What's this you've brought me?"

"A Jezebel to be cleansed!" Phoebe shouted back. "A wicked woman. Look at 'er. You 'ave the baths, Bessy Farrer. We want 'er brought forth cleansed, meek, and 'er evil tongue cut off."

"*Mother!*" Gideon interrupted.

Phoebe, to whom God had given a voice, raised her arm again to the sky. "There is One—"

"A Jezebel," Gledhill told Queen Bess. "A Mary Magdalene. Stop your ranting, Phoebe Greave. We want 'er brought forth later, Mrs. Farrer, prepared for conversion."

"God's holy water! Have you become dippers, all of you?"

"Not a Baptist amongst us!" answered Phoebe, insulted and shocked. "We're all true followers and believers."

"Then why waste God's water scrubbing the woman? But leave 'er to me, if that's what you want. Go on, go away . . . it's not visiting day. Get on wi' your praying."

• • •

Bessy Farrer closed the door on them. She looked over Mary the Scar, who looked back at her, boldly.

"What a place! Everyone's mad. I thought they were going to kill me." Mary, straightening her dress and hair, spoke to Mrs. Farrer as if she were a fellow human being.

Queen Bess did not like that. "So we're a crazy lot in Lady Well, are we? And who are you, madam, to call folk crazy? You know where you are now, do you? I'll show you, madam!"

Mrs. Farrer, her big iron keys swinging loose at her waist, gripped Mary's arm. She pushed her down a short passageway, then through the main room, where a dozen poor women had been set to spin. It was an unnecessary business now that the factories did the work, but the abandoned females did not mind. They would have unpicked all their work and started over again, with the same smiles, or lack of them. Life in the workhouse was the same meaningless disappointment, no matter what one did. They became silent and more brisk as soon as Mrs. Farrer's voice filled the room.

"Annie Drew, you're dropping threads! Do you want a maid to clean up after ye?"

"No, Queen Bess."

"Answer me back, you fucking cow, and I'll 'ave you scrubbing the floor after my lunatics."

Mary was led down another passageway. It was gray and damp, smelling of years of airlessness. Down a side passage she heard the noises of the infirmary.

"Listen to them!" said Mrs. Farrer. "I'll give 'em growling and moaning, not letting anyone sleep! Don't you try any tricks whilst you're in 'ere, neither. We know what to do about it . . . You're not going to be ill?"

"No, ma'am."

She gave Mary another push. "Keep going, then. Never mind leaning on walls, pretending to look sick. What's your name?"

"Mary Wylde."

"I thought they said something else."

"That's my name. Honest, that's my name."

"Where are you from, Mary Wylde?"

"From 'ereabouts originally. I've lived in London and a lot of other places."

Mrs. Farrer touched Mary's arm, and softened her voice. "I'm your friend. I won't let you get into their clutches. Trust me."

"Thank you, ma'am. I'm but a poor 'elpless woman, traveling in search of my brother."

"Poor 'elpess woman, eh?" Mrs. Farrer was shouting again. "No such thing, madam! If you're in 'ere, it's your own fault, and you deserve what you get. We can all 'elp ourselves, can't we?"

"Yes, ma'am."

Mary, nauseated by the stench of the workhouse, was bent over, clutching her stomach.

"Are you with a baby to get rid of? Is that what you've done?"

"It's that smell. It makes me dizzy."

They were going along a corridor where paupers were whitewashing the wall.

Bessy Farrer gave Mary another push. "That's better. Is someone looking for you?"

"No!"

Mrs. Farrer raised her arm threateningly but did not let it fall. She smiled, as Mary winced.

"You don't do yourself any good, not telling me the truth. Then I can 'elp. I'm your friend, Mary."

Mrs. Farrer, still getting no response, shouted, "You don't say anything! You damned cow! You fucking whore, do you know what I can do to you? I've 'ad 'em all in 'ere . . . murderers, thieves, poisoners, embezzlers. I know 'em all. You'd better trust me and do as I say, if you want to stay safe."

Mrs. Farrer put on her soft voice again. "It's only to satisfy my own interest that I want to know. I won't tell anyone . . .

"You still don't say nothing! Well, it's your funeral. Go on! Get in there. Yes, down there. You fucking blind? Or is it the cockroaches scare you? You look as though you might try to be fancy."

Mary was shoved down a flight of steps into a cellar, which had a damp stone floor and barred windows high in the wall. Their bottom sills were level with a garden, where the bare feet of paupers could be seen. The room was filled with steam and smoke. It was mostly smoke, from an iron pot, a "set-pot," built into the stonework over a fire, the stone breast of a chimney curving upward behind it.

In the center of the room was a pump. Along the wall was a row of five stone baths. A channel took the water out through a culvert in the end wall, and thence down the hill. There was a big scrubbed oak table at the other end. There were no chairs, other than a regal-looking "Windsor" with curved arms, in the corner near the table, where the workhouse mistress could sit and watch through the smoke, the steam, and the flying specks of soot.

When Mary was brought in, an attendant in a pauper's blue uniform ceased to poke sticks under the set-pot. She went to close the shutters, which were so splintered and old that they still let some light through. The other bath attendant, who had been sweeping the spilled water toward the drain, lit a lamp on the table.

Queen Elizabeth Farrer sat in her Windsor chair and took out a clay pipe. She produced a tobacco pouch, tinder, and flints. She packed her pipe and lit it.

"Now then, get undressed. Don't keep me waiting! 'Aven't you learned yet? Everybody 'as to 'ave a bath when they come into the work'ouse."

Mary took off her boots and cloak, then she turned to the wall to remove the remainder of her clothes, as slowly as possible.

After she had taken off her cloak, both dresses and her petticoats, the sight of her pantaloons made the others laugh, for they themselves did not wear anything under their outer clothes. Mrs. Farrer slid the lamp closer.

"Looks French. Wonder what old Bony Part'd make o' that!"

Then she saw that Mary was wearing officer's pantaloons, worn back to front.

"Stolen them off a corpse?" she smirked. "Or from some poor soldier kneed and elbowed on 'is way out of the public 'ouse?"

Bessy Farrer slipped back into her chair and appeared to fall into a doze. Thinking that the mistress was not looking, Mary pulled forth the cosmetic box, the hairbrush, and one of the purses from her underclothes and slipped them under her cloak, which was heaped on the table.

"You carry a lot of things about your person," Queen Bess said quietly.

"They're all my own."

"Are those your savings in the purse? And the 'airbrush? Good silver on it, too. And lovely lace 'andkerchiefs."

"Everything's mine, ma'am. I spent my years in service since I was nine, at seven pounds a year, to save that up. I only want to retire in peace, ma'am. The roads are full of robbers. I hope I'm safe now. I 'ope I'm with friends. You said I was."

"How much have you got 'saved up'?"

"Fifteen pounds."

"You must have been in a high class of service to save that much. What were you doing? Stealing the tea?" She pointed at Mary with the stem of her pipe. "You've not saved up that way, my lady. Who've you robbed whilst he was otherwise engaged, as you might say? What's in the little box hid under your clothes, that looked so fine? You got stolen jewels in there?"

"That's my cosmetic box. Look!" Mary pulled it forth and sprung it open. "I 'ave to keep myself looking a lady, for my prof— Please, ma'am."

"I'll tell you what I'll do . . . Oh, I weep for you! An 'andkerchief, please."

Mary handed over a lace handkerchief. Queen Elizabeth Farrer dabbed at her eyes, which were indeed running, because of the smoke, then tucked the lace into her own pocket.

"Fifteen pounds you've got there, you said?"

"Yes."

"There's many a starving weaver could keep a large family for a year on that. Well, it's none of my business 'ow you've come by it. You've got to take your bath now, to make you fit for the Good Lord's sight. It's a great responsibility for me to look after all that money whilst you're otherwise engaged."

"Thank you, ma'am. You're a good woman, I'm sure."

"That's right. I'm a lady. An 'andkerchief, please, my eyes are sore."

Mary gave her the second of her three lace handkerchiefs, which like the first disappeared into Queen Elizabeth's clothes.

By now, the hot water had been rationed into the bath. An attendant stood waiting, hands on hips.

"Time for your scrub," Mrs. Farrer said. "They need you to work the pump now. Put your clothes and stuff at this end of the table. I'll try and see that the loonies don't come near it, but I can't promise."

Mary, in her comical pantaloons, went to work the pump and fill a bucket to pour into the steaming bath. Trying to keep one eye on Mrs. Farrer, she walked across with one bucketful after another.

"You'll have it cold," said an attendant.

"I don't like 'ot water."

"Make sure it's 'ot, and scrub 'er proper!" Mrs. Farrer yelled. "You arguing?"

Mary skipped away from a blow from one of the attendants. She returned to deposit her final item of clothing, her pantaloons, on the table. Queen Elizabeth did not even look at her, but sat with her arms folded. Mary crept back to the inevitable bath. Both the attendants were tipping in more hot water.

Mary stood in the bath. Each attendant held a large scrubbing brush, of the kind used for floors.

"Start with my feet," Mary said. "In the best society, I believe it's always a lady's 'abit to start low down. There's a moral in that. Ow!"

The larger attendant, taking Mary unawares, pushed her down into a sitting position. Then she started on one of Mary's thighs. She held her knee with one hand and scrubbed with the other. Her assistant did likewise on the other leg. They roughly scoured her, as they would a pig. They did not speak. It was as if she was a carcass.

They turned her over and scoured her back and bottom. She twisted about, but they knew how to hold her. They turned her over again.

She was sick, dribbling onto her breasts. She tried to climb out but a hand pushed her down so that she slipped under the water. " 'Ere, are you being difficult by any chance? We know 'ow to deal with you if you are, don't we?"

Mary's stomach, breasts, all her flesh, was on fire.

"You bitch, you cow you, you fucking old whore, get down, you . . . give me the shears! The shears, quick!"

"No!" Mary buried her face in her breasts and tried to hug her knees. Before she realized it, her hair was hacked. Handfuls were thrown onto the floor, and a few clumps dropped into the bath.

With the stump of hair that was left, her head was pulled back. The two scrubbing brushes were applied to her face and scalp.

At last, they let go of her. She sat spluttering and coughing. Though the water was hot, she was shivering.

For the first time in many years, someone clearly saw the birthmark on her face.

"So that's what you've been hiding! And nobody knew! Quite a Devil's hoof you've got there, miss."

"Let me out! Let me out! *Let me out!*"

"Now, let's dry you, then we can show you to the chapel folk. What will they make of what the Devil did to you, do you think?"

Mary stumbled out of the bath. While they dried her with a rough and dirty towel, she tried to turn her head this way and that, away from them.

She clasped her thighs together, ashamed of her nakedness. As soon as they released an arm, she put it up to grasp the hair that was no longer there, wanting to pull it around her face. She did not want to be seen, and she could not bear to look at them, either. She felt that she was an obscenity, raped and naked, ashamed, reduced to nothing, unable to look anyone in the eye.

When they let go of her she stumbled, half-blindly, toward her clothes, cowering in shame. Why was she shivering so much? Why so cold? There were goose pimples all over her flesh. Her face might be crimson, but the rest of her skin was gray.

She climbed into her pantaloons, petticoats, and two dresses as quickly as possible, still turning her face away.

"You're not well," Mrs. Farrer said. "Your skin's not 'ealthy. I know what makes it that color. Show me your gums."

"Christ, it's cold," Mary muttered. "You wouldn't think there was a fire lit, would you? . . . in the month of May."

Queen Elizabeth Farrer stood up. "Did you hear me? Show me your gums."

"I'm cold, I'm cold," Mary whimpered, like a child. "Christ, I'm so cold."

Mrs. Farrer shouted to the attendants. "Over here! Pull back 'er mouth."

A spasm of revulsion and shame ran through Mary's body.

" 'Ere, you bitch, don't show any temper in 'ere." Mrs. Farrer slapped her. "We've got straitjackets, if we need 'em. 'Aven't you learned yet that we get our own way? I want to see the state of your gums."

Mary was still quaking. Her lips were roughly pulled back, and Mrs. Farrer peered in her mouth. "Lead," she said. "How long have you been using it? How many years?"

"Always."

"Speak up! I can't 'ear!"

"Always! Always! Always!"

The attendants and the workhouse mistress looked at one another, thinking of the straitjacket.

But they let Mary continue to dress herself. She was still trying to hide her cheek, although everyone had seen it. She felt naked for the first time in her life. She was angry.

"You got a dropped wrist yet? Show me. Come on, don't look as though butter wouldn't melt in your mouth. Show me."

Mary extended her arm. She was confronted by the fact, felt but hastily disregarded in the past—when she had waved goodbye to someone, or leaned in a doorway, or held money out in her palm—that her wrist ached.

"You're sick! I'd say my prayers if I was you. The only cure is acidulated water."

"That makes your teeth drop out. I don't want to lose no more teeth."

"I've never known acid do 'arm, not diluted. Are you trying to tell me my business? I've been in this work'ouse for twenty years, apart from a year or two away in York . . . where I was set up . . . I 'adn't done it. My parents were master and mistress 'ere before me. You aren't in a position to tell anyone their business anymore, you Devil's spawn."

"No, ma'am. But your teeth drop out with it."

Mary received another slap. "Don't talk to me like that! I'm mistress 'ere."

Mrs. Farrer turned to the attendants. "Go and fetch the lunatics. Leave this one with me awhile."

When they were alone, Mrs. Farrer brought forth Mary's purse. "Go on, look in it!" she commanded. "Never mind turning your head away. Do as I tell you."

Mary took a glance, and looked away again.

Mrs. Farrer smiled. "One of the loonies has stolen your money, hasn't she?"

"Ma'am?"

"I said, one of the lunatics has stolen your savings. But you're not going to say anything to anyone, are you? Because if you do, the constable will want to know where it came from in the first place. You'd rather be in the infirmary safe for the night, in a bed, wouldn't you, than in the 'ands of that mob of praying wolves in the street? . . . Why can't you look me in the eye? You're ashamed o' the mark of the Devil on your face, that's why. I don't like people who can't look others in the eye. A pity about your money, isn't it? . . . Isn't it?"

"Yes, ma'am."

"As if it never existed. Why, I do believe . . . Let me look at you. Turn your face!"

Mary angrily turned to Mrs. Farrer. She flushed and hunted for cover again, where there was nowhere to hide, in the cavities of her own shoulder.

"Yes, I thought so. Crocodile tears! What's there to cry about? You've got a nice infirmary bed for the night. Oh, I know your sort. Stop your sniveling, ma'am! I can't stand crying."

Mrs. Farrer stood up. "I'm going to leave you now, so don't you dare say a word about that money, or I'll see you 'ung for defaming me."

Three female "lunatics and refractory paupers" were brought into the cellar. They were mild cases, kept in chains only part of every day, merely to remind them of what would happen if they caused trouble. Lunatics notoriously suffered from short memories.

The attendants knew them well and treated them more like children than like animals. They looked forward to laughing at the loonies' antics in their weekly bath, when they threw the water all over the place, fought and argued sometimes, but did not attack anyone else.

When they came in, the one who enjoyed stoking the fire rushed to it immediately. Another carefully examined the row of baths.

The third "lunatic" was a child, lagging behind because she could not walk properly. Margaret had been left to sleep until an hour before. She had been put among the mad people because she persisted with her "obscene talking that would send 'er off to 'ell." As she came into the room she was still dazed, staring, with her legs apart, putting her feet forward slowly to prevent chafing.

Ahead of her, her two companions knew what to do and how much they could get away with. One was running her finger inside the baths to see which was cleanest. When she had decided, "This one," she said, "I'll have this one today," and started to work the pump. The other was throwing sticks onto the blaze, until she was running with sweat.

The attendants looked after Margaret's bath. Her rags had been taken away and she had been given a pauper's gown; as they disrobed her, they tried not to hurt her. They knew quite well what had happened, but had to pretend otherwise.

Mary, left in peace for the first time, was cowering in an out-of-the-way corner, wanting only to hide. She saw the frightened child, with her legs apart, a tranced look on her face, and realized what had happened.

"Can I wash 'er?" she asked.

One of the attendants smiled. "I wouldn't say it was too early to lend an 'and. It'll take a few edges off you, my lady, and get you used to what 'as to be done in 'ere. You're already a bit quieter than you were."

Mary rose, and walked through her own hair that had been dropped so carelessly on the floor. They were curls of flame red hair, in sad contrast to the ugly black stubble on her head.

Mary smiled at the child but did not receive a smile in return. "I won't 'urt you, chicken," she said.

The attendants, occupied with the lunatics, were not looking, and Mary used plenty of soap. Margaret at last began to smile. She was white-skinned and frail as snow. Mary thought of Harriet.

"What's your name?"

"Margaret. Why are you crying?"

"How old are you?"

"Twelve . . . eleven. I don't know. What're you crying for?"

Mary paused before speaking. "Mr. Horsfall 'as done something to you, 'asn't he?"

The child stiffened with fear. "They hit me when I said that."

"The beast! Someone should put strychnine in his silver spoon."

"Tell me why you're crying," Margaret asked yet again.

"I'm not."

" 'Ave they 'urt you? Did they spit in your mouth? Did they stick their fingers in your ears?"

"No, lamb."

Nothing so bad as what, so Mary had heard, happened in a factory. And to children. That's where this one's been, to think of things like that.

"Why are you crying, then? I can see you're crying. I can see it. 'Ave you been bath'd?"

"Yes."

"It's nice, being bath'd. But it hurts."

"Oh, poor lamb! The beast, the stinking beast. Come on. Out you go, my lamb. You're shivering." She called to the attendants, "Hey! A towel! Where's a towel for the mite?"

Mary realized that, for a moment, she had forgotten her own shame.

One of the lunatics threw a towel. When she had dried Margaret, her voice became subdued again. "Let's put something on you to keep you warm."

She led the child across the room to the big table, by the clothes. Mary fished out the child's pauper uniform from the others and dressed her.

"Look, I'll show you something." Mary opened her box, took out her mirror, and held it before Margaret's face.

Margaret touched the mirror handle, twining her fingers in Mary's. "My 'air's fair, isn't it? Look at it. 'E didn't believe me. 'E'd believe me now. Why don't you look at yourself? Go on. Take a look."

"I don't want to."

"Go on, take a look. Then you can see what your face is like."

Margaret turned the mirror around. Mary instinctively jumped back. Then she froze, staring at herself. For years, she had not scraped the cosmetic completely off. She had kept a flattering layer of white lead. Now, here were displayed her naked features, as she had not seen them since she was a child; since the time before a rich young man picked her up, and on their second night introduced her to the cream that hid her blemish. If she should ever forget it, there was always her nickname to remind her. Mary the Scar—shouted after her by children, written down in military reports. It was a crimson hoof-shape, the two horns reaching to the corners of her mouth and eye, the bulk spreading down her cheek to her neck. As a matter of fact, the other cheek now looked the worst. It was a yellow-gray color, with black specks.

Perhaps she had finished being a clown, painting her face. Her daubed features were worse than her natural ones. But nobody could look as bad as she did today, with her scrubby hair, unhappy eyes, and harrowed features.

Yet what did she most need now, to survive with an unborn baby to care for and maybe no husband? She needed her pride. She needed her true self again, after a lifetime as an exotic freak of the whorehouse, and now possibly the madhouse. It was ironic that her desire for reality came at the time when around her she saw artisan families seeking refuge in the madness of religion.

"What's that on your face?" the child asked.

"It's something I was born with."

"You've got some paints in your box!"

"They're for my face."

"Why don't you put them on it, then?"

"I don't want to, anymore."

"Why not? Can I 'ave some on *my* face?"

"No. It's poisonous."

"Gi' it me. I want some. Ladies use it, don't they?"

"Just a little, then."

Mary ground a little red pigment on her palette and brushed it on Margaret's cheek. Margaret picked up the mirror.

"Hurry up, you two," shouted an attendant.

"That's what my mother looks like," Margaret said. "She 'as all that color on 'er face. She's in London."

Mary put the mirror back in the case. "Would you like to go there, chicken?"

"That's what Mr. Pickles told me 'e would do. Take me to London."

"Pickles! You met 'im! Where did 'e pick you up?"

"In Liverpool."

"Oh, my! Where did 'e come from? Did 'e climb out of the slime at the bottom of the sea? Oh, my Gawd. Did 'e treat you all right?"

"Yes. But 'e brought me 'ere. I was waiting to go to London, but 'e brought me 'ere. That's not fair."

"Well, 'e would. 'E'd betray 'is own mother, Pickles would, if there was a penny to be made from it. 'E's not even good at it, neither. Never 'as been good at nothing, Pickles. 'E used to 'ave a business, but 'is documents and papers were in a mess. Cheating and lying, 'e got locked up. Pickles! Shit! *Ptttt!*" Mary spat. "We'll get you out of 'ere. You've 'ad some bad experiences, meeting Pickles, and then 'Orsfall."

"You can't 'ave your fallen woman, after all," Mrs. Farrer told Phoebe, Gideon, Joshua Slaughter, Gledhill, and the others of Lady Well. "She's sick. You couldn't take 'er into a clean place. She's poisoned with lead and mercury. You'd never bring that one to Christ, never. The mercury makes them mad. You must 'ave noticed she was a bit crazy."

"Jezebel!" said Phoebe.

"And when I wasn't looking, she painted up a child that was in 'ere."

"There is One above . . ."

"Let us pray," Gideon said, in a whisper as ringing as a church bell.

Upon the workhouse steps they knelt to pray for the child, and for the prostitute.

" 'Ow will I get to London?"

"I've got some money, my chicken. Don't tell anyone, though. I'll put you on the stagecoach."

It was Monday morning. Mary and Margaret had done two hours of chores and were eating oatmeal porridge in the main room of the workhouse. Mary had been set to do some whitewashing. Her hands were wrinkled and dry with the lime and her clothes were flecked. But she knew they would be out on the roads soon.

Mrs. Farrer had given back one of her sovereigns. "Go away as far as you can from Lady Well and take that child with you, and you can 'ave your sovereign back," she said.

"Are you coming to London with me?" Margaret asked.

"No, I must stay 'ere. There's someone I want to find."

"What shall I do when I get to London?"

"Listen, my chicken. You must face it. You may not find your mother. She might be worn out by now. If she painted 'erself like this, she probably . . . well, you just don't last for long that way, though you 'ave a good time whilst you're 'ere. I'm talking to you like your own mother now, my lamb, you can trust me. What were you doing in Liverpool before Pickles picked you up?"

"Can I really tell you?"

"You can tell me. I promise. Poor thing, you've met some evil types, I can see that. But be careful who you do tell the truth to. Generally it's safer to tell a lie, because if they discover it, you can always invent another one. But there's only one truth, and when they find that out, they've got you. But you can tell me, all right. I'm like your mother."

"I was 'ere in Lady Well before. I was a factory 'prentice and I ran away to Liverpool with Edwin on the night of the raid."

"Edwin? Edwin Greave?"

" 'Ow did you know 'is name?"

"My Gawd! You knew 'im! So where's 'e now?"

"On a ship to America. 'E stowed away on it. 'E wanted me to go with 'im."

"From Liverpool? Well! Edwin Greave! Oh, my lamb. 'E's all right?"

"Yes."

" 'E's all right!"

"I just told you."

"Oh, my Gawd . . . I'll 'ave to . . . You don't know what you've told me. I can't believe it. You must tell me all about it. Poor lamb. What a life we 'as."

By midmorning, they were out in the streets. Margaret was in her rags again. It was quiet now, with most people at work. Mary being scrubbed and shorn, hardly anyone recognized her as their victim of yesterday. A few threw stones at her. Margaret wanted to fling some back.

"Don't bother, chicken. Don't take any notice," Mary told her.

She followed the directions Mr. Binns had given to his house. His door was open and she could hear the cobbler at his work. They stood in the doorway.

"It's you! God bless us, what 'ave they done to you? 'Ave they all gone mad in this town?"

"I've been in the work'ouse."

"So I've 'eard . . . but that they should do that to you! Oh, I'm glad Mor Greave 'asn't come back, to see this. 'E loved it so much 'ere. Who's the child?"

"She was in the work'ouse, too. Horsfall dumped her there."

"Horsfall? Why should 'e do that?"

"I'll tell you what Mr. Horsfall does, Mr. Binns. 'E collects little girls from wherever 'e can and does what 'e wants with 'em. That's your big man of Lady Well for you. I think you should spread the news."

"Horsfall! We all know 'e gets up to something in that big 'ouse, but I didn't think it was that. I thought it was just . . . 'Ow do you know?"

"Because I've been in there myself. Nobody saw me go in and out because I was told not to be conspicuous. Mr. Binns, we need a cart to take us to Halifax."

"I can find you a cart, ma'am. I'll send my lad to the alehouse, they've got one . . . No, ma'am, I don't want your money. Put it away, do. It offends me, that stuff."

He got up from his bench and went into the recesses of his house.

Mary took Margaret to the wall at the far side of the road. She lifted the child up so that she could look over.

"It's beautiful," Mary said. "Isn't it?"

"There's the mill," Margaret answered.

Mr. Binns came back, and crossed the road to them. " 'Ere's a hat for you. You can't go about like that," he said. "Greave used to stare over that valley for hours, too. Rapt. 'What does 'e find to stare at,' we used to wonder. Nobody ever dared ask 'im, 'e was so absorbed . . . 'E's better off with his memories. All their noise would break 'is 'eart."

"I'll tell you something else," Mary said, pulling the cap tight over her skull. "Margaret, tell Mr. Binns about Edwin."

" 'E's gone to America."

"She's talking about Edwin Greave," Mary said to the incredulous Binns.

"I saw 'im onto the ship. We walked to Liverpool. We walked all the way."

"Will you tell Phoebe Greave where 'er son's gone?"

"I don't like the woman, but she ought to know," Binns said. "She probably won't believe me . . . No, put your money away! 'Ere's your cart . . . No, no, I said! I don't want money. Let me 'ave the satisfaction of doing a woman and child a good turn. I want at least one good memory after this past weekend."

He could not take it all in. They left him confused, but smiling, leaning on his stick in the middle of the road.

"Where did you come from?" Margaret asked Mary when they were in the cart.

"I'm from nearby, chicken. When I was a baby I wasn't supposed to live, but I did, against all the odds. I've gone on like that. Let that be a lesson to you. Because of the mark on my face, they didn't want to show me to my mother, so they told her that I was dead and buried. But I was carried off to foster parents. You ever 'eard of Anne Wylde?"

"No."

"She was my mother."

"I like stories."

"When you get to London, I'll give you the address of my friend and a note to take there."

"You can write notes? You must be a lady, then."

"I learned on the way up. If I was you I'd try to learn too, but don't ever tell anyone. It's surprising what people leave around when they don't think you can read it. And you'll meet all sorts of important people when you're in London. Keep your eyes and your ears open, because anything you find out could turn out useful and maybe save your life. When you get to London, go straight to my friend in 'Olywell Street. It's not far from the stagecoach stop. Don't talk to any men or women on the way, because they'll be looking out for a child like you, and don't go down any back alleys. You go straight to 'er door, not looking left nor right, give 'er my note, and she'll look after you. You might see some strange things going on, but don't get frightened of anything, because my friend'll take you in and look after you. She'll probably make you 'er maid, so that you'll learn the ropes and you can watch what goes on without the danger of being touched for a while."

"Touched?"

"Yes," Mary continued hurriedly. "But my friend won't let anything 'appen to you until you're ready. She'll teach you things that in the end'll make you a real gentleman's . . . an aristocrat's . . . 'Ave you ever 'eard of Lady Hamilton?"

"No."

"Oh, that's a story. There's love! Well, you could easily become a second Lady Hamilton. I wish I 'ad my time over again. You'll learn 'ow to play an 'arpsichord."

"What's that?"

"Bless you, child. You'll soon learn what an 'arpsichord is at Mrs. Rawdon's London establishment, and learn to play it marvelous too. Clementi, Mozart. You might meet a general through it. You'll even be taught to compose your own songs and perform them. You'll learn to dance."

"Dance? Me?"

"And to act. Already you can talk well. I don't know where you've learned it, but you're good at it. There's a gentleman to be found for every peculiarity under the sun, but what none can stand is being bored."

They had reached the coach stop in Halifax, where years ago Mary had listened to Joanna Southcott.

"Edwin was always talking."

"That's where you've learned it, then. There's no one I can't talk to. I can take 'em all on."

Mary paid the driver. When no one was looking, she handed Margaret the sovereign that Mrs. Farrer had given back. Margaret, in her rags but clean, was kissed and patted, then stowed in the coach.

Margaret was waving to her, waving and waving, a little golden-haired thing laughing out the window of the coach until it sank into the dip toward the parish church. It could be Harriet.

Mary wondered if the child would cry later. Mary had got used to the companionship of the child, and now with Margaret gone, she might as well have been in a desert, without another soul near her. Where was Mor? Not in Lady Well, evidently. Would he want her, if she found him? Could she persuade him to believe her? Should she go on looking for him? Would he even believe what she had to tell him about Edwin?

Reality. Reality was that she was a worn-out prostitute, pregnant and poisoned. With half of her money still hidden in the lining of her cosmetic box, she had enough to last for a year, but not enough to set up her own house, like Mrs. Rawdon's. She ought to spend her money on an abortion and eke out her remaining cash for as long as she could, offering herself at cheaper and cheaper rates to rougher and yet rougher soldiers and artisans. There was nothing else for her but lying to, and lying with, soldiers.

Perhaps another Mor Greave would come along, as the first one had, sitting in the corner of a public house, waiting for her to walk toward him.

No, there wouldn't be another one. She could still conjure the smell of him on her body. And the taste of him, too. The taste of his particular sweat clinging to her tongue.

She had worked out her plan while she lay in the workhouse infirmary bed, among the cockroaches. Already her steps were in the direction of Delph; sooner or later a soldiers' cart, or that of a farmer or merchant, would turn up to give her a lift.

She would go back to Gartside. In his care, she would bear Mor Greave's baby. Gartside would be happy, serving her, washing the baby, and tending the house. He was an educated man, and suitable to bring up Mor's child. Gartside had his own modest means of livelihood. Her own savings would last for many years when sharing with Gartside.

She could get Gartside to set down her memoirs for her, to sell in Holywell Street. That wouldn't be no "Beggar's Complaint," that wouldn't! That'd be a novel worth looking at; make her famous and a lot of money.

She had always said she'd end up with a reformed homosexual, for the sake of a quiet life. She didn't actually mind if Gartside reformed or not, that was his business entirely. She'd keep a tight rein on him in other respects, the domestic especially. She would make him happy, and in the liberty he did need, she'd provide him with a cover. That was all the "rights of man" that she could see was necessary. He could say the baby was his own, and pretend that he was a proper married man. She'd back him up in that.

Most important of all: if or when Mor came looking for her again, she was certain that the place he would go to, to pick up her track, would be where he had last seen her—at Gartside's.

She couldn't see how life might have offered her a better plan. It made her laugh to herself as she trudged along the road.

When Mor left Mary in Delph, his plan was to get into Lady Well without being observed, sneak in to see Phoebe, reassure her, and escape to the hills again.

After he had walked through the dark for several hours, he hitched a lift in a cart for part of his way, and walked the remainder along secret ways, avoiding farms and villages, tracking over moorlands and pastures under the cascades of morning lark song.

At last, he skirted the upper fringes of the woods and dropped toward the river, well downstream of Lady Well. By now, he was in the midst of a fulsome early summer morning that was lightly boiling with bird song. Yellow currents of buttercups ran through the grass, and the fields lay under a misty foam of seeding grasses, light purple and ready for mowing. Across the meadows, he could see stretches of the river, in a curving, broken line.

He ignored the notices, the messages of which he had read a thousand times before, and climbed a new-made wall. Wanting to take something home with him, he waded through the grass with the excitement he never could restrain when approaching a river.

There it was, his river, brown and white. He stared at the water gracefully sliding by, taking upon its back the buttercup petals that overflowed out of the meadows. Pale green flowers of alder and willow dripped from overhead, and the swell upon the pools gleamed with scraps of blue, fallen from the sky.

He dug around in the bank, until he found some grubs and worms. He took out of his bag the length of line he had stolen from Mr. Burton's. With soft, reverential tread, he crept along the bank. Putting his fiddle and bag in the grass, he paid out his bait in one or two places with no luck. He knew they were not good spots in which to fish, but he had to keep out of sight of farms, cottages, and the road.

He reached a place where the water slid in a thin glaze over a sandbar on the far side, but moved swiftly, dark brown and deep, close to him. At the edge of this fast water was a thick swathe of weeds. Here the best trout would lie; they had a channel with plenty of depth in which to maneuver, cover nearby, and fast water full of oxygen that brought down plenty of food.

He crept along the bank to where he could float his bait downstream to this spot. He knelt and threaded his line into the current, as delicately as a woman threading the eye of a needle.

The snatch of a two-pound trout took him by surprise. There was a jolt on his hand, and then with terrific speed the fish leaped a foot clear of the water, curving upon its tail. A trout sometimes jumps in sheer joy of a summer's day; with the same leap, desperately fast, it now expressed its anger and frustration at being caught. With a great splash back upon the surface, it plunged into the depths again. Fortunately for Mor, it did not retreat into the weeds, but made a fast, commanding line across the river. He could read its pain and anger from the silver thread creasing the dark surface, the fish itself being hidden. Back across the current; back and forth, making fierce, silver cuts.

As it weakened, Mor pulled it in. The trout made sad little coils of its body on the surface of the water—weak, desperate, final resistances. *Sic transit gloria mundi.* A minute ago it was a king, glorying in its health and power in the river. Now it was upon the bank, in Mor's hands, trying still to resist its death, thrashing about in an element that finally it could not defeat. The chaos of a creature drowning in air, dropped off the edge of its world, had a maddening, disruptive effect on Mor, too. He, who thought that he drew in the fish, was drawn by the fish into its own chaos.

It lay still for a second, panting. Its gills and mouth were throbbing, useless. For a brief moment it tried to use its tail, but it, too, was useless. Mor, gripping its fat sides, inserted his thumb down its throat and bent its head back, to break its spine.

The trout tried to leap, to find its life again. But with no water to spring from, the effort ended in a desperate wriggle of its head and tail.

It had put up its last, violent resistance to death. Mor's grip loosened. His thumb slipped about in its throat. The fish's mouth and gills filled with blood. Its soundlessness, other than the squeak of its flesh and the crunch of bone, was awful. Mor, frantic to end its pain, found an anchorage for his thumb in the well of blood, and with a last effort he broke its back.

He looked quickly around. Listened. A lark was singing in the distance. Another small bird was whispering peacefully among the alder twigs. Nothing else. He removed the hook from the trout's mouth, and wiped his bloody hands on the grass. He wrapped the fish in broad leaves of water irises and put it in his bag. He washed his hands in the river, then dried them on the grass once more. After looking about him yet again, he slung his bag and fiddle over his back.

He was not looking where he put his feet, and the steel jaws of the mantrap shut upon his lower leg. The crash of metal startled moorhens from the reeds and sent a pair of wild duck shooting into the sky. There was a frozen numbness in his calf, then a pain bolted through his thigh, his loins, and his spine. He stumbled, so that his flesh was torn further on the jaws. He twisted sideways as he fell, to protect his fiddle. He could not rise again.

He was plunged into the same chaos, fallen over the edge of the world, that he had made for the fish. His muscles quivered; his arms were covered with the gooseflesh of fear. He rid himself of his encumbrances, putting them at his side, then he heaved at the great jaws.

He could prise them no farther than a quarter of an inch. It was just enough to release the first spurts of blood, which flooded around the steel teeth, as it had flooded in the mouth of the trout.

Horsfall's traps *would* have sharpened teeth, damn him! In a second, he had to let go of the jaws. All he had achieved was to ease them far enough to enable them to spring back deeper into his flesh. Yet, like the fish that had struggled in his hands, he must try again. In anticipation of pain, he clung to the jaws, like someone gripping the edge of a cliff.

As he grew tired, the spring seemed to tighten. His arms were quivering and his back aching. His blood was fountaining around his fingers. He tried to release the jaws gently, back into his flesh, but the moment he eased the tension they sprang back, and he fainted.

He came choking out of his faint with vomit in his throat. He was lying on his back, with a bright silver glaze of sky above him. He had to turn on his side, or choke to death. He dribbled vomit over his clothes and onto the grass. A pain shot through his head. His leg was throbbing, but around the wound the flesh was numb.

He lay on his back again. He tried to ignore the thought of the hours, perhaps days, he might have to lie here. He might end up eating grass, insects, and raw, rotting fish.

He put out his hand and drummed his fingers on the sounding board of his fiddle. Tall grasses swayed above him, and red sorrel in shifting disks of inflamed sunlight. Absurdly normal sounds reached him. The tolling of church bells and, he thought, snatches of hymn singing from Lady Well. Rooks were swarming and circling the nub of a hill.

He fainted again. He awoke to the throbbing pain. He put his hand out to his fiddle and bag. He half-dozed, or half-fainted, once more.

Thus he endured through the afternoon. He was dizzy from hunger as well as from pain. The light, after it had silvered, began to yellow. Sleep overtook him once more.

When he awoke, it was in darkness, and he was being lifted at his shoulders and feet by two men. They carried him away, trampling through the meadow grass unheeding of the problems they were making for the mower. The one at his feet took his bag, the other his fiddle.

The jolting gave him such pain that he almost swooned again. He tried to steady himself by fixing his attention, but the stars were reeling, the rocks on the crest of the hills, the trees against the sky, were jumping up and down. He stirred as little as possible, and pretended to be still unconscious.

They took him to an isolated barn, carrying him in at the big cart-doors. Half a dozen soldiers and a recruiting sergeant were inside, wearing red tunics made redder by the firelight. He glimpsed several other figures, dressed in murky clothes like his own, among the shadows.

He was tipped onto the straw. He screamed, and fainted again.

When he came around, the sergeant held the coil of fishing line over him. "You've been poaching Mr. 'Orsfall's trout. You'll be transported for this."

A surgeon came up and knelt at his leg, picking at the wounds with tweezers, pulling away bits of grass and rust. "You are a rogue, sir!" he said. "Sergeant, have some hot water brought."

While waiting for the water, the surgeon continued to poke at Mor's leg. "Only bruised and torn," he murmured.

"He's brought his own dinner with 'im out of the river, though," the sergeant said, rooting in Mor's bag. " 'Ere, soldier, take this and clean it for us." Then he found "The Beggar's Complaint." " 'Ere, what's this? I can't read it. What about you, Doctor?"

"Later," the surgeon answered. He took a glance at what the sergeant was flipping open before him. "Sedition! The place is rife with it. I think we might have an interesting customer here, Sergeant."

"Anyone 'ere can read?" the sergeant shouted through the barn.

Hot water was brought at last, and the surgeon cleaned Mor's wound.

The sergeant had by now found someone to read the manuscript. He returned to his captive and reported what he discovered to the surgeon.

"So as well as being a thief, are you also what is termed a 'Luddite'?" the surgeon asked as he vigorously shook a blue bottle. He poured the solution on Mor's wound. Mor screamed.

"You show 'im, Doctor . . . 'Ere, look at this!" the sergeant said, pulling something else from Mor's bag. "A lace 'andkerchief. Now what lady did this belong to?"

Someone, Mor couldn't see who or where, was playing his fiddle. He winced because it was being strummed so badly.

The sergeant was watching the expression on his face. "You play the fiddle, then?" he asked. "You play it well? You must, to carry it everywhere with you, even when you go poaching, and to pull such a face when someone plays it badly.

"Listen, my friend. They'll 'ang you for stealing trout, when they know you're a Ludd as well. 'Ow would you like to be a soldier of the King instead? You're not much good to us, but I can use a fiddler, to keep the lads quiet."

"The King is mad."

"It's either the mad King's army or the 'angman, comrade, after what you wrote. 'The whole of England is turned over to the profit or the sport of a gang of knaves who run Parliament without being elected by the people.' That's what you wrote, isn't it? 'Our future has been sold to the manufacturers.' You Ludds 'ave 'ad it, friend. You're doomed. General Maitland came to Manchester with seven thousand more men last week, to settle your business. The sight frightened 'em to death in Manchester. I'll give it to Maitland, 'e knows 'ow to cut a dash. 'E put two thousand of us in one camp on the edge of town. What a sight! It chilled the blood. There were three regiments. One was Catholic, one Church of Scotland, one Church of England. That was so we wouldn't get together and start a revolution in the army. I don't give a bugger myself, but we 'ad a fine time off-duty, fighting about the fucking Virgin Mary. They know 'ow to set us up, this 'gang who run Parliament without being elected,' don't they? And we're a lot o' silly sheep, fighting about the Virgin Mary just because we like a scrap. Well, it's off to Napoleon with your fiddle and your bit o' lady's lace, old man. That's the best I can offer you, take it or leave it. You could say, your fiddle's saved your miserable life. You're lucky."

On Monday, Mor rested all day on a pallet in the barn, with a bloody bandage around his leg. On that day, too, he took the King's shilling and swore the oath.

Day after day, others were brought in from forays among the hill hamlets. They dragged in refugees and suspects. Many of the finest men were already in the forces, and though the gang were not very pleased about the health and stature of their catches, it didn't matter. The recruiting gang knew perfectly well what was most wanted: to dispose of rebels as cannon fodder.

The smoke in the barn made Mor's eyes sore; but at least he was excused from drilling because of his leg. He watched what was going on in the barn, and met up with one or two old acquaintances who were dragged in to become recruits. He had his food brought to him, and he could think. He was no longer "his own man"—that indeed had been brief—but on the other hand he liked the company, and he had more time for playing his fiddle than he had ever enjoyed before.

On the day before they were all to be moved off to Leeds to be given uniforms and arms, he got hold of some paper and wrote to Phoebe. Gideon would read it to her.

"I expect to be transported overseas soon to take up arms against Bonaparte, but thanks to the truth of the things in which I have believed, I can trust that fortitude will not desert me . . ."

"Are you going to take that stone with you?" asked the recruiting sergeant. "What are you going to do with it, holding it all the time like it was a lady's breast? You going to throw it at Bony Part when you meet 'im?"

At that moment a private came running in. He leaped in the air and scrambled through the barn, shouting for the sergeant.

"Perceval's been murdered, Sarge! They're singing and dancing in every village in the land! Crowds are mobbing Parliament! Liberty's come! There'll be reform in the army!" He grabbed a recruit and twirled him in a waltz. "No more cat!"

"Who is this Perceval?" asked the sergeant. He was thinking it must be some mill owner or magistrate, or perhaps an army officer.

"The Prime Minister of England," Mor told him.

"I've just 'eard the news from someone come on the stagecoach from London," the private continued. "They're dancing in the streets in every town between here and London, I was told. Mummers are out. Bonfires lit. They're composing ballads."

"I've always 'eard it was Castlereagh was Prime Minister, you swine," the sergeant growled.

"Well, it doesn't sound as though it's Perceval anymore," Mor said.

" 'Friend,' I was told, 'he died like Caesar. Fell lifeless in the lobby, cut down at the 'ands of King Ludd.' Where's the lobby?"

"In the House of Parliament," Mor told him.

"I've just 'eard the whole account . . ."

"Be careful," warned the sergeant.

"Of course—sedition, Sergeant. Of course. I understand. We don't want none o' that. Don't want to break ranks, Sarge. We're 'ere to defend the country, aren't we? Our dear Prime Minister, God bless 'im, gave up 'is dearly beloved soul, so I 'eard, at the 'ouse of Lord Colchester, then was taken by 'is tearful family to Downing Street nearby. That's where they live. There was not one dry eye in the Parliament. Nor should there be. 'Lord Castlereagh could not give a dry utterance to 'is sentiments,' they said. Instead they give fifty thousand pounds to Mr. Perceval's children and two thousand a year for life to Mrs. Perceval." He laughed. "What do you think o' that, Sarge?"

"Be careful, I said."

"Right, Sarge. I don't know 'ow the nation will recover, but we'll do it. Trust the lads."

Elsewhere in the barn, a recruit passed the word on, with a smile. "Parlyment's been shot dead in their beds!"

"That's a good idea," someone replied.

"It's true."

The sergeant was surveying Mor. "At the 'ands of Ludds, eh?" he said.

"Mr. Perceval was about to debate an act making the taking of Luddite oaths punishable by 'anging," the private said. "You know 'ow they talk first, before they go and 'ang someone. Stands to reason who assassinated 'im, don't it? And so they should—string up Ludds, I mean."

"Then they'll be 'anging 'is desperate fellows in these parts, and even more of them than they intended," the sergeant said, still looking at Mor.

He pulled the confiscated "Beggar's Complaint" from his own bag. He went to the fire and burned Mor's manuscript.

He turned to smile at Mor. "Evidence," he said. "They don't like it, even in the army."

Mor flushed with anger. *My immortality!*

Then he remembered what Mary had said: the only sayings of ours that will be remembered are what we confess to, when they hang us.

"There'll be a new Constitution for England, Sarge! An end to flogging in the army! The war'll be over! We'll be at peace with the French at last!"

The sergeant gave a slow wink at Mor. " 'One who suffers, 'opes. And one who 'opes, believes.' What do you say, weaver?"